A DIFFERENT KINGDOM

Also by Paul Kearney

Different Kingdoms
A Different Kingdom
The Way to Babylon (coming soon)
Riding the Unicorn (coming soon)

The Monarchies of God
Hawkwood's Voyage
The Heretic Kings
The Iron Wars
The Second Empire
Ships From The West

The Monarchies of God
Omnibus Editions
The Monarchies of God, Volume 1:
Hawkwood and the Kings
The Monarchies of God, Volume 2:
Century of the Soldier

The Macht
The Ten Thousand
Corvus
Kings of Morning

The Sea Beggars
The Mark of Ran
This Forsaken Earth

A DIFFERENT KINGDOM

PAUL KEARNEY

This edition published 2014 by Solaris
an imprint of Rebellion Publishing Ltd,
Riverside House, Osney Mead,
Oxford, OX2 0ES, UK

First published in the United Kingdom
in 1993 by Gollancz

www.solarisbooks.com

ISBN: 978 1 78108 187 7

10 9 8 7 6 5 4 3 2 1

A CIP catalogue record for this book is available from the
British Library.

Designed & typeset by Rebellion Publishing

Printed in Denmark

For Mary-Ann Kearney

PROLOGUE

WHEN HE HAD been very young, he had told people of the things he saw. His aunt, his grandparents; anyone who would listen. And they had smiled that peculiar adult smile which was not so much amusement as uneasiness, as if to say: *what an imagination.*

There was no one else to tell; there would not be for quite a while. And even when that someone appeared, she would be as unbelievable as the other things. So he spoke to no one.

How could he make them believe that there were wolves in the woods surrounding his grandparents' farm, that when he stood on the brim of the stream there, he could hear the sound of voices, people speaking in an unknown tongue, harsh and savage? Voices from the Other Place. And he could not tell them, for his tongue stiffened in terror when he tried, that he had seen a werewolf padding silently in the back yard in the dead of night, sniffing at the locked doors with its eyes reflecting back the light of a gibbous moon.

No. There was nothing he could say to make them believe, so he said nothing. And they never remarked on the fact that he always kept his window shut at nights.

Antrim

PART ONE

ONE

To an adult, with the weariness of the world in his veins, the land is as detailed and defined as a ship in a bottle. Ireland is a small country, its northern province smaller still. Sea surrounds it and from the highest of its hills a man can see half its breadth at a glance.

But to a child the land is amorphous, vast, huge beyond measure—if anyone should need to do anything as absurd as measure it. It is a horizon of blue mountains on all sides, looming woods deep with secrets and running streams pouring out of ken to a distant, guessed-at sea. For the child, a trip three fields away is an expedition, following a mile of stream akin to paddling the Amazon. A small land, then, but not for children. It is wide enough for fairy tales.

Deep as the peat, the history lies in layers. There are arms caches in desolate places, some forgotten for half a century, some slick with preserving grease and ripe for future murder. A flickering warfare has tilted to and fro across the meadows and woods, the streams and villages, for years beyond count. It is as ritualistic as the turning of the earth, a bloody libation to old, unsatisfied gods. It is a way of life.

Dredging the rivers turns up pale, Celtic gold or, even older, shaped flint, flaked to fit a hand gone to dust ten thousand years before. It is an old country, this Isle of Emerald, millennia in the shaping. War, famine and religion have marked it irrevocably, staining the minds of the people, filling the shadow of the standing stones, seeping into the peat for future fuel. It is his home.

He lives amid the acres his family has occupied for generations. They have multiplied through the years, growing from a single unit into a clan, a tribe. Sons have built houses and scraped together farms in their fathers' shadows. Daughters have married neighbours. Exiles have been and gone, have sailed away and returned to die where they were born. His family has roots here as old as the hill fort nestled on the highest of the pastures. They have possessed the land, raped it, nurtured it, cursed it and been enslaved by it.

His parents have been killed by it. He was orphaned by a bomb meant for someone else. A shopping trip to Belfast in the car his father had just bought and was so proud of...

He lives with his grandparents now, the memory a mere blur in his young mind. He does know that outside this world of his the larger world is growing darker, and in the discussions of grown-ups there is talk of *rights*, of *equality*. He does not know—nor does anyone—that in the next decade this quiet world will explode.

For the present, however, his grandparents' farm is the star his life circles. The farm is a scattered square of buildings, white-washed and red-roofed, thatch only recently replaced by scarlet corrugated iron. There are small, forgotten sheds filled with fascinating rubbish, the jetsam of past seasons. There are lost corners, hidden nests, sudden smells, the stink of decay and fermentation, dung and hay, animals and humans.

The farm is a city in miniature, the citizens everything from the field mice in the dairy to the pigeons in the stables. There are chickens pecking in the stone-paved back yard, sly felines sleepy by day and psychopathic at night, barking collies trying to appear busy, calm-eyed horses unaware that their time of pulling and ploughing is over and that they are kept out of sentiment (though this is never admitted). There are sheep in the lower meadows, a rancid goat in the top paddock that was once a lawn, a heavily pregnant sow grunting happily to herself among the oaks and acorns of the bottom inch, and half a dozen kittens that no one has yet had the heart to drown.

But that is not all. Down by the river that cradles the farm there are water rats and voles by the score. Foxes slink across the fields at night, unnerving the chickens, and there are badger setts in the woods at the bottom of the hills. At least one kingfisher darts for stickleback, and minnow from the alders that overlook the riverbank, and curlews call constantly, arcing over the hills like arrows into the heart of the mountains in the west. The world is a busy place, thriving and writhing with activity, but for all that it is a quiet one. Horses on the roads are not yet uncommon, and cars are still a means to an end. The roads themselves are bad, potholed and crumbling, water-riven in winter and dust-baked in summer. It is two miles along them to the nearest village, which is itself nothing more than a hamlet with a public house and three churches. The town with the market that is visited once a week is eleven miles away.

Between the blunt peaks of the Sperrin mountains where the sun always sets, and the stony, gorse-ridden heights of the Antrim plateau to the east, the wide river valley of the Bann opens out for twenty miles, encompassing two counties. It is dark with woods and intaglioed with fields of barley and potato, kale and turnip, and the rich rolling pastures and meadows with their attendant hedges. Villages are spattered over all, islands in the green mantle of the world. There are no towns worth speaking of, and the sprawl of housing estates will not infect the land for another twenty years. It is a last breathing space, a final look around at the soon-to-be-felled woods, the rush-choked bottom meadows, the fields with the wild flowers that have seeded for a thousand years and which knew the feet of the Druids.

But this is beyond his knowledge. The village, the market town, these are to him immense distances away, and beyond them he knows only rumours of America, land of exiles. The farm, the river, and the fields and woods about his home; these are his kingdom.

TWO

Even then Michael's grandmother seemed old, older than his grandfather whom she would one day outlive. She was a big woman with large hands and a mop of white hair that escaped every clip and band she installed to imprison it. Inclined to stoutness, she called herself 'big-boned,' and would glare round when she said it, as if daring anyone to contradict her. Her eyes were a bright blue, the whites of them slowly yellowing with the weight of years, but she kept her own chickens and milked her own goat and darned endless socks with complacent skill. She cooked huge meals effortlessly, bringing in vegetables from the garden with the mud clinging to them and bullying anyone who was near to carry in wood for the big range that shouted with heat at one end of the kitchen, taking up almost the entire wall. Its top plate was never cold and there was always a villainous pot of tea stewing there that would be as dark as clay in the cup and which Michael's grandfather downed daily by the gallon. Coffee was unheard of, and breakfasts were massive affairs of spitting bacon and fried eggs and soda bread. The men—family and hired workers—would congregate in the stone-flagged kitchen and eat mounds of steaming food before turning out to the fields and stables while mist was rising up out of the meadow bottoms and the last star was considering quitting the sky. There were cold mornings, stiff with winter and dark as pitch, when the men took swinging lanterns out with them, electricity not yet having been wired to the byre and the stables. And there were soft summer dawns when the sun would be a ball of molten fire inching its way up a flawless sky and pouring flaxen light over the waking land like a benison.

And if Michael's grandfather, all six feet five inches of him, was lord of the farm and the fields, the labourers and the crops, then his grandmother was mistress of the house, provider of meals and stern guardian of manners. Hands were washed before meals with the strong carbolic soap whose reek would haunt Michael the whole of his life, and boots were scrubbed free of mud. The house and the farm seemed all of a bustle in those days, with people coming and going, boots clumping in the hall, his grandmother calling out in the yard for the men to come for their dinner—or if they were too far away then Michael would be sent scurrying out to the fields where they would be scattered at their jobs, sweat on their faces, scythes or halters or buckets or shovels or sacks or pitchforks in their hands. He remembered evenings like that, haymaking evenings, when there were clouds of midges floating like gauze in the air and a cow's low would carry for miles in the stillness, and he would be plastered with hayseeds and specked with liquid dung from his pelter through the meadows to fetch them in.

'You've shit on your nose,' he would be told calmly. 'What have you been doing, snowballing with it? Go on with you. Get in and scrub, or your gran will have your hide.' And he would not see the grin they threw at his running back.

Michael Fay, with shit on his nose, had been running back like that one day in the middle of a waning summer when he tripped, and fell down, and slipped, and slid, and had his life picked up and thrown around and put down again in a different place. In another world.

* * *

He could smell the rich earth as he slipped along it, tumbling down a steep incline with his short limbs flailing. He smelled wild garlic and river mud, and when the world had stopped turning he found that he was on the slope leading to the stream at the foot of the bottom meadow, had cartwheeled down twenty feet of steep, hazel-covered bank and had left the sunset-lit evening behind, up in the meadow. Here it was gloomier, with the trees—alder and willow—edging close to the water like animals come to drink, and the twilight already deepening in their shadow.

He sat up, dusting himself off with stubby hands. He could feel twigs lodged in his hair and beetling around inside his shirt, and his clothes were green and black with mud and mould. He grimaced, peering at his black palms, then at the river hollow, loud with water noise, swamped with an early dusk. He trolled for minnow here often, during the long afternoons when his grandmother released him from the swarm of jobs she found for him every day. He knew this river—for to him it was a river, though barely ten feet wide and shallow enough to wade. If he followed it for a few hundred yards upstream, he would come to the old bridge, where a seldom-used road crossed it and the heavy masonry was sunk in the water like the wall of a castle, with nothing but black darkness and skipping water rats under its arch.

Michael shivered, and then froze like a startled rabbit. For there was something different about the river this evening, something strange. The trees seemed thicker, bigger. The willows seemed older, their hair dipping lower into the bickering water. And there were no longer any stumps on the slope he had just fallen down.

He looked behind him. It was true. His grandfather had thinned out the hazel there so the sheep could make their way to the river and drink. Cattle would never have made it down the steep slope without slipping, but sheep could. There had been stumps there to trip the unwary, tangled with ivy and covered with moss, but not one had interrupted Michael's downward slide, and he could see none now. Odd.

But it flitted out of his mind as quickly as it had come. In the grown-up world there would be an explanation, as there always was. Here it did not matter. He sat for a moment, listening to the river and half smiling to himself. Above him the evening star climbed unnoticed over the heads of the trees. All thought of dinner and his errands was leached out of his head. He sat as if waiting for something.

There was a movement in the trees on the other bank of the river. He sat still, though his heart began to beat an audible tattoo in his head.

Branches swung back and forth; something heavy was blundering through them. He stared, but could make out nothing in the fading light. Of themselves, his muscles began to tense under him and his hands gripped fistfuls of leaf mould, dirt grinding in under his nails.

He heard a snatch of talk—a voice, and then another answering. He could not understand the words. They sounded deep, snarling, guttural; but rhythmic as a song. He got up on his haunches, ready for flight.

Something burst into view in the brambles opposite, on the other side of the river. It was the grinning mask of a fox, the eyes alight and the teeth shining, but under it two more eyes glittered and there was a streak of teeth set in a wide grin. Shock took the air out of Michael's lungs and he fell backwards, scrabbling through the twigs and leaves. There was a bark of something like laughter, and more movement along the riverbank; a dark flickering of shadow. Something plashed into the water, and he caught a glimpse of a prick-eared shape, wading the stream upright. There was more talk, more of the song-like chanting and another rattle of hard laughter, like the sound of a woodpecker at work.

'God!' he squeaked, kicking soil and leaves into the air as, without thought, he propelled himself up the slope with his backside dragging in the earth. There were more shapes crowding the stream now, though none had yet reached his bank. They were man-like, crouched, wrapped in furs, their limbs gleaming with sweat or paint, and fox faces on their heads. Two of them bore a long pole on their shoulders, a dark shape swinging from it. Something like a hat rack was bound up to the pole. Antlers. And as the air moved out of the river, pushed by a stray breeze, he could smell them. They stank of urine, of rotten meat, of woodsmoke. Their dripping burden reeked of blood and offal.

His nerve broke. He turned his back to the river with the air whooping in and out of his lungs and tears of terror flashing unnoticed on his face. His feet slipped in the muck and mold, his fingers gouging the soil for grip. He clawed his way up to where the trees thinned and the light grew, up to the meadow where he had left his world behind. And as he did, he stubbed his groping fingers agonizingly on a moss-covered tree stump and fell to one side, crying, waiting for the shapes in the river to pounce on him, for that evil stink to surround him. He shut his eyes.

But nothing happened.

He opened them a slit, saw nothing in the gloom, and then stared wide-eyed down the bank.

There was nothing in the river. A bird sang evensong to itself and the brightness of the water was unbroken. The trees were quiet, undisturbed. He sniffed, stifling sobs, and heard across the fields the sounds of the men walking to the house for their dinner. He looked out and saw their shapes walking dark across the dimming fields, the sudden glow of a cigarette, like a tiny eye, winking at him. He crawled out of the well of shadow that was the river course and lay there on the edge of the meadow a moment, spent, his chest heaving in the slow air of the evening. A wood pigeon was talking softly to itself somewhere. One of the men laughed at something—a wholesome, safe sound. He heard the metallic clink of a gate and knew they were entering the back yard, where the lights of the house would be yellow in the windows though it was not yet dark. He got up unsteadily, glancing behind him, and limped away wiping his eyes, blowing his nose on his sleeve. He could feel the mud caking on his cheeks, stiffening under his nails. His grandmother would certainly tan his hide for coming in like this.

* * *

AND SHE DID. And afterwards she scrubbed him from head to foot at the kitchen sink until his ears were glowing, his cheeks shining and the smell of soap stinging his nose. He sat, in his nightshirt and slippers, at the table with the rest of the household, the remembered contact of her hard palm making him treat his seat gingerly. But he had not cried. The memory of what he had seen at the river was still merry-go-rounding in his head and his crying had been done there, when he had thought himself lost.

He ate his food ravenously, wolfing down potatoes and carrots and lamb lashed with thick gravy, moustaching his upper lip with great gulps of milk. His grandmother darted sharp glances at him now and then in a mixture of disapproval, affection and worry. Michael never noticed. His nose was buried in his glass and behind it his thoughts were whirring like a Catherine wheel. Were those things he had seen at the river what his grandparents called 'terrorists'—the sort of things that had killed his mammy and daddy? He paused in his swallowing at the thought. He had a vague picture of a terrorist as a mask-wearing, night-loving monster which killed people for fun. And they probably smelled, too. Maybe he had better tell...

He looked around the table, feeling strangely guilty. His grandfather had pushed back his plate and was now lighting his pipe in a flare of match flame, its light throwing into relief his big, roman nose and the chiselled lines of his face, like a sea cliff that has weathered many storms. The hair on his head, though pure white, was as thick as it had been thirty years before, and his back was still poker-straight. The hand that held the pipe was as huge as a spade, brown and liver-spotted. The hired hands called him 'The Captain' because he habitually wore a pair of old cavalry breeches and leather leggings. His boots struck sparks off stones when he walked, a thing which never failed to fascinate Michael.

His grandmother was clearing the plates from the table, helped by her two daughters. His Aunt Rose, not much more than a girl herself, winked at him as she left for the scullery, balancing a tower of dirty plates. He began to swing his legs under the table, careful to avoid Demon, his grandfather's bad-tempered, ageing collie, who crept under there at meals in the hope of scraps. It was the only thing he had ever seen his grandparents disagree on: the grey-muzzled dog under the table at mealtimes. Michael disliked the animal. He was coal-black, lean, sharp-nosed, and he worshipped his master and held the rest of humanity in contempt. But though the house was grandmother's kingdom, the dog was grandfather's workmate of a dozen years and so he stayed.

His Uncle Sean was rolling himself a cigarette, humming under his breath. He had the face of a film star, and his sisters doted on him. He popped the finished fag in his mouth and fumbled unhurriedly for his matches, smiling at Michael's pink face. People said he looked like Clark Gable, with his thick black hair tumbled over his forehead and those sea-grey eyes which were the hallmark of the Fay family. The local girls congregated around him like wasps on a jam pot when he appeared, polished and brushed, at the dances that were held in the church hall at every month's end. But he seemed never to notice them. He was caught up with the farm, preoccupied with ways of improving it—often in conflict with the views of his father. Michael had heard some of the labourers talking about him one morning. Too much of a bloody gentleman was Sean, they had said, and one had sniggered, saying if he'd been offered as many cunts as Sean his John Thomas would have been worn away to a button by now. Somehow Michael had known that this was not the sort of thing he could bring up at the dinner table, though he had thought of asking Aunt Rose, who often fished with him in the little river and took him into her bed when the thunder was loud.

Chairs were being pushed back and there were a few belches. (His grandmother was still in the scullery or they would not have dared.) Tobacco smoke spun blue tendrils in the light of the lamps. There was an electric bulb dangling forlornly from the ceiling, but it was saved for special occasions. And besides, Michael's grandparents hated it. It had no soul, they said, and they continued to light the oil lamps at dusk despite the protests of their children. Electricity was saved for visitors.

The hired hands said their good nights and left for home, slapping their caps on their heads as they went out of the door and sniffing at the starlit air outside. One or two would eat a second dinner cooked by their wives, but most were bachelors and were going back to empty cottages or parents' houses. There were quite a crowd of them around the farm at this time of year, with haymaking and the harvest approaching. Those inside could hear the scrape and tick of bicycles pushing off from the wall of the house, and then the door had been closed again and Aunt Rachel was drawing the curtains on the night. Demon sidled out from under the table and flopped down before the range with a contented sigh. Old Mullan lit his pipe and sat opposite Michael's grandfather with a leather halter he was soaping. That was his privilege. He had been with the Fays since the Great War, when he had returned from Flanders a young man with one leg shorter than the other.

Clattering plates and women's voices came from the scullery. Michael felt sleep hovering around his eyes. He would tell someone tomorrow, perhaps—tell them that there were terrorists with fox faces down by the river waiting to blow everyone up. But it seemed less real here in the solid security of the house. Like a dream. He yawned, and his Aunt Rose pounced on him.

'You're half-asleep, yawning there in your nightshirt. Bedtime for you, Michael-boy.'

He protested sleepily as she dragged him from his seat and took his hand in hers. His grandfather nodded at him over pipe smoke and the *Irish Field*, his grandmother kissed his forehead and Uncle Sean waved a hand absent-mindedly, whilst old Mullan merely paused in his soaping for a second. Rose tugged him up the stairs, talking all the while. He liked her to talk, especially if it was a thundery night and he had burrowed into her arms in the girl-smelling bed. She would talk then to keep him from fearing the thunder, though she loved it herself. It made her hair crackle, she said.

He realized suddenly that she was asking how he had come to be so dirty that evening, what had happened to him. He told her he had fallen, had slipped and fallen down to the river, which was the truth and so he had not sinned. And she put him to bed with a kiss, tucked him in and told him to say his prayers. But he tumbled off to sleep forgetting them, with the fox faces grinning at him across the river, telling him he was theirs now. Their little boy.

THREE

THE SUMMER OF 1953 was long and fine, the afternoon of the year winding down to autumn and harvest. For Michael a summer was a living thing, an entity of its own which set him free of school and gave him endless hours of daylight to use. It was long and slow and benevolent. In summer the rings of trees grew widest.

The skies remained perfect, blue darkening almost to purple at the zenith, dust and shimmer hazing the horizon so that the mountains could only be guessed at much of the time. Dust hung over the roads also, kicked up by the hoofs of horses and the carts they drew or thrown about by the passage of shiny cars. Looking west to the Sperrins from the first heights of the Antrim plateau, the valley would appear to be an almost unvarying patchwork of hedge-lined fields, the barley ripening in the sunlight, the woods dark and cool, the Bann a silver flash of slow-moving water in the midst of it. Here and there would be the white wall of a house, smaller than a sugar cube, but it was only at night that it would be possible to see the hamlets and villages and townlands of the counties, when they would become a confetti-glitter of lights in the darkness.

Drinking his buttermilk at the table in the morning with the crumbs of his breakfast on his chin, Michael's vision of the day before seemed less real than ever. Already it had been demoted in his memory, moving from the realm of fear into that of curiosity. His head was filled with things to do for the day, and he was eyeing his grandmother's back as she worked at the range, wondering if he could slip outside into the bird-loud morning unnoticed.

'And where do you suppose you are off to?' He could not. He turned dutifully. 'Just out.'

She nodded. 'That's fine, so long as you pump me a couple of buckets when you're out, and then bring them in again.'

He left by way of the larder, where the buckets were kept, and hauled two round to the pump which supplied their water. He actually enjoyed pumping the stuff and watching it churn clean and clear in the pails. It tasted of iron; hard water, cold and delicious, not like anything out of a tap. The spring it came from had never failed, not even in drought years.

He hauled them in and left them, spilled liquid specking the stone floor. And after that he was free, released, and left to the morning. He skipped out of the back yard like a colt, making for the fields.

He met Rose first. She was surrounded by hens and was tossing them yellow meal by the fistful, clucking softly all the while. They had pecked and scraped their paddock into a pale bowl and their nests were scattered throughout the surrounding hedges. Only Rose and her mother knew where they were. Half wild, the birds could often be seen flapping in the lower branches of the trees. They were wily fowl, and seldom fell prey to the foxes that roamed the hills at night. But thinking of foxes made Michael uneasy and his flesh prickled in the warm sun.

'Sleepyhead,' his aunt said without looking round; and she shushed the chickens, who were a little alarmed by Michael's approach.

'I had the eggs to gather on my own this morning,' she went on, but he knew she was not annoyed with him. His usual contribution to egg-gathering was one or two from the most visible nests. She liked him along for the company, and to see the early morning with. He watched her throw the birds their meal and debated telling her his secret, but thought better of it. For the moment he wanted to keep it his alone.

'Fancy fishing this afternoon, then?' she enquired carelessly, and threw another fistful of meal for the hens to scrabble over. Her arms were long and slim, tawny with sun and speckled with golden hairs. She was barefoot, and the dew had wet her feet so the dust clung to them.

'Aye,' Michael piped.

She nodded to herself, still clucking occasionally to her charges. 'Down by the bridge there are trout, young yet but worth going after. I've seen them when the light shines through the water. They keep to the deep part, where the willows are.'

'Don't let your shadow fall on the water,' Michael said automatically. It was something she had taught him, and Rose smiled as she heard it.

'Mammy finished with you for today?'

'Aye.'

'What are you for doing? I'm busy till after lunchtime.'

He felt suddenly furtive. 'Don't know. Go to the bottom meadows maybe, see the river there.'

'Mind that slope.' This time it was Rose who spoke automatically. 'You could break a leg on those hazel stumps.'

I couldn't, Michael thought, now bursting to tell his secret. They weren't there. And he was filled with an exhilaration which almost giddied him. He skipped on the dew-wet grass, making the chickens flutter nervously.

'Watch out there, clumsy! Go, get lost, and I'll see you later.' And she soothed her brood with soft words. Uncle Sean said that Rose had a name for each of the hens, though she denied it indignantly. Michael was not sure. She called them strange things under her breath sometimes.

He scampered away, the wet grass beginning to be felt through his old shoes. It would be hot today, and there would be dragonflies by the river.

Someone was limping up the long slope towards him with a pitchfork over one shoulder, a bucket in one hand and a cloud of blue smoke trailing behind him. When he saw Michael he waved and sat down on the sward, spearing the pitchfork into the ground. It was old Mullan. Michael joined him. The grass was ablaze with buttercups, so that they sat in a gently swaying yellow sea, and the pollen was already beginning to powder their legs.

Mullan scraped a match across one boot heel and sucked the dim flame into his pipe. It was an apple-bowl Peterson, a beautiful thing, the brown of the wood so deep it could nearly be a dark scarlet. Even the scrapes and dints it had received over the years had mellowed, becoming part of the shape. The mud and blood of the Somme had left no mark. Mullan was an old Inniskilling Fusilier, though Michael's grandmother said he was an old Blow. He was the only one of the hired hands she would let sit by the range after dinner, however.

'Well, Mike,' he said, puffing contentedly. He was also the only person who called Michael that, and he liked it. He felt it was a grown-up's name. 'What have you been up to? I saw you come in last night, muck to the eyebrows and your face as white as a sheet. You looked as though you'd seen a ghost, so you did.'

Michael plucked a buttercup and watched it reflect a gold light on his palm.

'I fell—down by the river where the slope is. I fell all the way down it.'

'Ah.' Mullan thumbed his bowl with a fireproof digit. 'Odd place, that dip, when the evening is coming on. It gets dark down there so quickly you can be caught out. And you notice the sheep never drink there, though your grandfather cleared that hazel.'

Michael raised his head, surprised. They didn't, either.

'And there are never any birds there,' he said. 'Why is that?' Mullan smiled. His chin was as bristly as a nettle stalk and his eyes two glints of blue in a maze of folds and wrinkles. He had been born in another century, before aeroplanes or cars or two great wars, before Ireland had been split in two. When Pearse had been on the steps of the GPO he and his comrades had been in the trenches in the spring rain.

'There are places,' he said, 'that are just plain odd. Ordinary places that are a wee bit different, so the birds shun them and people feel uncomfortable there. There are places like that all over the country, or there were when I was a boy.' Somehow he made that sound a very long time ago. Another age.

'What are they?' Michael asked, wide-eyed. 'What's wrong with them?'

'And did I say there was something wrong with them? There are differences, maybe; wee things you can feel now and again, on the right kind of day. At dusk or dawn. And if you sit still long enough in them you'll maybe see something—something out of the corner of your eyes. Fairies, Mike. The Little People.'

Michael was disappointed. The things he had seen by the river were most definitely not fairies.

'Aren't they supposed to have wings and stuff, and pointy ears?'

Mullan chuckled, his humour a spit of blue smoke. The Peterson gurgled happily to itself.

'Oh, aye. Wings and things—like dragonflies, shiny and buzzing.' And he began to laugh.

'You're making fun!'

'No. Not me. I'm dead serious.' But he continued to wheeze.

Michael reddened and the old man stuck out a hand. 'Hold on, there. Wait a minute.' He coughed and spat something semi-solid into the buttercups. 'Jesus. No, listen, Mike, I'm not mocking you. I'll tell you a story. Listen to me...' For Michael had half stood up, his eyes outraged. Mullan's hand grasped his forearm and brought him down to earth again in an instant's mist of buttercup dust.

'You're just laughing!'

'Remember the field across the river, the one below the bridge?'

Michael nodded suspiciously.

'Well, Pat—your grandfather—he found an old sword there once that the Romans had left behind, and it had writing on the blade he couldn't read.'

'I know that. Everybody does. It's in the museum in the city. Sure there's nothing to do with fairies in that.'

'Aye, but your grandfather told me that when he found the sword it was lying on the grass, just lying there, and that he could swear there were things watching him from the trees at the river. It was near dark, and he was so sure they were there that he was going to go and see, for he was thinking it was trespassers or the Campbell boys—they're a bad crowd—but something put him off. He had old Demon with him, except he wasn't much more than a pup then, and the dog was snarling and growling and carrying on something desperate; and damned if he would go into the trees, even when Pat threw him a kick and cursed him up and down. So your grandfather picks up the old sword and says to hell with it, and runs—*runs*, Mike—back into the house with the dog whining at his heels. So what do you think of that, then?'

'He never said that to anybody. He said he found it under a bramble.'

'Aye, well, do you think a grown man, nearly sixty years of age when it happened, would talk about how he had been as scared as a baby by some shadows?' Mullan smirked triumphantly and settled his point with a sweep of his pipe hand. A few ashes scattered from the bowl and drifted off into the air.

'You're making it up.'

'Maybe I am and maybe I'm not. You can take it or leave it. I'll tell you this, though. When I was your age, if I'd turned the word on any of my elders, I'd have got a thick ear.' For a second Mullan looked almost fierce, and it was possible to see the young soldier who had gone over the top on a long-ago July morning.

'Sorry,' Michael said sullenly. He had been going to tell the old man about the fox faces by the river, but he was sure it would be indifferently received. Still his secret, then.

Mullan levered himself upright on the pitchfork and retrieved his bucket with a clank. 'Never you mind it. But remember that there are more things in heaven and earth...' He trailed off. 'Aye. More things than you can poke a stick at. Listen to your elders and maybe you'll learn something. Now I'm off. Stay out of mischief.'

And he lurched away with the pitchfork slung over his shoulder as if it were an Enfield, humming 'Tipperary' and towing smoke behind him.

* * *

WHEN MULLAN HAD gone, Michael wandered his way down to the dip of the river in the bottom meadow. Despite the brightness of the day, it was dim there in the shadow of the trees. He stood undecided on the lip of the slope and stared down to where the river plashed and burbled to itself. Hazel stumps stood like square-topped stones in the litter of the wood floor. He began thinking... What if?

What if there *were* Little People in the woods, like in the stories Rose told him? What if there were wolves and bears and trolls, wicked witches—and fairies, too? But not ones that lived in flowers. What if they were big and silent and gleeful, more like goblins? They would have a goblin kingdom, castles and mines. And there would be knights in armour with swords and women in towers with long hair. What if it were all real, all true?

And something like a picture entered his mind—someone else's memory, perhaps—something which had happened a long time ago in another place. Or something which had still to occur.

THE HORSES WERE spent, head-hung and exhausted. The stink of their sweat was steaming the air as Michael and Cat dismounted, their own leg muscles trembling in sympathy.

'We've not lost them,' Cat said, pushing the wet hair from her face. Michael nodded. He was almost too tired to care. Fear had carried them far, but tiredness was dulling even that.

'Fire,' he said. 'I'll get a fire going. The light's failing. Night is coming.' There would be a moon again. The full had waxed and was on the wane but it was still thick and silver in the sky. Enough to quicken the blood of the pursuit. Enough to hunt by. Soon the woods would be a dappled maze of moonlight and shadow, a silver chiaroscuro.

'Lord, I'm sick of trees,' he said.

Cat did not reply. She was unsaddling the horses, wiping them down with the sodden saddle blankets. No picket pins would be needed tonight to keep them from straying.

Darkness. It was creeping out of the trunks of the trees, seeping up out of the leaf mold, bleeding into the snow-leaden clouds. He was sick of darkness, also. Two thirds of every day seemed given to it.

There was dead wood in plenty about the feet of the silent trees, and small drifts of dry leaves in the crook of roots. Elsewhere gobbets of snow on the wood floor marked where the canopy was thin. The ground was cold, clay below the humus sucking the heat away. They needed the fire. It was both a defence and a heartener.

He skinned a knuckle on the steel and cursed softly. His weak hand made things awkward. Spark after spark leapt into the tinder, smoked a moment and then died. At last, though, one caught and glowed; He bent his face to the ground and blew with infinite care until he had a flame, fragile as blossom, curling into the leaves and twigs. Bird-nest linings made good tinder, feathers and all, if they were old and sheltered enough.

The flame spread. He eased wire-thin twigs into it, coaxed it around them. And when he straightened, back creaking, he saw with a shock that it was almost fully dark.

Cat unrolled their bedding, and even across the fire he could smell the damp staleness of it. Too many rainy nights, too much clay underfoot. They drew less warmth from it than from each other's bodies. And even with that closeness they had not loved in many days. Someone had to watch, all the time. So they would not both be woken, as had happened three nights ago, by the screams, and sit up to see the eyes in the dark beyond the firelight, hear the grunting snarls that were almost speech.

They had nearly died.

The fire caught well. He could toss wrist-thick branches on it now and watch the sparks spiral into the air like just-forged stars. The warmth was a blessing on his wind-scoured face, soothing the long ache of his scarred limbs.

They ate dried beef and bannock, washing it down with a mouthful of wine. Good red stuff from the tiny vineyards that men had planted in the woods down near the weald, not much spoiled by the skin. From the amphora it had been wondrous. They were down to their last quart, a cause for mourning. When he smelled the stuff it put the fetor of the dank woods out of his nose, and he was thinking of sun-pale hillsides heavy with vines—places he had never seen, flagged stone hot to the touch. He smiled at Cat, knowing she too was a summer creature, a warmth lover. She was so white and pinched in the middle of her cloaks that he drew her close, feeling the spare, bird-like build of her. Hollow bones, he thought.

'We'll have peace tonight,' she said, leaning her head into his shoulder. He felt a yawn tighten her jaw.

'How so?'

'They're slow by day. They keep to the deepest woods. They'll be walking five miles for every one in our wake. It is rough country behind us.'

Indeed. They had almost killed their mounts. He wondered how much longer there would be a way for the horses to battle through the lower trees and the brambles. Their legs were scratched and scored, and yesterday the grey had come down on one knee, opening it on a vicious tree root. He was lame, and would not improve whilst their flight continued. The chestnut, Fancy, was not much better off; once a high-stepping, spirited animal, his grandfather's pride and joy, she moved now like a warped clockwork toy. Neither of them had ever fully recovered from the ordeal in the Wolfweald.

'We'll be afoot yet,' he prophesied gloomily.

'Soon, yes, but if we can win clear of the trees and hit upon the first heights of the hills, then we have a chance. There are cliffs there, gullies and caves. Something to put our backs against at nights. And they don't like the open sky above them, even at night, much less the bare slopes. It's the woods they love to skulk in.'

'The damn trees.'

'Yes. The damn trees. But they don't go on for ever. And Ringbone is to try and meet us near the edge, take us as far as the Utwyda.'

'What about the Horseman?' Instinctively his voice had lowered as he asked. Cat hesitated.

'We haven't seen him for days.'

'That's why I ask. Will he be waiting for us, you think, when we break free of the trees?'

She lifted her head from his shoulder. 'Ask the moon. I am no oracle.'

'You brought me here.' His tone roughened despite an effort to keep it soft.

'And now I take you home.' Her eyes flashed in the firelight, the flames a little turning hell in each one. 'Besides, you wanted to come. And it was not I who found a quest to follow in this land, a maiden who needed rescuing.'

'I was a boy, a child. I knew nothing of what it would be like.' And I was in love with you, he thought but did not say. He marvelled that the thought had come in the past tense, and wondered if that presaged some future revelation.

'Fairy tales have teeth. Even children know that. The big bad wolf must eat.'

'Yeah, okay.' He rubbed his eyes, too tired to argue. Tension had been flickering between the two of them for days, like far-off summer thunder, and it was a wearisome thing to bear. There was so much they did not talk about, so much pushing them apart. His decision to return home. The events in the Wolfweald. All there, hanging unspoken in the air between them. And he so wanted her warmth pliant in his arms tonight, her arms around him. There were few worse things than her lying there, stiff with resentment. If she had enough energy for even that.

The fire cracked and spat as a faggot collapsed into its molten heart. He drew himself up as slowly as a geriatric.

'Need more wood.'

'Take the sword', she said automatically, eyes still lost in the flames, lids already drooping. It was plain that he would be taking first watch tonight, and the prospect made his face ugly for a second. It was marvellous what the body could bear in the way of wet and wind, injury and agony, but lack of sleep was the worst thing. It had become a physical pain to him at times to keep awake through the nights.

The sword was in its scabbard, beside it the barrel of the shotgun—useless, if it had ever been of any use. Its few remaining cartridges were soaked through and through. He patted the carved wooden stock. His name was there in copperplate, along with the date: 1899. A lovely weapon. He carried it for sentimental reasons alone now, and the prestige that the iron barrel brought amongst the tribes. Excess baggage. It was beginning to rust. He rasped the sword out of its scabbard instead. It was heavy and cold. He could make out rust on the blade, too, near the hilt, and scraped it with a nail, frowning. The edge had dulled. They had used it to chop wood; an unforgivable thing. It needed work. He knew now the difference between a strike with a sharp blade and a blunt one, the artistry in the swing. His prowess with the blade—an iron blade—was all that had kept them alive. The lead of the shotgun pellets had been good merely for hunting.

I've been well educated of late, he mused. I can doctor a horse and skin a rabbit. I can tan leather and stitch wounds. I can kill men. And a little while ago I was a schoolboy, a squeaker, a dreamer.

He shook his head, wondering how much of his life he had lost in the woods and the hills, the wild places. He would get it back, of course, would walk out of this place the morning he had left—but would he remain the same? Would he walk into the kitchen a hulking savage, scarred and bearded, or would he be a boy again? Would that childhood be returned to him?

His fingers scratched through the white hairs of his beard as he shambled to the edge of the firelight. The years had added themselves to him with every mile deeper they had gone into this place, years piled on to his shoulders in a few months. And Cat had aged, also. She was no longer the girl he had met in the wood. That was his fault, his alone. Mirkady had warned him of that, one night in a fairy howe.

He gathered wood with a wandering mind. He was thinking of his grandfather's farm, the swallows in the stables, a fire in the hearth. Pots of tea and bacon and eggs. Clean sheets—Mother of God!—a bed that was dry and warm with the night beyond a window.

He yawned enormously, the bones in his face cracking. He had an armful. It would do an hour or two. Cat could gather more later. He hungered for the fire. For her, as well. Despite his dog-weariness, the thought of her skin under his hand appealed. The last time they had loved they had both fallen asleep before the finish and had lain like Siamese twins, still connected in the morning.

But no. Too risky to chance it. No time for love when the beasts are on your trail.

She was asleep, as he had known she would be, one hand in a fist at her throat. He set the wood down and covered her, the sword digging into his ribs. First watch. And more than likely he would take the dark one before the dawn too. A long night, but as Cat had said, the pursuit would have had a rough time of it today. He had perhaps a few hours of peace.

The damn wound was acting up again. Another day and he would open it, cauterize it for the umpteenth time. It was on the big muscle of the upper thigh, deep and angry. The smaller punctures beside it had already closed. Perhaps there was something of the beast's tooth remaining there. It hardly bore thinking about. He knuckled it savagely, wishing away the deep ache and glow. The wild riding did not help.

'Ach...' He stabbed the sword into the fire and watched the dull iron cradled by the flames. The blade needed to be reheated properly, in a forge, and then dipped in urine. Though clay would do, he supposed. The interlacing pattern of the iron writhed and turned like part of the fire, and the maker's name was etched in runic lines upon the metal. *Ulfberht*. An old weapon this, the work of a master. It deserved better. Other, worthier hands had darkened the bone of the grip. It had come a long way to end up in the paw of an Ulsterman.

The Ulsterman had come a long way also. A long way from the valley of the Bann. And an ever farther way back, it seemed. If there was a way back. Now there was something to gnaw on in the long nights, something to keep him awake with a vengeance.

How could he have been such a damn fool?

He turned and looked at Cat's pale face, serene in sleep.

Because he had been only a boy, and he had been in love for the first time in his short life. In love with a girl no one else could see, and the fairy tale she promised him.

Likely enough the fairy tale would end here, in these woods, and the Ulsterman would leave his bones here. He rubbed his forehead and saw that the edges of the sword blade were cherry-red. Damn pattern welding. The thing lost its edge so quickly, and needed to be quenched every so often to harden the carbon-rich iron.

For a moment he thought of a round-faced priest who had tempered it once in a woodland forge. Then he shook his head. Best to forget.

The pressure in his bladder was almost painful. He had been saving it up all day for this. When the deep blush of heat was through the blade he whipped it out of the flames, scattering sparks and swearing at the heat of the hilt. Then he tossed it away and leapt up, gasping at the pain in his thigh. He fumbled with his breeches and let rip, groaning with relief. A veritable torrent gushed out of him in an unending stream and exploded on to the red-hot metal, billowing at once into clouds of ammoniac steam. He coughed and sputtered. In mid-flow he halted himself—not the easiest of tasks—and toed the blade on to its other side. Then he let fly again.

Next time he would use clay, he promised himself.

MICHAEL DID NOT go down to the river's brink. Now was not the time, he thought obscurely, and that knowledge was both weird and familiar. His own notion, but from another time. A grown-up thought, and thus not one to be questioned. He accepted it without argument, and let his feet take him elsewhere.

In the afternoon he and Rose set off for the bridge with sandwiches, nets and jam jars; their fishing equipment. They sat close to where the old stones were sunk into the bank, and the sun spangled off the water like white flame, spotted every so often with the iridescence of a dragonfly. The river was sleepy here, the water brown with depth and slow as syrup. It looked cool and calm. Michael, peering past the unbroken reflection of his own pudgy face, could see weed waving like a far-away forest in a gale, and freshwater shrimps scuttling along the bottom in trails of silt like horses galloping along dusty roads. Maybe there were little countries down there, where eels were dragons and trout great airships hovering above. He looked up again, and saw the black maw of the bridge in front of him. Near the entrance reflected light writhed snake-like along its roof, but farther in there was nothing but darkness. The bridge was not especially wide, but it bent slightly in the middle so that it was impossible to see the light at the other end. Because it had once been below an off-set crossroads, his grandfather had said, but one of the roads had fallen into disrepair and was gone now, its only remnant long ruts in the neighbouring fields and this queerly constructed bridge.

There was a plop beside him, and Rose had set her net in the water. She was kneeling on the bank with her skirt pushed up around her thighs, her free hand tucking hair behind one ear. Her knees were almost as scraped as Michael's.

'Missed the bugger!'

'What? Where?'

'Right below your eyes, dreamer. A trout as long as your hand, but he's made off for the deep water by the bridge. Just as well; he'd never have fitted in the jar... Are you here to fish or to stare at your reflection?'

Hurriedly he sank his own net into the water, twiddling the bamboo pole. He was stirring up a hurricane down there. The shrimps were scattering in all directions and a great whirling cloud of silt was enveloping the weeds.

'Watch it! You're dirtying up the water.'

'Sorry.'

They trolled in silence for a while, Rose stopping once to nudge Michael and point surreptitiously to the kingfisher that was perched on an alder spray just downstream, watching them with his head cocked to one side. He darted off like a cobalt jewel in flight, seeking a less crowded spot. Rose and Michael grinned at one another.

'Ah, you bugger, you wicked little shite, I've got you!'

'What is it?' Michael craned to see.

'An eel, half a foot long if he's an inch. Look how he twists!' Rose's catch was a silver coiling snake in the mud and weed of her net. 'Reach me the jar—no, put water in it first, you fool. Hold it up. He'll have it over. There he is!'

The jam jar was full of brown soup through which they could catch sight of the eel as it pressed itself against the glass in its attempts to get away. A dragon, Michael thought. We've caught a dragon and put it in a magic cage.

They regarded it in silence for a few seconds, until Rose sighed in disgust. 'It's no good. He's too big for it. Chuck him back, Michael.'

He tipped the jar into the river and the eel poured away. The dragon released, soaring through the air above the lands below. It wiggled off and disappeared under a submerged stone. Back to his lair. Perhaps there was gold in there, and he was coiled up on top of it.

'God, it's hot,' Rose said, sitting back and letting her net loll in the water. She watched the mayflies dancing over the surface of the water like gossamer-winged fairies, then started as a trout broke surface to snap one up. In the deep part, by the bridge. She had told Michael that there was a pike in there her father had almost caught a score of times. An old, wily grinning killer fully three feet long. Perhaps he lurked now in the mud of the bottom, biding his time.

'Is there anyone about, Michael?'

He looked up from the muddy broth his net was stirring. 'Don't think so. They're over the other side today.'

'Then I'm for a swim. Coming?'

'All right.'

She took his hand and led him over to the sheltering spray of a riverside oak, and there they threw off their clothes, giggling. Her skin was very white where the sun never touched it, and the sable curl of hair below her belly button drew his gaze for a moment.

'Rose, why—?'

But she tugged his hand, half dragging him along, and with a whoop had plunged into the water, taking him with her. He felt a moment of panic as the coolness covered him, closing over his head. His hands flailed. Then Rose's arms were about him and he was lifted above the surface, the river streaming off his face in blazing sunlight, his ears full of her laughter. The panic trickled away, and he laughed himself, feeling the soft push of her breasts against his chest, nipples hard with the cold water. She kissed him.

'Now, Michael-boy, can you float on your own or do I have to carry you everywhere?'

He realized that she was in her depth, standing with her feet planted in the silt of the bottom and the river lapping round her shoulders.

'Don't let go of me.'

'Ach, you've no courage. Did I not teach you how to swim last summer?'

But last summer was a year ago, a lifetime to a child. He shook his head.

'Well here, then. Grab hold of this.' She pulled down a slim branch of the old oak for him to hold. 'Got it? Good. Now don't let go. Hold on there while I splash about a bit.'

He clung there blinking water out of his eyes and feeling the current move lazily around him. His feet kicked for a moment and the liquid forced his toes apart. What were they thinking, those underwater knights and ladies, those dragons? He shifted uncomfortably as he thought of eels, pikes—who knew what?—powering through the water to nibble at him.

Rose was scattering a shower of sun-kindled spray as she splashed and kicked in the middle of the river. Behind her the black arch of the bridge loomed like an open mouth. Michael saw her head go under and her buttocks flash as she dived, and the river quietened, ripples plashing and spreading, lapping the banks.

'Rose?' he called, alarmed, but she broke surface seconds later with black hair plastered over her face.

'I can see down there,' she called. 'I can see under the water. It's clear as a bell, Michael, like another world.' And then she had dived again. Her pale form was a blur under the river, sinuous as an otter.

She could be a fairy, Michael thought. All she needs are wings. A water fairy. Were there such things?

Rose stood up in the shallows, waist deep. Water poured off her like liquid flame. She raised her arms to wipe the hair from her eyes, grinning, and for a second the water that streamed from her shoulders, sunlit, looked like two transparent wings, and Michael gurgled with happiness.

But something tore his stare away, drew it to where the stone of the bridge was covered by the trees. Movement, a white blur. A face disappearing quickly into the shadow there. Someone watching.

'Rose!' he yelled, lifting one chubby arm to point. His other hand slid along his oak lifeline, leaves torn free by his slipping palm, and he was floating free—no, sinking freely, his astonished eyes filling with water, the river's cool clutch easing over his forehead as softly as a caress.

He batted at the stuff surrounding him, kicked and wriggled, and felt himself rise. Then there was a grip in his hair and he was hauled into the air, the pain making him cry out.

'You wee twit, Michael! What did you want to do that for? What was it anyway?' She hugged him tightly, and he would remember afterwards and replay endlessly in his mind the way she felt against him. Cold with the water, her arms hard around him, his kneecap tickled by the soft pelt at the top of her thighs.

'There was somebody there, Rose. Somebody was looking at us, up by the bridge.' No fox face. Just an ordinary one. A real face, but gone in a moment, quick as shame.

'Oh there was, was there?' Oddly, she smiled, a curious, inward smile. 'It doesn't matter, Michael. I don't care and you've nothing worth hiding.'

'What's so funny?'

'You.' She released him. 'Your face when you went under the water. I thought the pike was tugging at your toes for a minute.'

'It's not right to spy on people.' Especially when they've no clothes on, he added to himself. There was an odd feeling in him, like a cold blush tightening under his stomach. He looked down through the clear water. 'Rose!'

She followed his goggling gaze and her eyebrows shot up her forehead. 'Dear me. You're growing up, Michael.' She kissed his wet nose. 'It's alright. Come on. I think it's time we got dressed.'

FOUR

Growing up... Terrible, frightening words. They were on a par with *dentist* and *mortal sin*. The feel of Rose holding him, and his unprecedented reaction. That dizzy, fearful excitement. These things wheeled in his head for days so he forgot about the face at the bridge, the fox faces at the river. They were placed somewhere in a back room, filed away until something should bring them to light again.

The bridge drew him. He was fascinated by the fact that it was impossible to see daylight through it. It seemed more like a long tunnel leading into the earth. A place for goblins, subterranean workings, mines and borings. But there was water there too, the river, as deep as a sapling and as slow-moving as cold honey. The place was like a green-walled cathedral, the oaks and limes standing back from the bank where the willow and alder clustered as if eager to drink. Light fell on to the water and filtered through the canopy like the rays running through the stained glass of a church. It was both shadowed and brilliant, sparkling and dim. And dominating all was the black mouth of the bridge, as lightless as a well. To enter the arch of the bridge one would have either to swim or procure a boat. Michael could do neither, so the blackness remained one of the fixtures of his young life, as unplumbed as the deepest Pacific canyon.

The river, the bridge, the meadows that surrounded them—these were the places where he frittered away his time, alone for the most part, for Rose developed sudden, unexplained absences over the following weeks which produced sharp words in the house, and one time Michael entered her room to find her sitting crying on the bed. This was a shock to him, a break in the natural order of things. He wanted to exit immediately and forget it, but then Rose looked up at him and he found himself hugging her clumsily, feeling like an impostor.

He was aware that his grandparents, and his Aunt Rachel too, for that matter, disapproved of Rose for some reason, and that she was fighting an obdurate battle against them, but the whys and wherefores of it were kept from him. He heard snatches of talk about 'bringing disgrace on the family' and 'not even one of her own kind,' but these merely baffled him further. It was Aunt Rachel's voice he heard saying these things. She was a big woman, like her mother, in her late twenties and thus ten years older than her sister. She was unmarried, austere, prematurely grey. Michael had seen photographs taken of her before he was born, and in them she had been a smiling dark girl with squarer shoulders and slimmer hips, one hand clasped round a prayer book and the other fighting to keep a broad-brimmed straw hat on her head in a wind from an older, black and white world. She had been 'disappointed in love,' Rose had told him once in a portentous whisper.

Michael came to know the warning signs. The family would take up what he had come to think of as their battle positions in the kitchen, with Rose bright-eyed and defiant, Rachel looking strangely vindicated, his grandmother haggard, her husband weary, and old Mullan sneaking out of the door with a shake of the head. It was grown-up business, a squall to be weathered.

Then there was the dreadful night the parish priest walked in, grim and ashen-haired, his black cassock sweeping the ground, and Michael had been hustled upstairs to bed. He was glad to stay clear of it.

Set against the tension in the house were weeks of the finest weather imaginable. In the fields the barley was being slowly touched with gold and the hay was paled steadily by the sun. A wet spring had meant a much later hay crop and Michael's grandfather had fussed and worried over this one as though it were a wayward chid. Field mice by the hundred had woven their hanging nests in the stalks, unaware of the coming apocalypse. Pat walked through the forest of stems with a smile in his eye, rubbing the ears between his hard hands and winnowing the result with a swift pucker. Ten acres of fine barley, four more of hay—very soon now, the haymaking—and the pastures thick with the dung his cattle had so kindly donated. With Sean's talk, it would be the last time perhaps that they would use the old horse-powered thresher for the barley.

He talked to Mullan of buying a horse, at one of the autumn fairs perhaps, 'just a wee, high-stepping thing for the trap,' whilst his wife listened in stony silence. There was such a thing as stretching sentiment too far. Mullan told a wistful story of seeing a British transport column moving to Ypres in '15; thousands of big heavy horses taking up the roads for miles, hardly a truck among them, towing wagons, ambulances, limbers, guns. And never a one to be seen now. Just damned tractors, keeping a man's feet from the earth, lifting him out of the furrow. You could plough a field these days without even getting its soil on your boots. And he shook his head whilst he and Pat shared a pouch of Warhorse, and even Michael's grandmother was seen to smile a little wistfully, which made Pat and Mullan share a private grin.

It was the calm before the storm, the storm being harvest time, that deliciously busy, back-breaking time of the year when the long, slow days suddenly contracted and seemed too short, when the men sometimes worked on into the nights and the women would bring them massive sandwiches and bottles of cool porter out to the fields. They would work by the light of storm lanterns, eyeing the sky nervously. When the hay was cut and lying, one day's rain was all there was between a fine crop and a ruined one, and in spite of Mullan's protestations they would be glad of the tractor then and the angular bundles that the baler tidily excreted in its wake. The tractor was an innovation, and the year before, Pat muttered about the square-built towers of bales that dotted the fields instead of the old blunt-headed ricks. Progress. Life was speeding up, he complained, like the cars on the roads. It took a wary hand on the reins to make the trip to the village, with the horse snorting at the passage of the metal monsters. He was a simple man, was Pat, his life built in black and white, as nostalgic as any Irishman when talking of his own land. To the hands he appeared to be absolute master, but even Michael knew how his wife prodded him on, like an old cob reluctant in the shafts. His son Sean was full of the ideas he had picked up at agricultural college. Farming was a science, according to him, whereas to Pat and Mullan, and to Michael's grandmother too, if truth be told, it was a way of life, as natural as the return of the swallows in the spring. It had resisted change for generations, but now it was succumbing at last, as was the land itself. It was being battened down and circumscribed, made smaller. The seasons were becoming elements in an equation.

MICHAEL KNEW NOTHING of this. He knew that there were more metal contraptions in the sheds than there had been, and that the smell of engine oil and petrol were becoming as common as the scent of leather and horse, but he drew no conclusions. He was about as analytical as one of the horses themselves. The day ahead was far enough away to look after itself, and the summer stretched like a golden road winding to infinity. There were far more interesting things capering under his very nose.

Grandfather and Mullan went to have a look at the 'wee, high-stepping thing' a few days later, whilst Michael's grandmother remained silent and disapproving and Uncle Sean thought it a waste of money.

'But the harvest will be a good 'un,' Grandfather had said, surreptitiously scratching the back of a wooden chair. 'We can afford it, and when we sell off the bullocks we'll have pasture and to spare.'

'For sheep, I'd have thought,' Sean mumbled, but Grandfather affected not to hear.

'The bottom inch needs a rest; one pony on it for a while will hardly strain it too much.'

'It's winter in a few months.' Sean made a last-ditch effort. 'What about feed?'

'God willing, this will be the best hay crop I've seen in ten years. We can spare enough for one more mouth.' He and Mullan exchanged a look of triumph. Sean subsided grumpily.

They took Michael with them to see the animal, trundling along at a snail's pace with Felix, one of the two heavy horses, clodding between the shafts. Demon sat in the rear of the cart, panting, his black coat livid with dust. A few cars passed them, making Felix throw up his head in annoyance, but he was an old hand and was not going to start playing at silly buggers in the middle of the road—so Grandfather said, anyway. There were others on horses, and they stopped more than once, blocking the road entirely, to share a chat with distant neighbours, the pipe smoke rising between them, the smell of Clan and Warhorse melting away in blue ribands down the breeze.

Twice they drove under Orange arches left over from the Twelfth, gaudy and woebegone. Michael had always been fascinated by the wooden images enshrined there, the man on the white horse, the red hand, the miniature ladders; but he understood also that there was something wrong about them. That was why Grandfather had spat without thinking into the dusty road as their shadow fell across the cart, though he glanced apologetically at Mullan the next second. Mullan was a Protestant. On the Twelfth of July he marched the roads with a chestful of medals and raised his good hat formally as he passed the farm as though they were strangers, though most of the family would be out in front waving at him. For that day he was in a different world, part of a different people that had nothing in common with them. On the thirteenth he would be Old Mullan again, cap-wearing and disreputable. That was the way life worked.

They reached their goal after a long morning in the heat and dismounted before the usual tangle of whitewashed buildings, slapping the dust from their clothes. A dog began barking furiously, and Grandfather laid a hand on Demon's collar. They heard children's voices. A door slammed, and a stocky, shirt-tailed figure stepped out of the house pulling his braces up over his shoulders.

'Ah, Pat, so you're here to have a look at her, then. I knew you would.' They slapped hands. The man dug in his pocket, produced a thumbed-out cigarette, jammed it in his lips, grinned at Michael with what teeth he had (not many, and most of them black), and then strolled off towards one of the buildings, jerking his head for them to follow. 'Brought her in specially today so's you wouldn't have to chase half across the field to look at her. She's a fresh wee thing.'

He clanged back bolts on a half-door and they heard the stamp of a hoof from within. Mullan struck a match off his boot heel as was his wont and sucked the flame into his Peterson.

She was a chestnut, two white socks and a blaze on her nose. 'Two white feet buy him,' Michael muttered, and his grandfather winked at him.

They waded through the thick straw of the box whilst the mare blew down her nose at the smell of strangers and retreated into a corner. Grandfather ran his hands over her gently, produced a stub of carrot for her to nibble, felt her legs, then lifted her hoofs and peered at the frogs.

'How old?'

'Just turned five, same as I told you,' her owner answered him. His stub of cigarette was lit and he was crinkling up his eyes against its smoke.

Pat lifted the upper lip, peered at the teeth, nodded. Noted the way her ears remained forward and there was no white in her eye. Even-tempered.

'How about a look at her moving?' he asked.

'Surely.'

The man threw a halter on her head and led her out of the swishing straw to the sun of the yard. Demon lay watching. The man trotted her up and down. She was unshod, but her hoofs were brought from the ground in an exaggerated prance. She was as perfect as a fully wound toy. Michael gaped.

'A real mover,' Mullan said. He and Grandfather exchanged a look, and Michael knew the horse was as good as bought. 'Fifteen hands, I'd have said,' Pat offered.

'Och, no.' The man was out of breath. 'Fourteen three.'

'Fourteen, you told me,' Pat said easily. 'Just a wee pony, no more.'

'Sure I knew if you thought she was this size you'd never even look at her. And she's worth a look, isn't she?' Pat stared at him with a look that was both annoyance and amusement, and the man grinned hideously, knowing he had been right.

They haggled whilst the mare stood uncomprehending but attentive, the muscles quivering in her flanks.

'Sixty pounds would seem fair.'

'Guineas would be fairer, and a few more at that.'

'What would you say, then?'

'Well, what would you offer? Be realistic now.'

'No, no. It is for you to say. What would you be wanting?'

The man stated a price which made Grandfather and Mullan sputter with mirth and wipe their eyes. 'So you're a comedian,' Mullan laughed.

The price came down. They argued. Grandfather made as if to walk away in disgust. Mullan pulled him back. They threw up their hands, drew attention to her height. This was a horse, not a pony. Ate more. Needed more careful handling. Wasn't quite what they had been looking for.

The price fell further.

The owner shook his head in despair. The beast was a family pet. His daughter would be heartbroken. Hard times forced such measures. Pat tried to bring the price down a last time, but it had hit bedrock. The man was obdurate. He and Grandfather looked at one another, gauging; finally Pat spat on his hand and stuck it out. They shook, each believing he had the better bargain.

'We bought her!' Michael cried.

Mullan patted his head. 'Two white feet, Mike, remember. We had to buy her. Now get you up on the cart.'

They were even slower on the way home, the chestnut tied behind, Felix plodding along in front, keeping to a walk to spare the mare's feet. A subtle gold came into the air, heralding the wane of the afternoon. Blackbirds darted out from the hedges in front of them, alarmed. The roads were quiet. Pat and Mullan were discussing grazing, winter feed, hay and tack. Horse talk, wholesome as apples. Michael looked back at the white-splashed face of the mare. She was staring wide-eyed at the woods to their left.

They were nearly home, and the trees wound about the little river. They could hear it churning in the quiet of the coming evening. The woods were thick here, perhaps half a mile above the bridge. They butted on to meadows and fields of barley.

There was movement there, in the shadow of the trees. Shapes were coursing along low to the ground, grey as smoke.

Demon growled deep in his throat.

Michael peered harder. Dog-like silhouettes loping along-the edge of the meadows. Were they after sheep?

With a clatter of cracked branches a great stag came leaping out of the woods, sprays of leaves caught in its antlers and the insides of its nostrils gleaming like blood. It was gasping and heaving, stumbling, its coat foamed with sweat and matted with briars. The other creatures gave a collective howl and changed course in pursuit. They were wolves.

One fastened on the stag's near hind and was flung away with a kick. The stag turned and lowered its head. A wolf was caught by a vicious swipe and Michael saw something like a dark streamer ripped out of its belly. One of its fellows darted in and fastened its muzzle deep in the stag's groin. It bellowed and spun around frantically, trying to claw forwards with a hind leg, the antlers swinging madly and dispensing oak leaves—

And then was gone. They had turned a corner round the wood and the duel was out of sight. Demon and the chestnut mare had quietened. Pat and Mullan were still talking horses. Michael sat back with his eyes shining. Wolves. There were wolves in the woods.

One day whilst negotiating a broad fire-scarred clearing they were ambushed and caught, the wolves sliding out from the ragged boulders and the shadow of fallen trees. It was rough, uneven ground for the horses, and they had not torn along two hundred yards before the grey went down with a scream and Michael saw Cat flung away like a doll. He hauled on the reins, dragging the chestnut from a full gallop into a tearing halt. His free hand whipped out the heavy sword from the saddle scabbard. There was a torrent of snarling and snapping behind him and he had to force the terrified horse round with what strength he could muster from his crippled hand.

The grey was already dead. Wolves swarmed over it like lice, bracing their forefeet upon the body and ripping out chunks of quivering meat with sideways jerks of their heads. Cat was on her hands and knees, groggy from the fall. The wolves were ignoring her for the moment.

Michael kicked his mount viciously, but the smell of the wolves and the blood was terrifying her. She backed away with her ears laid against her skull. He hammered the flat of the sword on her head and then on the flank. Cat was looking around her with dawning comprehension. Any moment now the wolves would notice her. Snarling wordlessly, Michael scythed the edge of the blade along his steed's rump, and she jumped forward just as the first wolves left the grey's corpse with red muzzles, smelling the woman crouched nearby. The horse powered forward, knocking them aside. Michael swung the blade, felt it tear through fur and muscle, swung again at one which was going for the mare's belly and clipped and crunched the skull. Cat leapt behind him and her slim arms locked around his waist. He stabbed the blade into a yellow-eyed face, and then staggered in the saddle as a heavy weight smote his left arm and clung there. The horse wheeled in panic-stricken circles, and Michael felt the maw of the wolf fasten deep, deep, in his forearm, the mad eyes glaring at him over the blood-soaked snout. He shrieked with pain and fear as the wolf's weight began to drag him from the saddle. Only Cat's arms kept him there, but his right foot left the stirrup and slid up to the horse's neck. The mare's body lurched as she kicked out to the rear, and with what seemed like infinite slowness he brought the sword round for a shortened stab, deliberately chose one of the glaring eyes and thrust the point into the socket. It grated on bone, caught for a second, then scraped free as the jaws opened and the wolf slid silently from sight. He kicked the chestnut onwards and she broke into a gallop. His left arm was numb, and he could see the blood dripping from it. Like that good wine we had, he thought muzzily. It was Cat who saved the sword as it slipped from his fingers, who took the reins from his nerveless hand, who kept him on the horse as they pitched along in mad flight with the wolves loping and snapping around them.

Michael was being scrubbed by his grandmother in the bath when she paused in her labour to wipe soap from her nose and fix him with a stare. He squirmed uneasily, thinking of how his body had betrayed him in the river with Rose that time. It hadn't happened since, but he wondered if it had somehow left a mark.

'You're eight now, Michael, aren't you?'

'Nearly. Will be in December.'

She shook her head. Her cheeks were flushed and tendrils of wet hair hung over her forehead. Michael saw that the whites of her eyes were ribboned with tiny red veins and the grey irises were cloudy.

'Too big for someone to be bathing you.'

Michael shrugged. Rose usually did it, and by the end they would both be soaked and laughing, the bathroom floor a mosaic of bubbles, the air opaque with steam. It was one of the high points of his week. But Rose was in her room, and he thought she might be crying again. He was afraid to go in, yet could not make himself avoid it. He knew he would knock on her door as he mounted the stairs to bed. And, besides, it had clouded over today and the thunderheads had piled up like skyborne anvils. His grandfather had snuffed at the air and prophesied a storm before the morning. It was in the house now, waiting to break. The air was hot, the sunset bringing no coolness. A thick haze had overlaid the western mountains, and the clouds were still piling. Uncle Sean was worried about the barley. It would be just typical for a storm to flatten the half of it, and it nearly cut, he had said.

'Michael, you're very fond of your Aunt Rose, aren't you?'

He nodded, eyes wide as a deer's. This was a new topic, and he was immediately defensive, wrapping his arms around his knees in the soapy water. His grandmother wiped his back absently with the sponge.

'Well, it might be she'll be going away for a time, Michael, and I don't want you to worry about her.'

'Why? Where's she going?'

'That doesn't matter. Never you bother your head about it. She'll be away for a fair while, but she'll come back.'

'When? How long will she be gone?' He could hear his voice shake and tears burned in his throat.

His grandmother hesitated. 'She'll be away maybe a year, Michael, but it'll soon pass, you'll see.'

A year. A year was an immense expanse of time. The rest of the summer. School, and Christmas. Would she be away for Christmas? And Easter, and then the summer again. A huge time. Hundreds of days. He bowed his head to his knees and his grandmother kissed his crown. 'Come on, Michael, get yourself out of the bath and dried. I'll leave you to do that yourself. You're a big boy now.' She hauled herself off her creaking knees and out of the door. Michael could have sworn by the tremor in her voice that she was near to tears too.

The storm broke in the early hours and from his bed Michael watched his grandfather and Uncle Sean battle across the yard with a swinging lantern to check on the horses, brought in from the fields that afternoon. The stables were a lovely place to sit out the rain, deep in straw, lamplit, warm with sleepy animals, the blue night roaring and splashing down beyond the half-door. Michael wiped at the glass. The rain had hardly begun and the air was close and stuffy. Then a bright burst of forked lightning raced down the sky and lit up his horrified face. He launched himself away from the window, some part of his mind counting seconds. When it had reached six the thunder exploded above the roof of the house, rolling from gable to gable, and he thought the glass shook. A whimper crept into his throat.

Another flare of light, garish across the spilled bedclothes, and another rattle of celestial artillery. He leapt from the bed like a hare, hit the wooden floor with a thump, scrabbled out of his door and darted along the hallway. Rose's door. It was closed. She had not answered his knock earlier in the evening. He opened it to another flash of lightning, and saw Rose pressed up against the window, the bolt burning through her nightdress so that for an instant she was a naked silhouette surrounded by gauze. Then it was wholly dark, and he bumped into her bed, dazzled.

'Michael! I thought I'd be seeing you tonight.' To his relief her voice was normal, even merry. She loved storms.

They climbed into bed together under a flickering barrage of lightning and thunder. He clung to her and she smoothed his hair.

'You're going away,' he said at last, muffled at her breast.

'It's all right, Michael, it's for the best.' Her hand strayed down to her stomach and he saw it caress herself there. He had a sudden feeling of panic, as though things were about to change irrevocably; and this strange mood of Rose's was part of it, the beginning of it, even. He wanted her to be herself again, ordinary and unafraid, making a joke of everything.

Why were these weird things happening? Maybe they were something to do with her, with the arguments in the family. Perhaps she should know.

'There are wolves in the woods, Rose,' he blurted out. 'And men with fox faces down by the river. There are things out there. Like the face watching us swim.'

But she was a thousand miles away. 'Watching me, he was,' she murmured. She took his hand and set it on her navel. 'Do you know what's in there, Michael?'

He struggled with the change of tack. 'Guts and things?'

She giggled. 'There's a wee girl in there, sleeping now, and when she wakes up she'll come out, and you'll have somebody to play with.'

He raised himself on to one elbow. 'Rose!'

'It's true, Michael. That's why I'm going away.' Her voice thickened but he hardly noticed.

'How did it get there?' He was still dubious. Her reply was drowned in thunder.

'And she'll come out... here.' She touched herself again, lower down. His hand pursued hers, below the nightdress, brushed the curly mat of hair, found a narrow dip and followed it until his questing finger was on a moist pout of flesh and Rose tensed. Her hand closed over his, lifted it gently away. There was that tightness again, a steady pressure below his stomach. Rose tapped it, then took it in her hand through his nightshirt, squeezed gently. He thought his breathing would stop. The thunder raged on forgotten. A tense, ecstatic, terrifying second, and she released him, kissed his nose. The lightning made her smile perilous. 'I'm a fallen woman,' she whispered in his ear. 'I'm in mortal sin, Michael.'

The words were grown up, frightening. The Devil is listening, he thought. Mortal sin. Rose was going to hell, then. And she would never come back to him again.

'I'll say my prayers, Rose,' he whined. 'I'll pray for you.'

She laughed loudly, the thunder roaring its way along the roof like a mad horseman. 'Prayers! It's the priest is sending me away, Michael. It's him that's making me leave home. Prayers!' She sat up in the bed, as electric as the racing clouds in the wind-bitten sky beyond the window. 'Say no prayers for me. Save them for the child.

It'll be a girl. I know it will be a girl. And they'll take it away like they drown the runt of the litter. It'll be a bastard, Michael. It has no father.'

Lightning forked in her eyes like luminous cat slits. She was as tense as a bent branch in the bed, blue light illuminating her face. When the lightning died Michael could see her eyes hovering disembodied before him, bright after-images.

'Don't forget me, Michael. And don't believe all that you hear. They're going to take me away, but if I don't return I want you to find me, to bring me back. Or my daughter,' she added in a whisper. And in the same low tone said: 'My soul.

'You'll do that? You'll look for me no matter what they tell you? Promise?'

He promised, fearful and puzzled.

She smiled brokenly. 'There are worse things than sinners in the world, little Michael. Much worse.' Then they embraced each other in the narrow bed and lay like lovers until sleep muffled the thunder.

THE FARM SLEPT, the rags of the storm tumbling off in the west like the rear of a battered army. Down in the kitchen old Demon twitched and sniffed in his sleep, smelling ancient smells, seeing things he had sensed but never known—old things that were lodged for ever in the hind part of his canine brain. Snow and ice, and great rime-coated beasts lumbering through the drifts. The drip of water in caves, the scrape of teeth on warm, marrow-sweet bone. He whimpered, his claws scraping the stone floor, but he was an old dog and did not waken.

Rachel slept also, her dark tresses unbound in the bed, the hard lines of her face relaxed. She was dreaming.

Dreaming of her beautiful man, her sloe-eyed suitor with the red lips and skin thorn-blossom pale. The dark man with his clothes elegant and fine on him, tapering from the broad shoulders to the slender hips.

Still sleeping, her legs scissored a pillow, pulling it in to her.

But he had left her. Even when she had... even when she had wanted it, had agreed, was aching for him in the grass with her prayer book thrown aside and her hair fanned out in the buttercups. The flower-print frock was up over her thighs, and if she had dared she would have touched herself where she wanted him to touch her, so desperate was her need. And he had smiled and wagged a finger. Left her without a word, her legs spread in the field and her clothes clinging to her.

Soundlessly and unconsciously, Rachel wept in her lonely bed. Old Mullan was dreaming too.

'That's a Papist name,' the recruiting sergeant had said, his UVF badges on his shoulders and his eyes as narrow as keyholes.

'I'm no Pape.'

'So you'd say *fuck the Pope*, then?'

'I—I would.'

'Say it.' And he had.

He was crumbling Flanders mud in his grimy fingers, as hard and pale as old chocolate in the baking sun. The sweat ran down under the lining of his helmet and the dust clung to it, streaking his face. His uniform was hot and sweat-soaked, hitched and itching, and his webbing gnawed at his young shoulders. The dried-out earth glued itself to the blue-black oily barrel of the .303 and powdered the wooden stock as though claiming it. Far off there was the crump of guns.

Agnes Fay, Michael Fay's grandmother, lay as still and straight as a felled tree in the conjugal bed, breathing softly to Pat's low snore. She was dreaming of boots. Boots kicking the door of her home and men in two-tone uniforms shouldering in, police tunics with soldiers' khaki underneath. Her mother in an agony of terror, her brothers white, whirling for the revolvers gleaming on the chair. And she had plopped her rump down on them as calm as you please, sat on their metal hardness and refused to move as the Black and Tans skeltered through the house and her father stood with his hands on his head. A girl, merely, she had almost wet herself with fear, but had sat on, her skirts hiding treason and saving her brothers from a bullet in the back yard.

Sean dreamed of shiny tractors ploughing ruler-straight furrows and belching smoke into the blue sky. Behind them the settling seagulls were pushed aside by the rising corn, and a man came scything, his blade like a horned moon brought into the sunlight.

Pat dreamed of horses, and smiled as he slumbered. Michael did not dream, because he was in Rose's arms.

His younger aunt was awake, feeling for a bulge that would not be there for weeks yet. Her knuckles skimmed over her boy-narrow hips, and she wondered if it were possible that a new life should burst out of them without killing her.

She remembered. He had stopped her up so that the slick clockwork of her monthly trickle had been dammed. As she was damned. A dark man, a faceless man, he had filled her with heat and pressed her into the cool leaf mould whilst the river had churned on like the rage of her swimming blood and the night rose dark and thick with trees around her. And now there was another heart beating in there.

Poor Thomas McCandless. Clumsy and eager, she had blamed him for it, let him have what he had been wanting this long time and then she had named him the father. Poor, gulled Thomas, fumbling and red-faced, afraid to look and yet as greedy as a child. A Protestant father of a bastard child, or so they thought. The real father had been a hooded horseman passing by, and as his mount pulled out of the river bottom in the next morning's dawn its hoofs had sent the crumbling bank tumbling into the water. She did not want to see him again, but thought she would if the baby split her apart in its journey toward the light.

'Souls are cheap,' he had said as he rode away, and she thought he had laughed.

In the rain-flensed back yard the stone was dimly glinting, the gutters pouring night-dark liquid into the rainwater barrels. The wolves padded the stone like ghosts, peopling Demon's dreams with fear and fellowship, sniffing at the animal smells. The horses laid back their ears in the stables and in the fields the sheep were crowded and alert, but nothing molested them. The farm cats watched luminous-eyed from dry corners. The pack milled about in the starless gloom, silent and searching. Once one pawed at the back door. Then they poured away towards the woods like feather-footed phantoms afraid of the dawn.

FIVE

FIVE YEARS PASSED.

Rose never came back, because she was dead.

The news filtered down to Michael some seven months after her hasty departure. She had been stolen in the night by the priest and a pair of stern nuns, and Michael had cried his heart out at her white face in the back of the big car, looking not much older than himself. For him she died the moment the door closed on her and the car was out of the front yard. She had left his world and was in another one. Death did not enter into it, and he was unsure as to what exactly it was anyway. Death to him was like a letter lost in the post. Someone had gone somewhere he could not visualize. For him death started ten miles from home.

No one would tell him how or why she had died; it was under-carpet material, a skeleton to find a closet for. He prayed for her, and for the child she had said she was going to get, but he was not entirely sure if she had been joking with him, even now. Rose had always been a great one for stories.

After a while, an immense while—three years at least—she receded from the forefront of his mind. Rachel took over with the chickens and made a hash of it, for they distrusted her and she could not find half their nests. So there were eggs for breakfast less often. And Grandfather had thrown one of the hired hands out of the house, Thomas McCandless, a youth who was almost a boy. Michael never learned why. He spent as much time as possible alone or with Mullan. It was safer that way. He had a vague idea, however, that Rose would come back some day, that he would go down to their pool by the bridge one morning and see her sitting there with her toes in the water waiting for him.

The five years saw him grow furiously so that his clothes crept up his limbs overnight and alarming wisps of hair began to appear where there had been none before. Where Rose had had some. That thought was absurdly comforting.

'You'll be growing out of your skin next,' his grandmother said to him, holding a shirt against his widening shoulders and pursing her lips. 'And that hair! It's like a shaggy dog on top of your head. What am I going to do with you?'

He roamed the woods and meadows around the farm like a gamekeeper, often in the company of old Mullan. He grew lithe and tall, gawky until flesh began to fill out the stretching bones. And work round the farm made the muscles under his skin move like smooth stones. The sun burnt freckles around the bridge of his nose and made his grey eyes startling in so brown a face. Rachel admonished him for being 'wild,' bent his head over the kitchen sink and scrubbed the back of his neck whilst he wiggled and squealed in her strong, stout arms. This was even though he had had the responsibility for keeping himself clean four years and more.

'You're not so grown up you can wander about a Christian house with a neck as black as peat,' she said.

The days and weeks and months washed back and forth like tides, taking and giving flotsam or jetsam. Demon died and was quietly mourned by Pat. He would no longer be an unseen presence under the dinner table. They buried him near the river without ceremony, though Michael's grandfather touched his cap to the grave in an odd gesture that was both farewell and salute. After a decent interval his place was taken by a pair of squalling pups, and soon they were running at Pat's heels like midget doppelgangers of their grey-muzzled predecessor.

The land remained the same. There were perhaps a few more cars on the roads to frighten the horses, and here and there a new house was built. One or two copses were slaughtered by farmers who wanted another half-acre of pasture to put some silver in their pockets, and there were the usual tales of outrages in the city, talk of the British Army being brought in, which caused a barely perceptible tension between Pat and Mullan for some days. But all that was too far away to worry about.

Sean's acquisition of the new tractor was much more newsworthy—a great, roaring McCormick Cropmaster that put their little grey Massey-Ferguson to shame. It reminded Michael of nothing so much as a scarlet, bug-eyed dragon that farted smoke. Pat appeared uneasy both at the smoke-bellowing apparition in his yard and the amount of money it had taken to put it there, but Sean was grinning and confident. Clark Gable on a tractor.

'It'll be a bloody car next,' Mullan prophesied gloomily, and went back to grooming the chestnut mare.

School continued to claim Michael for two thirds of the year, much to his frustration. He walked the two miles into the village five mornings a week with his books and his lunch in a bag and in winter a bundle of turfs for the stove on his back. He hated maths, science (what there was of it), geography, grammar, and everything else except some bits of history (Celts, Vikings and Normans, his island's heritage), and reading, when there was something interesting to read. He sailed through Lady Gregory, the Brothers Grimm, Jules Verne, Robert Louis Stevenson and even some Conrad. He was an anomaly in the class (apart from being a head taller than any other child). He loved reading—only certain things, perhaps, but he loved reading. The teacher was a Miss Glover, and she had been across the water. A comfortable, round-faced spinster, she spoke with an accent that the children (and most of the surrounding district) assumed she had picked up in England. She could be imperious when she forgot herself, but mostly chose not to because she was aware that it secretly amused the children. Michael had seen her annoyed and even cross many times, but never furious enough to hit a child, which was unusual in the extreme.

He made few friends at school, none that were even remotely as close as Rose had been. A fair few of the class were relatives; the Fays were a numerous horde. But he had little to do with them. He was 'odd,' and would have had a hard time of it were it not for his precocious height and strength. The two-room school bordered on to the first heights of the Antrim plateau so that behind the paved playground was a long reach of gorse-scattered heath running up into boulder-strewn hills above. The village it belonged to was merely one straggling street stretching from the Bann bridge in the valley to the first folds of the eastern hills. The school was at its eastern end, set far back from the road. Michael's grandfather had been schooled there a half-century before, and some of the books the children used still spoke of the British Empire and the Raj. It reminded Michael of Mullan's war tales; how he had seen Indian troops shivering in the mud of the trenches, and Old Contemptibles, the remnants of the Regulars, trying to speak to the Belgians in Urdu or Hindi, confident that one language sufficed for all foreigners. Brown men, tanned by the sun of Africa or India or Afghanistan, meeting their end in the chill drizzle of Flanders. The end of an Empire, Mullan had said sadly—but then Mullan was a Protestant.

The fox faces had returned to the river hollow.

Like Rose, they had belonged to another time, when he had been someone else. It was strange that Michael could begin to forget Rose's face, and yet remember every nuance of that moment when she had hugged him naked to her in the river. It paraded through his dreams in the nights and filled him with inchoate desire.

The memory of the Fox-People (as he came to call them) filled him with a mixture of dread and curiosity. There were strange things in the woods and fields, the meadows and hills, and only he was aware of them. His literary diet primed him for them, and his ceaseless wanderings inured him to the sudden sights that would skitter out of the shadows at odd times and disappear again—never harming him, no matter how fearsome they appeared. Only the wolves bothered him. Worried, he had asked Mullan, who was as close to the land as it was possible to be without being buried in it, whether he had ever seen anything strange in the trees, any tracks, bones, signs. And the old man had looked at him craftily and asked him if he had been seeing fairies again.

'Dogs. What about dogs, a pack of them? Any signs?'

'What are you getting at, Mike? Are you trying to tell me we've lost some sheep?'

'No. No. It's nothing.' But he worried when Mullan stayed out all night after pheasants, and wondered what would happen if he stumbled across a feasting pack of wolves. It never happened, and Mullan, close to the earth though he was, never noticed anything out of the ordinary.

Perhaps they were his alone, then. Michael's wolves.

SOMETHING FROM AN old, old nightmare hung over him, making him cry out. A fox's mask with a dirt-dark face below it, breathing fetid air on him. He tried to sit up but was pushed down again and a hard, deep voice barked strange words at him. The forest language. Ringbone. His head lolled to one side and he saw that his forearm had been bound with birch bark, black mud oozing out of the crude dressing. The mud stank of urine. He closed his eyes. He could hear people around him, the crackle of a fire, the wind in the branches of the trees. Underneath him, his bedding rustled as he shifted. He felt a cold palm on his hot forehead.

'Cat?'

'It's all right, Michael. Ringbone and his people found us again, drove off the wolves. You're going to be all right.'

He'd heard that before. Such phrases were very cheap. He dragged open his eyes. Wood poppies. The bastards had drugged him. But he knew Ringbone. He was almost a childhood friend. He raised his good arm in salute to the lean fox man who squatted at his side, reeking of sweat and carrion. The white teeth gleamed briefly in answer.

'Are we safe? The wolves—'

'They've drawn off for the moment,' Cat said. 'Ringbone's people are keeping watch.'

'It wasn't a manwolf bit me—tell them that—they know that, don't they?'

'Of course,' she said soothingly. 'It was just an animal. They know... You're all right. They won't eat you.' And she smiled that famous Cat smile, Cheshire Cat, leading him through Wonderland. She looked less tired. There was a pale sun in the air, like a gleam of spring, or autumn jetsam. Her hair was washed and her breath smelled of mint. He felt the old stirrings and laughed at himself.

She set a hand on him, down where the breeches were, confining his erection.

'Tonight, maybe,' she said. 'The Fox-Folk can watch for us.'

'Who will they watch?' he asked lightly.

'Whoever they like.'

I've become a savage, he thought. No modesty left. I'd take her now, in front of them all, if I had the strength.

She seemed to know. She bent low and her mint-tasting tongue entered his mouth, stabbing like a wet snake. He felt the leaves pushed from her mouth into his, tasted the chewing-gum flavour of them. She withdrew.

'Tonight,' she said, grinning. 'We're almost home, aren't we?'

'Almost.' Her grin faded. 'Not out of the woods yet, though.'

He closed his eyes, ashamed of the sudden fear that had been assailing him. This was not the first time Ringbone and his folk had saved their lives. And yet he could not help but remember a butchery, a grisly feast seen by firelight in a wood haunted by the howls of wolves. Ringbone's people setting one of their kin to rest after he had been... tainted. A thousand years ago, it seemed. Another world, another life.

IT WAS AN evening in the autumn, over four years from Rose's departure, and the first prickings of adolescent irritability had helped drive him from the supper table to the stables, and then to the open land beyond the farm. A blustery evening, the clouds pouring across the sky and the wind roaring in the half-nude limbs of the trees. The dark creeping up more quickly, the long days of summer far behind, the hay gathered in and built brickwise in bales under the hayshed roof. The grass was wet and gave slightly underfoot, the ground swollen with rain. Even as he stood watching the blank slate where it was usually possible to see the mountains, the rain started again and he cursed (something he had picked up recently), heading for the shelter of the trees by the river, half wondering if there would be anything in them.

'You're too grown up for your own good!' Aunt Rachel had shouted at him, after he had made a remark about her soda bread that had caused even his grandfather to smirk helplessly. But she had not stopped there. 'Hanging around with Rose as if she was your sister, and her ten years older, that's what ruined you, boy.' And there had been a shocked silence in the kitchen. Michael had blundered out with treacherous tears stinging his throat, but not too quickly to miss Pat's voice raised in anger, Rachel's shrill reply.

As always, it was dimmer under the trees, a darker, grimmer shade than the green swaying dimness of summer. He scuffed through leaves for a moment, thinking of Rose with a baffled, angry confusion of grief and desire, and then shifted into his wood mode, watching his step. It was possible there might be something in the wood on an evening like this. Dusk and dawn, Mullan had said once, and he had been right.

Michael had seen huge deer in these woods, and something that might have been a beaver once, slapping in the river—and wolves, of course. They were dark, the wolves, blacker than those he had seen in animal encyclopedias, with larger skulls and bonier frames, their legs like long jointed sticks. Built for speed, like greyhounds. He had watched them from the branches of trees, stinking of woodsmoke to hide his smell. Mullan had taught him that.

There were around a dozen of them, though the numbers varied, and they most often were encountered moving north to south, swimming the little river without a thought and casting about the undergrowth as though following a scent. Once he had seen them in the open fields below the upper meadow, a distant crowd of loping shapes, tiny as ants in the failing light. For the life of him, Michael could not figure out where they had come from or what they were doing here. He knew that the last wolf of the British Isles had been killed in Scotland in the eighteenth century. There were no longer beasts in the fields to be afraid of, and in Ireland at least there were no wildernesses left. The puzzle fascinated him.

But there were no wolves here this evening. He could hear the river, full and rushing between its banks. The undergrowth was dying off with the approach of winter and the ground between the trees was almost bare, clay covered with leaf mold, cold and damp.

It was the sound of voices that halted him.

He crouched, the ground cold on his knees, and saw on the other side of the river a flicker of yellow light. A fire. He edged forward, knowing who it must be, afraid but curious—and still bloody minded from his tangle with Aunt Rachel.

They were in the dip on the western bank of the river. He could see their shapes squatting in front of the flames, backs to him, the evening becoming dark enough for the fire to dazzle him. He closed one eye and crept forward, felt his palm slide in muck and then sink in freezing river water. Around him the trees soared up and the rain dripped off them in a pattering susurration. He was covered, sight and sound. And smell, for he could smell them, the same smell as before, and he was a frightened child again for a second, rigid with one foot shin deep in the churning river, smelling the musky reek of them. But he was almost thirteen now, an old thirteen, a big thirteen, not far off six feet and as lean as a cat. He was invincibly young, and pig-headed to boot. He waded out across the river.

The rain grew heavier, trickling down his neck and soaking his shoulders. The fire flared as someone threw another faggot into its heart. The light shone off rain-slick forms and the smell grew thicker. Wet bodies, unwashed and wood-filthy. The talk subsided abruptly, and for a panicky second he thought they were aware of him, but there was a moan, a savage grunt of deep pain, and then the talking started again. If it was talk. It sounded like the muttering of discontented hounds.

He was barely twenty feet from them when he halted, unwilling to trust his woodcraft further. Their fire cast a tiny dome of yellow light in the blackness of the wet trees, lit up the falling raindrops as if they were sparks come from some overhead forge. Four of the Fox-People squatted around the flames, their masks making them into prick-eared shadows, the eye sockets strangely lifelike. They were huddled in thick furs. (*Bear*? Michael wondered. No. Not thick enough. He looked again. Wolf. They were clad in wolfskins, with the spiky neck ruffs pulled round to their napes so they appeared hunchbacked.)

He could see the paint on their faces, pale as lime. White across the eyes and then some darker pigment rubbed in on the nose and mouth. There were other skins under the wolf furs. Fox, probably. He thought he saw the end of a brush peeping out towards the fire. They had rawhide belts and slings, roughly sewn pouches (mostly empty), and beside them on the sodden leaves were spears and knives, some of cruelly sharp flint, others of what might have been bronze, green and slick.

The Fox-People had fallen into silence. They were not cooking anything, though there was a crude spit across the fire, and a good store of wood at its side drying out close to the flames. They looked utterly weary and downcast. One in particular fingered his flint dagger as though he meant to cut his own throat with it.

Movement on the edge of the firelight drew Michael's attention. Something struggled there on the soaking ground, and he heard again the moan of pain that he had heard earlier. There was a man pinned to the earth like an insect, his hands jerking uselessly at his bonds. He was a fox man, but he had been staked out, and his headdress lay beside his cheek. There was the dark shine of thick clotted liquid on his naked chest, and Michael saw more of it bubble and pop out of the hole there as he writhed. Michael's stomach did a long, lazy roll and he reswallowed a gulp of vomit, feeling it sear his throat.

A wolf howled, long and forlorn, off in the distance. The Fox-People twitched at that, glancing up through the trees to the heavy sky. It was wholly dark now, and there would be no moon visible through the cloud, though it was almost full.

At last they seemed to come to some sort of unspoken consensus. They got up from the fire, hefting their weapons, and made their way over to where their comrade struggled on the ground. One of them carried a spitting branch from the fire that threw a kaleidoscope of shadows along the boles of the trees. Then they stood looking down, as if waiting.

The bound man growled deep in his throat, making Michael jump. He crept closer.

He could see little. The lying man was threshing and tugging at his ties, and the growling sounds were becoming louder. One of the fox men backed away a step as though in horror. Michael stared in disbelief.

The man on the ground was changing, darkening, lengthening. He was growing a black fur as quickly as steam mists a window, and his body was bending, arms flexing at non-existent joints, his growl becoming a gargled bellow of animal rage. Michael saw his face change, the snout push out and the ears lengthen. There was the glint of teeth, impossibly long. The head snapped from side to side and two yellow lights lit up in the eyes.

'Jesus!' Michael whispered.

He was no longer a man, but some huge, misshapen animal, barrel chested, long limbed and black with hail. One hand, a paw now, came free—

And a spear was thrust with incredible force into its chest, pinning it to the ground. The man-animal screamed, and from the surrounding woods Michael heard more than one wolf howl in answer, a desperate, despairing note in the sound.

But the thing's struggles were weakening. Other spears were being jabbed into its still living body. It was impaled half a dozen times. The huge head stopped its snapping. The eyes dulled.

Immediately the fox men knelt and began working on it with their knives. Michael thought he heard one of them weeping, but the rain was too loud in the wood to be sure. He was soaked to the bone, but hardly realized it. His whole attention was on the bestial scenes at the border of the sinking firelight.

They stood up, one holding a slippery, steaming mess in both hands. Then they repaired to the fire, leaving the gutted wreck on the ground behind them. A two-fisted gobbet of meat was slipped on to the spit and the blood streamed from it to sizzle in the fire. The men licked their fingers and squatted on their haunches once more. Two of them covered their faces with their hands. All began keening softly, a low wail of grief. They watched the thing's heart char over the flames, turning it with the prick of a blood-sticky knife. They were covered in blood, soaked with it, and their face paint had bleared in streaks down their filthy faces.

When the meat had hardly been seared they cut off chunks of it and ate, holding the gobbets up to the tree-covered sky before swallowing them with great solemnity. They ate the entire heart, shaking out globs of coagulated blood sometimes, jerking off bites with twists of their head. And when they had finished one of them produced a bulging skin bag from his furs and drank from it, passing it round. Even from where he sat Michael could smell the spirit stink in the air, potent and flammable. They each took a long swallow, wiping their sticky faces, and then two of them went over to the corpse again and began carving it up, skinning and gralloching it as though it were a butchered calf. There was the grate of stone on bone, a sharp crack, and the hideous head rolled free on the ground, the teeth catching the flames for a second.

'Michael! *Michael!*' A familiar voice carrying over the rain and the sizzle of the fire. Michael started. His grandfather's voice, coming from the fields beyond the wood. The Fox-People gave no sign that they had heard it. It was not part of their realm, Michael realized. He backed away slowly, conscious of the numbing chill that the rain had beaten into him. He was clumsy, tired, but the rain covered his blunderings. The flame light receded and then disappeared as though a switch had been thrown, and he could see the slightly lighter patch where the wood ended and the fields began, the figure there with a lantern burning, bright as the fire he had left. Pat, his grandfather, tall as a hill in the pouring night, calling for him. He plashed back across the river, left the dank woods and laboured out towards the meadow, weary as a whipped hound, his mind in a whirl.

AUNT RACHEL KEPT out of Michael's way for days afterward, and was tight-lipped in general. He shrugged it off as one of the countless idiosyncrasies common to grown-ups. He was not yet old enough to bear grudges or to understand exactly what they were.

He wanted to go back to the river and take another look at the site of the Fox-People's grisly feast, partly to assure himself that he had not been dreaming, and partly out of morbid curiosity. But he found that the shortening days, combined with the drudgery of school, homework and the 'wee jobs' that his grandparents set for him conspired to keep him in the immediate vicinity of the farm. Mullan, too, off-loaded his unfair share of tasks, from grooming Felix (the old man spent too much time by half currying that fancy bloody chestnut, Michael thought) to soaping rarely used tack and harness. Mullan would sit in the tack room smoking sometimes, and stare at nothing for minutes on end, explaining only when Michael asked him what he was about that he was having a last look. 'This sort of stuff'll soon only be in museums, Mike.' It made Michael scoff, but the old man would not be budged out of his fit of melancholy, until, perhaps, he had the chestnut harnessed to the light trap, when something like a gleam would appear in his eyes again.

It was over a week after his last visit, then, that Michael finally got away to the woods and the river hollow. A Saturday, the absence of school meaning he could go in the middle of the day instead of creeping along in the half-dark. He had grown less fond of the dark since he had seen the fox man transformed into an animal on the ground. A wolf. So he was a werewolf. And the realization was like a sliver of ice in Michael's gut. He should tell someone, a grown-up. Mullan, maybe. Yet again he felt an ache at the memory of

Rose. She would have believed him, or if she hadn't she would at least have been willing to wait in the wood with him, and watch. Maybe then she would have been convinced. Why had there been no funeral, no wake? Not even a mass to go to. Unless she were not dead after all.

The wood was filled with a faint rushing of air, the creak of tree limbs, forlorn birdsong. A blackbird burst out chittering in front of his knees. Hysterical birds, he often thought, always pitching about in a panic. But he moved more warily after that.

The wood changed. It happened often when he was in it, usually when he was about to see something unusual, something from what he had come to call the Other Place. The trees seemed older, though they were no larger, and there was a different feel to the air, cleaner and sharper. His nose seemed to take on a new sensitivity, twitching at the sour mold and wild garlic, the green tree smell which he found impossible to define, but which was like a vastly subtler version of new-cut grass. And he was able to note the holed hazel shells where a squirrel had had a snack, the peeled bark where a deer had feasted, the bony, crumbling pellets of an owl.

And there, in the soft earth, the imprint of a padded paw. He straightened, but the wood was quiet, and there were hours of daylight left, even if it were only a dull, late autumn daylight. He considered breaking himself a staff from the ruler-straight hazel, then thought better of it. Before him was the river, still full, white between its banks.

He stepped on stones this time, at leisure and unwilling to wet his toes. Then he was across, leaving the roar of the water behind, moving deeper into the wood. The river coursed in a horseshoe here, enclosing a great arc of trees. If he carried on he would find it again eventually, more sedate as it ambled into the mouth of the old bridge where he and Rose had fished.

He stumbled across the ruins of the fire without effort, footing the ashes almost before he was aware he had found them. Bones, here, amid the black butts of sticks. Ribs, they looked like, a heap of them. Longer ones split for the marrow.

He looked up suddenly. The wood was silent, even the birds quiet. But then they usually were around this place. They seemed to shun it. He thought he could hear the faint rushing of the river, but that was all. The wind had fallen. He poked with the remains of the spit and dug at the fire scar. More bones, buried in loose earth and ash, wood burned to charcoal.

He picked up a stick of charcoal and then, half smiling, scored a thick-line across his face with it, streaking his cheeks and nose. He was a savage now. He wondered what Aunt Rachel would say if she could see him.

Wild.

He dug deeper, levering out earth and bones with his makeshift pick. The point jarred on something like a large stone, and he discarded it, scooping and scrabbling with his hands.

The skull.

He heaved it out with his fingers in the eye sockets. There were shreds of blackened gristle clinging to it, long, coarse black hairs stuck in the clay, and what might have been the withered, leathery remnant of one ear, sharp as a horn.

The teeth fascinated him. Longer than Demon's had been, thicker at the base. The skull was huge, heavy, frightening. The fire had burned it black. He wiped ash and hide from it, staring in wonder. A werewolf's skull. Would he be believed now? Maybe they would put it in a museum like they had the sword his grandfather had found. He could be in the paper.

But the idea faded away as he stared at it. He had a notion that it was still alive, and it would take little imagination to see it snap, the eye sockets light up like candles. He had a sudden urge to bury it again.

But no. That was what he had come for. Evidence. Something real out of everything he had seen. He was not leaving it behind.

There was a long, distant howl, way off in the sombre depths of the trees.

He stood up at once. Wolves.

The skull hung heavy from his fingers. Was there a distant swishing of feet in the wood? A pattering, an irregular rhythm? He tensed.

The first wolf came into view two hundred yards away through the wood. It looked horribly black against the trunks of the trees, like a burnt corpse. Instants later there were six more flickering in its wake.

Michael turned and ran.

He was no more than sixty yards from the river, though it was invisible through the trees. He doubted if they would follow him as far as the walls of the farm.

No distance. No distance at all.

He heard a clatter and yowling behind him and dared a look. They had reached the fire scar and were snuffling among the bones.

His feet flew over the fallen leaves, brambles and low branches rasping at his face, plucking his sleeve. Where was the river?

No good. He must have come in a circle or something. He paused, gasping. There was no sound for a second, except the confused snarling behind him.

There was no sound of the river.

An edge of true panic entered his mind. He knew this wood in and out, winter and summer. It was impossible that he should be lost, impossible that the river should be unheard, for it was full and fast at this time of year, the noise of its rush carrying to every corner of the wood.

A horse nickered behind him, and the wolves gave tongue like a pack of hounds. He whirled and saw something new towering through the trees. A man, black as pitch, on a black horse. His face was shrouded by a hood and he was swathed in what seemed to be ragged lengths of cloth. Even his hands were wrapped, like a leper's. He held a whip in one of them and was blurring through the tree boles at a trot, urging the wolves on.

It's the Devil, Michael thought. And he's going to catch me.

He ran again, following his nose and gulping frantic air into his lungs. The skull was a dead weight that ached his wrist, but he refused to give it up.

He could see dark shapes out of the corner of his right eye, and behind came the solid thump of hoofbeats.

Tears flashed from his eyes and his back slimed with sweat. His heavy shoes weighed pounds and pounds.

He tripped, fell headlong and rolled. The skull swung in the air and came down to crack him on the head. His sight swam for a second, then he was up again, dizzy and staggering.

A black-mawed shape rushed up on him with a snarl. He swung the skull with all his might and heard it crack against the wolf's jaw, jarring his fingers. The animal's lip split under the impact and it yelped. He hit it again on the snout, then ran on. The whole wood seemed full of the cries of the hunting pack, the hoofbeats underlying them; and they were somehow more frightening; directed, implacable.

The wood was alien to him, strange and unknown, vaster than was possible in his own world. He had slipped into the Other Place. He was lost. Sobs threatened to rack his chest and steal his air.

Then he saw Rose, plain as day, standing before a clump of impenetrable hazel and bramble. She was beckoning, an urgency in her face. He almost laughed with relief.

'I knew you'd come,' he gargled, staggering towards her.

It was not Rose. He caught only a glimpse before she slipped into the darkness of the thicket, still beckoning to him, but he was sure it was not her. This girl was taller, darker-eyed, slimmer, and she wore a white shift that left her arms and neck bare.

He crashed into the hazel and pushed his way through, the skull snagging on twigs.

'Wait!'

Behind him the wolves howled in anger and disappointment.

He cackled madly, the breath like an ebbing tide of hot sand in his throat, scraping and scalding his lungs...

'Where are you?'

...And tumbled down a steep incline, rolling, the skull banging loose from his tired hand. To splash with a shock of cold water in the river. His head went under and he thrashed around, fought it above the surface. It was deep, icy cold. He began to hyperventilate, screamed aloud, beat for the shore—and stopped. The skull was under the water somewhere.

He dived. Swimming was something he had taught himself since Rose had disappeared. His fingers fumbled in mud, upturning stones, one fastening on the wriggling flash of a fish. Then the hardness of the skull.

He surfaced, whooping for air. His shoes were weighing him down. He made the far bank, hauled himself out of the water like an old, old man and lay there with the grass at his cheek and waited for his heart to slow from a sprint.

'God,' he croaked.

He was on the eastern bank of the little river, and ten yards away the arch of the bridge gaped like a dark and empty gateway.

SIX

'MOTHER OF GOD, Michael! What in the world is that? It gave me the fright of my life!'

He groaned, turning in bed, muzzy-eyed. His grandmother shook his shoulder. 'Where did you get it? You can't keep things like that in the house.'

Stupid with waking, he told the truth. 'Found it near the wee river. It's just a skull.'

'A skull! And what would you be wanting with a skull in the house, sitting on top of the wardrobe? I hope it's not old Demon's head that you've dug up, or your grandfather will be none too pleased. Grave-robbing, is what it is.'

'It's not. It's some other skull. Some other dog.' He yawned, though he was now fully awake. Outside the morning was blue and murky, and rain drummed on the window.

'Well, you'd better shake a leg. Your grandfather's already at his breakfast and Mullan is setting up the big trap. We don't want to be late on account of one sleepyhead.' She moved towards the door. 'Skulls now it is!'

Michael hauled himself out of bed. His body ached all over, and he felt grimy. The skull grinned at him, black bone in the corner. God, it was big.

Sunday morning. Mass. He groaned again.

THE RAIN WAS blinding on the way into town, the water spinning off the wheels of the trap. Sean muttered about getting a car and moving into the twentieth century, but Michael's grandparents seemed not to mind the rain. Bundled up in oilskins and hoods, they looked more like sailors than churchgoers.

Michael and Aunt Rachel hung on grimly at the rear with the water streaming into their eyes. Michael could feel the collar of his good shirt slowly getting colder and colder with the rain. Rachel ignored him, holding down one end of her hat with a work-red hand.

The Horseman was in the field next to the road, close to the hedge.

Michael could have touched his horse's muzzle as the trap rattled past. No one else appeared to have seen him. He was even blacker with rain, his mount's coat flat and slick. His cloaks and wrappings clung to him like a second skin, and he was lean and wiry under them. The whip dangled from one gloved hand. His steed threw up its head and snorted against the insistent rain, but the rider might have been a corpse propped up in the saddle. Except when the hooded face turned to follow the progress of the trap down the road.

THAT NIGHT THE sky cleared and the wind fell. It was a cold night, the promise of frost in the air. Michael lay in bed staring at the skull on top of his wardrobe. At his feet the window opened out into blue darkness. The farm was asleep, but he could not drop off. He felt he was on the border of another country, that he had peered through a door not often opened and it had remained ajar after him. For things to come through.

The skull stared at him, sneering in the dark. He should have left it where he had found it. He knew, now, that this thing was his alone, that no one else would ever share in it or see the things he saw. A dog's skull, he had said, and his grandfather had looked at him with disconcerting shrewdness.

'Been a whole load of farm dogs buried on the banks of the river through the years, Michael. Our family, my father, my grandda. There's probably a dozen of them lying down there, fifty years dead. It's no bad idea to let them be. You wouldn't want somebody digging up Demon, would you?'

And he had shaken his head dumbly.

Old Felix whinnied in the night, the sound carrying in the starlit air.

He threw aside his bedclothes and crawled along the bed to the window. His eyes were already accustomed to the dark of the room and the yard seemed almost bright by comparison, the farm buildings shrouded in shadow. He grabbed his alarm clock and squinted at the arms with the face close to his nose. Just after four.

Something tall and angular moved quickly from one patch of darkness to another, disappearing behind a corner.

He stared, eyes wide as an owl's.

The thing came into view again, on all fours this time, with its nose close to the ground as if following a scent. It was black-furred, lean, deep-chested with a long thin muzzle and large upright ears. It stood up again, well over six feet, its forearms too long for its body. It had no tail.

And it loped across the yard with its nose tilted up towards Michael's window.

He drew back, sick with fear. The window was open six inches and he thought he could hear it snuffling below. Can werewolves climb? his racing mind wondered. He felt a scream creep up into his throat but it lodged there, choking him into silence.

The thing reappeared, near the stables. The half-doors were closed and it pawed the bolts with clawed hands. Felix began whinnying in earnest, and the other horses joined him. There was a bang, loud as a gunshot, as one of them kicked the stable door. The werewolf drew back hurriedly. Michael heard voices from his grandparents' room.

Then the back door slammed and Mullan limped out into the yard with a shotgun broken open in his hands. He stuffed a shell into it and clicked it shut. The werewolf had sidled round the corner of the stables. Michael could just see it, crouched down along the wall with its mouth open, panting like a dog. He banged his window to warn, but still could say nothing. Mullan spun round, eyebrows going up his forehead as he saw Michael at the window—and in that instant the beast leapt away from the stable wall, out of the yard. Mullan spun again and fired the shotgun from the hip like Audie Murphy, the recoil knocking him back a step. The shot was shockingly loud, the flash scattering Michael's sight with after-images. Mullan broke open the gun once more and limped steadily out of the yard in pursuit, fumbling in his pocket for another shell. A flood of light filled the yard as Sean and Pat came out of the back door bearing lanterns, long stock coats thrown over their pyjamas. They almost collided with Mullan as he came back into the light with the shotgun over his shoulder. Michael caught snatches of their talk.

'—Some dog or other, big one too.'

'Need to have a look at the sheep.'

'—Woke the whole bloody house up.'

'—Scared Rachel half to death.' And the three of them laughed there in the light and dark of the lantern-lit yard. Sean turned and waved at Michael's window, his black hair tumbled down over his forehead.

'Did you get it?' Michael squeaked.

'It got away,' Mullan said, tapping the shotgun. 'But I frightened the living shit out of it, that's for sure. It was just a stray, Mike. Go back to bed.'

He did, but he locked the skull in the bottom of his wardrobe first, listening to the men pottering in the yard, checking on the horses. He hoped none of them would venture far from the farm before dawn. It was Michael's monster, but if they could see it, then perhaps it could... Perhaps it was real for them, after all. A werewolf wandering the fields. He closed his window tightly and drew his curtains against the blue night, longing for sunrise.

* * *

It was no use, of course, him trying to tell his grandparents that it had not been a dog in the yard that night. He made an attempt, but found that halfway through his description of the creature he had seen—clearer than any of them, too—his grandfather began smiling indulgently whilst exasperation glittered over his grandmother's face, and so he ground to an ignominious and stumbling halt. He left, hearing his grandmother from outside: '*That boy's imagination... spends too much time alone... needs someone his own age.*'

He spent the day at school, thinking of wolves, of the Horseman he had seen twice, of Rose... of the girl in the wood who had shown him the way home.

The year continued to turn at its usual rate despite the weird events that shaped it. His astronomical growth rate slowed a little. He began to fill out, became less of a scarecrow. His grandfather looked at him appraisingly one evening as his wife was fitting some of Sean's old clothes on him, and told him with a twinkle in his eye that wherever he was going, he was going in a hurry.

For a while the happenings that Michael had come to think of as belonging to the Other Place became less frequent, and his life drifted back towards normality. Occasionally, though, he would see a dark figure at the edge of the woods in the evenings, sometimes mounted, sometimes afoot. He never dared approach, and so could not be sure who it was. And he would feel watched, sometimes, when in the woods alone, as though there was a face to be seen behind him if he could only spin around quickly enough. He gradually grew accustomed to the idea that he was seldom truly alone when near the river or in the trees, or near the bridge. Sometimes he wondered if it were Rose's ghost that was haunting him, but he thought the sensation too strong for that. And he did not believe her ghost would snap twigs or giggle as it watched him, as this presence did. He thought again of the willowy, dark girl who had saved him from the wolves.

An armistice of sorts was wordlessly signed between himself and Aunt Rachel. Rose's name was never mentioned again in the house. It was as though she had never existed. Her room was cleared out, her things boxed away in the attic, her clothes given to the St Vincent de Paul. She became a taboo subject. The closet skeleton.

SUMMER CAME AGAIN, and through some shenanigan or other Pat managed to wangle a massive, glinting horsebox for a day, a monstrosity of a thing which awed the entire family and came complete with a greasy, fag-smoking, flat-capped driver called Aloysius, or Ally to his friends. And we are all friends here, he assured them with a nod and a wink and a leer at Rachel which made her glare at him and heft a Thermos flask thoughtfully. The family piled on board along with Felix, Pluto—the other carthorse, thick-limbed and amiable—and the chestnut mare, which had been nominally christened Trigger but was mostly called Fancy. Then they were off for the coast, to the long sands for a picnic and a damned good gallop as Pat said, until his wife nudged him for swearing in front of the child.

They rattled along like a lost component from some circus, the old Bedford as noisy as a rocket and leaving about as much smoke behind. Felix and Pluto clamped and stomped and blew down their noses nervously, but Fancy seemed to take it in her stride. She put her nose to one of the side slats and sucked the rushing air in through flared nostrils.

In Rasharkin they picked up a foursome of cousins or great-uncles and aunts or something. Michael was not sure. He did know that he was forced to leave his seat in the tack compartment of the vehicle and take up a cramped position in the space at Felix's broad rear to make room for them all, the great dinner-plate hooves clumping and shifting in front of him.

The rear ramp was lowered and the wooden gates hauled open half an hour later. He found himself joined by a brace of children his own age (and half his size, which was usual these days), and surmised that they had picked up another gaggle of distant relatives at their last stop. It never failed to amaze him when he saw people he had never seen before (or hadn't for years, which was much the same thing at his age) greet his grandparents with grins and smiles, hugs and claps on the back, and find that they were brothers or sisters. That they had grown up in the very place he called his home, moved away long years in the past and separated themselves by insuperable distances of forty miles or more.

Mullan pushed into the stall rear that Michael and the silent children occupied. (They were staring at him shyly, their best clothes already hayseeded and beshitted. Both girls, to be ignored.) The old man's Peterson was dangling unlit in his mouth. He braced himself against the lurch and swing of the farting lorry by pushing against Pluto's massive behind. He looked disgruntled.

'World and his bloody wife is climbing on to this thing. We'll not make Portrush with this load, Mike, you mark my words.' But they did.

There was a collective sigh at the front and the sunlight slanting and shifting into the horse-smelling rear brought with it a distant rush and hiss, a smell of salt, a tang in the air that galvanized the dancing dust in the sunbeams. The two girls suddenly began bouncing up and down with their ringlets hopping on their shoulders. 'The sea! The sea!' they chorused. Michael glared at them with distaste and the horses shifted restlessly, snuffling at the unfamiliar odour.

'Have a look, Mike,' Mullan said, and a horny hand helped him off the cramped and perilous floor to peer out one of the side slats.

They were driving down the flank of a hill, the road cutting into it and opening out on Michael's side to a steep slope of marram grass and pale sand. Other, smaller sandhills tumbled and crept to a white—as dazzling as sun on water—stripe of beach that was fringed with the breakers of the Atlantic, beyond which was the deep, vast blueness of the sea itself. Gulls called overhead and the salt tang filled Michael's lungs. Behind him, the horsebox was a clamour of voices. He stuck his nose farther out the narrow gap, drinking in the air, listening to the sound of the foam hitting the beach, and laughed aloud.

The lorry made hard going of the sand until they off-loaded the horses, Felix throwing his head up like a colt, and put their shoulders to its rear. Even then they would have had a time of it if Mullan, reeking of smugness, had not thrown a line round Felix and Pluto's shoulders and got the big animals to haul the machine out of the ruts its tyres had carved for itself. There was much laughter at that, though Sean seemed not to know whether to laugh or scowl. He settled for shaking his head ruefully, and the lorry chugged on without further event, though the driver was prudent enough to make everyone disembark before continuing along the beach, and they trudged in its wake with the two ringleted girls on Felix's broad back, looking a little like the retreat from Moscow.

There were others on the sands, car windscreens glinting like beetle wings in the bright sunshine, tartan rugs sprawled with red-faced, lotion-slimy people, Thermos flasks dotting their picnics like blunt-nosed artillery shells and their children digging happily, rearing up ephemeral castles. Kingdoms in the sand.

The Fays came to a straggling halt in the lee of a slab-sided dune, and then began the battle to organize what was in effect a campsite. Agnes, Michael's grandmother, started to take charge, she and her sisters and their children unloading hampers and rugs and balls and buckets and spades and bathing costumes and windbreaks. Whilst Pat and the male members of the family (Michael included among them, not one of the children, he noted with immense pride) rubbed the horses down, for the ride had sweated them up. The mare in particular was white-eyed and prancing. There were too many people about, Mullan complained. She needed a bit of peace. He led her off the side of a dune. Pipes were lit, matches fighting the sea breeze. Pat took off his boots and rolled up his trousers. The giggling girls hid naked behind towels as their mother slid swimming costumes up their thin legs. Michael leant on Felix's rump and stared out to sea. It was a long way from the trees and the smell of leaf mold, the river and the looming bridge. It was clear out here, open and empty, a place to lose cobwebs. Rose had always loved the seaside.

Mullan brought the chestnut back and saddled her up, looking at Michael enquiringly. Michael nodded, bridled Felix and then hauled himself on the great back, kicking him forward. The pair of them sauntered through the sand, Felix's huge hooves throwing it aside in sweeps, Fancy stepping through it as though she were wearing a frock she refused to muddy. Mullan's Peterson lurched up and down in his mouth, scattering ash to the breeze. Children stared and pointed, parents peered from underneath shading hands. Michael and Mullan ignored them loftily.

Mullan had a struggle with the chestnut mare at first, for she was fresh and the sea wind seemed to intoxicate her. She pranced and danced and pirouetted whilst Mullan cursed atop her and Michael grinned from Felix's back. After a time, though, she settled and picked her away alongside the carthorse amiably enough.

'Speed and to spare in this little bugger,' Mullan grunted, the sweat inching down below his cap. 'Needs a firm hand.' He spat copiously and the breeze shunted it away. They rode in silence for a few moments, the horsebox already the better part of a mile behind them.

'Mike, remember that dog I shot at a while back—the one that was prowling in the yard?'

'What about it?'

'Hell of a thing that was... Steady, lass, steady.'

'Why?' Michael asked, though he knew.

'It was damned big, for one thing. Big as a bloody calf. Like a St Bernard or a wolfhound or something. And I could have sworn I had the barrel lined straight up with it when I let rip.'

'From the hip,' Michael said off-handedly, though he thought his ears would visibly prick up if he paid any closer attention to what the old man was saying.

'From the hip, aye. But it was a matter of a few yards. I could have sworn I hit it straight on. It should have been blown to bits.'

'Would have been a hell of a mess,' Michael said.

'Mmm.' Mullan seemed lost in thought. 'Exactly. I'd have thought the spray would have got him with at least a few pellets, but not a drop of blood was there. As if they had gone straight through the bastard... Mike, you asked me a long time ago about dogs hanging round the sheep or in the woods. Have you been seeing anything out of the ordinary, then?'

Michael almost laughed. Where should I begin? he wondered.

But no. It had gone too far for that. Once upon a time he might have told Mullan, but it was too late now. Rose was mixed up in this thing, he was sure, and he did not want to bring her name into anything, even though it would be easier with Mullan, he being a Protestant and not related. Strange, that.

'Nothing,' he said shortly.

'What about that skull you dug up? Your grandmother said it was a huge great thing.'

'It was just a dog's skull. Probably one of the old farm dogs that are buried down by the river.' He felt a chill rake his backbone as he wondered if what he was saying was close to the truth.

'I see.' Mullan seemed put out. He bared his teeth for a second around the stem of his pipe.

'I only ask, see, because it's been on my mind again lately. There's something in the woods is scaring the sheep. They keep to the southern edge of the bottom meadow and they've chewed the grass down to the roots. There's good grazing yet on the side of the field that borders on to the trees, but they won't go near it. Your grandfather can't understand it. Him and me is thinking of waiting in the woods a few nights to see if we can't bag whatever is wandering about in there.'

'No, you can't.' The words were out before Michael could stop them.

'Why, Mike? You tell me why. You know something about this, it's plain.'

'I don't. I don't know anything. Wouldn't setting traps be better than sitting there all night?'

'You've a point there,' Mullan said. 'Need bloody big traps if we're to catch the dog that was in the yard that night. If it was a dog.'

Michael looked at him sharply, but the old man's eyes were narrowed, his thoughts elsewhere.

They reached a long, shining stretch of empty sand and there Mullan's pipe disappeared into a pocket. He kicked his mount in the ribs and shouted wordlessly. Immediately Fancy took off like a chestnut rocket, throwing up scuds of sand behind her. The old man bent low over her neck and hallooed back at Michael, who was bumping up and down on Felix as the carthorse lumbered into a trot, then a rolling canter, his back tilting like a ship in a heavy sea. The air whistled past Michael's ears as Felix picked up speed, an equine juggernaut that sprayed sand. He guided the horse over to the firmer footing nearer the sea, and there was water splashing under Felix's hoofs. Ahead Fancy was hock deep, a seahorse, neighing shrilly, Mullan yelling like a boy. The water exploded around them in a deep furrow as they galloped, ploughing the waves.

THEY RODE OUT of the river in a thrash of spray, the chestnut labouring up the steep bank. The land levelled off then fell to a long slope of hazy forest that stretched for miles into the afternoon sun. Immediately before them was a glade, barely a hundred yards wide, woodsmoke rising blue from thatched buildings shrouded in trees. A bell tolled in the quiet, and dun-robed figures paused to watch the newcomers.

Michael slipped off the exhausted horse, leaving Cat clinging to the saddle, yawning. Around him Ringbone and his men were sidling out of the river dip as silently as voles, the jet eyes of the fox masks catching the sun. They fingered their spear-throwers nervously, eyes wide and white in the paint and filth of their faces.

Ringbone set a hand on Michael's shoulder and looked at him, questioningly, asking in the forest patois if this place was safe.

His three companions hung back, murmuring. A Christian bell and men in robes. This was a Brothers' retreat all right.

Michael nodded and made encouraging gestures. It was maddening the way the language was leaving him the nearer the edge of the wood came. Ringbone felt the frustration, too. They had shared so many things together and now could no longer speak the same tongue, but must mime like lunatics. It was Cat who, exasperated, spoke quickly to the fox men in their own language. Michael glared at her. 'What did you tell them?'

'That they can camp near the river, at the wood's edge if they choose, and be eaten by the wolves or they can seek the sanctuary of holy ground along with us.'

Michael grunted. The fox men looked sullen, Ringbone touching his ivory neck charm uncertainly.

'I'm damned if I'll sleep under a tree tonight, anyway,' Cat said, and kicked the mare forward to where a trio of long-skirted figures was approaching. Old men, bald-pated and full-bearded, the sunlight behind them throwing their faces into shadow. Crosses made of unsquared twigs swung from their waists. Michael stared at her. She hated the Brothers, always had. Even Nennian she had distrusted, but she was willing enough to partake of their hospitality now that the Forest-Folk had shunned her. She made him feel oddly ashamed.

'*Pax vobiscum.*'

The fox men backed away at the sound of the secret language, the Church tongue of magicians. Michael shrugged and joined Cat.

'*Et cum spiritu tuo*,' he mumbled. A priest had taught him that in the depths of the Wolfweald a long time ago. It fell off his tongue like a flint, but the Brothers smiled as one, faces crinkling.

'A Christian couple—in odd company, it is true. And you have travelled far. Enter the Retreat and be refreshed.'

Michael looked back, but Ringbone and his men had disappeared in a twinkling. Must be back in the trees. Damn fools. And yet he could not blame them. The Brothers and their Knights had been responsible for much of the violence in the wood. For a moment he thought of returning to the depths of the trees. Ringbone was his friend, after all. But it was himself and Cat the beasts were after. To return would be folly. He cursed under his breath, and hoped the proximity of the Retreat would keep the night's evil from them. Then he sighed and knelt before the tallest of the Brothers of the Wood, the one who had spoken, and felt a leaf-light hand on his head. A blessing.

'*In nomine Patri...*'

They would have peace tonight, at any rate.

The community was a mere circle of thatched huts huddled against the loom of the surrounding forest. The chapel was the only substantial building, log-walled and chinked with clay. The others were a sprinkle of wattle and daub and turf with birch bark and sod roofs. There was the pungence of a herb garden, orderly rows of cabbages and an orchard with bee skeps silenced by the season. Michael was sure he could scent the strong whiff of fermentation. Cider it would be, cloudy and potent. There was no wine to be had. The blood of Christ would come from the juice and pulp of apples, His body from barley bannock.

'We eat no meat here,' one of them had said. But it was good to tuck into fresh vegetables and fruit, bread that could be torn between the hands, butter and buttermilk. They must have a stretch of pasture here somewhere, off in the trees. No need to fear the wolves with the chapel rearing its blunt tower above the wood, the crucifix hovering over every corner. For a moment Michael envied the Brothers their faith, and remembered going to mass at home, the heady incense that made him think of Byzantium, the red flicker of the sanctuary light. Childhood.

His forearm twinged, itched. Smelled. Ringbone's poultice had been disagreeable but effective. He was aware of how he smelled. Cat, too, for that matter. They smelled of the forest and their own overworked bodies, of horse and old rain. The Brothers were as clean as pins. He longed for a bath. Still some manners left, he thought with a smile.

They ate and ate. More Brothers trooped into the low length of the refectory, blessed themselves and joined them. Most were old. Some even bore the facial scars of the tribes, the tattooing of savages. It took all sorts, he supposed. It would be easy enough to tire of life in the woods and the wilderness, to come here seeking peace. No women, though. A sad state of affairs. He noticed they avoided Cat's eyes, which seemed to amuse her. As discreetly as he could, he levered her mischievous hand from his thigh under the table.

When he had wiped his wooden plate for the second time, watched approvingly by the beaming Brother Kitchener, he found a youngish man standing before him, obviously ill at ease.

'The Brother Abbot would be glad of a few words when you are done,' he said. His gaze strayed to Michael's sword, hanging at his hip. 'He will not keep you, and we have a tub rigged for bathing and a place for you—for both of you— to sleep.' The young brother was blushing and Michael realized that Cat was probably treating him to a lascivious wink.

'I will take you to him when you are ready.'

The Abbot was not so old either, oddly enough. He was a vigorous man in early middle age with a broken nose and the build of a boxer. Michael would have bet he had once been a Sellsword or Knight; he had that look about him. His eyes were as blue as cornflowers, widening a little with interest as they gauged the pedigree of the Ulfberht.

He walked Michael through the orchard. Cat was off for her bath and would lounge in it until the water was tepid if Michael knew her at all. The trees were almost bare but the sun gave the lie to winter. It was like clear amber, as warming as a flame. They sat amid the bee skeps and crossed their legs like warriors.

'The wolves are close,' the Abbot said directly. 'We can sense them on the edge of the hallowed ground. You bring trouble in your wake, traveller.'

Michael felt a sudden stab of anxiety. 'Our friends—the Fox-Folk. They were afraid of this place. They stayed in the trees—'

'They are within our protection, never fear. But I cannot answer for either you or them once you leave the Retreat. One horse will not carry you very far.' There was an unspoken question in his statement.

'The edge of the wood is near. I'm hoping they'll leave us there.'

The Abbot nodded. 'Two days, if your going is good. You are much battered, and you bear the sword of a master.' He seemed unable to frame a direct question.

Michael smiled faintly. 'I... picked it up in the south, from a merchant there. We've been travelling for months. At the wrong time of year, too.'

The Abbot let his chin fall on his chest. Michael saw a long scar that puckered his tonsured scalp. Definitely an old soldier, not a tribesman. He was somehow too squarely cut for that.

Better not to reveal where the sword had truly come from, if the man had not already guessed.

'There are worse than wolves in the woods,' the Abbot said. 'A horseman has been seen by several of the Brothers, prowling our borders in the nights. There is power in him such as I have never experienced before. And evil, too. I fear he hunts you also.'

Michael's face went flat. 'I fear he does.' So the Horseman was here ahead of them, waiting. The Devil, as Michael had always thought of him. 'We go back a long way.'

The Abbot looked up at that. 'I have my own people to consider. You are welcome to everything we have, even mounts, if a mule will serve your purpose. But—'

'We won't be staying long. Until tomorrow, no more.'

The other man nodded, face twisted with... shame? Relief?

'Have there been other travellers on the tracks?' Michael asked.

'Few, very few. As you say, it is a bad time of year. Some pedlars, one caravan from beyond the great river in the south, a heavy escort with them. The tribes are quiet, the Badger-People lie low every winter, the Roamers stay close to home. The woods are full of wolves, black wolves. Some say—'

'The spirits of the dead are in them. I know. I've heard.'

He had heard it from every tinker and traveller between the river and the mountains. It irritated him to hear it from this man, this man of faith, this old soldier.

'Don't worry,' he said brusquely. 'We'll not stay long.'

And this time the look in the Abbot's face was undisguised relief. Michael felt like striking him, the saintly bastard.

* * *

HAM SANDWICHES, FIZZY pop, rock buns, ice cream. Sand gritting in the mouth and crumbs in the lemonade bottle. The Fays had gathered like the Israelites in the Wilderness and were crowded in the shelter of a line of windbreaks, lolling on a series of rugs and munching happily. The horses had been rubbed down and watered and were deep in nosebags, tied to the back of the lorry. Its driver, Aloysius, was eating thick-cut sandwiches daintily, his fingers leaving black smears on the bread, the sweat cutting streaks of cleaner skin down his face. It was hot out of the sea wind, though the children had come in from the water goose pimpled and shrieking until towels were draped round their shoulders. Their hair hung in tails and sand stuck to their wet limbs.

Michael sat on the edge of the throng—it could almost be called a throng, he decided—and shut his eyes occasionally as perverse eddies of wind sent sand scudding in his face. Sand everywhere. When they got home it would be as though they had carried half the strand back with them, in the lorry, in blankets, clothes, hair, teeth.

Pat was slugging porter in tune with two of his brothers. They also were tall men, beak-nosed, brown-faced, hair grey and thick, eyes the shade of a heavy sea. Sean sat with them, the wind throwing his quiff of hair about. The little girls stared at him, agog.

The women were in their own group, drinking tea. They were all old and Rachel was the youngest, though she had no problems fitting in. Their talk was of the parishes, chickens, relatives who had died or were about to, though there was no mention of Rose, of course. They spoke of scandals, sometimes whispering and wagging fingers, shaking heads, pursing lips; a body language of disapprobation. Michael turned away and looked out to the clean sea.

And saw the girl there, tall and slim, paddling in the waves. She turned at almost the same instant his eyes fastened on her, met his look, smiled.

She wore a white shift that left her arms and neck bare; the same he had seen her wear in the wood. Her black hair streamed out behind her like a flag. The wind pressed the shift against her like a second skin, and the bottom foot of it was soaked by the waves and clung to her calves.

Beside Michael Mullan was nursing his pipe and staring out to sea, but said no word. She was invisible to him, Michael realized. To all of them.

He was up and away a second later, as fast as the chestnut with the sea wind in his teeth.

He saw her face light with humour, then she had gathered her shift round her thighs and was off across the sand with that mane of hair flickering behind her.

She disappeared behind the shoulder of a dune.

He stopped, the air rasping in his chest. There were no footprints to follow. The sand was unmarked, though he had seen her heels throw it up. She was gone, just like before. She was playing hide and bloody seek with him. He punched marram grass in frustration.

'Damn!'

He had had enough of this—this weirdness. He had been frightened for too long. He would be fourteen soon, though he knew he could pass for older. He wanted some answers. One way or another he would get them.

SEVEN

A SUMMER EVENING, the fourth running he had spent down by the river. The trees were quiet, their tops moving in a faint breeze, but down here no wind penetrated. The wood floor was overgrown and tangled, a riot of ferns and brambles, reaching saplings and the stumps of rotten, root-thick trunks. He could hear the river, though the undergrowth rendered it invisible. It was calm and slow at this time of year, alive with minnow and stickleback, the stones rising above its sleek surface in smooth humps. No birds. Rose's kingfisher was nowhere to be seen.

He wore old, wood-coloured and smoke-smelling clothes and strong boots, and carried a satchel with bread and cheese, matches and a bottle of milk so warm now as to be undrinkable. By his side was a shallow-curved sickle, the type his grandfather used for trimming hedges. Across his legs lay a hazel staff with a sharpened point. The tree at his back was easy to climb; he had made sure of that. He had not seen the wolves in weeks, but he was taking no chances.

'You're odd, you know that?' his Aunt Rachel had told him as he came in night after night in the gathering dark, for he was not yet ready to spend the whole night in the wood alone. 'Out in the woods till all hours, filthy as a gypsy. It's no wonder you have no friends. And you never even gave your cousins the time of day at the seaside.'

Mullan had offered to accompany him, but he had refused. There were traps set in the woods, big ones that would crunch the foreleg of a dog or a fox. Or a wolf. He knew where they were, and his time here had been spent listening and watching, waiting. He felt as keen-sensed as an animal himself. He felt he would smell something happening before he saw it.

Laughter, light and high as a ripple of silver bells. It was upstream, carrying over the water.

At last.

He rose carefully, tucked the sickle in his bag and hefted the hazel like a spear. Again he heard it, and splashing.

He pushed forward, edging through the snatching briars, rolling his feet across the brittle twigs. The running water covered sound. He made slow progress, though, for it seemed to him that his limbs were shaking, as unsteady as an infant's. A drift of dandelion down sailed across his face, lit by the slanting rays of the dying sunlight. He listened to the harsh screech of a jay off in the trees, the first bird he had heard that evening.

There was no change in the wood, no feeling of having left or arrived, but he knew with sudden certainty that he was in the Other Place, that he had passed through some invisible gateway and had left his own world behind. He no longer knew where he was, save that the river was somewhere ahead, buried in trees. As always, his senses seemed to sharpen even further. He could almost taste the air, feel the season moving against his skin. He crept forward with new caution, knowing that this other world had its beasties and goblins, its big bad wolves.

There was whimpering, a muffled squeal, something like a gasp in the ferns ahead where the ground dipped. He moved forward quietly and peered through gaps in the thick leaves and stems, a blur of movement catching his eye. Someone was lying there in a tangle of limbs.

Two people, one spread eagled, the other on top, his lower body thrusting and pushing in time to a series of sighs and groans. A pale pair of thighs stuck up on either side of the man's hips like two bark-stripped stumps. His trousers were down around his calves. The woman below him was Michael's aunt, Rose.

Rose!

Her face was set away from his nuzzling mouth; she was staring up into the branches overhead, moaning as the man pushed deep inside her. Tears spilled down the sides of her face to her neck.

Oh, Rose.

Michael buried his face in his arm and wept, shock, grief and joy, all mixed and muddled, spiralling in his mind.

But when he looked again she was gone. There were two stumps embedded in the ground: pale birch, with a darker log lying between them.

'You liked that, Michael?'

The girl was here beside him with an avid grin on her face. So close he could feel her breath on his neck. He sprang away in terror but she followed his leap and caught him. Slim arms went round his waist and they tumbled into the ferns and leaf litter and the grasping brambles. Her hair flew across his face like a black scarf. She was laughing, the same silver laugh he had heard earlier. Her chin dug into his navel.

'Hold hard there, my warrior. I will not eat you.'

She was wet, he realized. Water sparkled in drops on her skin as though she had been in a shower. She climbed up him like a monkey and lay full length on his body. Involuntarily, his hands settled on her back. Wet, the thin shift was like skin under his fingertips.

She kissed him, her mouth pushing over his, hungry, still laughing.

But Michael threw her aside, tumbled her to the leaves and fumbled for the hazel spear.

He saw a light leap in her eyes, vulpine, perilous.

'Who are you? What do you want?' he demanded, the crude weapon pointed at her stomach. Her eyes were green, but the pupils had dilated so as to make them almost black. They seemed to shine in the dimness of the darkening wood.

'*What* are you?' he whispered.

Her fingers encircled the haft of the spear loosely, caressing the smooth bark. The smile was back on her face.

'A friend. Come, calm yourself. I mean you no harm.'

'What was that I just saw? Those two—' He cursed the hoarse up-and-down of his breaking voice.

'A memory. Something the wood remembers. No more.'

He lowered the spear. 'You know my name.'

'I've watched you for a long time.'

'You're part of it, aren't you? What this is all about. The wolves, the—the things in the woods. I don't understand.'

She shrugged as if it were unimportant. 'No one can understand everything. You ask a lot of questions, little Michael.'

'I'm not little.' Hotly.

She drew close, her nose six inches from his own. If she was shorter than him it was by a hair's breadth.

'Believe in fairies, then, do you?'

'Is that what you are?'

She spun around, her shift mushrooming about her legs.

Bare feet. A mole on one calf, the muscles sliding below it. Michael felt a pang of lust so acute it dizzied him, adolescence in a buzzing rush. He gripped the spear till his knuckles whitened, which seemed to amuse the girl. Everything about him amused her, he realized with irritation. He could still feel the imprint of her teeth on his lips.

'Well?'

'Well what?'

He felt absurd. 'Are you a fairy?'

'If you like.'

'What's your name?'

'Call me Cat.'

'That's a stupid name.'

'You're a stupid boy.'

Silence. Maybe he was. He had no retort for her. He stood watching her with a mixture of glumness and rising excitement. He wondered if she would kiss him again.

'Have you anything to eat?' she asked.

He was trying to decide what she smelled like. There was a fragrance off her, something familiar. 'Bread and cheese, and milk—too warm.'

'Put it in the river to cool.'

'All right.'

It was as if a test had been passed, a hurdle leapt. He set the bottle in the river where it sparkled over the stones and was less warm, then opened his satchel to her. She drew back from the sickle in distaste and was reluctant to touch it. He offered her the food and she ate ravenously, cramming it into her mouth, crumbs trickling from her lips. They were dark lips, he noticed, so dark they looked almost bruised. Her nose was neat and upturned, her eyebrows heavy and black, almost meeting in the middle. There was a fine down of colourless hair where a man's sideburns would be. Her skin was sun-ripened, flawless but for scrapes and dirt. Freckles spattered her nose. She seemed to him one of the loveliest things he had ever seen, long-limbed as a boy, her hands slim, the nails short and grubby. He could have stared at her all day.

He fetched the milk, and only realized then how dark the wood was becoming. Not his wood, either. It was time to be getting back. Cat wiped her white moustache away and gazed at him with those strange eyes.

'You saved me from the wolves,' he told her. 'You showed me the way home.'

'Indeed?' A smile curved one corner of her mouth.

'Can you do it again? Can you show me the way home now, before night?'

'Leaving so soon?'

'I have to. They'll worry.' He did not want to go. It was not that he was no longer afraid, but what is frightening for one can be an adventure for two. And he did so love looking at her.

'All right.'

Gorse blossom. That was what it was. She smelled of yellow gorse blossom, a summer smell, bringing to mind short-cropped grass and high cirrus.

'I saw you on the beach,' he said. Her eyebrows were two black bars in the fading light and her hair shaded her face like a hood. Her grin was predatory, frightening almost, but he felt no fear, only a rush of exhilaration. He did not even start when the wolves began to howl in the blooming twilight.

'Poor souls,' Cat said, her eyes switching off into the distance of the haunted forest. The wolves sounded lost and forlorn. Damned.

'The Devil rides a horse in this place,' she said to Michael suddenly. 'Gathering souls. We must always flee the sound of hoofbeats when we are here.'

'He has Rose,' Michael said, the words like lead in his belly.

He had no idea where the knowledge had come from, but he knew it was true. Rose, or her ghost, was deep at the heart of this place.

Cat shivered, her gaiety gone for the moment. 'Come. I will take you out of here, back to your own place.'

They rose together, a sudden dread constricting them at the same time. The wood was black with shadow, pools of murk brimming under the overhanging branches. Something which was as dark as the shadow and yet apart from it moved between two trees. Upright, long-muzzled, sharp-eared. It halted and stood still barely fifty yards away, watching them. Cat took Michael's hand, her eyes showing the whites like a horse smelling fire.

'Run!'

He remembered little later of their headlong flight through the wood, though he would bear the scars of the briars for weeks. He remembered her hand locked on to his, pulling him onward, her hair flying in his face, the white shift like a ghost in the crowded darkness. He felt as though it were all a dream. A fairy tale in which the princess was rescuing him rather than the other way around.

They laboured up wooded hills that he had never seen or climbed in his life before, plashed through streams which could not exist.

They covered the better part of two miles in a wood he knew ended a hundred yards away. And always the shadow was behind them, swift and silent, now running on all fours, now upright. Behind it the wood was alive with the cries of the pack.

Time passed and died. He grew exhausted, though Cat seemed built out of untiring sinew and bone. Or sugar and spice, perhaps. In the end she was half supporting his weight, and absurdly he noticed even then the springy suppleness of her body as it moved with his.

A last hill, she told him. Nearly there. And they found themselves above the trees, looking out on a starlit night at a blue, sleeping earth. It was the Bann valley where Michael lived. He knew its contours as well as the profile of his own face, from the long slope of the plateau in the east to the river and then the low hills leading to the Sperrin mountains in the far west.

Not a light was to be seen across the whole landscape. Not a house, not a village or town. The land was as dark and empty as an undiscovered wilderness.

That was what it was in this place, he realized. Wilderness. And sometimes his world and this one met.

As he watched, he saw a tiny bead of flame-like light strike up miles away in the hills leading to the mountains. A bonfire, perhaps; a big one, to be seen over twenty, twenty-five miles.

Cat was tugging at him, her voice a low hiss of urgency, but he resisted her pull for a moment, staring out at his own country gone wild, drinking in the weirdness. It was his to travel, if he wanted to, and if he was fit for it.

The wolves were close, the shadow that led them a rippling black shape powering through the trees with two eyes burning yellow and its maw agape.

'Mother of God!'

Then Cat pulled him down what seemed to be a deep hole, a dark pit leading into light at its end. A tumble... did he always have to fall through these things?—and he was lying on leaves with a tree root digging into his neck and the sound of the river peaceful and endless at his side.

He got his breath back. 'Cat?'

But she was gone. Back into Wonderland, perhaps.

Answers... well, he had a few of them now, but they only made him think of new questions.

Back in the world he thought of as his own, where there were clocks and guns and flying machines, where wolves paced in zoos and girls wore shoes, the long days continued to go by, unaware of anything out of the ordinary. Each was as distinct as a portrait miniature, their procession merging into a larger canvas, a picture painted by memory. Midsummer was weeks gone and there was a barely perceptible shortening of the golden evenings as August drew on and Michael's holidays ran away from him like sand in an hour glass. Cat did not choose to reappear, and though Michael prowled the wood like a savage, he saw nothing unusual. Or almost nothing. He did come across tracks and managed to persuade Aunt Rachel to get out library books on nature, on woodland and forest wildlife, and an old one on prehistory: cave-men stories, as Rachel labelled them. But she and his grandmother were nonetheless impressed that he was reading books during the holidays.

The tracks were of the usual animals of north-western European woodland, except that they were a thousand years out of date. According to the book's identifications, there were boar and wolf, beaver and great deer, wild oxen and bears in the woods. Bears! And yet they were silent and invisible, ghost animals, their only record the footprints in the soft clay of the wood floor.

Mullan's traps caught themselves a fox and a pair of rabbits. There were signs that one had caught something larger but whatever it had been was gone, leaving the snare bent and broken behind it, the surrounding vegetation thrashed to shreds. Michael, Pat and the old soldier stood staring at it one bright morning in the tail-end of August. Pat pushed his cap back on his head and whistled softly.

'Something made a right mess here.'

The trap was still affixed to its ground peg, but the links of the chain had been stretched almost to breaking point and the jaws were bent.

Mullan eased his old bones down to look closer. He picked off a tuft of coarse black hair that was sticking to the metal.

'Badger?' Pat asked.

'Not likely. It's too long, too dark. And even a badger would be held fast in a snare like this, or he'd worry his leg off to get away... No, I'm damned if I know what it is, except some bloody big dog. But there's no blood around. You'd think it had bent open the jaws somehow, not scraped free. Curiouser and curiouser.'

'He'll be after the sheep next,' Pat said grimly. 'I'd best warn Sibbet and McLoughlin that there's a big stray on the loose, gone feral maybe. Lambing's long over; that's one thing... Easy, boys. Calm down, for God's sake.' This was to his pair of collies, which were whirring and snarling a little way off, refusing to come near. They seemed frightened one moment, angry the next.

'Useless buggers,' Pat said, not without affection. He clapped Mullan on the shoulder, staggering the older man as he was in the process of getting up. 'So much for your traps. There's a few ten bob notes down the drain there.'

'Rabbit pie tomorrow, though,' Mullan said sulkily. He wheezed and spat, putting one brown fist to the small of his back and grimacing. 'Never seen anything like it. Maybe it was kids skylarking.' They both turned to Michael enquiringly.

'I haven't seen anything.'

They laughed, two old doors creaking on their hinges.

'There's a guilty conscience if ever I saw one,' Pat said. 'But then they always are at that age.' Michael scowled.

'So what now? We just keep an extra lookout?' Mullan asked.

Pat nodded. 'No great deal, this time of year. You and Michael could scour the woods again if you like, sit out another night or two.'

'What we need is a bloody good hunt,' Mullan said, producing the Peterson from his pocket. 'A lather of horses and hounds pounding through here. That'd flush him out, wherever he is.'

'No ground for horses here,' Pat disagreed, looking about him at the dense undergrowth and the low-hanging trees. There was a light in his eyes at Mullan's suggestion, however. Winter hunts—they were a great occasion, fifty horses thundering across the fields and the hounds baying in a pack. Pat had not ridden in one for years, the last hunter having been sold off when Michael was a mere infant. Felix and Pluto were workhorses, and even Fancy could be justified to an extent, but Sean had drawn the line after Pat's last hunter, a wicked-eyed giant of a horse, had died. Dog food, now. And Pat was getting too old for tearing about the countryside and leaping everything in sight, so said Michael's grandmother.

'Never clear these woods,' Pat said absently. He accepted a black twist of tobacco from Mullan and rubbed it between his fingers. 'Been here longer than the farm has. They used to be twice as deep when I was a boy, but these parts are too up and down, too wet. Best to let them be.'

'Sean would clear them,' Mullan said, smiling toothlessly round the stem of his smoking pipe.

'Sean would skin a gnat for its hide,' Pat retorted. He looked at his grandson quickly, guiltily. 'Damn it, Michael, you're going to be tall.'

Michael shifted uncomfortably. 'Not my fault.' He felt that his grandfather, and Mullan too, were waiting for him to say something, to communicate some revelation. He studied the ground stubbornly. His grandfather filled the silence with lighting his pipe, the blue smoke a streamer reaching through the trees.

'Fay bones. Always been tall, our family.'

'Always been horsemen,' Mullan added.

'Aye. That too. Used to be fifteen horses on this farm, cobs and Clydesdales. A Morgan once, bad tempered and black. We sent four off to the war, gone for good. A waste.'

Mullan clamped his lips, though Michael was sure there was a comment hovering behind the pipe. He coughed, and said at last: 'Cows need watering. They're drinking like fish these days.'

Pat inclined his head. 'You'll keep an eye out?' he said to Michael.

'Sure.'

'Fine. I want this bastard shot before winter comes. He'll get hungry then, if he stays around, and the next thing you know we'll have lambs disappearing.'

It was with his grandfather's approval that Michael began handling the shotgun, learning the principles of safety, marksmanship and cleaning. There were three of the weapons in the house. Two were side-by-side twelve-gauges, the third an old over-and-under, intricately carved and as light as a toy. It was Russian-made, the wood gleaming with age and polish. Pat's father had picked it up at a fair before his son's birth and carved thin copperplate letters in the stock: *Michael Fay, Ballinasloe 1899*.

'You're young,' Pat had said to him, 'But sensible enough. And it has your name on it, my father's name, so it's only right you should have it. But if I catch you firing it anywhere near the house, or near any of the stock, then you lose it. Understand me, Michael?' And Michael had nodded, eyes shining.

There was no need to fear the wolves now. With this in his hands he could blow them to kingdom come.

He built himself a hut on the western bank of the river, south of the bridge, for this seemed to him to be the place where the weirdest things happened, where the tracks were thickest. It was a crude affair, three sided and roofed with ferns a foot thick. Michael reburied the werewolf's skull by its open side, and over it constructed a hearth with stones from the river. He hoped the fire would keep it there, though he sometimes saw it in his dreams—snarling, skeletal, shrivelled, remnants of gums pulled back from the blackened teeth.

He watched, and waited, saw September enter the year and tint the leaves, felt the wind pick up in the heights of the trees. He checked Mullan's traps daily, shotgun in hand and game bag slapping at his side, but the wild creatures shunned them no matter how he moved or disguised them. He took them up in the end, leaving the wood clean and untouched once more. Over his horizon school loomed like a dark cloud.

The wood was an eerie place in the shortening evenings, full of the rushing of air and the whispers of the trees. He heard a voice singing there once, lovely as a summer blackbird, but the sound of it made the hair rise on the back of his neck. It was singing an old, old song, making it into a dirge, a coronach for dead dreams.

I overheard my own true love,
His voice it was so clear.
Long time I have been waiting for
The coming of my dear.

Sometimes I am uneasy
And troubled in my mind.
Sometimes I think I'll go to him
And tell to him my mind.

And if I should go to my love,
My love he will say nay.
If I show to him my boldness,
He'll ne'er love me again.

Perhaps it was the Banshee, and there was a death to come in the family. But the death had already happened, he told himself. Perhaps there had even been two.

He knew this: there was a life to the wood, an awareness. It remembered things, and it was watchful. He could feel eyes on his back every time he entered it. They were not hostile, but they were wary, gauging. He felt as though he were being weighed in a balance. But he could not guess what purpose he was being considered for.

EIGHT

THE EVENING THE girl called Cat reappeared, he was sitting outside his hut with the fire bright and crackling at his feet, experimenting with weapons. The book Rachel had got out of the library for him had pictures of cave men wrapped in furs and carrying spears and odd-looking axes, flint knives and scrapers. Cro-Magnon man, tallest of the prehistoric humans who had wandered north after the retreat of the ice some sixty thousand years before. Michael was trying to lash a sliver of stone on to a hazel staff, for there was no flint to be found in this countryside. His fingers were becoming raw with the effort. String was not strong enough. He grunted irritably as once more the stone blade shifted awry.

And when he looked up again, Cat was standing on the other side of the fire, watching him.

His heart thumped briefly and one hand fell to touch the shotgun he always brought here. She raised an eyebrow, smiling, and sat down opposite him without invitation. She wore the white shift, even in this biting autumn weather. She was human enough to relish the glow of the fire, he noticed. He put the spear aside and rummaged in his bag. 'Hungry?'

She nodded.

An apple, a squashed ham sandwich and the dregs of a flask of tea. She wolfed them down, gulping the tea straight from the mouth of the flask. Her elbows were bloody, Michael noticed, and it irked him to see her loveliness marred. If truth be told, she smelled. Not of gorse blossom this time, but of herself. An unnameable smell, at once repulsive and exciting.

It began to rain, the drops pattering on the thinning canopy of the trees and dripping down on their heads. The evening was falling fast, cloud gathering. Michael threw another chunk of wood on the fire, making the sparks sail up, and withdrew into the hut's shelter. Cat looked up at the sky in something like resignation. She seemed tired, he thought, and he saw now that she was muddy and grimed.

The rain grew heavier, hissing in the flames.

'Come inside,' Michael told her. Already the water was beating dark hair lank against her temples.

'I like the rain.' Grinning. 'I hope it thunders and storms!' And she appeared so like Rose for a moment that Michael blessed himself.

It became a downpour. Runnels of water were carving channels in the fallen leaves and the bare clay, and the wood was deafening with the rattle of rain beating the trees. Drips began to come through the roof of the hut, but Michael had seen out other showers within and knew it would stand up to the weather. There was an old blanket he kept there for a floor and he shook it out, beckoning to Cat.

'Come on, you'll catch your death.'

She had her head tilted to the rain and was catching it in her open mouth, her tongue stuck out to suck it in. She paused to look at him for a moment, then shrugged and joined him in the hut.

It seemed suddenly very crowded in there. She was wet through. What was it she liked so much about getting wet? The smell intensified. He could feel the warmth of her, and steam was already beginning to curl from her bare arms. A dark nipple looked ready to pierce the wet material of her dress. She pressed against him and he drew the musty blanket round both their shoulders, dizzy with apprehension, drunk with her nearness. Her dampness sank into his clothes. Her hair smelled of earth, rain, and a catch of that gorse blossom, summery as mown hay. He kissed her wet temple, her eye, the lid quivering under his lips. Her hand slipped inside his coat, wormed its way past his jumper to lie cold against his ribs. She had chilled fingers, though the rest of her was steaming, warm, reeking.

She was asleep. 'Cat?' Whispered.

Nothing.

So even fairies had to sleep. He leaned back against the wall of the shelter, hearing it creak ominously, and watched the fire fight the battery of the rain. Cat grew cold, goosepimpled, and he drew her across his lap, hugged her tight to his warmth and wrapped his coat around her.

I'm in love, he thought, and laughed quietly at the rain and the empty wood.

THE RAIN STOPPED after a while and he shifted his burden to let his arms breathe again. She was awake instantly, eyes open and pupils wide and black in the dimness. The fire was down to a lump of glowing log that smoked fitfully. Night had come upon them in the wake of the rain.

She sat up, shivering, her hair in wet rats' tails. Michael was damp, too, and cramped. An hour, she must have slept in his arms. He creaked his way out of the hut and stood up, stretching. Overhead branches dripped water on to his face. The fire was all but dead. He should be getting home.

Cat was sitting with her arms about her knees and the blanket over her shoulders, staring at him. 'What's the matter?' he asked her.

'Not a thing... Well, I'm cold, if you must know.'

'You should wear decent clothes.'

'*Decent*, he says.' She rubbed her raw elbows gingerly. 'It's all right for you.'

'What do you mean?'

'It doesn't matter. Get the fire going. This is not my season. Chill rain, the leaves dying, nights a day long. Oh, no.'

Michael set about resurrecting the fire, wondering what she was talking about. She seemed suddenly petulant, snappish. Warmth would cheer her up, he decided.

Yellow light flickered over their faces. Cat's shift was still dripping and Michael wondered if he dared suggest she take it off.

A crow of laughter, ending in a giggle. She had found his spear.

'A mighty hunter you will be, with a weapon such as this!' She wrenched the stone blade from the shaft with a flick of her wrist.

'Hey!' He was outraged. He tried to wrest it out of her grasp, but she wriggled like an eel and sent it flying out of the firelight. He bore her to the wet ground and set his weight atop her, not entirely sure what he was doing, but before he could decide she sent a narrow fist flying into his nose and stars exploded in his head. He rolled aside clutching at his face whilst her laughter rose in the night.

'A little over-eager there, Michael!'

'You... bugger,' he muttered, feeling the slow slide of blood down his upper lip. It smeared the back of his hand.

She was beside him in a flash, knees sinking in the wet clay.

She touched his battered nose with her fingers.

'I'm sorry. I did not mean to pain you.'

'Aye, right.'

She pulled him close. 'I would not hurt you, Michael.'

Was the fire somehow in her eyes or was there a light there, yellow as candles?

She licked the blood from his lip like a cat lapping milk. He could taste it as her tongue pushed inside his mouth. There was that tightness, that blooming warmth below his stomach. Her fingers brushed him there and he flinched, the breath sawing in his throat.

'Who are you?' he whispered.

Her mouth silenced him. They lay down beside the crackling fire and she tugged her shift above her waist. He saw the dark pelt between her legs, thick as fur, and fumbled with his trousers. Cold air and warm flame on his naked skin. He lay on her and she guided him, spoke to him in a low voice as though he were a horse to be calmed. And he was there, in her.

'God.'

He pushed and thrust, something within him taking over. Her hands were like claws on his shoulders and he heard her whimper as he pressed her buttocks into the cold earth. The wind was in the trees, oddly like the sea in a seashell: the circulation of his churning blood. And then there was a paroxysm that shuddered through him. He cried out into her shoulder, feeling her hand on the back of his head.

He was in the wood, *inside* the wood, spliced into the fabric of the trees. And it was within him also, its roots the network of his arteries. For a brief moment he thought he knew what the Other Place was, where it lay.

But it was trickling away. His elbows were deep in mud, his face buried in the hollow of Cat's collarbone. He slipped out of her, flaccid and spent. It was wet down there, slick as melted butter.

'Mine,' Cat murmured.

'What?'

The sudden grin was an inch from his own. She kissed his nose and her legs scissored his waist. 'All mine.'

Fornication, he thought. That's what it was. The biblical word made him shiver. He stood, ashamed of the wet sheen that plastered him. He pulled his trousers up hurriedly. Cat twitched down her shift.

I've fucked a fairy, he realized, the awful, forbidden word twisting like a snake in his mind. Was that a mortal sin? He ruminated momentarily on confession, what the priest would say about this in the little dark box. What had he said to Rose when she told him?

'Will you have a baby?' he asked Cat. She was poking the fire composedly.

'Do you want one?' She seemed amused.

'What we did. That makes babies. I know.'

She began to laugh. 'You worry too much, Michael. Sit.'

He did as he was told. Her back was filthy from the wood floor. He brushed leaves from it and found himself leaving his hand there, savouring the taut muscle under the shift. The dark hair was a midnight cascade down one side of her neck, thick with the detritus of the trees.

'What do you mean when you said "mine"? That I'm yours?'

'And I'm yours too,' she said, her eyes fixed in the fire. 'We belong.'

Baffled, he took his hand away. He needed to pee, but could not while she was here.

'Listen, Michael.' She became animated, twisting round to face him. She took his hands in hers. 'How would you like to go somewhere? Somewhere strange that you've never seen before, somewhere far away?'

'The wolves...' he began doubtfully.

'It's not just wolves. There are other things, too. Castles and cathedrals, cities and sailing ships. It's a whole world, Michael.' He remembered the glimpse he had been given, the empty land of the Bann valley with the single light off in its darkness.

Werewolves and wilderness.

Dream or nightmare? He didn't know. But this was real, here: this girl and what they had done. She was as real as earth and wood and stone, as solid as himself. Though only he could see her.

'I don't know.' It was late. His grandmother would be worrying. How long had he been out here?

'You think it's a fairy tale, Michael, but it's not. It's out there, all of it. I could show you things.' Her hand caressed his stomach.

'I—I don't know. It's late. I've got to go.'

'They'll worry. You've said it before.'

He felt strangely guilty. 'Are you still cold?'

'You warmed me.'

His face burned in the firelight.

'Come with me,' she said. 'Stay with me.'

He stood up, retrieved the shotgun and his bag. The desire to urinate was a hot pressure.

'I can't. I can't, Cat.' He had a moment's vision of the pair of them riding along a bright road in sunshine with the pennants of a castle flickering on the next horizon. The knight and his lady, like in the stories.

The wood was silent and dark, water dripping from the leaves. His clothes were thick with mud. He felt stupid, heavy-headed. Cat's eyes were like dark holes in her face. He wanted to do it again, and was ashamed of himself.

'I love you, Michael.'

His heart leapt for a second and he had to smile. Seeing that, she grinned that wide grin of hers and stood up also. The shift was a disrupted pattern of light and dark, white cotton and black earth. Blood there too, he noticed, a patch like a strawberry at the top of her legs. Had he hurt her?

She hugged him as though he were a child, as Rose had hugged him in the thundery nights. Their eyes were level. I'm tall, he thought. Not a baby any more. A man, then?

'I'm not going,' he said as she manoeuvred him into the hut and her deft fingers unbuttoned him.

'Oh, I know.'

He no longer had to go to the toilet. He saw her stand and let the shift fall to the ground around her feet like pale water. Then she was with him, on him, under him, her smell all through him, and he was marvelling at how fine it felt to touch those forbidden places.

'Mine,' she breathed as he coupled with her. 'All mine.' They let the fire die, and were blind to the rising of the moon.

IT ROSE OVER a vast forest.

Leagues upon leagues carpeted the world in a dark sea that lapped at the shoulders of the mountains. They reared their hoary branches to the stars and at their feet moon-silver rivers wound patiently towards an unknown ocean. Hills and valleys alike were covered by the thick growth, and in the dips of the land mist gathered like lambs' wool.

Here and there the turrets of a fortress jutted above the grasping oak and elm, lime and sycamore, horse chestnut and yew. In the river bottoms were willow and alder, brakes of thorn, and where the land rose there were birch, Scots pine and spruce. At their feet briars and bracken nestled, awaiting spring.

Roads ran through the forest, and there were clearings hacked and burnt along their length, clusters of buildings usurping the hegemony of the trees and woodsmoke rising in the moonlight. They huddled together as if fearful of the dank woods, fenced off by palisades, guarded by crucifixes. In the midst of every hamlet the steeple of a church sprang up like a spike. But no men were abroad in this wide land, this moonlit kingdom. They locked their doors against the night, and in the darkness the beasts roamed unafraid, peering at the light behind windows, ruling the depths of the forests.

Michael lay naked with the girl in his arms. The fire was dead, one solitary glede mocking him like a red unwinking eye. She was asleep, but he lay listening to the night sounds. Pheasant, with its harsh whirr, and the keewick of a hunting owl. Other, distant sounds he could not name. And once the deep, full-throated growl of some huge beast. The wood was alive with sound, a plethora of rustlings and shufflings. He thought if he lay still enough he would hear the very beat of this land's heart; enormous, bestial. Some night creature snuffled at the base of a tree yards away, invisible, and then padded off into the depths of the forest.

'Cat.' Soft as a summer zephyr. 'Cat, wake up.'

She stirred. He saw the dark eyes open.

'You made it happen, didn't you? You did it. We're *there* again.'

She sat up, pushing him aside. He thought her nose was sniffing the air. How far was he from home? How many miles or years or worlds away. He shook her roughly. 'Cat!'

'Ssh!' Her fingers bit into his arm. Their lower bodies were entangled. His penis lolled like a severed umbilical across his thigh and he could feel the cold air bite into the sweat that still marked him.

'Jesus, Cat, what have you done?'

'Be quiet!' As sharp as a slap, but low, afraid of being heard.

He could see nothing beyond their livid limbs. Their clothes were beneath them but the shotgun was invisible, off among the leaves somewhere. Fear shrunk his belly. He felt like a cave man at the world's dawning. Cro-Magnon man shivering in the prehistoric dark.

'Get dressed.' Her voice was a hiss.

They sorted out their clothes, fumbling and stumbling. He had even taken off his boots. There were dead twigs in them and leaves and old bark stuck to his coat like burrs. In silence, by touch, they dressed. He explored the leaf litter until his fingers struck the chill iron of the gun barrel. At once, he felt safer.

'Davy bloody Crockett,' he muttered.

They stood for a moment, listening. It seemed reckless to speak aloud, to make any noise. Cat bruised his lips with a kiss and then pulled him along by the hand. 'Come.'

She can see in the dark, he thought. Those eyes. A cat, indeed. He stumbled in her wake as they left the hut behind.

A few yards in the impenetrable gloom, and he had forgotten where the hut had even been. His hand tightened on Cat's fingers. If he got lost here, that would be him lost for ever. Disappeared. His family would never know where he had gone.

How did it happen? How was it done? One moment he was a quarter of a mile from the walls of his home, the next he was in some primeval wilderness. A dark fairyland, complete with wolves. The magnitude of the puzzle kept him silent as he shuffled along after Cat.

There was something behind him.

He knew it as surely as a blind man knows the direction of the sun. It was big—he thought he heard it expelling quiet breaths far above his head—and almost entirely noiseless. Like a horror film, the ones in the pictures where the hero is grabbed from behind.

He let the weight of the shotgun ooze through his grip until his fingers were curled around the trigger guard.

Crackling footsteps in time with his own. He tried to say something to Cat, but she seemed intent on the way ahead, wherever that was. And his throat had seized up and puckered.

He would turn around and give it both barrels like Audie Murphy, as Mullan had done with the werewolf in the back yard. Except that the werewolf had escaped unscathed.

Magic or no magic, two shotgun rounds at point-blank range would settle anything's hash.

He tore his hand loose from Cat's, pointed the gun and fired. The recoil threw him back into her and they both fell. He was deafened, blinded, bruised. Got you, you sneaking hairy bastard, he thought gleefully, but all that came out was a strangled wail.

For a second he saw a massive torso lit up by the flash, man-like but not human, and what might have been a face above it, brutish, hulking. Then utter dark took him. He lay not replying to Cat's cries, her searching hands. Something crashed away through the trees in a chaos of breaking branches, but there was no other sound—unless it might be a cavernous muttering, bad-tempered thunder.

'What did you do? What did you do?' Cat's fingers pried into his painful shoulder.

'Ow, let go. It was a monster. I shot it.'

'A monster? What kind of monster? Did you see?'

A giant, memory told him. A troll. But he shook his head in her invisible face. 'I'm not sure, but I got it. It ran away.'

Her ringing slap sent lights flaring across his vision again. For a moment he was too shocked to do anything, then he reached out to where he thought her throat might be, but encountered only empty air. 'What was that for?' Tears of fury stung his eyes.

'You're not at home now, Michael. You can't slaughter things with your brave guns. There are different rules here. Listen.'

He did, still smouldering. The woods were silent—deathly silence, the hush like that of a desecrated church.

'It doesn't mean you have to slap me. A bloody girl, too.'

'Oh, be quiet, you stupid boy.'

That word again. He gritted his teeth. He'd get her back for it.

'We have to put some distance behind us, and quickly. We must leave this place. They'll be flocking like bees.'

'Who?'

But she ignored him. He was tugged to his feet and yanked along like a recalcitrant child, and he felt like one, sulking and chastised.

Brambles raked his face and the lower branches strove to gouge holes in his skull.

'How do you see in this?'

Again he was ignored. They ploughed through the midnight forest in silence.

By the time they halted he was staggering with tiredness. He no longer cared where they were or where they were going. The shotgun was a dull ache of weight. Cat grasped his free hand and set it against the rough bark of a tree.

'Climb.'

'You must be joking.'

'Climb, if you want to see the morning.'

'I can't, holding this.' He brandished the shotgun in the darkness.

'Blast you. Give it to me, then.' He could have sworn she shuddered as she took the weapon from him.

'I can't see a thing—'

Noises off in the trees, distant growls. A long, high-pitched howl.

'Climb!'

He did as he was told. The rough bark tore his palms. He straddled it and hauled himself up with quivering limbs, encountered a stout branch and clung to it, grunting. There were others here. He hauled himself on, feeling his way, running his hand up the trunk of the tree until he met something his fingers could grip. Once something small and clawed scampered over the back of his hand and he almost fell. He gave in to cursing, low and venomous. He was too tired. His arms would not support him and there was nowhere for his right foot to go.

A hand, guiding his ankle. 'Put it there.' And his foot was safe, taking weight.

'That's enough,' she said after a while. 'Ease out along the branch.' He inched out fearfully, the drop an unknown height in the blackness. His branch was a yard thick, and others arced close by. He was able to sit back and relax. He heard Cat rustle beside him and then the cold weight of the shotgun was plumped into his lap. 'There. Now we can sleep.'

'Sleep!'

A palm caressed his cheek, and then she was kissing his ear, the corner of his mouth, and her hair tickled his nose. 'I'm sorry, Michael.'

'Aye.' Mollified, despite himself.

She slipped a slim arm about his shoulders and he felt safe as houses. He dipped his head under her chin. Bloody hell, he was tired, sleepy as a child.

He did not hear the pack coursing below them later in the night, the hoofbeats that battered the empty air above the tops of the trees, the trolls calling out to one another.

THE LIGHT IN his eyes woke him. He prised open his gummy lids, stiff as wood all over and beginning to shake with cold. For a second he was utterly bewildered by the swaying branches, the birdsong and the brilliant early-morning light sifting through the leaves. Then it flooded back. He shifted in Cat's arms and the shotgun slipped out of his lap and fell to the ground with a far, muffled thump.

'Bugger.'

Cat stirred but did not waken. His leaning weight had made her arm blue and cold and he rubbed it gently, coaxing the blood to move. She was severely beautiful in the dawn, though dirt smeared her cheekbones and thorn scratches lined her skin. He brushed a sun-brilliant beetle out of her hair. His stomach rumbled and complained and he thought wistfully of bacon and eggs, hot tea, soda bread. And a bath.

But there was something fine about being here on talking terms with the birds, seeing the sun come up. And having this girl beside him. In a strange way, his hunger made it more immediate. Once he had ground the sleep out of his eye sockets he felt as sharp as a knife, and licked dew off a coppery leaf to moisten his tongue.

When he looked back she was awake, her eyes enormous and filled with sunshine, like the shallows of a summer sea. She was flexing and stretching, pointing her dirty toes.

'Is it safe now?'

She yawned and smiled. 'Safer, maybe. We can get down. You slept well.'

'Where are we going?'

'I'll take you home. You're not ready for this yet.'

He surprised himself by feeling let down. Perhaps it was the crystal clearness of the morning air, the jewel light of the sun, the bird-loud trees. Adventure. Wonderland.

'Can you explain any of it?'

She shook her head, vastly amused. 'Not in your terms. Why seek reasons?'

'I don't know. There's a reason for everything.'

She began lowering herself to the ground. They were a surprising way up, he saw, at least thirty feet. A red squirrel regarded them curiously from a nearby branch, unafraid.

He retrieved the shotgun, cleaning dirt from the muzzle anxiously whilst Cat sniffed the air and peered through the trees like some lithe animal. He wanted her again, but could not bring himself to say anything.

The forest floor was a lot less congested than it had seemed the night before. There were bare spaces under the trees, the brambles dying back with the turning of the year, and the sun flooded the ground through the thinning leaves. Wood pigeons somewhere, and a thrush. Other songs he could not identify. Apart from that there was near silence, broken only by the clamour of his empty gut. He was filthy, and so was Cat. She seemed not to mind, wood creature that she was.

Michael broke open the shotgun and pocketed the spent shells. Cat shot him a disapproving look, and he snapped the weapon shut without reloading. There was a glass rattle in his game bag and he knew that the flask was broken.

'I'm for it,' he said with a groan. Out all night without a word. His grandmother would flay him alive.

Cat beckoned impatiently and they started off into follow-my-leader again, a steady lope through the trees.

'How do we go from one place to another?' he asked when his breathing had settled a little. The shotgun jigged painfully on his shoulder.

'We walk, being poor,' she replied shortly.

'No. You know what I mean. From my home to here, this place. How do you do it, how do you get us through?'

'It's not my doing.'

'Whose then?'

'Yours, maybe?'

'Don't be daft. Tell me, Cat. Or do you not know yourself?'

She slowed to a walk and allowed him to catch up. 'There are holes here, leading to where you have your home. There always have been. They move and shift, disappear and reappear, but some are permanent. And we can go through them.'

'How do you know where they are?'

'I just know, like I know which way is north, or where open ground lies.'

'Is it all forest like this over here?'

'Mostly. The forest stretches for uncounted leagues in all directions. Beyond it are hills and a great river, and mountains to the south. Huge mountains no one has ever climbed.'

What about towns, villages, people?' *Fox-People.*

'We have those also.'

'What are they like?'

'You will wear me out with questions, Michael. These things you will find out soon enough. For now I am keeping a lookout for breakfast.'

'Breakfast!'

'Hush! Not so loud. Breakfasts are caught on the hoof in this country.' Her eyes danced at him and his throat tightened with... love? Lust? The feeling was powerful enough to dizzy him. He felt like shouting aloud.

'I'll shoot you something,' he said. 'We can roast it on the spit.'

'You will not. There will be no bangs and blasts in this place. The forest will not like it. Did you learn nothing from last night?'

He remembered the hulking shadow, the flashlit face. Human and yet inhuman, like a giant Neanderthal. 'What was it?'

'Troll, most likely. Hard to tell if it was a good one or a bad one. You didn't give it a chance.'

'Good and bad trolls,' Michael mused. 'They didn't have those in the stories.'

'This is more than a story.' She stopped. 'Have you flint and steel?'

His fell fell. 'No, I'm sorry. Only matches.'

She giggled. 'They will have to do, I suppose. What about a knife?'

'I've a penknife.'

'How splendid. Give it to me.'

He handed it over doubtfully. 'What's it for?'

'Breakfast. Light us a fire. I will be away a while.'

Then she stripped off her shift and rolled naked in the earth and leaves of the forest floor whilst Michael gaped. When she rose again she was a matt-haired brown-skinned savage, the knife blade glinting in one fist. She winked at him and scampered off, as silently as a—as a cat.

'Bloody hell,' Michael said. He set about building the fire.

A LONG, HUNGRY morning inched along. There was a stream nearby, a transparent rivulet hardly a foot wide. There Michael drank and scrubbed himself, stripping to the waist and gasping at the coldness of the water. He dried sitting by his little fire. There was dead wood littering the ground among the trees and he had a respectable pile. He had even fashioned a crude spit, breaking branches between his fingers. The fire was smokeless, the air above it shimmering with heat.

He wondered what she was trying to catch for them to eat. Not bacon and eggs, that's for sure.

He whipped round, staring. Something in the trees, darting behind a trunk.

'Damn you, Cat.' His hand crept to the shotgun.

There was a flickering movement. He could hardly catch it, and he thought he saw spider-like limbs scrabbling in the beech leaves.

A face, there, in the crook of a branch, black, triangular and leering, with slits for eyes and pointed ears sticking up through a thatch of moss-coloured hair.

Gone again. A hoot of high-pitched laughter, like that of a demented child. The wood was still, but for a distant patter like rain on a canopy of leaves. Feet? Impossible to tell. That laughter again, distant this time, merry and disquietening. It faded, and was gone.

He reloaded the shotgun.

—And spun round at the noise, but it was only Cat dumping a dead animal on to the leaves and glaring at the levelled shotgun with eyes narrow in her mired face.

'There was something in the trees,' he told her lamely.

'There are many things in the trees. You can't shoot them all.' She bent and without further ado began cutting into her catch. It was a large piglet, Michael saw, dun-coloured except for black stripes running along its body from nose to tail. He watched in horrified fascination as she slit the throat and held the body up by the hind legs while a thick stream of dark blood gushed out. It had hardly finished steaming on the ground before she sliced into the skin and gralloched the animal, pushing the steaming entrails to one side.

At last she jointed it, licked her fingers, and began to sharpen sticks of firewood.

Breakfast. Somehow the edge of Michael's appetite had disappeared.

'How did you catch it?'

'Easy.' The fire hissed as she placed the skewered joints over the flames. 'Their trails are simple to follow, the young as simple to snatch if you are fleet of foot. It is the mother you must beware. They are good mothers, the wild sows.'

'You're a mess.'

'I'm a huntress. Mind the meat, and I will make myself presentable.' She snatched up her shift and made for the stream. His gaze followed her as she went, the tangled hair flowing down to her buttocks, the smooth movement of muscle in her calves, the tight curve of her hip as she knelt by the water.

Behind him the stink of blood and fresh entrails was being drowned by the appetizing odour of roasting pork. He felt hungry again.

Cat was humming as she splashed, a dark sound, sweet as honey. The tune he had once heard being sung in the wood at home. He grimaced. She was rubbing a handful of green leaves over her arms, breasts, belly and thighs, crushing them to the skin. He looked away, swallowed, and twitched his trousers into a more comfortable position.

When she rejoined him, dressed and wet-haired, he had to sniff at her to confirm the smell he had caught over the roasting meat. 'Chewing gum!'

She shook her head. 'Mint leaves. I found a few along the boar track, faded by the season but still with some goodness in them. See?' She thrust a forearm under his nose and he breathed in the tang of spearmint along with the slight woman smell that underlay it. He kissed the forearm and she laughed, then began retrieving pork from the flames.

It was black and seared on the outside, white underneath and pink at its heart. They chewed in silence, their faces smeared with grease, juggling the hotter pieces in singed fingers.

'Tell me about the things in the wood,' Michael said when they had finished gorging themselves.

She sucked grease off her fingers and wiped them on her filthy shift. Once white, it was now the colour of beech bark.

'People fear the wood. Your kind of people. They build barricades to keep it out and burn the trees so the branches will not touch their houses. They stick up crosses everywhere to keep off the beasts, and never venture out after dark. They grow crops and herd animals, build things and haggle over money. But there are others. The tribes, the wanderers who roam the forest at will, setting up a village here and there for a few days, a week, a year, and then moving on. They build huts, fish the streams, hunt the boar and wolf. Live free.'

'Like you.'

She frowned. 'Not like me. They are *people*, you see.'

'So what are you?'

'A fairy.' She struck a pose.

'You're no fairy. Fairies are tiny, with wings and such.'

'Ach, what do you know? And there are the other folk, the tree folk who keep to themselves, helping or hindering as they please. And the trolls, of course. Wood trolls, stone trolls, good and bad. Odd things, half beast. The forest is alive with them at night. That is when they hunt. In the day they are stones or tree stumps.'

'Who is the Horseman?'

She fired a black-browed stare at him. 'The Devil. He seeks souls. The black wolves follow him sometimes, and the manwolves.'

'Manwolves? Werewolves, you mean?'

'Whatever. They are the worst of the beasts. They carry disease with them and increase their numbers with infection when they've a mind to. Terrible things.'

'One came after us.'

She nodded. 'Terrible things. Servants of Satan, the village folk call them. They steal babies and drink blood. And then there is the forest itself. It knows things. It lives just as we do, and remembers all that it sees.' She paused, looking up at the kaleidoscope of branches above. 'I love the forest.'

'I love you,' he said on impulse. Simple words, fearful and grand.

She cupped his face in her long hands, unsmiling for once. 'I know.'

She would not speak further, but began stuffing what was left of the piglet into Michael's game bag.

'Put out the fire. Piss on it, if you can. Cover it up. The blood, also. Time to go'

He beat out the low flames and buried them with damp earth.

When he had finished, Cat sprinkled the scar with leaves and twigs until it looked as undisturbed as the rest of the wood floor. In the air the smell of burning remained, and under it was the tang of blood. Cat's nostrils quivered like a deer's.

'Best to make some haste. The blood will bring things here, even in the daylight.'

'Are you taking me home now?'

'Indeed.'

'So where is this hole, then? This way back?'

'A fair tramp. A day's amble, no more. Pick up your knife.'

The morning had worn on. It was noonish, he guessed. His grandmother would be cooking the lunch.

They set off again, Cat free and unencumbered, swinging her arms, himself weighed down with weapon and bag, boots and coat. Michael Fay, intrepid explorer.

THE AFTERNOON CAME round and the sun slanted through the trees to dapple their way, a shifting leopard-skin carpet. It was warm when they walked, autumn a mere guess of wind and colder air above the canopy overhead. They glimpsed scurryings and movement in the thicker undergrowth, the startled flight of deer, and were eyed once by a massive horned owl from the limb of an oak. They stumbled across other things also: a tree wound round with garlands of dog rose and honeysuckle, the blossoms dead and fallen. And at its foot a pile of bones and broken spears. Michael retrieved a beautifully flaked spearhead from the pile, leaf-shaped and keen as a razor. He looked at Cat but she frowned and gestured that he throw it back. It was a place sacred to one of the tribes, she told him, best left alone.

Later they walked into a small clearing in the wood that was slowly being reclaimed by saplings and thick briars. There, mouldering amid the riotous vegetation, were the remains of wattle and daub walls, thatched roofs, crude stone hearths, discarded skins and a midden high with bones and bluebottles. And here, with its back to a tree, was the leathery skeleton of a man, all smell gone from it now. The seasons had washed him clean and for some reason the beasts had left him alone. Empty sockets looked out on the lost village from a black face, the scraps of hide drawn tight as a drum over his skull.

The clearing was silent and still, and the sun had gone in.

Michael felt there had been something unpleasant here, some disaster. He and Cat hurried on without a word, leaving the corpse to its vigil.

The forest grew thicker, darker, and overhead the clouds gathered. They began to fight their way through thickets, Michael cursing the game bag which snagged on everything, and beating branches aside with the barrel of the shotgun.

Rain. It started as a drift of moisture where the leaves were thin but soon strengthened into a pouring drizzle, flattening Cat's hair to her back and making her shift transparent. She began to shiver and Michael gave her his coat to wear. Then they slogged onwards, Cat correcting their path every so often from the rear.

Evening. It was beginning to gather in the shadows. Michael doubted if they had come a mile in the past hour.

'How much farther?'

'I don't know it in yards,' Cat snapped. She wiped the dripping rain from her eyes. 'Too far to make today.'

Another night in the forest. And Michael was already wet through. He swore, and as he did his voice cracked into a deeper tone, startling them both. Then Cat began to laugh.

'I hope your wonderful matches are dry, my love, or it will be a miserable night.' She hugged him to her, teased his lips like a bee brushing a foxglove. Her face was cold, rain gathering in the hollows of her collarbones and trickling between her breasts. He kissed it away, tongued a pebble-hard nipple through her shift. Then she lifted his head gently.

'Time enough for that later. For now we need shelter, and a fire.'

'We're not sleeping in a tree tonight, then?'

'We'll risk the ground. We need the fire, and it'll help keep the beasts at bay.'

A long, hard time, cold as flint, the woods dark and loud with pouring water. He had his coat laid over the little pyramid of twigs and his shivers would barely allow him to strike the matches. Match after bloody match, damp and dead, until one caught and he nurtured it in the palm-rubbed moss that was their tinder. Smoke stung his eyes and reeked his hair. But it had caught.

Cat had rigged up a shelter, a framework of branches covered with drifts of leaves and caulked with fistfuls of squelching mud. It looked like a great hairy molehill and was so close to the flames that the smoke sailed in, but they huddled inside to eat the cold pork, grey with congealed grease, and soaked up the warmth, building the fire until the flames were a yard high.

They made love there in the damp smokiness of the firelight, and this time Cat's fingers were as tight as ivy on his shoulders and she screamed into the rain and the rushing trees, so that he paused, afraid he had hurt her. But she urged him to go on, not to stop, and his climax was like a burst of brightly lit blood in his head, a sea wave washing over them. Her tautness relaxed under him and she kissed his eyes, murmuring words in some language he could not understand. In his nostrils was the smell of mint and mud, woodsmoke and sex. Ever after he would associate the act with those smells, and the sound of branches tossing in wind and rain.

There had been, or would be, another time, however, when those smells would be part of his life, and the deep trees would be the only world he knew.

In the morning of that other time there was snow on the hills and the hide of their shared bag was stiff with frost. It seemed that even with the dawn the life of the forest was in abeyance, sleepy and torpid with cold.

They were close to the edge here, nearing the end of the trees and the open land beyond where there was a hole in the mesh, a way back through a cave mouth they had emerged from—so long ago, it seemed. Despite his heavy weariness, Michael's senses kicked into a higher gear. They were close. It would not do to get caught so near to the finish.

In the late afternoon a dark shape rose out of the side of a tree and Ringbone was before them as he had promised he would be, his rank smell making the mounts sniff and blow down their noses. The long ears of Cat's mule twitched.

'*Ca spel, ycempa*?' Michael asked him. *Spel* was the word for news, an Anglo-Saxon word, but Michael had long ago given up any attempt to classify the languages that the forest peoples spoke. Old Gaelic mixed with Saxon and Norse, and a smattering of bastardized Latin. It pulled at the mind, flickering just out of comprehension. Old words, buried like gems in the subconscious. It was a huge effort to drag them out of his mind, though once they had been the very tongue of his dreams. It was because he was so close to the finish, so far from the heart of the wood. Mirkady had warned him of that: that the wood sent roots and feelers into the mind as surely as the trees put out their branches. They were receding, pulling back, but he thought some of them would always be there, no matter what road he might walk in the years to come.

Ringbone told them that the land was deserted, the weather change sending the forest creatures to their burrows. Even the trolls were lying low until the cold snap passed. But scent would persist for a long time in weather such as this. Good weather for hunters.

The snow crunched and Cat had kicked the mule forward.

She threw back her hood.

'Best to make hay while we can. We should keep going, Michael, find the wood's edge before setting camp for the night. This is the last chance they will have to come at us out of the trees.'

He nodded sombrely. She spoke to Ringbone in his own language, Michael glowering and frowning at his own inability, and the fox man seemed to agree. He jogged off through the trees, beckoning. Ringbone was alone. The rest of his kin—those who had survived—had departed, for this part of the world was outside their ken.

The trees thinned after a while, the open spaces between them thick with snow. It was a relief to ride without having to be wary of snatching branches, to look up and see the first of the icy stars a deepening gulf of night away.

And then the trees ended. Michael and Cat dismounted and stood gazing out from the last vestiges of the forest towards what seemed to be an expanse of infinite space, a rising land of low, snow-covered hills that glistened in the starlight and rolled endlessly to the edge of sight. Open country, at long last.

'Utwyda,' Ringbone said in a plume of breath. *The Place Beyond the Wood.*

The cold ate into them after a few minutes and they began to busy themselves with the well-worn routine of setting up camp. Fire, sentry, horses—each had their set task. It was a brief half hour before they were sitting around the hissing fire and the yellow light was carving shadows out of their faces. They ate—a hare Ringbone had snared the day before—and then reclined like emperors with the trees a brooding blackness around them, the slightly lighter patch to one side where they had ended and the hills began. They would put forty miles behind them tomorrow, but for now they unrolled their bedding amongst the leaf mold one last time. This was Cat's place they were leaving behind, the land she knew best and loved most. It was Ringbone's also. In the morning the fox man would go his own way. Michael wondered if Cat would rather be going back with him, back into the forests and the hazy fairy-tale existence she had known before.

She pushed into Michael's arms and lay there like a child whilst he nuzzled her glorious hair, tangled and greasy now, and her buttocks nestled against his groin.

There, in the travel-weary quiet of the firelight, Ringbone told them a story. It was one Michael had heard before, though from other points of view. It seemed to be the seminal myth of all the forest peoples, the story of their beginnings. He could even pick out the meaning in the words because he knew them so well. He thought Ringbone might be telling it to comfort them, and himself, out here on the edge of his world.

It was a tale of his people, of all the peoples of the wood and the hills. His tribe were once warriors, he said, and they had been in service to those folk who lived in the villages and fortresses. But they had tired of their task, the patrolling of the stockades and the escort of caravans, and they had set out into the wood to make lives of their own, taking some of the village womenfolk with them. They had split up, splintered and sundered like a tree struck by lightning, and had become the tribes: the Badger-People, the Fox-People, the Boar-People. They had dwindled, worn down by the beasts of the forest, and whilst they were away more men came from the north, where the trees ended. These men were lost and confused, and they had a speech of their own. They were fleeing the raiders from the sea, they said, leaving a land in flames behind them, and the village folk had nodded at this, remembering their oldest legends. Some of these new men wore robes and carried crosses. The crosses kept the unholy amongst the beasts at bay and the people of the villages welcomed them. And so the churches were built, and the Brothers of the Wood set up their retreats. But Ringbone's people they denounced as pagans, little better than animals, and they were denied the villages except when there was a mart or fair when their trading goods of skins and amber, hunting dogs and river gold, were welcomed. But the tribes remembered that they, not the Brothers, were the true guardians of the land, from the time when the Old Man, the lame one, had brought them across the terrible heights of the southern mountains, through the dank terror of the Wolfweald and through the southern woods. They had come from a place of fear and persecution, and the Old Man had vanished once the passage of the mountains had been forced, returning to the snow-clad peaks which the village folk said marked the world's end. They had forgotten, because of the words and worship of the Brothers, who said that all men came from the north, from beyond the Utwyda. But the tribes remembered the truth of it, that these Brothers were from a different place, another world, perhaps, whereas the true home of all Men in the Wood was south, beyond the terrible mountains, a land of burning and horror where lost cities rose on great hills and monsters worse than the trolls of the forest roamed the deserted streets. The tribes had been god-like there, wielding strange weapons of wood and the black metal—iron, the metal that slew the Wyrim with a scratch, if they had no yarrow to bind to it.

Here Ringbone reached a hand into his pouch and brought a doeskin lump into the firelight. He unwrapped the bundle carefully. This was part of such a weapon, he said, handling it with reverence. It looked like an outsized ring of ancient iron, pitted with corrosion, paper-thin with age and three fingers in diameter. Michael had seen a few others like it, kept as heirlooms by the tribes to remind them of what and who they had once been. Knights, he thought. They went from being Knights to being savages, and it is still there in the back of their mind after all this time.

'Temuid gewenian,' Ringbone said at last, replacing the artifact in his pouch. *We will return.* And his story was done.

Michael took first watch, and built up the fire to keep their last night in the woods at bay.

In the dripping, bird-loud morning a two-hour walk brought them within sight of the little river and the wet, massive stone of the bridge. It darkened as they approached, the early light thickening into the gloom of evening. They passed the humped shape of Michael's hut as the first stars rose. As though it had been a dream, and the time lost in the Other Place had been returned to them.

There were cattle lowing in the meadows beyond, and here Cat kissed Michael goodbye.

'I'll come back,' she said, and was gone.

NINE

'TIME,' CAT WAS to tell Michael, 'is like a lake. You can go and haul out bucketfuls of its water, throw them about, drink them, pour them off, and then go back to the lake and find it the same level as before, with even the ripples you made wiped away.'

He walked in the door of the house the same evening he had come out of it, the grime and mud of two days in the Other Place still upon him. He was late for supper, and Aunt Rachel threw her hands in the air when she saw him.

'Jesus, Mary and Joseph!'

After that there was the broken flask to explain whilst his grandmother folded her heavy arms and listened to his lies and half-truths with what seemed to him like perfect comprehension. Grandfather and Mullan remained smoking thoughtfully by the fire, though Michael saw Pat's old eyes range along the dirty length of the shotgun barrel speculatively.

A bath was drawn and he was hustled into it. He had dirt ingrained, it seemed, even below his clothes. When he snuffed at his arm he smelled mint, girl and woodsmoke. He let the steaming water cradle him and wondered where she was now, in what world, under which trees.

There was cold pork in the game bag, he remembered. He would dump it in the morning.

A different morning, in another world. He had left a wood minutes ago where the sun was slanting high and bright in the sky, and yet here there was blue darkness outside the window and he could see the flash and tilt of lanterns in the yard as the men went out for their nightly check of the stock.

He was tired, though. Sleeping in the wood seemed somehow not like sleep at all, more like a semi-conscious awareness. He yawned in the hot clutch of the bath.

Where was he being taken? What was this place she brought him to, with its monsters and forests? And how much of it was here, in his own world? Was there a barrier wearing thin between the two, or was it merely him, his fancies that no one else could see?

Something had bent that trap in the wood, something big.

And he had seen the hideous shape in the yard that night. He had dug up the skull of one of its kind.

No. It was both real and unreal. It was *there*, waiting for him, and Cat wanted him to enter it, to view the marvels. To travel Wonderland.

School took him.

It was a marvel the way the days flew, flitted, tumbled past sunlit and ordinary, and wore down to autumn. The turning of the year seemed to have arrived in a wheeling rush. Now it would slow again, as Michael waited out the waning days within the confines of the schoolroom with the smell of chalk, the must of books, the voices of other children. But always, the knowledge that there was more—a whole world mere heartbeats away—there, brooding in the corners of his mind like a pot bubbling on the back of the stove.

Grammar, algebra, trigonometry, Irish, religion. These he was taught, plodding in unison with the rest of the chanting class and eyeing the amber-pale field, the crops cut now, beyond the narrow windows.

History, prehistory, the taking of fire from flint and wood, the flora and fauna of long-vanished wildernesses, tool-making, burial rites, the construction of dolmen. These he taught himself in a crazy-quilt of patchwork reading and talks with Mullan. It was a dappled, magpie education, riddled with gaps and deep in the wrong places—but wholly necessary, he was coming to believe. It fed his growing appetite for strangeness, but nourished his fellow pupils' belief in his eccentricity. Miss Glover seemed to him a confused mix of encouragement and censure. She had lent him books, but they were the wrong books and he returned them unread. Nothing she did seemed to suit him, and he remained determined to dig deep in his own chosen fields of study, scraping only desultorily at the topsoil elsewhere. From bafflement she passed into irritation and anger. Michael began to be kept behind after school, remaining alone in the ticking silence with thorny mathematical problems on his pad, Miss Glover baleful and intense at her desk and the bright day wasting away outside.

Again and again this happened, his grandparents and his aunt adding to the punishment when he got home so that he began to feel caged, surrounded, savage. He even wondered if Cat had put some spell on him, blunted some self-preserving instinct to do as he was told.

For she had gone and left him. There was no sign of her by the river or the bridge, and the wood was empty. Perhaps, he thought, it was something to do with the season, but the wood seemed deserted of almost all life. Birds had never been common there, but there had always been other things—rabbit droppings, squirrel-gnawed nuts, owl leavings. And the tracks, of course. Now there was nothing but the rising wind in the trees. The husks of ten-foot giant hogweed swayed brittle and fantastic down along the river and the air was full of the onion-smell of ramsons. The roof of Michael's hut had fallen in on itself and the embers of their fire were black, stone-hard and cold.

There was something here, though. The hut had not collapsed. It had been torn down, the supporting sticks splintered and smashed.

And here, in the ground beside it, a blurred footprint, manlike but with claws at the end of the toes and no arch at the instep. Padded, like a dog's.

Michael straightened from his perusal of the ground, staring out at the blank faces of the surrounding trees. They were nearly bare already, and the wood was full of falling leaves. He felt he was not alone, that there was a watcher out there, unfriendly, malevolent. He no longer trusted the gun as a defence, not since he had shot the thing in the wood that night and heard it blunder away unharmed. Different rules operated here. That was another reason to seek out Cat. He needed to know things, things he had not found in books. How to fight werewolves, for instance. How to ward off evil.

THE EARTH SLOWED, wound down to a darker season. In the hedges be-dewed spiders' webs swayed and swung like strung pearls, and the early light caught them in a dance of linked gems. September trickled by, the air full of the flitting leaves and the first coolness falling on the world. Soon the mornings grew sharp, white with frost, the grass crunching underfoot as Michael set off for school. And in the schoolroom itself the breaths of the children would be little clouds until their body heat and the labours of the stove had generated a comfortable fug inside.

October came, snapping at Michael's sleepy limbs when he threw off his bedclothes and chilling the water in the taps. In the Fay household the first fires were lit, cautiously at first, like the trial of a newly knit limb, and then banked up as the cold snap remained. Michael loved those mornings, coming down to porridge in the big kitchen, the table crowded and full of talk, the fire leaping red and friendly out of the opened range. Then there would be the crispness of the air outside, the way smells seemed to hang in the air, frozen. Treacle and creosote, dung and hay, oats and pipe smoke. They pervaded the mornings like some tangled perfume, and underlying them was the tang of the cold, the fallen leaf. Autumn, and winter creeping up on its shirt-tails.

To spend such mornings in a schoolroom seemed to Michael worse than a crime. He chafed and fidgeted and shifted, cursed under his breath and felt his mind lock up and seize. He received extra lines for not paying attention at least once a week, but that was far preferable to having a note to take home. And then Rachel, afterwards, watching him like a well-fed hawk and keeping him at the table until the stupid letters that were supposed to be numbers had resolved themselves. By then, of course, it was dark and the day was gone. He could stand out in the back yard with a pool of lamplight spilling out of the door at his back and listen to the river churning in the night, the call of an owl, the squeaks of the wheeling bats taking their last flights before winter hibernation. That was where he was meant to be, where he belonged—with Cat beside him. And he would dream of her at night, her fingers tight on his shoulders and her body answering his in the leaf litter and the rushing trees.

October passed by and November inched on to the stage, dark and damp. Michael always thought of October as a beautiful month, a coloured tumble of warm days mixed in with the bite of crisp cold and the end of the long evenings. A harbinger of what was to come, but a benevolent one.

November was a dark month, a cold month, when there was likely to be the first flurry of snow. It seemed to Michael to be the end of the year, a limbo time that would not end until Christmas—or midwinter, depending on how you looked at it. November heralded the real start of the cold, the days that made walking to school a chill misery. It was during the night of one of these days that Michael lay in bed listening to the wind pounding the gables. The gale had swooped down on them in the afternoon so that he had had a weary battle home from school and had arrived soaked to the bone with wind-driven rain, his cheeks glowing, schoolbooks beginning to crinkle with damp. He lay now with the covers pulled up to his chin, looking out of the window at the foot of his bed and tracing the glimmer of the racing clouds beyond the black shapes of the farm buildings.

One of them had a tracery of rectangular light shining faintly around the cracks in its door—Mullan looking in on Fancy, probably rubbing her down with a twist of straw. She always got sweated up on stormy nights. The other buildings were dark. The wind was a roar overhead that whined around the roof and made the rafters creak. It pushed at his window, trying to get in, and circled in odd draughts around the floor, for this was an old house, well acquainted with the seasons. It seemed to have compromised with the wind, allowing in the little eddies and draughts but standing hardy as a crag against the worst blasts. If he closed his eyes Michael could almost believe himself to be at sea in some storm-racked ship, the hull groaning but adamant, the wind bending the masts. An unknown shore to his lee and the surf booming white and murderous at its foot.

Except he was not imagining that sound: banging close by, and a rattle as his window shook.

He sat up and was immediately dazzled by the silver moonlight flooding in the window. The moon was up and half-full, the clouds galloping past its horns, but there was a shape silhouetted at the window sill, perched there with one hand spread against the glass and two green lights glowing in a hood-like tangle of hair.

'*Let me in, Michael.*'

'Jesus!' He blessed himself.

The window was thumped again with an open palm and the face turned to look back down in the yard. He saw the profile then, the one he knew. Her eyes seemed to ensnare the moon, like a cat's eyes reflecting lamplight.

'Michael, please! They are here, below. They smell me. Let me in!'

He was paralysed. She crouched on the sill like some tensed animal waiting to spring, and that awful radiance made her eyes like those of a fiend. The moonlight sculpted a savage skull out of her face, light and dark with the hair whipping round it.

'*Please!*'

The spell snapped at the pleading in her voice. He leapt forward over the bedclothes and fumbled at the catch. There was eagerness, fear in that face an inch away on the other side of the glass—but something else also. Triumph?

He shoved the sash window upward and immediately the storm blasted into the room with him, pelting gleefully along the walls. Cat's eyes were fixed on him like unwavering candles.

There are worse things than sinners in the world.

Why was he suddenly so afraid, shaking with fear and cold, and she sitting there on the window ledge as though she were about to pounce?

'You have to invite me in, Michael.'

'What?'

'This is an old house, and the faith in it is strong. I can't come in unless you invite me. Ask me to come in. Quickly!'

I'm a fallen woman. I'm in mortal sin, Michael.

Why were these things in his head?

'Michael! Ask me inside!'

'Come in, then. I—I invite you in.'

She was over the threshold in a second, banging the window down after her. At once the storm receded, becoming a distant roar in the roof. Michael edged away along the bed until the headboard was at his back. Her eyes were still green, luminous. She looked like some sleek predatory animal, the black mane falling around her face. There was an overpowering musky smell about her that was as heady as wine. Some far voice of calm in Michael's head wondered what kind of thing he had invited into his grandparents' house.

She crawled up the bed on hands and knees, the moonlight behind her and those eyes alight. But as she left the window their glow faded. She was grinning at him, her teeth a white flash in the shadow. Her hair brushed his face as she straddled him, leant down and nuzzled his neck, licked him there, kissed him hard on the mouth so that he could feel the bruise of her teeth. Her smell was all about him, intoxicating.

'I told you I would come back.' The voice was as low as a purr.

'Who's outside? Who's after you? The wolves?'

'Yes. They're prowling the edges of your world. They chased me from the border of the wood. But it doesn't matter. I'm safe here. They cannot cross the threshold. I must stay here till morning, Michael.'

She unbuttoned his pyjama top and kissed his chest, moving up and down on him so that a delicious tension built, like a charge of static electricity.

He heard the wolves howl outside in the yard... or was it merely the howl of the gale? He tensed, but Cat soothed him with low words. In one swift movement she pulled her shift up over her shoulders and he saw her nipples dark against the paleness of her skin, her navel a blur in the shadowed muscles of her stomach. She was thin, the bones of her pelvis sharp and the line of her ribs visible. He ran his hand over them, feeling the bones.

'Are you all right, Cat?'

She paused, smiling—a real smile with less of the predator about it. A forefinger touched his nose.

'Strange times, Michael. For everyone. On the Other Side all is astir, everything in the air.'

'Will you take me there again? I want to see it. I want to go back.'

She seemed suddenly tired. The electricity died. Her skin was cold under his hand.

'Let me sleep. Let me in beside you tonight.'

He thought of his grandmother in the morning. Tomorrow was a school day. Again that feeling of being trapped surrounded him.

He tugged her down beside him and pulled the covers over them both. She pushed close, that black hair in the hollow of his neck and shoulder.

'Dawn will see me away,' she said quietly.

Away again. 'For how long? When will you come back, Cat?' She mumbled something, halfway towards sleep. Out in the yard the stable door slammed shut. Mullan coming back into the house. The wind was a shrieking banshee about the buildings, pushing at his window.

'Cat, I'm coming with you. I'm going too. I don't want to stay here any more. Cat?'

Asleep. He kissed the top of her head. Her face was buried in his flesh so he could not see the smile.

It was the black hour before dawn. The wind was still battling round the farm as Michael dressed by candlelight, Cat sitting naked on the bed with her arms around her knees, watching him. He chose his clothes with care: warm, outdoor things, thick socks and sturdy boots. He thought of his grandparents, Mullan, Sean, even his Aunt Rachel.

'I'll be back before they know I'm gone, won't I, Cat?'

She shrugged, pulling her shift down over her head. And finally he thought of Rose, that Devil's grin of hers which was so like this girl's. Where was she? Was there a place on the other side of things where she remained yet, watching him? In a different kind of hell, perhaps. That was another reason to go.

Cat kissed him, cupping his face in her long hands and brushing his eyes with her lips.

'Come. The wolves may still be about. We will have to be swift.'

They moved out on to the landing together, Cat gliding over the floorboards, Michael's boots clumping loud enough to make him wince. But the storm drowned out the small noises. The rain had been blown away, but the wind was savaging the trees down by the river. Even here they could hear the tossing branches and aching trunks.

Down to the kitchen, leaving the sleepers upstairs. There was a low red glow in the grate of the range, clothes set out to dry before it. It made Michael shiver to think of leaving the security of the house for the baying night outside.

He collected an old oilskin cape his grandfather had given him, his game bag and a dozen articles to make life in the Other Place bearable: matches, a knife, candles, soap (which made Cat raise her eyebrows) and the shotgun with a box of shells (which made her frown).

Cat went to the scullery and rummaged there, clinking and rustling.

'What are you doing?' he asked in a hiss.

She emerged with an iron saucepan, a large bulging sack and a length of baler twine with which she fashioned a crude sling. 'Provisions and such. Take this, and I'll try the door.'

He was weighed down, struggling and encumbered, and cursed under his breath.

Cat opened the back door a scant six inches, peering out cautiously. The wind pushed hair back from her forehead. It was blue darkness out there, night giving way to morning, the sky swept clear.

'They're gone, I think,' she said at last. 'We can go.'

'Are you sure?' He felt a definite reluctance now, had an idea that this was his last chance, the place where the road forked once and for all. If he went out of that door the homely kitchen would never be as safe again. His world would have changed.

'*Come on*, Michael!'

Cat was already out of the door, her hair flying and whipping like a live thing and the wind billowing her shift around her thighs. There were leaves spindling and rocketing in the yard like the ashes of some old fire, and the clamour of the wind-beaten wood was a steady roar.

'All right, all right.' He stepped outside, and the wind banged the door shut behind him.

They started across the yard, eyes slitted. He thought of the wilderness he had glimpsed once before, the wide tangled emptinesses, and had a mad idea.

'In for a penny, Cat!' he shouted into the gale.

'What?'

He clanked back the bolt on the half-door of the stables, releasing a warm waft of horse and hay. Fancy stamped invisibly inside.

'We'll take a horse with us, Cat. We can ride it over there.'

'Michael, wait—'

But the idea had him. He fumbled with tack, bridle and saddle, and pushed his thumb in the mare's mouth to open her teeth and slipped the bit in. Cat's urgency had caught him and he worked with speed. It was dizzying to be doing this, this madcap thing, and his reservations were blown away. He laughed as he saddled the startled mare, cinching the girth tight and finally leading her out into the tempestuous yard.

It was brightening, the navy blue of the sky becoming pale over the mountains. Dawn was not far off and his grandfather would waken soon, if he were not up already. Cat gathered Michael's belongings, and they clattered out of the yard like drunken thieves, the mare yanking at Michael's grip on her bridle. She seemed to smell what was afoot.

'Where are we going?' Michael demanded.

'The bridge. Through it is the clearest way.'

The bridge. 'But Cat...'

She ignored him and ran on like a wind-flung leaf towards the dip where the trees were roaring and the river foamed white in the gloom.

'Damn it, Cat!' He ran after her, the mare prancing at his shoulder. It was harder going once they hit the wet grass of the meadow. He left the gate open behind him, which was unthinkable, but Cat was becoming a livid blur in the trees, leaving him behind.

'Hold on!'

He cursed, stuck a foot in the stirrup and hauled himself into the saddle as Fancy circled in confusion. Then he dug in his heels and shouted a wordless cry of exasperation. The mare leapt forward into a gallop towards the trees. They rushed up like a wall, but he did not slow. He bent over her neck as the first branches raked through the air above his head, flaying his face with twigs and briars, and kicked her on.

The ground dipped sharply, and the mare ploughed down the steep slope almost on her haunches, taking short bounds over stumps and fallen trees. Michael let her have her head. She was *raised*, the ears laid back on her skull and the whites gleaming in her eyes. Her hoofs were skidding and slipping in the muck and leaf litter.

Then she gave a lurch and twist. He had an impression of free fall for an instant, there was an eruption of ice-cold white spray around them and water soaked him up to his crotch. They were in the deep part of the river, and the current was racing them along to where the bridge loomed, as stark and massive as the barbican of a fortress, the water disappearing into its maw.

Fancy was striking out, nose in the air and the water foaming along her neck. Michael slid out of the saddle and clung to her mane, the freezing liquid threatening him with hyperventilation. He swore foully between his chattering teeth, deciding that Cat had deserted him and had led him here to drown.

But there she was on the bank with his things lashed about her, making a dive into the turmoil of the river.

'Cat!'

And she was here, clinging to the saddle with her hair plastered over her face like seaweed. He shouted over the rush of the river and the wind.

'Where did you go? Why did you run ahead?'

She pointed to the western bank. Blinking the water out of his eyes, he saw the Horseman there among the trees, the paling sky silhouetting his head, watching them.

'Holy God!'

Then they were past, the current carrying them onwards, into the dark depths of the bridge and through to another world.

The Other Place

PART TWO

TEN

HE LAY FOR a moment watching the patterns the car headlights made on the ceiling, listening to the hubbub of engines and people's voices, even at this late hour; the sounds of the city.

He was alone in the bed. Decent of her to go before morning made things awkward—as long as his wallet hadn't gone with her.

It had not. He padded naked across the tiny room and peered out between slits in the blinds, one hand fumbling on the dresser for his cigarettes. The room was hot, and he could feel the prickle of sweat in his armpits; but if he opened the windows the buzz of traffic would become a roar and the fumes would sweeten the stale air. Better to boil. Even now these night noises could keep him awake, creaks on the landing bringing him bolt upright in bed.

The dream again. That was what had woken him.

He lit a cigarette and sucked in the blue smoke gratefully. His fingers were trembling and he dropped ash on the floor. After all this time it was the same. How many years?

He scraped a hand through his hair. Still a bit drunk, his mouth dry-and sour. Briefly he wished his head were not so hard. It was an expensive business, this alcoholic lark, and Christ knew he could barely afford to keep it up. He had a vague idea his health was going, too. That cough in the mornings, the shortness of breath that had taken him of late when climbing stairs or lurching into an unaccustomed jog. Perhaps it was the city. He breathed it in day and night, absorbed the stuff of concrete and smog so that he felt his blood thick with it, sluggish in the arteries. He thought sometimes that if he were to leave, to go back to trees and grass and growing things, he would cough it up and be eighteen again. Now there was a fancy.

But there were shadows under the branches of trees, he remembered, and back there only the moon lit up the night. 'The Wolfs Sun,' Cat had called it. He turned away from the window and flopped back on the bed, wishing now that stupid girl had stayed to see him through the dark hours, to hold him and talk empty-headed rubbish until the dawn.

Not fair, though, to think she would have robbed him. She had been sweet enough, young and a little credulous. It was the dark eyes that had reeled him in along the bar, conjuring his neck hairs upright. Another mistaken identity. He would file it with the rest. He was a sucker for a certain look, a slant of eyebrow, a shade of hair. It had become a habit.

What had her name been?

No matter. The other name was too strong in his head. That face, the grin. Cheshire Cat, and his trip through Wonderland.

She was gone. He had left her behind, watched her shape grow smaller and smaller as he drifted away. To his own place. She had led him through a strange country, a terrible place that had almost killed them both, hence the dream. That awful dream, taking him back to his childhood and another land. Christ, he hated the dark, the open spaces. Only in the bright chaos of the city did he feel safer, even now. But it was strange—and disquieting—to find the memories returning so clear and fast. He was remembering things he had thought long forgotten or blocked away. Odd.

There was grief there, also. He had never been sure what exactly about his past had marked him so, had set him this road to tread in all the following years. Perhaps it was the simple, impossible disorientation of it all. To live a life twice, to grow old a second time. He smiled sourly. The mind of a man in the body of a boy. Maybe.

Or maybe it had been the things he had seen and done. The killing. Or maybe it had just been a memory of Cat. And there her face was once more.

He sucked on the cigarette again. Years spent forgetting, denying it had ever happened (and God knows it might well have been a dream), but there was no getting away from the nightmare. Brother Nennian's face before he died. The horror of that day.

You cannot strike deals with memory, he thought. It holds all the cards. There are no bargains made.

He scanned his watch. Nearly three. Dawn in less than two hours, and work to go to in the morning. Terrific.

But there was a wash of malt left in the bottle, he noted.

Something to deaden his mind. He swallowed it in three gulps, feeling the fiery stuff burn his throat and set his insides aglow. That was better. That hit the spot.

He lay down again, frowning. Had he actually managed it that evening, or had he merely slumped there—hence her precipitate departure? Damned if he could remember.

To hell with it. Another nameless face and another sleepless night. Police sirens careering beyond the window, whining off into the farther streets. A bottle smashing, laughter and the rush of feet. It's all happening, he thought muzzily. It's all here.

He remembered cold water, and the mare shaking herself like a dog. He remembered Cat's shining face, and the sight of that first dawn light over the forests and hills of another world.

'WE'RE THERE,' SHE said. 'Back again.'

He hauled himself to his feet, chill water filling his boots and running down his back. There was a shiver starting, for they were in the shadow of a stand of trees and the sun was only a sliver of brightness somewhere in their crowns. Night coolness filled the water hollow along with the splashing river. Beside him Fancy shook herself, spraying droplets over them. She seemed bemused.

They had come out of a cave, it seemed. The river was quieter here than in the place they had left behind, sliding out unbroken around stones and tree roots, plopping and gurgling smugly to itself. The cave was dark, deep as the maw of the bridge on the other side. It looked somehow ominous.

'Come on,' Cat said. 'We'll freeze here.'

She started off with Michael's shotgun, sack and other paraphernalia swinging from her thin shoulders, her hair dripping. Without a word, Michael took the mare's bridle and followed, icy water squelching in his boots.

They struggled up a steep slope covered in Scots pine, needles soft and dry under their feet. The sunrise was huge and silent in the sky, light beginning to flood the trunks of the trees. It was clear as glass, picking out everything in brilliance and shadow, and there was no sound in the wood save for their laboured progress. The silence was like a great buzzing in Michael's ears. Perhaps there was a faint rushing of air in the very heights of the tallest pines, but that was all.

They reached the top of the slope, Fancy blowing out through her nose and sniffing the luminous air. And here they paused on what seemed to be the edge of infinite space.

The trees opened out and became sparse, dotted clumps scattered over a great rolling expanse of broken hills and valleys that stretched for perhaps thirty miles away at right angles to the sunrise. There the trees regrouped, and became at once a dense darkness of thick forest that covered the slopes of the land to the south for as far as the eye could see. Mist had gathered in miles-wide banners where the land hollowed, and the dawn set it alight, made it into a golden shimmer so that the forest seemed almost to be steaming in the sun, the mist and haze making each hill into a silhouette and the air so clear that Michael thought he could make out clearings, glades, even individual trees. It was like looking at an impossibly detailed painting through a magnifying glass.

'*Weoldwyd*,' said Cat.

'What?'

'The Wildwood, Michael. It runs almost unbroken from here to the great mountains in the south. In the foothills it becomes the Wolfweald, a bad place where there are manwolves and other things that lurk in the trees. I told you of the people who live in the wood—the tribes and the villagers, the wanderers. And the Folk of the Forest, of course: the Wyrim.'

A wind came searching through the pines and Michael shivered again.

'What about the Horseman? What's to stop him coming through the same way we did and chasing after us?'

Cat shook her head. 'I don't believe his purpose is to catch us, either of us. He shadows but he never closes. He is only watching, for the present. It is his minions, the wolves and suchlike, who do his work for him.'

'Great,' Michael muttered. But he was feeling oddly cheerful.

It had happened before on coming here, though it seemed now more tangible. It was the crystal air, perhaps, the light in the early dew; or the smell of pine resin on the wind and the vast panorama at his feet, everything coming to life under the dawning sun as though this were its first morning and he and Cat the only ones to see. He felt like singing, but settled for kissing Cat's cold lips and was rewarded with her famous grin.

'We'll turn to ice standing here. I've a mind for a fire and a breakfast of sorts. What say you?'

He nodded readily, and they started down the slope to where the trees gave some shelter and they would find wood in plenty.

Not piglet on a spit this time, but close enough: bacon spitting in a pan and bread to mop up the fat. Michael had been wise enough to keep the matches in a waterproof tin, and the dead branches lying around were as dry as tinder. Their fire was almost smokeless, built high and hot. Around it they had clothes steaming on ground-stuck branches and they sat nude, soaking in the warmth while the mare grazed contentedly nearby. The land around them seemed entirely deserted. There were birds—Michael recognized the songs of both blackbird and thrush—and a hare had sat upon its hind legs to stare at them for a moment, but no sign of people. No roads, no smoke, no noise.

'No school,' Michael said happily. 'No algebra, no trigonometry, no grammar.'

Cat cocked one dark eyebrow at him curiously, but she was busy with the bacon, wincing as the dancing fat landed on her skin.

'I'm free,' Michael went on. 'I can do anything I want.'

'You can give me a hand, then,' Cat told him. 'Hold the pan—there. Almost done.'

They ate breakfast in the immense stillness, wiping out the pan with mops of bread, grand as kings. A goldfinch warbled at them from a nearby tree and finally plucked up enough courage to hop around their feet in search of crumbs. Michael's laugh startled it away. He stood warmed by the fire with the sky a cobalt dome above his head and the grass cool between his toes. He felt invigorated, invincible, the very air he breathed as sweet as a draught from a spring. Cat laughed up at him and he pounced on her. They rolled, giggling, in the dew and made love as though it were an accustomed overflow of spirits, swiftly and without thought.

'Where, then?' he asked her when they were quiet and her head was on his chest. 'Where to now?'

'Anywhere you want.'

Anywhere. He could spend a lifetime here, in this place, and then go home the morning he had left. They had all the time in the world.

'Cat, you know where we are, don't you? You know your way about this place?'

'We are in the hills to the north of the Wildwood, far from anywhere. I have no say about where the doors leave us. The bridge on your side is an enduring gateway, as is the cave which is its counterpart in this world, but the rest shift and fade, blink out and reappear with no rhyme or reason. We take our chances with them.'

'What about getting back?' Michael asked, anxious despite himself.

'To return to the same place and time that we left we would have to swim through yonder cave. We would come out at the bridge again in your own world.'

That, at least, was reassuring. Michael stared at the empty sky. There was a coldness to the air, an autumnal bite, that even the flowing fire could not keep from him, though Cat was warm and slight atop his torso. Nearby Fancy was cropping grass as though she were in the meadow at home. The sight was obscurely comforting.

All that day they spent in the shelter of the trees, drying their clothes and taking stock, pondering where to go and what to do. Michael had an odd feeling that he was not here merely to sightsee. There was a reason behind this, he was sure, and he was positive that it would manifest itself in time.

'You must have cleaned out half the bloody larder,' he told Cat as the afternoon slipped into twilight and the evening star rose high and bright over the horizon. He was rummaging through the sack she had brought from his grandparents' house. Bacon and bread, apples and jam, cheese, oatcakes, and a mashed apple pie, his grandmother's glory. 'No tea,' he said. 'What do we drink?'

'Water. What else?'

'Sure... Hey, wait a minute, Cat. That's thieving.'

She eyed him innocently, sliding a pair of his Uncle Sean's breeches over her thighs. One of his old collarless shirts lay to one side.

'I needed a change, Michael.' And she buttoned the breeches close over her navel, tying them around the waist with twine. Her breasts swung as she bent for the shirt and she looked arch at Michael's unabashed stare.

'Manners, my dear.'

Michael mumbled something about a lack of shame, then shook his head and left the fire to fetch the mare in closer to the light. The dark was sidling in on them. He had a sudden picture in his head of Cat in a pretty dress, shoes on her feet and a hat on her head, but it was Rose's face under the brim. He realized that he could no longer be sure it was Rose he was imagining. In his mind their two faces had become the same, and the thought disturbed him.

Fancy nuzzled him and he gave her an apple core to munch, running his fingers down her mane. For such a highly strung beast she seemed remarkably at ease. Maybe it was the quiet here, though there was a breeze picking up again. He could hear it in the branches. The land loomed out to the south in a vast expanse of nothingness. No lights, no cars; no noise here but for the waking owls. Mullan would love it. It was the country before Man had made his mark—beautiful and untouched. Dangerous, too, he reminded himself. Odd things walked in the moonlight. As well to remember that.

'Are we safe here?' he asked Cat on retuming to the fire. 'Are there things we should watch out for tonight?'

She was heating up the broken pie in the greasy pan they had used for breakfast, and the night air was full of the scent of apples and pastry.

'We're all right out here. It's in the wood we have to be careful, as you should know.' She tilted her face to the blue night and the overhanging branches of the copse. 'But here we'll have peace, unless you are afraid of owls.'

He sat down beside her and together they picked out pieces of piping pie, burning their fingers and putting it into each other's mouths. Cat's new clothes smelled of home, despite their ducking in the river. Of ironed linen and soap. Her own rich scent—if that was the right word—rose from the neck of the shirt, incongruous as a wolf in a drawing room.

After they had eaten they lay pillowed by Fancy's saddle with the saddle blanket thrown round them, while the flames leapt and cracked before their eyes.

'Tomorrow we'll head for the Wildwood,' Cat murmured into Michael's arm. 'Get under real trees again.'

Michael yawned. The open air was getting into his head. Woodsmoke and apple pie, horse and linen. The fragrance was as good as a lullaby.

'Anything you say,' he told her, and promptly fell asleep.

* * *

A FROST STIFFENED their hair in the morning and made the world into a brittle white fairyland, the sun picking it out in brilliance.

Michael jumped up and down, shuddering, whilst Cat grumbled at the lost warmth of his body. She spied on him disapprovingly with the tip of her pink nose just over the rim of the blanket.

'Get the fire going, Michael, for pity's sake, and stop hopping around like a frog on a hot stone.'

His teeth were chattering too much for him to reply and great clouds of his breath hung in the air like steam. He settled for coaxing the ashen warmth of the fire's heart into flame. Another of the precious matches was used to resurrect it.

'Done,' he said to Cat. 'You can come out now. It's a beautiful morning.'

'It would freeze the tail from a dog, and I'm not getting up till the frost is gone.'

Michael shrugged and greeted Fancy, who seemed none the worse for wear, and stood staring southwards to where the hills became covered with the frost-pale carpet of the trees.

The Wildwood.

Cat's arms came around him, cold fingers linking on his stomach and warm breath in his ear.

'It is wild, Michael. We must remember that. It is not like the forests in your world. Man is not the master in there. There are things older than him in the deep woods, and not all of them friendly.' She kissed his nape where the hairs had risen.

'What are you, Cat? Are you one of those things, a changeling or something?'

She dropped her arms, releasing him. 'Never you mind.' She turned to the fire. 'You'd best saddle that animal of yours. We have a fair step to put behind us today.'

He watched her as she scrubbed out the pan with a twist of rime-covered grass. 'Do you know why I'm here, Cat? Why this is happening to me?'

She paused and sucked her teeth for a second. 'I know the Horseman has some link with you. He wants something from you.'

'What?'

'How would I know that? He's not someone I pass the time of day with very often.' For an instant it seemed she was going to say more, then she clamped her mouth shut in a thin line.

'Who is he?'

'The Devil.'

'Are you sure about that, Cat? Do you know what the Devil is?'

The sun caught her eyes as she stared at him, and the light in them was as green as emerald, the pupils mere pinpoints.

'Some say he is father to all the Wyrim in the Wildwood, that we are his children. It is the village folk who say this.'

'Wyrim?' He made it into a question.

'Some you have met. The troll. The manwolf. They are both of the Wyrim. And the morning I killed the pig. They were watching you then, the tree folk, but they left you alone because I was with you.'

He remembered hooted laughter in the branches, spidery limbs, the glimpse of a pointed face.

'What are you then, Cat? You look just like me. Normal.' Most of the time, he added to himself.

'I'm one of them, Michael. I belong to the land, too; its sap courses in my veins. Tree sap and old magic—they're the stuff I'm made of. I don't know when I was born or... or from whom, what manner of home I had or how long I have been upon the earth.' She gazed down at her slim hands for a moment. 'There are others like me. The villagers call us ghosts, changelings. They shun us once they know our true nature—but I'm as real as I can be when you are here. I love you, Michael. Is that not enough?'

Tears had set her eyes alight with green fire. Surprised, Michael bent and took her in his arms.

She was real; she was muscle and bone under his hands, warm flesh and blood, and he would follow her to death's door if need be.

They took turns riding Fancy south, one of them always striding through the wet grass of the hills at her side whilst the other perched like a lord on her back. It grew warmer as the sun climbed; a fine, clear day reminiscent of an early September.

There were deer wandering and grazing in groups along the hills, kestrels overhead and hares streaking through the grass at their approach.

'No people,' Michael said. It was odd to see land as good as this unused. No hedges here, no fields. It constantly amazed him.

'No one lives this far north, because this is where the most doors are between this world and the others. Strange things come through them at times—not only men such as the Brothers, but odd beasts as well. To the men of the wood this is a sorcerous region.'

Michael shook his head, frowning.

'What is it?' Cat asked.

'Now I know where the fairies and stuff came from. They were from here, these Forest-Folk you talk about, and werewolves and all sorts. They've been made into myths back home, but they're here, plain as day.'

'Plain as day,' Cat repeated. She seemed preoccupied, taken up with the dark line of forest on the southern horizon.

They kept marching and riding through the day, munching oatcakes as they travelled and drinking their fill from streams. Cat managed to tickle a trout from one in a twinkling, leaving Michael agape. Mullan had always said it was possible, but he had never believed it.

They went on through the lengthening shadows and halted in the eaves of the Wildwood. It was pitch-black under the trees except for the glow of fireflies and luminous mould, and Michael felt himself grow wary. He loaded the shotgun despite Cat's glare and they had their trout for supper along with the last of the bread and cheese. Then they lay in each other's arms before the fire and listened to the wood noises whilst Fancy stamped nervously in the leaves and sniffed the crowded air.

'They're here, Michael,' said Cat.

'What? Who?' His hand sprang for the shotgun, but she caught his wrist and pinioned it with startling strength.

'Be still, love. You are all right so long as I am here.'

'Who is it, Cat?'

She did not answer him. The hair on his head rose up stiffly and his heartbeat became an audible swish in his throat. He began to mutter an Our Father.

Cat squirmed as if in pain. 'No! None of that. Be quiet.' She laid a hand across his mouth.

There was noise in the trees, a rustling that might have been a momentary breeze.

'Mirkady,' Cat said softly.

'I'm here, sister,' a voice said out of the blackness, making Michael jump. At once, all around him there was a chorus of titters and chuckles, some as high-pitched as those of an infant, others a deep baritone.

'What *have* you done, sister?' one said.

'What company she keeps,' a second gurgled.

'See how he glares,' a third put in.

'I smell iron off him,' a deep voice said, and then there was silence again. But Michael thought he could sense shufflings and shiftings in the dark, rustlings of movement. And there were eyes out there in the night, scores of them around the limit of the firelight. Some were as large as golf balls, others subdued firefly flickers. They moved incessantly, blinking and winking at him. He stared about wildly and saw that they were high up in the trees, peering down at him. A twig came whizzing through the flame light and bounced off his skull, producing a ripple of merriment. Cat's arms tightened around him.

'Leave him be. He's mine.'

Something plucked at his foot. He caught a glimpse of a black spindly form, small as a child's. There was more laughter.

'Stop it, Mirkady,' Cat said, and her eyes flashed with a light to match those glowing in the trees. 'Leave him alone.'

'What game is it you are playing, Sister Catherine?' the voice Mirkady asked, reedy and high-toned as a flute. 'Why do you bring an iron-bearing mortal into the Wildwood? Have we taught you nothing?'

'I claim his eyes,' a voice said.

'His teeth I'll have—a necklace of them.'

'No,' Cat said steadily.

'He is from the place that spawned the bald men. I smell it on him.'

A long, collective snarl eddied round the tree trunks. Michael sprang to his feet, tearing out of Cat's embrace. His instinct was to run, but before he could go a step something hissed round his head and a rope of some sort had lassoed his torso, pinning his arms to his sides. He was jerked forward into the dark beyond the fire while a medley of catcalls and shrieks broke out, and behind him Cat's voice was raised in fury. He crashed to the leaves head first, his mouth and nose full of the stink of decaying humus, and struggled there while bony hands pinched and pulled at him, tugged painfully at his ears and poked at his eyes. Angry as well as frightened now, he battled to his knees and roared at his tormentors. Laughter rose around him like a ripple of bells, and he was jerked to the ground again. This time a tree root smote him between the eyes, filling his head with coloured lights and bringing the smell of blood to his nose. He grunted with pain and felt the weight of what seemed a child tap-dancing on the small of his back. Then there was a squawk; and the unseen dancer had gone. Hands helped him upright with gentle but irresistible strength. He blinked the tears out of his eyes until he was able to see.

There was Cat, holding a spitting branch from the fire, the light of anger in her eyes and her black brows thunderous. Beside her was a fantastic, scarecrow figure, no more than three feet high. Its skin was black, the eyes upward-slanting slits filled with green light, the nose sharp and angular as a chisel, the ears pointed and long, a mop of curly hair so fine it might have been moss on the head. It wore rough clothes of tanned hide decorated with strips of fur, reams of shining beads, lumps of quartz and amber, and what had to be the skulls of tiny animals—shrews, moles, squirrels and voles. It stank of leaf mold and earth, the reek of autumn, of the very forest itself.

Michael's attention was drawn to the hands holding him upright. They were massive, four-fingered and hairy, with thick, sharp nails that were almost claws. He twisted his neck to look and found himself staring up—and up—at a broad, ugly face with a huge nose, beaming eyes, pointed ears and a lower lip that hung pendulous and wet because of the two great fangs poking it open.

'Jesus, Mary and Joseph,' he said.

'I am Mirkady,' the small figure said, grinning so that Michael could see the even, yellow teeth that seemed to stretch from ear to pointed ear. 'My friend there is Dwarmo, a good-hearted soul, if none too bright. Sister Catherine here has persuaded us that you should be shown more deference.'

He nodded to the hulking figure behind Michael and the thin cord fell loose, dropping to the ground.

'She has also persuaded us that you may need something in the way of help in the Wildwood, so I'm thinking we can maybe sup a little and sip a little and think the matter over, and maybe wager a little when the needs of the body are satisfied. What say you, tall man?'

Beside Mirkady, Cat was looking intense and concerned, as if she wished to say something, but the guttering branch so confused the shadow and light amid the trees that it was hard to tell. Michael fingered the footprints in his back.

'All right, then.'

The grin widened until Mirkady's face seemed all leering teeth and glowing eyeslits. 'Then we will invite you home'—there was a babble of voices in the darkness, instantly stilled—'and offer you the hospitality of the Folk of the Wood.' And here he bowed deeply, one skinny leg thrust forward until his long nose was touching his kneecap. Without warning, Cat's burning brand went out, and there was only the glow of the campfire, strangely distant. In the faint light Mirkady's features were as hideous as a gargoyle's. He came forward a step and beckoned Michael's head down with a long curl of forefinger.

'Your consort worries over you, you know. Best to keep her sweet. She's a fine lass, but a touch impulsive.' He laid the forefinger against the side of his nose and gave Michael a conspiratorial wink.

'What?'

But Mirkady had already skipped away.

'To home, to home—to Gallow's Howe!' he cried, and the shout was taken up by a crowd of voices. Behind Michael, Dwarmo's deep bass joined in, chuckling like a good-humoured bear. Cat took Michael's hand.

'Cat, what is going on here? Who are these people? They know you.' *Sister Catherine.*

She squeezed his fingers until the bones grated.

'They are friends, Michael. Stay close to me and you will come to no harm.'

'*To home, to home, to Gallow's Howe!*'

'Do we have to, Cat?' His superstitions, deep-rooted as a religion, were crowding his throat.

She stopped and took his face in her hands, kissing his mouth quiet. 'We have no choice.'

'*To home, to home, to Gallow's Howe!*'

ELEVEN

FAIRIES. THAT WAS what these things were supposed to be, except they were like no fairies out of any book Michael had ever read. There were no gossamer wings, no diaphanous robes and slim, pale limbs. No butterfly-like maidens offering cups of honeydew. These things were as angular and odd-shaped as the denizens of a Bosch canvas. They capered and pranced and danced through the black wood so that Cat and Michael travelled as it were in the midst of a feverish Rackham illustration, made all the more fantastic by the light of a thousand fireflies that circled and spun in squadrons like tiny Chinese lanterns come to life.

Goblins, Michael decided. They were goblins. And trolls, he added to himself, looking up at the hulking shape of Dwarmo and his long-fanged grin.

Mirkady had called Cat 'Catherine.'

They walked for hours hand in hand, Michael leading the mare by the bridle. She seemed unperturbed by her fantastic company, and even when the more boisterous of the Forest-Folk swung through the branches close to her head she did not shy. It was as if they did not exist. Cat, however, gripped Michael's hand until it pained him. He would have sworn she was afraid, if he had ever known her to show any fear—and yet she had said these were her friends.

'Leave the horse,' Mirkady commanded.

'What?' They had stopped. He felt thick-headed with wonder, dull as an oft-used knife.

'Leave the horse. It cannot enter the Howe, it being a creature of the sun and suchlike. Come now, sir, are you so ignorant?'

'Thick as young oak,' something said.

'Indeed. A clodpoll,' said another.

'I'm not leaving her out here in the middle of nowhere,' Michael said, becoming heated. Already he was tiring of being a butt.

Cat took his arm. 'She'll be all right, Michael. Nothing will harm her in the bounds of the Howe.'

'Except cross-magic, and Latin, and holy water,' a voice squeaked.

'Silence!' Mirkady shouted, his mouth opening wide enough to show the deep red within. The eerie glow of the fireflies was all around, and the air was full of the rich smell of freshly turned earth, like that of a new-dug grave. There was a sweet stink underlying it, however, a hint of putrefaction which made Michael wrinkle his nose.

'I don't see any Howe.'

Laughter beat about the trees. 'Well might he not!'

'Someone open the front door for him!'

Mirkady bowed deeply again, and the fireflies clustered around his temples like a burning circlet.

'Your pardon. Our manners are not all they might be. Let me be the first to welcome you to Gallow's Howe, Michael—?' He made it a question.

'Fay,' said Michael, just as Cat's elbow drove the breath out of his ribs.

'Fay.' Mirkady looked strangely thoughtful. 'Now there's a name to conjure with. Is it apt, I wonder?' And his hellish eyes studied Michael with something like seriousness.

'You know how he is called now, Mirkady,' Cat grated. 'He gave the name in blind trust. If you abuse him I swear I'll have it out of your hide.'

Mirkady held up a long hand. 'Fear not, Cat. It may be I know more of this whole drama than you.' He smiled a smile that seemed almost human in its warmth. 'Let the door be opened.'

A hush fell, and beyond the glimmer of the fireflies Michael saw that they were at the foot of a mound. It was dark and bare, the grass free of the leaves that carpeted the wood floor, and at its summit a stark old tree squatted, its trunk as thick and round as a hay rick. The branches splayed out overhead, and from them dark bundles swayed and swung, some small, some large—and from these the sweet decaying smell drifted.

Corpses.

Some were men, some small enough to be children; but there were dogs and cats, sheep, even a horse, all hanging cadaverous and rotting from the huge limbs of the tree. Strips of long moss and ivy hung there also, like torn funeral shrouds, and here and there in the grass Michael could make out bumps and hummocks that were the remnants of other offerings, fallen like overripe fruit from the boughs.

But there was a new thing. A blade of light appeared like a misplaced sunbeam, stabbing from the mound itself. There was a snatch of music, exquisite as a ripple of silver bells, and the light broadened, rays lancing out to throw Michael and the others in relief and send shadows streaming behind them into the trees. A door rose out of the mound, flooded with light, and all the while that maddening, beautiful music tinkled, tugging and evocative. Michael walked forward into the light without a thought in his head save the music, and was conscious only that there was a great crowd, a host, a throng, pressed around him and laughing, saying welcome.

He remembered tall walls rearing up in sunshine, white as chalk. There were battlements and flapping flags, and men in bright armour mounted on huge horses. There was a bridge spanning a wide, glittering river with girls plashing and diving, sleek as salmon.

And there was a vast hall hung with golden tapestries and gleaming weapons, its long table set with silver goblets and sparkling crystal. The bread he ate there melted in his mouth, and the mead filled his belly with fire. The people were beautiful: stately and royal. Mirkady was a wise king, grey-haired and venerable, his fingers sparkling with rings and a crown of bronze oak leaves on his head. Dwarmo was a broad-shouldered knight whose dark curls cascaded around a shining cuirass, and who clinked glasses with him and laughed like a gale. Other lords and ladies sat in robes trimmed with ermine and beaver, circlets of thin gold around their brows. The men were athletic, dark, the women coy and graceful, like half-tame deer, and they shot veiled glances down the table at Mirkady's guests.

Only Cat remained the same, dressed in her stolen clothes and smelling of sweat and earth. Midnight hair hung round her face like a hood, and her eyes were emeralds in a face still smudged with smoke.

Wonderland. He had found it.

Things became blurred. He remembered leaning on Dwarmo, the pair of them drunk as coots, a dizzy gliding drunkenness that made Michael's tongue free and easy. They stood on a battlement that looked out on to a sea, an ocean of trees extending away out of sight, hung over with a golden haze to infinity. Michael had the feeling that he had gone *deeper*, had travelled down some tunnel into a more far-away place, and he knew with sudden certainty that there was an infinity of such places, one for every dreamer in the world, perhaps. But the moment was smothered with laughter and the feel of Cat, warm but unyielding beside him. That was somehow sobering.

'Where is this place?'

It was the king, Mirkady, who answered.

'The Wildwood, where else?' Then he smiled at Michael's puzzled face. His eyes were green, like Cat's, but a darker, murkier green, like the weed that floats on a stagnant pond.

'Think of the world as a glove,' he said. 'One garment, many fingers, each leading away to its own place, and the glove itself is meant but to fit something larger.'

That made no sense, and Michael's bubbling happiness was marred by bafflement.

'The world is the ground beneath your feet. As long as it stays there you can walk on it. It is a road the same as any other.' It was Dwarmo. He looked like a statue hewn out of silver and the goblet was as small as an eggcup in one knotted fist. When he smiled Michael saw that his canines were longer than they should have been. Muzzily, he wished he had not drunk so much mead at the feast.

Feast?

'Who is to say where you are?' Mirkady asked lightly. 'Some say there is a different world for every story ever told or untold, that there is no such thing as the here and now, only the unfolding of infinite possibilities, all of them real in some place or other.'

'In which case,' Dwarmo said, vastly amused, 'there is no such thing as a mistake.'

Michael was lost. The battlements, the forest, these companions, they blurred in his eyes as though they were on the verge of metamorphosis. He dragged his gaze away.

'Cat.' She at least was real, unchanging. She appeared as stern as a nun in the golden sunlight—like the nuns who had taken Rose away in the black car. The black car driven by the tall priest into the night...

Rose.

He could no longer remember his aunt's face. When he tried to summon it up all he could see was Cat. They were almost twins in his mind. But Rose was dead—wasn't she?

She had died having that baby she had told him about. She had never come home.

A voice singing a coronach off in the trees... Dead love, a lost lover.

I'm in mortal sin, Michael. I'm a fallen woman.

The mead (had it been mead?) was fogging his mind. He felt he was on the edge of something. It was on the tip of his consciousness, hovering like a swimmer about to dive.

There had never been a funeral. Why?

Unless she was not dead. Unless she had simply disappeared somewhere...

Michael's eyes widened. The other three regarded him unsmilingly. Was it imagination, or were King Mirkady's ears pointed, his mouth too wide to be human?

Rose.

'She's here,' he said, the knowledge bursting in on him. 'This is where they took her. They brought her to this place.'

'Who?' Dwarmo asked. His armour was somehow dimmed, ragged at the edges.

'You knew about Rose, Cat. That's why you brought me here. *You knew!*'

Again, that resemblance, the almost-recognition.

There were no battlements, no white walls. They were standing in an earth-ceilinged cavern with tree roots lacing the black soil like old bones. In their hands were wooden cups, and up and down the cavern old hides and furs covered the bare earth. They were spattered with clay plates and jugs, gnawed bones, discarded scraps. A host of nightmarish creatures of every shade and form sat busily around a flaming fire pit, the lights of their eyes as green as jade and their hubbub an indecipherable din of noise.

'Bravo,' Mirkady said, and he winked one brilliant eye at Michael.

'My God,' said Michael weakly, and the din at the fire lessened.

'Your God,' Mirkady agreed. 'Not ours.'

Michael ignored him. He grasped Cat by the upper arm. 'Who are you, Cat? Where did you come from?'

'I was not baptized,' Cat said. 'That is all I know. It is how the Wyrim were able to take me in.'

'Infants left out by the villagers to die, unwanted and cursed, we claim as our own,' Mirkady said. 'It was the Horseman left Sister Cat here, at the Howe, shouted the name "Catherine" into the trees and then rode away. But he always comes back to claim his own—Michael Fay.' Mirkady's voice was almost a sneer. 'You make our sister mortal, so that she feels cold and hunger. You make her human, and so the Horseman hunts her.'

'Is it true, Cat? Did you know?'

But she would not meet his eyes. She looked disturbing in his uncle's clothing, at once seductive and child-like.

'The Horseman sired her, as he sired us all in the beginning,' Mirkady went on implacably. 'We are kin to the wolves of the forest. Everything in the Wildwood belongs here, but you and your kind.'

'The Brothers,' a low murmur from the fire pit said, and there was a general growl of agreement.

'The tribes, the villagers. They were all one once, the remnants of a proud people driven over the mountains from the lands beyond and led by a crippled man into the Wildwood so long ago that they do not remember themselves. So they clear the trees and burn the ground and rape their crops from it—call it theirs—while we, the dark folk, who have been here always, are pushed into the deepest parts of the Wood, to lurk in the impenetrable fastnesses there. Some worship us as the spirits of the woods and the earth and hang their offerings in the trees, but more often we are hated, feared as children of the Devil.'

'So call me a changeling, then,' Cat said bitterly and pulled her arm out of Michael's grasp. But he was hardly aware of her, of any of them.

Rose was in this place somewhere, still alive. He was sure of it.

He could find her and bring her home.

'That's why I'm here,' he said, dazed. Cat broke away from them and squatted at the fire pit to swill from a discarded cup. She stared into the flames as though she were contemplating some private hell.

'We have to go,' Michael told Mirkady. 'I have to find her if she's here. She's...' He glanced at Cat. 'She's family.'

'Blood is thicker than water,' Mirkady said, his mouth a lipless gash across the triangle of his face. 'Do members of your family make a habit of wandering between worlds?'

'She was brought here. My aunt. Years ago. She was going to have a child and was taken away.'

Mirkady's interest seemed to sharpen. 'The father?'

Michael's face burned. 'A labourer who worked for us.'

Thomas McCandless. That much he had guessed at as he grew older. The young Protestant man his grandfather had thrown out of the house.

The man who had been atop Rose in the wood, pushing her into the leaves with his thrusts.

'So it seems you have a quest to follow in this world, young Michael. A maiden to rescue, perhaps. But what of our sister?'

Michael swallowed, met the green stare squarely. 'I love her.'

'Indeed! How noble of you. Do you know what the Wildwood can be like to a wandering mortal, my fine friend? I think not. Even the tribes have scant idea of what lurks in the thickest parts, the shapes that wander there. Nightmares prowl the trees in this land, and the Horseman will be hunting you. He has followed you from your world to this. I'm thinking he has plans for you both. And his steed can walk on the wind.'

'We'll survive,' Michael said, more firmly than he felt. He thought he might be in a dream and would wake up in bed at home to hear the wind whistling round the gables. It was too strange, even after all he had seen. It was the stuff of sleep. And yet he could smell the earth around him, sniff the woodsmoke from the fire pit and the roasted flesh there. This land was solid under his feet, as Dwarmo had said.

'Can you help us?' he asked Mirkady and the little goblin laughed.

'I was wondering when that would come! So you would ask a boon of us, or several if you dared. And you love our sister.'

He paused, and Michael realized that the others in the cavern were silent and Cat was watching him with almost painful intensity. Her look made him feel somehow ashamed.

'We are not sages, nor seers either, despite what some of the villagers think of us. We will give you no magic to aid your journey, nor charms to ward you on your way. But some things we can bestow, for our sister's sake.'

Mirkady was sober now, the laughter gone from his voice. 'Food, some gear, even a weapon or two, so you will not have to let off that iron monstrosity you left tied to your horse. Clothing, also. It becomes cold, and so long as our sister's path lies with yours she is as human as you are.'

'She's human anyway,' Michael said.

Mirkady shook his head. 'You have a lot to learn despite the promise of your name, Michael Fay. Catherine is as a princess amongst us, and we value her. I would not willingly let harm come to her.' His tone made the words into a warning. 'When the folk you meet realize the blood that is in her, you will be shunned. You may be attacked. Our kind are not popular amongst the Christians of this world.'

Michael shook his head. 'Who are you people? The castle I saw. The hall and the knights. You were a king.'

Dwarmo chuckled nearby and wiped his wide lips. 'Sup with the Wyr-Folk in one of their Howes, and what does a mortal expect to see?'

'Indeed,' said Mirkady. 'We can be anything you want us to be, or anything your mind expects. Cat cannot, because of the human in her. She and her like are caught between the worst of both worlds. And it is worse yet if they fall in with a mortal whom they come to... love. Then they forfeit any protection their forest blood gives to them, and the Horseman pursues them.' He stopped and looked at Michael closely. 'And they begin to age.'

Abruptly he turned his sharp face upwards, glancing to the root-held ceiling overhead.

'Evening lingers in the world above. It will be night soon. Since you are eager to take this thing upon yourself, we will leave when the sun sets.'

'We?'

'Indeed. Talk to our Catherine—your Catherine, I should say. I have things to do.' And he skipped off into the shadows to disappear.

Your Catherine.

When he joined her at the fire pit her eyes were full of the yellow flames, as amber as a wolf's. He knew now that there was a link, a kinship between her and the werewolf, between her and every monstrous creature he had so far seen, but the thought no longer disturbed him. He set a hand on her nape and stroked the soft hair there. To his relief, she leaned into his arm.

'Tell me of this aunt of yours,' she said.

'I thought you knew about her.'

'Only a little. Only what the woods themselves remember. That she was dark, and tall, and loved the land. That she came here seeking something, but lost her way and the Horseman took her.'

'Where, Cat? Where did he take her?'

She shrugged. 'They say there is a place in the Wolfweald where the Horseman has a castle, and there he keeps souls. But that is in the deep part of the Wildwood, the worst part, where even the Wyr Folk are afraid to go.'

'I'm not afraid,' Michael said.

'I did not bring you here for this, Michael.'

'For what, then?'

'What do you think? You wanted to come, and I wanted to have you—to show you this country, the marvels and the wonders. I cannot live in your world, so I brought you to mine to share it with you. And now you announce you have a quest, no less, this lady to rescue.' There was a leap of the old flame in her voice and her eyes flashed. Michael grinned.

'You're jealous, Cat.'

'Jealous! She is kin to you, this woman, and older.'

'So she is.' But unbidden in his mind came a picture of Rose in the river, with the sunlit water cascading from her naked shoulders.

THERE WAS NO music when they left the Howe, no glory of yellow light or ring of voices. The earth opened in a widening circle before them to let in a night breeze full of the smell of rain and clay. The trees were thrashing and rushing in a high wind and the milling air seemed full of spray. Michael screwed up his eyes against it. Fancy was standing patiently at the foot of the Howe, ears back to the rain and her bundles strapped to the saddle. He felt a surge of guilt, and ran out to her with the wind and water beating about his head, but found she was hardly damp. She nosed his new clothing with interest.

'How long have we been in there?' Michael yelled at Mirkady.

The creature was closing the door to the Howe. Even as he watched, the opening with its light narrowed and drew shut like a curtain. There was a brief twinkle of the silver music, a final blade of light that struck out through the trees, and then they were alone with the trees and the gale-bitten night.

'A moment or two, no more. In my kingdom we can give you all the time you want!' His grin was diabolical, black skin as slick as wet ebony in the rain.

'Yeah, sure,' Michael muttered.

He and Cat were dressed in close-fitting hide tunics that came down to mid-thigh. They seemed to be a coarse kind of suede, but the raindrops rolled off them like marbles. Deep hoods hung from the shoulders—Cat had hers drawn up over her head—and strings drew them shut at the neck. The fit was perfect. Part of Mirkady's boon. Cat bore a long, wicked-looking knife of black stone in a scabbard at her hip and a skin bag of unknown weight was slung on her back. She looked medieval. The picture was completed by an unstrung shortbow and a leather quiver that bristled with black-fletched arrows, each over two feet long. Michael had handled them and had been shocked by the cruel barbed flint of their heads, the runes and symbols incised upon the shafts. At his own waist was a broad-bladed bronze dagger, the hilt cast all of a piece with the blade, and a leather thong wrapped around the grip. It was a heavy, ungainly thing, the nicks in the greening blade testimony to much usage. He had asked Mirkady about it and the little goblin had been amused. A corpse's shaving knife, he had called it, which made Michael handle it more gingerly than ever.

He felt suddenly lost, adrift, and a pang of homesickness smote him as he stood there in the dripping dark of the forest with his not-quite-human companions. He thought of his bed at home, the range in the kitchen with the tea brewing on its top plate, his grandparents. Mullan. There was a tightness in his throat which he fought away by drawing his hood up over his head and knuckling the rain out of his eyes. The path had forked; he had chosen one way, and could never go back and re-find the other.

He was thirteen years old.

THEY WALKED THROUGHOUT the night. When Michael asked, quite reasonably he thought, where they were going, he was ignored. So he plodded along, leading the mare by the bridle, whilst his legs became soaked by the wet vegetation of the forest floor. It was almost impossible to see or hear anything. The wind abated after a while, but there was still the rush of the rain on the canopy overhead. Soon Michael was cursing to himself, tripping over invisible obstacles, plucking at the back of Cat's tunic to avoid being separated. She and Mirkady seemed to be able to see in the dark. When the goblin looked back at him Michael could see the glow of his eyes green and feral in the darkness. And Cat's seemed to shine also. Their light transformed her face into that of an animal, something unguessed and wild.

Dawn seeped into the air like a cold liquid, filtering down through the trees and distinguishing shadow from object, imagination from reality. Unseen birds sang in the treetops and the rain ceased, water continuing to stream and drip and trickle everywhere, runnelling round their feet. Michael was stiff and tired. He had to lean against the horse or he would have swayed where he stood.

Cat and Mirkady seemed to be in conference. She was stooped over him with her ear close to his mouth and her hood thrown back, looking for all the world like Maid Marian taking advice from a leprechaun. Michael chuckled aloud at the thought, intensely glad that the night was over. What next? he was wondering.

'A mount,' Mirkady told him when they were sitting chewing fairy bread (more wholesome than it sounded) and slugging deep red wine from the mouth of a skin, relishing the alcoholic buzz and warmth. Behind them Fancy was discovering fairy barley, and from the sound of things finding it as filling as the bread.

'We've got a mount,' Michael said with his mouth full.

Mirkady sighed. 'We are more than one person, however.'

Stubbornly Michael said, 'The forest's too thick to ride in. Your head would be at the pommel the whole day. I thought one horse would be good for baggage and stuff.'

'The forest is not all as thick as this,' Cat put in. The wine had coloured her lips; they were dark as bruises.

'It is open in places, and there are glades and clearings. And then there are the tracks that men make. We can follow them.'

Michael shrugged. 'Fair enough. Where are we going to get one? And what are we going to buy it with?'

'Iron,' Mirkady said.

'What? You can't buy a horse for a piece of metal. And we haven't got any iron anyway.'

'You can and we have,' Mirkady said smugly. 'Iron is rare here, a precious metal. And that metal club you have tied to the saddle with the wooden head—'

'No,' Michael said, realizing at once. 'That was my great-grandfather's. I'm not giving it to some woodland savage to use as a club. It's a modern firearm. You need a licence and everything.'

'The barrel is worth its weight in gold here, Michael,' Cat said impatiently. 'We need it.'

'You're not getting it.'

She glared at him. Mirkady merely laughed. 'You will remain penniless then, and become footsore before long.'

'We'll steal one,' Cat said.

'We can't...' Michael trailed into silence at her stare. He had an odd desire to seize her face in his hands and crush those lips with his own, but could not with Mirkady there. Cat smiled at him, eyes dancing as though she had read the thought.

'We'll steal one from the next village we come to; a priest's horse. They always have the best.'

Catching some of her mischief, Michael grinned. 'So we're going to be horse thieves? All right. How do we find the horse?'

'Not a problem,' Mirkady said. 'We are close to a village here, scant miles from the South Road that runs almost the length of the Wildwood. We can be there before the middle of the day.'

'Darkness is the best time for thieving,' Cat said, and the little goblin nodded.

'The best time for our kind to be abroad, but we must be wary now we are out of the bounds of the Howe. All sorts of things roam the woods at night, the hunters and the hunted. Myself, being what I am, most of them will ignore, but you pair have the reek of human blood about you. A sweet drink for many of the night prowlers.'

Michael had the feeling Mirkady was trying to goad him, so he said nothing. The bronze dagger hung heavy and cold at his hip, but he could not envisage himself using it. He vowed to unpack and load the shotgun when he had a chance, to stick to a civilized weapon.

'And we had better find ourselves some wolfsbane to crush on your blades, just in case,' Mirkady added.

TWELVE

Wolfsbane.

The pub was crowded at this time of day, the tables full and the spaces between covered with people. Their noise and warmth clouded the air and the smoke of their cigarettes was a blue haze in the fading sunlight from the windows.

He was sweating, deciphering three demands at once and tugging down the pump to bring brown beer frothing into a pint glass. In his mind he added up figures, remembered orders and calculated the time left until he would finish. He could smell the yeasty reek of the beer and his own sweat, the smoke in the air. His feet felt flat as slates from long standing. Two feet away from his nose a line of customers pressed against the wood of the bar with money clutched in their fists, clamouring for attention. Just another Saturday.

But he was glad of the crowd. He hated silence as much as he hated darkness, and the press of bodies was comforting. Nothing could touch him here; nothing that was not a part of pavements and tarmac, offices and exhaust fumes. He was safe.

He was tired, too, and the flesh of his stomach was a bulge over his belt. Too much beer, he thought as he set the foaming glass on the bar and reached for another. Too little exercise. Always it had seemed to him that his body operated best on nothing but the essentials. It made use of every scrap of nourishment and rest it was given, wasting nothing. And now there was a surplus: there was too much. He had become soft—a big, soft man with full red cheeks and too much flesh under his chin. A paunch ahead of its time, and a heart gone to seed along with his smoke-stained lungs.

No piglets on a spit here, he thought, listening with a blank face to the shouted order of another customer. None of the diamond clearness that had been a part of his senses as he had travelled through the Other Place. He had been an animal then, had been chipped down like a flint spearhead, and while the process had been an agonizing one it had left him sharp and hard, clear-minded as the bleb of an icicle—and afraid almost every moment.

His lungs ached for a cigarette; he clamped his mouth into a thin line and hauled his attention back to the work in hand. He pressed tall glasses up to the optics, dug into the ice bucket, pulled more pints and poked unendingly at the cash register's noisy buttons, the cash drawer hitting his stomach every time it opened as though to remind him it was still there.

Still there. He felt that there was a skeleton inside him—not locked in some closet, but in his very flesh—a different man, another adulthood. He had seen himself grow up twice. The first time he had grown into a woodsman, a warrior, an acquaintance of savages and fairies.

Fairies. Such a childish name. The Wyrim. Odd how it had taken a mental effort to remember it. Some things he had forgotten much as he had forgotten the forest language the farther from the wood's heart he had gone.

But this was his other adulthood, his real life, he reminded himself harshly. This was the reality of the world he would remain and die in: these faces with their slurred urgency across the bar, and the stink of the beer, the rumble of the traffic outside. This was his own world, without wonders, grey and tired with striving; a potbellied, short-of-breath world. That leaner, deadlier man that he might once have been was as dead as a half-forgotten dream. And in any case, he did not want to go back. The nights were bad enough as it was, here in this urban labyrinth, this tamed place.

He was given a break after four hours and walked out of the back of the pub for a breath of fresher air, fumbling for his cigarettes as he went. Out here there were red-bricked walls and overflowing dustbins; a cat cleaning its paws. The sky was bricked off, a mere square far above him lined with jet trails and deepening now into a street-lit night. Other buildings soared up on all sides, metal fire escapes hung with washing. There were children's voices up there somewhere, a baby crying, the sound of a young woman's laughter.

He smoked the cigarette down to the butt and lit another, setting his backside on a dustbin. It would be a long night. He was there till the end, the last shift, and one of the night's final tasks would be throwing out the reluctant drunks. The manager had given him the job because of his size. They never argued. Perhaps even now there was something in his eyes which told the quarrelsome to walk away. The thought pleased him. Still a trace of that hardness there, the man who had been Cat's lover, Ringbone's friend and a killer of men.

The evening was quiet for the city. Something—a cat—crashed off a dustbin, clattering the lid and yowling loudly. The alley backed away into thickening shadow filled with rubbish, peppered with vertical and horizontal bins and the wreck of a discarded and stripped van. It was empty.

His cigarette glowed like a hellish eye as he sucked on it. Winos slept in this alley sometimes, huddled in old newspapers. They rooted in the bins, competing with the rats, and were as furred and foul-smelling as animals themselves. Perhaps there was one out there tonight, curled like a foetus in its womb of trash, watching him.

Hard to believe that a brick wall away there was a crowd of people drinking and talking and doing the things people enjoyed doing in the city. It was so still out here, still as a wood on a windless night. From the surrounding buildings a few faint lights glimmered, and on one ceiling he could see the blue flicker of a television. But it seemed almost as if there was a thickness of silence, a depth of it as thick as smoke, down here where he sat amid the rubbish, the papers and the dogends, the scraps of littered food and wrappers of chips and sweets. The flotsam of the streets.

He blew out smoke that was becoming invisible in the gloom.

Something moved down the length of the alley, furtive, lurching. As his hand came up to his lips again ash fell on his shirt. His fingers were trembling.

One of the winos rummaging for a bed or the leftovers from someone's snack.

Because something *was* watching him. He could feel its stare crawl up and down his plump body. He knew he was not alone in the alley.

Behind him he heard a burst of ragged laughter from the windows of the pub. They were pools of yellow light now, and made the alley seem all the darker. Had he been out here so long? Best to be getting in before he got told off for skiving.

Something there, in the shadows.

He backed away with the cigarette hanging from one moist lip. His heel clanged against the bin and he cursed ever so softly.

Not here. Not now. That was done with.

There was a snarl in the shadows, a low, liquid growl coming from deep in some massive chest. The cigarette dropped from his mouth. He turned and ran for the safe throng of the pub.

THEY HIT UPON the village near midday and at once climbed one of the surrounding trees, the shotgun bumping at Michael's back, to take a look at the lie of things and see what they were up against. Fancy they had left tethered half a mile behind them, much to Michael's misgiving, but Mirkady told him that no Wyrim would touch an iron-shod horse with more iron in its stirrups and a bunch of holly—they had found some in the thickets—tied to the pommel. The animal was safe from any non-human forest dwellers who happened to chance by, and few people ventured so far from the villages or the Great South Road. Cat had reinforced his argument and Michael had given in, though was uneasy about the idea of the ordinary fauna of this place. Lions and tigers and bears, no less. Nothing would have surprised him. And he placed little faith in the pungent plant Mirkady had crushed on the blade of his dagger.

The village huddled without rhyme or reason in the bow curve of a fast, clear stream. The trees had been cleared to a hundred yards from the outlying huts and the ground there was thick with stumps, reclaimed by fern and briar and nettle. Around the corner of the stream Michael could glimpse other clearings green with pasture and dotted with animals. A haze of woodsmoke hung over the place, blue and grey, and from a midden rose the steaming scent of dung and carrion.

The buildings were wattle and daub or wood logs chinked with mud from the stream bank. They were roofed with turf and tree bark, their doors animal skins weighted with stones.

One building was different, however. Built of squared planks and roofed with shingles, the church stood on a small rise to the north of the rest of the village, and beside it was a finer, larger hut that must belong to the priest. There were crosses on the church's gables, coloured glass in the tiny windows, and the brass glint of a bell in the stubby tower that was not even as high as the surrounding trees.

The village seemed quiet, the menfolk out in the tiny fields, perhaps, or hunting in the forest. Children played by the stream dressed in undyed linen and wool, barefoot and grubby, and a small group of women was drawing water and talking some tongue that carried strangely in the stillness. Others worked on tall looms that sat under lean-tos close to their huts, or scraped at small vegetable gardens with crude hoes. An old man was smoking a clay pipe in the beaten dirt before one house, spitting contentedly now and then and kicking out when a foraging pig came too near.

Pigs, chickens and dogs roamed freely, mingling with the children. They were scrawny creatures on the whole, the pigs half wild, the chickens thin and fierce and the dogs lean creatures that looked scant generations away from wolves.

The village was surrounded by a rough palisade of sharpened stakes, sometimes with a gap of as much as a foot between them. It straggled along the eaves of the outlying huts and crossed the river, ending in a crude gate which was hanging open on leather hinges. It was unguarded. The place was peaceful, sleepy.

'Nice as pie,' Mirkady whispered with relish.

'But where are the men?' Cat wondered.

A burst of distant shouting gave them their answer. Its source was hidden from them by the curve of the woods. Michael saw the women at the stream pause and straighten. One shook her head.

'Something's going on,' he said, the curiosity kindling in him.

'Nothing to do with us,' Mirkady told him. 'See the grey gelding in the pen behind the church? That's ours, the one we're after. A noble beast indeed, but inside hallowed ground, alas. I cannot enter. It is your own wits you must rely on from here on.'

'Listen,' Cat said, ignoring him.

Hoofbeats, and a surf of voices. Mirkady's eyes brightened.

'Trouble. Now is the time—'

A crowd of people both horsed and afoot came into view at the far end of the village. A pair at the front seemed to be tripping and stumbling as they came... no, they were being shoved from behind. One tall, bald figure in a brown habit was waving his arms. He shouted something about devil worshippers, savages.

'I can understand what they're saying,' Michael breathed. Neither Cat nor Mirkady seemed to have heard him.

'One of the Brothers,' Mirkady spat, making the word into a curse. His twig-like fingers jabbed out hornwise at the approaching throng.

There were shouted words, which this time Michael did not understand. His comprehension ebbed and flowed. He was aware that the language being spoken was strange. He could feel the unknown quality of the words in his head, but here and there they burst clear-lit into his mind like cloud-broken sunlight.

The villagers plashed across the stream in a mass. There were at least three or four dozen of them, and the tall priest stayed at the forefront all the while. The objects of their invective were two ragged and barbarous looking figures who were tripped up in the stream and fell with an explosion of spray. They were tied, Michael realized, arms bound tightly to their sides.

They were fox men.

'So the priest has taken offence at some tribes people,' Mirkady murmured. His eyes glittered like wet jade. 'What will it be? Drowning, burning, or a mere beating?'

The horsemen thrashed through the stream and bent in their saddles to drag the two fox men out of the water and on to the other bank. The pair lay there struggling feebly. There was blood on their faces, and one had lost his headdress.

They were not frightening any more, but seemed oddly vulnerable, like mistreated scarecrows. They were a long way from the terrifying shadows of Michael's past.

'Why are they doing this?' he asked. Instinctively he sided with the underdogs.

'They have no love for the tribes, do the bald-headed Brothers of the Wood,' Mirkady said. 'And the tribes fear them for their cross-magic that keeps the Wyrim at bay. Sometimes there is a slight, real or imagined: an insult, or a theft maybe. They have different ideas about the rights and wrongs of things, the tribes and the villagers. Then this happens. The fox men will be lucky to see another dawn.'

Outrage flared in Michael. 'They're going to kill them? We can't let them do that. We have to do something.'

Cat and Mirkady looked at him.

'We're here to steal you a steed, or had you forgotten?' Mirkady asked archly. 'And, besides, see the men on horses?'

There were perhaps half a dozen of them, their mounts hardly larger than ponies but thick-limbed and shaggy. The riders wore leather armour that flashed with odd pieces of bronze and were decorated with strips of fur. On their heads were rough helmets of hide and horn, guards coming down from the brims to encircle the eyes and make beaks out of noses. They appeared predatory, capable. They bore lances of bronze-tipped wood and long daggers.

One had a sword slapping at his thigh in a wolfskin scabbard and all of them had the scarlet shape of a cross dyed into their jerkins, rusty as ageing blood.

'Who are they?' There was something elemental about the horsemen, something unrestrained. They were laughing as they rode in circles round the two prostrate tribesmen, and when one of the fox men levered himself to his knees the butt of a lance sent him sprawling again. The priest stood preaching with his arms in the air and the villagers quietened. Even from here Michael could see the glee in some of their faces, the unease in others.

'They are Knights Militant, the military branch of the Brothers,' Mirkady told him. 'The Protectors of the Villages and Saviours of the Church. They are animals.'

'They know no mercy, Michael. It's best to steer clear of them,' Cat said, though her eyes were fixed and glaring at the scene below.

'They're killing them,' Michael protested, horrified as he watched lance butts hailing down on the prostrate fox men. 'What kind of priest is it who can watch them murdering people?'

'The Brothers are from all peoples,' Cat said. 'Both good and bad. They have been here a long time—centuries, perhaps. Some of them were of the tribes themselves once. In the main, though, they see such folk as savages. *Hiethyn* is the word they use. They do not like the villagers to have dealings with them.'

'Wisht! See now,' Mirkady said in sudden excitement. 'Here's a turn-up. There'll be sparks a-flying in a trice I shouldn't wonder.'

Something had alarmed the villagers and the horsemen. The priest was gesticulating more wildly than ever. 'The tribes come!' Michael was able to understand. Then something dark appeared in the priest's throat and he toppled backward.

The villagers froze in shock for a second, then abruptly scattered. The Knights had to fight their horses through the milling throng, shouting and belabouring with their lances. Michael saw a flicker of movement in the treeline and then a line of fox men had burst out of cover and were sprinting across the stump-filled clearing, shrieking as they came. A burning torch was flung over the palisade onto a hut and at once the roof took light, grass and bark blackening and smoke staining the air. The fox men halted at the rude stockade and fired arrows through gaps in the stakes. The villagers cowered behind buildings or ran away, though two of the braver were struggling to drag the body of the priest from the bank of the stream.

The horsemen galloped upstream, nearer to Michael's tree.

They were making for the gate, meaning to outflank the tribesmen by going round the outside of the palisade. Michael could see the drawn sword of the leader flashing as bright as lightning. An iron sword, not the yellow of bronze.

He dropped down from the tree, making the Knights pause, but then they galloped on. He heard Cat shouting behind him but ignored her. Blood was singing through him. He felt as light and fiery as a wind-borne ember, and could understand the flung shout of the lead horseman: '*Stay together. Let none through!*' It was as clear as if Cat had spoken to him. Something in him had leapt into place and found its home. He loaded the shotgun automatically as he ran for the gate.

He met them as they powered out of the gateway, watched the glaring eyes of the leader behind the helmet guards, and then saw the man's chest erupt as the first shot hit him fair and square in the breastbone. He remembered no noise or recoil, but was vividly aware of recocking the weapon, the click impossibly loud as another Knight spurred past his falling leader with lance thrust forward.

High, this time. The shot took the top of his head off, the helmet splitting and flying away along with fragments of skull and brain and a dark gout of blood. The horse cantered past Michael with its dead rider sliding down one shoulder.

The four remaining riders were crying out, their mounts backing and bucking away from the roar of the shotgun. Methodically Michael broke the weapon open, ejected the two smoking shells and reloaded. It was like a dream.

More shouting, from the village this time. There was a pall of smoke in the air, the crackling of flames, women screaming. Michael stepped forward and fired again—too low. The shot exploded the side of a horse's face and it went down at once, throwing its rider forward. Something like warm rain kissed Michael's face as the animal struggled a few moments, its awful ruined head swaying about like a flower on a stalk, the bone glinting and blood rising and popping in great bubbles. The air was suddenly rank and sickening with the stink of slaughter. Michael hesitated, the euphoria leaching out of him. His next shot went completely wide, and he dropped the weapon from nerveless hands as the dismounted Knight lunged at him with bared teeth and glittering eyes.

—And halted with his dagger in midair. The air thickened and dark shapes blurred past Michael, childhood nightmares running under the sun. The fox men were all about him.

The riderless Knight snarled and was buried under a fusillade of swinging arms. There was a barrage of sodden thuds and the fox men ran on, screaming, leaving a corpse behind them.

The remaining horsemen turned tail and fled into the burning chaos of the village. Michael bent and was sick on to the bloody ground. It was happening too quickly. Too fast.

He reloaded and shot the maimed horse with tears burning in his eyes, smoke smarting his throat. The dead leader's sword lay glinting on the ground nearby and he picked it up, avoiding the gaze of lifeless eyes, the glint of bone. There was a breast split open like a Sunday joint. He stood in the gateway and stared into the village.

More houses were burning. The fox men had fired the church and flames were creeping up the tower. A pig ran squealing and knocked down a hysterical toddler. Shapes struggled in the gathering smoke, horses nickered and spun, metal clashed, men and women shouted and yelled. A body bobbed in the stream. Ashes and cinders blew through the air like gliding crows.

'My God!'

'Your God,' Cat said, and he spun round, sword in one hand and shotgun in the other.

'You stink of blood and iron,' Cat said with distaste.

He turned back to the terrible show, shaking his head. 'Why, Cat? Why do they fight like this?'

'It is the way the world works. This world. You do not like what you see, Michael?'

'I loved it. For a minute there, Cat, I loved it. I really did.'

The fighting seemed to be dying down. The rush and crackle of the burning buildings was the loudest sound. The church tower collapsed in on itself with a crashing roar and an explosion of outflung gledes. Smoke veiled the village as thickly as fog, acrid on Michael's lips. It grimed his skin, along with the stiffening horse blood.

Out of the smoke a shape trotted, wide-eyed and breathing hard. Cat caught it, uttering a laugh that Michael had not heard her use before. She soothed the terrified grey gelding and stabbed Michael with her dancing, green-blazing eyes.

'We got what we came for, at any rate.'

Other shapes loomed out of the smoke: a line of men. Michael backed away.

'Cat—'

Fox men. They carried four of their comrades on their shoulders and seemed tall beyond belief, with the bestial masks on their heads and the sharp ears pricking. They were black with smoke and their eyes were white and glaring in the paint and filth of their faces. Severed heads swung bleeding from their waists and they dragged weeping girls behind them by the hair. When they saw Michael they gave a shout and broke into a run.

They had come for him. He had known they would since that first evening he had glimpsed them down by the river. He was theirs.

'Cat!' Despairingly. He could not move.

They were around him then, their teeth flashing and their miasma rising to join the smoke. Up close they were smaller—shorter than he was. Bone ornaments clicked and swung; blood and hair clotted their flint axes. Michael's stomach heaved, but he swallowed it down. The shotgun was a dead, slick weight in one hand, the sword a bar of lead in the other.

'Help me, Cat.'

'You need no help, Michael. I believe they mean to thank you.'

And she rattled off a speech in the weird tongue that Michael half understood. A soldier, she said he was; a warrior of standing from a far-off land. A friend of the Wyrim.

One fox man taller than the rest pushed forward, his fellows making room for him. The only sounds were the muffled sobbing of the women and the crackle of burning.

The fox man said something, something Michael did not catch. Cat translated for him.

'The sword. He says it is a good one; an iron sword of the type made by Ulfberht.' She grinned. 'He says to take care of it. It will be good for killing Wyrim if the magic of your fire-stick ever fails.' The fox man put a fist to his chest and said something else. 'He says his name is *Oskyrl*, a warleader of his people. In your tongue that name would be Ringbone.'

THEY LEFT THE village to burn, and slid off through the forest while the surviving inhabitants fought to save what was left of their homes. It was frightening to watch the fox men move through the trees. They seemed to be built out of sinew-covered bone, unrelenting and untiring as wolves, and their feet made no sound. They loped through the forest in half a dozen parallel files, the captured women struggling along in the middle of each. The women were quiet now, their eyes red-rimmed and their faces blackened. They followed their captors as if too shocked or tired to be anything but resigned. When one stumbled her captor usually helped her to her feet with a swift flash of an arm. Sometimes, however, she was tugged on by her ragged clothing until she could scramble upright. No one spoke. They moved through the wood like a swift wind.

'*Michael. Michael Fay.*'

A whisper like the hum of a bee in his ear. He turned to catch the iridescent flash of a dragonfly that was perched on his shoulder. He flinched and was about to bat it away when the thin voice came again.

'It's me, you fool. Mirkady.'

'Mirkady! Bloody hell!'

'Not so loud. These tribesmen have hearing like gnats. And they distrust the Wyrim almost as much as the villagers.'

'What is it? What do you want?'

'To give you some advice. I'm going. You seem to have found yourself some new friends, and they will be more useful to you than one of the Forest-Folk could ever be. Listen to me now. Cat has gone.'

'I know. Where?'

'To fetch your prancing mare. She will meet you in the woods ahead in a little while. But I must tell you this: you are hunted. My people have sensed things shadowing you in the woods. And the Horseman is near. You are being watched, young Michael, and Cat also. And as long as she is in your company she is just another human—in most things. You must be careful. Learn all you can from the Fox-People. They are loyal to the death, and the hardiest of folk in the Wildwood. It comes of what they once were.'

He paused.

'There is magic in this place, Michael. The Wildwood thrums with it. Only in the cross-guarded sanctuaries of the Brothers are you safe. That village you left behind: if its priest is dead, then half its survivors will be carrion by morning.'

'Why?'

If a dragonfly could be said to shrug, this one did. Its eyes glittered like sun-caught prisms.

'Revenge, perhaps. Even the folk of my own Howe will be happy to see one more part of the forest reclaimed, the cross-magic overthrown. The beasts will close in on them tonight.'

'And you?'

'I am sickeningly soft-hearted at times. It comes of loving a halfling like our Catherine.'

'Mirkady, there are things I have to know. There's a reason for me being here, I'm sure.'

'Oh, yes. Nothing happens without a reason.'

'The Horseman. He follows me?'

'Undoubtedly.'

'But—'

'I am going now, young Michael. I am not a seer to be consulted on the secrets of the Wildwood. Even the Wyrim do not know everything. Some things you will have to find out yourself. Some of our people I will set to watch over you when I can and I will look in on the pair of you myself. But that sword you carry—you had best learn to use it. Iron is the surest killer in this country, more sure even than that thunderous fire-stick you carry. And remember that holly and wolfsbane are your friends. Kingcup, also. It keeps witches at bay. And yarrow for healing iron-made wounds. Remember these things, Michael.'

The dragonfly buzzed, wings a-blur.

'Mirkady—wait a minute...'

The insect took off, wagged its wings impishly and then wheeled away into the heights of the towering trees.

After perhaps three miles they met up with Cat. She was standing between Fancy and the stolen gelding. A shaft of thick, honeyed sunlight was falling on the three, making her face into a white blaze. They were a golden triptych from some other time. But the sunlight faded, and he could see the dirt that smudged her cheeks and grimed her tunic. She smiled.

'Now we'll travel in style.'

THIRTEEN

TRAVELLING.

A long way, they had gone, until all his life it seemed he had been under trees, staring into fires in the night, feeling the hard ground under his back and tasting smoke-tainted meat. A long time—enough time to put far behind them the smell of burning and the vengeance of the Knights. Enough time to strip the adolescent roundness from his face, to pump out the birthing muscles of his gawky frame and proportion it anew. Rein, knife and sword hilt rubbed callouses on his palms, and his shoulders were pushed farther apart.

Ringbone taught him things: tracking through the dense woods, recognizing game trails; stalking. Killing. And as more and more of the forest language surfaced in Michael's mind, so he slipped more and more easily into the tapestry of the Wildwood. He picked up the ways of the wood, and found that for the most part they were there already, locked inside him the same way the language was. A hidden bud blossoming. These things he saw and learned; and as he did, he aged.

It was the fast-growing down of hair on his chin that drew his attention to it. Ringbone's people went clean-shaven and crop-headed following some ancient tradition, so there was no shortage of flint razor and goose grease to take it off. But it thickened and bristled, grew harsh and rasping. He let it grow in the end, though Cat disapproved, and became a bearded man before his fourteenth birthday. That frightened him, but Cat refused to talk of it. It was then she told him that parable of time being like a lake. He wondered if it were truly so inexhaustible, if this place were drinking his years away.

They followed Ringbone's tribe as it moved with the hunting and the seasons. He saw the morning frosts give way to snow that made the deep woods into a pristine, monochrome wonderland where white owls hunted in the night, and rime-furred wolves padded the drifts. He killed a bear—a day to be remembered—and the skin made robes for Cat and himself. He dug squirrels out of their dreys, rabbits from their warrens, and scavenged his way through the lean part of the year. Ringbone's people settled for the winter by the banks of a half-frozen river far from any village or chapel or troop of Knights Militant. Here they reared up shelters of brush, hide, turf and anything else which came to hand. The kidnapped women of the burned village settled into their new way of life with surprisingly little trouble, learning from the women of the tribe—some of whom were captives from past raids themselves. They smoked meat and cured skins and gathered firewood and water uncomplainingly, though the cold grew more intense as the months darkened. The wolves prowled between the huts at night, and once one darted in an open door flap to snatch a sleeping child. The forest things were hungry, too.

Other beasts stalked the snow-filled woods. The men gathered in the biggest hut around the fire pit to talk over strategies for spring, and ultimately to reminisce about past winters, the terrible, dark times. Four winters ago a manwolf had stalked the village and killed a woman. They had hunted it into the next spring, and in the hunt Fuinos had been taken, though they had killed the beast with wolfsbane-poisoned spears. But Fuinos had lived, and so they had had to kill him as he changed, the werewolf blood blackening his veins; and then they had eaten and burnt the beast he had become, out of respect for the man he had been.

Other things also. There was the time the Knights had come in a great troop to push the tribes southward into the haunted woods, and they had been trapped with their back to the river and to cross had had to bargain with the troll who controlled the ford. Thus they had laboured to decipher riddles whilst the enemy had closed in. The troll had been a hearty sort. He had enjoyed telling the answers as much as he had enjoyed posing the questions. He had let them pass—the Wyrim had a greater tolerance for the tribes than for any other humans—and he had then baited the Knights as they galloped up, drowning three who had tried to cross without considering his riddles.

The winter settlement which the tribe would occupy until the turning of the year was small, and Michael came to know that the group of men who had attacked the village had not all been of the Fox-People. Some had been Badger-Folk, others stag men. They were all one people in the end, splintered back in some ancient time. They did not hate the villagers. Occasionally they even helped them, when the Brother who lived with them was willing and the Knights were far away. But more often there was an uneasy truce between the two peoples. The pair of fox men caught in the village had been there to trade, but they had been cheated by the villagers and had lashed out, injuring one. The villagers had been about to burn them as there was a troop of Knights in the place. At any other time, and with a less zealous priest on hand, things might yet have been settled more peaceably. But the Fox-Folk had gathered up men from the neighbouring tribes with swift runners, and a huge force of at least forty warriors had been in on the attack. The Fox-People numbered only some three score individuals, of whom fewer than twenty were fighting men. They were dwindling, they said, as were all the tribes. Slowly the beasts and the Knights and the seasons were wearing them down, and soon they would be gone.

They were an odd people, convinced of their own doom and yet refusing to yield to any outside force. They could have settled down decades in the past and become villagers like the rest, but they had refused because of some obscure tradition now lost. They were soldiers, they said. They did not work the land. But when asked where this knowledge had come from, they could not say.

Ringbone, Michael found, was the perfect teacher and mentor. He was sombre, sober, but endlessly patient. Only rarely would a grin light up his filthy face, making him seem almost young. It was impossible to guess his age, as it was impossible to guess the age of any but the oldest and youngest of the people. They were all lean and dark, but broad in the shoulder and incredibly quick, as sure and swift of movement as wild animals. The women were slight and dark also; beautiful when young, but growing old quickly. Swollen joints and rheumatism plagued the old people, and they would wander off into the trees when they felt their time had come. Sometimes their body would be recovered and burned, sometimes it would be lost, a feast for the animals. The Fox-Folk were not a sentimental people, though they valued their children above everything.

Cat was as able as a hunter as any of them, and sat in on their councils, her pale face a sharp contrast to their dark ones and the tangle of Michael's beard. They were a little in awe of her, Michael thought, for she could outrun many of them and had a way with the forest animals which was unique. They considered her to be something of a witch because of how she loved the wood. They said the trees spoke to her. She and Michael were together always. She was his shadow, the flip side of his life.

Michael's 'fire-stick' remained unused, though it and the sword gained him much respect from the men. The respect survived even his first clumsy attempts at hunting and snaring. He was something of a warlock to them. Perhaps it was because they would glimpse movement up in the trees when he was out with them, or hear laughter far off in the wood. The Wyrim watched over him, they said. And they considered him lucky.

He would find things in his path in the wood—a posy of heartsease, a pheasant hanging from a branch, a ribbon-bound twig, a pair of magpie feathers—and he would know that Mirkady was keeping his word. The Forest-Folk were out there, overseeing him and looking after Cat, who was almost one of them, after all.

And he saw the Horseman once, whilst out hunting in the chill dark before dawn. He was sitting still as stone in a clearing under the fleeing stars with his mount a raven-black statue beneath him. Werewolves grovelled at his feet and gore crows circled around his hooded head. Michael had lurched away stiff-faced and quaking, knowing that he had not gone away. That he would never go away. Some obscure umbilical connecting them had not yet been cut.

So time passed, unrecorded and unaccounted for. He lost track of the months, but was conscious of a disharmony, a thing half-forgotten at the back of his mind, and as the snows melted and the woods began to flame with buds and birdsong, the feeling grew. He had to be moving on. He had to journey deeper to the heart of things. He had not lost the conviction that his Aunt Rose was here somewhere; perhaps in the Castle of the Horseman that Mirkady had spoken of. His *quest* drew him.

THE MEN OF the tribe had a meeting in the biggest of the huts to discuss the spring move. It was crowded inside, rank with the smell of unwashed bodies and woodsmoke, but there was a welcome warmth from the close-packed crowd and the yellow flames which were the only light. Cat was there, pressed against Michael's side. Some of the younger men, no more than boys if truth be told, stood around the walls for want of a seat, stooping because of the low roof. Scraps of bark and mud fell from above constantly; the burrowing mice had woken with the change of the season. That, Ringbone told them, was a lucky sign. It meant a good spring, a fruitful year.

The men were leaner than ever, the firelight making skulls out of their faces with the eyes a deep glitter in cavernous sockets, the cheekbones sharp as pebbles. It had not been an especially bad winter, but this close to the heart of nature all living things suffered in the dark half of the year. Once, for Michael, winter had been snowballing and sledging, coming in out of the dark to hot cocoa and a blazing hearth. It was more now. He could feel the season in his bones, in the lines his ribs carved out of his skin. He could see it in the sunken look of Cat's face. It was a thing to survive, a test. At least three of the very old and the very young of the tribe had not passed it. That was the way this world worked.

The meeting was entirely democratic. The men knew that Ringbone was the man who knew best where the Knights were likely to be and what their intentions would be with the breaking of the snows. Semuin was the best hunter, who knew the widest game trails and had the movements of the deer herds mapped out in his head. And old Irae knew what places to leave alone, those sacred to the Wyrim. He knew what offerings to make to the Forest-Folk to pass through their barriers and territories, though he seemed rather disgruntled because Cat was present and would probably know these things better than he.

No one ordered anyone else. Everything came in the way of a suggestion, which could be agreed with or discarded. There was a kind of drift of argument as one by one the tribe's most knowledgeable men gave their opinions. The Knights would be out in force soon, seeking the despoilers of the village; the Fox-People would not be able to trade with any of the nearby settlements this spring, but must move south into the empty forests where the game was most plentiful, even if it meant moving closer to the Wolfweald. The Knights would not follow them there.

A few of the younger men, clearly full of themselves, said that they should not run from the Knights; they could beat them in a fight any time they liked, especially with the Farsider's fire-stick.

There was a silence after this, the older men unspeaking. *Utwychtan*, the Farsider, was what they called Michael, as they called Cat *Teowynn*, the Tree-Maiden. It was a name that pleased her immensely.

It was not good to bring the Farsider into a quarrel that was belonging to the people alone, Ringbone said. The Farsider might want to go his own way some time, and to do that he would not need a troop of Knights on his tail. He no longer looked like the boy who had slain the Knights in the autumn, and so they would not touch him. Better to leave it that way.

Ringbone met Michael's eyes across the fire, and Michael knew then that the fox man did not expect him to remain with the tribe another winter. He was giving him free rein.

'I will go south with the tribe,' he said. He thought his path lay that way in any case, and he was reluctant to begin journeying with only Cat for company. He felt like a child in this land and knew that he had vast things yet to learn.

He could feel her eyes on his face in the dimness. She gripped his arm through the heavy robe.

'Are you glad to be going south?'

He could not answer her.

'No one goes in or out of the Wolfweald but those who are taken by the Horseman,' she said, as though reading his mind. 'Not even the Wyrim go there. And his castle may be only a tale, a legend. None knows.'

'It's there. I know.'

'How?'

He smiled. 'Because in fairy tales there's always a haunted castle.'

'You fool.' But her grip on his arm remained. She laid her lovely head on his shoulder.

So THEY MOVED south, through the melting drifts and the sound of running water. Sixty souls labouring through the birthing forest with their belongings, their very homes, lashed to their backs or perching on the backs of the two horses—thin, their coats long and tangled and the bones long ridges under their hides, a relief map of hunger.

The men ranged far ahead and behind, and off on the flanks to ware against any sudden enemy. They looked like strangely upright apes when glimpsed through the trees, wrapped in furs and hide, the fox headdresses barbaric on their heads. When they hunkered down to spy they disappeared against the black tree trunks, and when they warbled softly through the wood the whole straggling column of women and children and old people would freeze where they stood and wait patiently. And Cat would talk in a low whisper to Fancy and the grey so that they would be still, the white breath pluming from their nostrils.

Days passed in this manner, and slowly but perceptibly the wood changed. It grew thicker, darker, with more yew and spruce, holly and Scots pine, birch on the higher hills. But they were able to take off their verminous furs as the weather slowly warmed and Cat scrubbed herself in a pool they found, though it made her pant with cold. The tribe camped for the night on its bank and chewed smoked venison around the fires whilst a patrol of the young men circled the area, wary of the beasts.

But the forest seemed deserted. Even birds were few and far between. And there were mutterings about the wisdom of moving to a part of the wood that was so scarce in game.

It was in the depths of night that Michael awoke to find himself staring up at stars and the black limbs of the overhanging trees. Cat was curled against him and the nearby fire was a low, red glimmer. Other shapes lay crumpled around other glows. It was piercingly cold, and his mind was as clear and sharp as a flake of flint.

What had woken him?

He eased himself out from under the bearskin, Cat murmuring to herself at the loss of warmth. He kissed her ear and stood up carefully, feeling for his dagger in the darkness.

Something there? But the sentries would have noticed. He picked his way out of the camp's perimeter, nodding at one of the warriors who was squatting at the base of a tree, a dark, amorphous lump.

'*Taim mae, Utwychtan. Aelmid na sytan.*' And the sentry's spear waved him on.

He placed his feet carefully in the frost-cracking needles of the wood floor and drew his dagger, wishing he had brought the Ulfberht. Iron might be better than bronze here.

Nothing. He was two hundred yards from the fires and the wood was as black as pitch, the stars glittering silently overhead and his breath a barely visible wraith of paleness around his face.

A fool's errand. Why had he left Cat's warmth? The cold leeched into his bladder and he pissed against the trunk of a nearby tree, the steam rising and the liquid pattering loud in the stillness.

Then he saw it: an outline against a lighter patch of branches. The ears were high and sharp as horns in the dark and the lights that were its eyes blinked once.

It stepped forward silently, and in the faint starlight he could see the long muzzle, the maw slick with teeth, the heavy bone over the eyes and the close fur that covered the enormous head. A dewlap of loose hide hung from its throat, down to the deep chest. He had an impression of lean massiveness, a towering blackness in the trees. And then those baleful eyes fixed on him, narrowed and brightened to brilliant pinpoints.

Involuntarily he stepped backwards, mind numb with terror. There was such malice in the eyes, such focused hatred and hunger, that he felt their glare almost as a physical jab.

As the beast leapt forward, he screamed with all the breath in his lungs and then turned and ran.

The starlit wood careered past him. Briars snatched at his legs and low branches tore his face. He felt as though he were afloat, adrift from the ground and being propelled by some weird gale. The air burst out of his mouth and then was sucked and dragged back in again, chill as meltwater. He heard an awful snarling howl at his shoulder at the same time as he saw the red fires of the camp ahead. The sentry was standing in his path, shouting.

'*Wyrwulf!*' Michael shrieked, and then a shattering blow raked down his back, something catching in the tunic Mirkady had given him and ripping it like wet paper, pulling him off his feet.

The air whooshed out of his lungs as he hit the ground, and as he lay there he was aware only of the stink around him, as sickening and sweet as a blown corpse—that and the vast shadow rearing above him.

More shouting, too far away to matter. The thing was bending over him, one arm reaching down. Michael felt a cold-clawed paw brush his face with horrible gentleness, and the reeking foetidness of its breath dammed the working of his lungs so that his heart was yammering and struggling and he was gaping like a landed fish, his stomach heaving and the white panic pumping adrenaline through him. He met the eyes from eight inches and saw that the cornea was luminous, yellow broken by tiny scarlet lines as fine as the veins on a blossom. And in the centre were black pupils, slitted like a cat's. They seemed enormous, big as tennis balls, and all their malicious power was bent on Michael's face like the rays of some diseased sun. The jaws opened.

Swift as thought, the beast straightened and with a sweep of an arm batted away a flung spear. There was shouting and the uncertain light of torches. It paused, the black lips pulling back from its fangs. Another missile went wide. A man came up close with a short stabbing spear, and the *wyrwulf* moved.

It poured forward and knocked the man's weapon to one side, jarring it out of his grasp. He stumbled backwards, hand going to his hip for a knife, but the beast caught him by one arm, whipped him to its chest and then bit.

The crunch and pop was loud in the night. The man was dropped, his neck bitten almost in half. A shout of grief and fury went up from the other fox men. They darted in and ringed the beast, jabbing with long flint-tipped spears. The *wyrwulf* snapped at one and champed off the blade. It grabbed at another, pulling its owner forward and severing his spine with another crushing bite. The body was thrown at his comrades, knocking one off his feet. The circle was broken. The beast thrust forward, tearing the face off a third man with one swift rake of its claws, and then it was running free. More spears were flung at its back but in the dark it was impossible to tell if they went home. It crashed into the trees and was gone.

* * *

He sat up in bed, shuddering and slick with sweat. The face—dear God!—that face inches from his own, the awful reeking breath in his lungs.

The room was quiet, the luminous digits of the clock telling him it was three-thirty. Even the traffic had calmed. The city was sleeping. He reached for his cigarettes, fumbling them off the night table, and then flicked on the lamp so there was a corner of brightness in the room, an oasis in the night.

Smooth smoke eased the catch of his lungs, slowed his battering heart. Werewolves. Bloody hell.

He was afraid, more afraid than he had been since travelling a wolf-haunted wood long ago. Because that wood, that world, was reaching out here for him. He was sure of it. Too many things—the growl of the unknown animal in the alleyway that night, these dreams, reliving all kinds of things he had forgotten—were reminding him of what it had been like, almost as though he were being prepared.

For what? Going back? God forbid!

Imagination, perhaps. His sense of paranoia playing tricks on him. Everyone had nightmares, and the thing in the alley might have been a dog. He had never even seen it.

He had taken a taxi home though. He had found it impossible to face the thought of that measly half-mile in the dark. And not true dark, either, with the street lamps and cars. More like an urban twilight, a half-world. Mad. Harder to believe in it over here. Easier back in Ireland, with the silent woods and the tiny fields, the empty roads. He had not thought the city had enough soul about it to shake him. And here he was, lighting his third cigarette in a row at nearly four in the morning, his hands trembling ash on the bedclothes and his eyes flitting fearfully to the window.

Those eyes. He could almost see them now, hovering out of the lamplight's circle. Strange how he had unlearned so much over the years until he could hardly remember Ringbone or Mirkady or Brother Nennian. Cat and Rose he had never forgotten—they had cut too deeply for healing—but everything else had become a haze, a childhood thing of dreams and imaginings and half-remembered stories. Until recently. Waking and sleeping, he was remembering more and more every day. And then there were these sightings... Last week at the station, in the scrum for the tube.

They had been packed like canned beans in the train, breathing in each other's faces and jutting elbows into other ribs. It had been hot in there, and still some damn fools were struggling to read the *Financial Times*. It had been fun watching them trying to fold the broadsheets in the midst of the cramped, swaying humanity. He had switched off, as he always did, and had been staring out of the grimy window. Black tunnels, dim stations, black tunnels, dim stations, and the tidal ebb and flow of people leaving and entering.

Then a wedge-shaped face on the other side of the glass, the eyes blazing slits and the mouth grinning redly...

The blood seeped from his face and his throat tightened unbearably. One of the Wyrim, here in the city.

Two, three feet away.

The door. With a snarl he pushed those beside him out of the way, toppled a trio of commuters like briefcase-wielding dominoes, dug his elbows in.

The doors were closing.

He rammed himself through them to cries of alarm and anger, levered them apart with the veins pulsing in his thick neck, and fell rather than stepped to the hard concrete of the platform, glaring about like a maniac. People backed away. The train began to pull out. It wasn't here! Where was it?

And the face had sailed past him, laughing, the white teeth bared. On a tube train, disappearing down the dark of a tunnel. He could hear it hooting and giggling with glee.

He had bent over to clutch his knees and sob for air as someone in a blue uniform asked him what the fuck he was playing at.

That had been three days ago.

A product of a fevered imagination? A nervous system strained near to breaking? Or simply the alcohol that was increasingly pickling his brain.

What was happening to him? Was it starting up again? The merest scratch from a werewolf kills, infecting the victim with the disease. Michael had come a quarter of an inch from death the night the tribe had been attacked. Only the thickness of Mirkady's tunic had saved him, though it had been ripped from his back.

That was how close he had been all the time, running along that knife edge with Cat for company. In the Other Place death had never been farther away than spitting distance and the distance itself had been life, a packed, raw life possessing one less skin than he owned now. A running life, vivid with fear and so riddled with violence that it had become second nature. A man broken open looks much the same as a beast.

But it was behind him now—and that was his mantra these days. Those muscles, growing up for the second time, had grown differently. He was a different man; even the beard was gone. These things had no right to come crowding back into his life. Werewolves, for Christ's sake! No right. Even Cat. Though a chance resemblance brought his heart into his throat sometimes, he did not want to clamber back on board that merry-go-round. Even with her it had not all been milk and honey. There had been times when he had seen the inhuman, the Wyrim side of her.

He prayed that it was not coming for him again.

FOURTEEN

After burning their dead they continued to move south, following the sparse game trails through the thicknesses of the forest. They were even warier now, scouring the land for wolfsbane to increase the effectiveness of their weapons. For Michael there was the unaccountable feeling that he had been *called* the night the manwolf had attacked, and he could not forget how its claw had touched his face, almost tentatively, before the fox men had attacked it.

Spring was in full force. Snowdrops beneath the trees were giving way to daffodils, bluebells as thick as carpet, bright primroses. The wood was brightening, coming to life before their eyes, and the nights were getting shorter. After the initial shock of their encounter had worn off, the tribe seemed to become cheerful. When two weeks had passed they traversed a wide game trail and some of the men left to try their luck at the hunt, for smoked meat was beginning to stick in their throats. Michael stayed behind. An inchoate dread had begun to steal up on him with every mile southwards they walked. He and Cat left the tribe's camp and wandered on to a wooded rise that overlooked a long, westward-winding valley. A sea of trees stretched out like a vast, long bowl to every horizon, stark under the sun but with the greenness just beginning to be picked out in the unfolding buds, and the darker patches where the tall evergreens stood unchanging.

'No people, no houses, no roads—nothing.'

'This is the Wilderness, Michael. What were you expecting?'

He looked at her. Cat got on well enough with the Fox-People, but had made no friends. They were a little afraid of her yet, he thought; they could see the Wyrim part of her perhaps more clearly than he could. To him she seemed as lovely as ever, slim as a willow wand, seasoned as a steel blade. It made his heart skip to see her lips quirk into a smile, those green eyes flash. She was wearing a doeskin shift, supple as silk, her skin pale as cream where the garment fell forward below the collarbone. The stone knife was tucked into her belt.

'None of the villagers come this far south,' she went on. 'The wood is too wild here, with too many beasts, and the Horseman riding the glades in the nights. Even the tribes seldom follow the hunt so far. We are scant leagues from the first eaves of the Wolfweald.'

'What about your people? Do they live here, or are they too frightened as well?'

She grinned at him without humour. 'They are all my people, the wolves along with the fairies. We are all the same.'

'That's not true, Cat.'

'Isn't it? Ask any of the Brothers, or the merchants who wander the great roads with their escorts. Ask the Knights. We are all the same.' She rubbed her eyes as if tired. 'Trolls there are here, the dark kind that cannot abide the sun. And... goblins, I think you would call them. They have strongholds in some of the valleys. They are a strange folk. Mirkady tells me they eat anything that lives and smelt their weapons from bone and marrow, but he may have been jesting. Sometimes they and the wolves hunt together.'

'Does Ringbone know this?' Suddenly the wood seemed secretive, furtive. He watched a kestrel circle and circle over the sunlit tops of the trees whilst his imagination ran momentarily riot conjuring up shadows beneath them.

'Of course. He lives here.'

'And I don't.' Ever the alien. There was a part of him that would always be the boy from the farm. He knew that. It was why he was not out hunting with the men. His heart was not entirely in it.

She kissed the side of his neck as he watched the kestrel stoop for the kill.

'These Brothers. They don't fit in here either,' he said.

'I think they are from your world. Not spawned by the same time, perhaps, but breathers of your air. Ringbone could probably tell you more than I.'

'Ringbone and his people are full of myths and tales. To hear him you would think they were descended from princes or warrior kings. They're savages, Cat.'

She teased his beard. 'And what does that make us, then?'

'Strangers. Foreigners. You have no more of a home here than I do.'

'This is my home—here at your side. If I am content with that, why cannot you be?'

He stared at her helplessly, watched her flush.

'This damned woman you think is here,' she said. 'Is that still in your head?'

'Mirkady thought she was here.'

'Mirkady would try to tell a fox how to fly. Not everything he says has truth in it. He has not your welfare at heart all the time, or anyone's. That is the way of his folk.'

'Your folk,' he said with a smile, but she did not return it.

'If this kinswoman of yours is truly here, Michael, then she is lost, gone for ever. This land does not go out of its way to provide happy endings. Death is all you will find if you take this quest of yours seriously.'

'I love you, Cat.'

She was silent, startled. On her face pleasure and annoyance fought for mastery until she laughed, a loud, ringing sound. 'You fool.' And she kissed him until his lips felt bruised.

'I want you to take me to the Castle of the Horseman.'

She was instantly sober again, and angry.

'Are you deaf? Do you not listen to anything I say? It is impossible, Michael.'

'Nevertheless,' he said doggedly.

'You're afraid. I can smell the fear off you.'

It was his turn to be silent.

'What demon is at your shoulder making you do this? Is it the only reason you came here with me?'

'No, Cat, of course not.' He did not tell her that one of the reasons he had come was because she had made it sound like some kind of medieval wonderland, not the harsh, brutal world it was.

Restless, they both began walking in the same moment, scuffing through the remnants of last year's leaves as though they were strolling through a park. They climbed upwards from their hill, up the slope that was the southern side of the valley, and by unspoken consent did not stop until they were at the top looking out from the encroaching trees on to the heavily vegetated coomb below with the odd glitter here and there of the river at its heart, and the almost vertical ribbons of woodsmoke from the camp rising out of the depths of the trees.

Michael tripped over something, kicking it out of a burial of leaves and earth. He bent and tore it free in curiosity. It was a human femur, shreds of cartilage and flesh clinging to it. He threw it down in disgust. Death and decay everywhere. Violent death—the bone was snapped off at one end. He footed it away. Cat stared, then switched into her wood mode and began sniffing and prowling round the thickets at the lip of the slope.

'Cat, come on. We should be getting back.'

'Wait a moment.'

He joined her as she scrabbled and snapped her way through a riot of dead branches and the crusts of lifeless ivy.

'What is it?'

'I smell something.'

And then he did too: a faint miasma on the spring air. The stink of corruption, old but perceptible.

They broke through to a small open space where the ground was almost bare and the branches arced so thick overhead that they were at once enveloped in a half-light and had to blink and squint to let their eyes adjust.

An old, old oak, so old it was only a stump, a shell black with rot but tough as an ancient molar. It was shaggy with sap-sucking ivy and wrapped about with dog rose. Around its roots the broad, hanging leaves of nightshade swayed at the intrusion. The smell of rot and decay became overpowering and Michael buried his nose in his sleeve, though Cat remained unaffected.

There were bones on the ground. Some gleamed white, others were green and grey with clinging tissue. A skull grinned at them from under a mat of black hair, and a skeletal hand lay like some great petrified spider. Long thigh bones had been split for the marrow and vertebrae were scattered like jagged stones. The place looked like a cross between a desecrated burial ground and the site of a cannibalistic feast.

'Michael. Here.'

He followed Cat deeper into the surrounding brake. Here was a taller tree, a beech, bearing a few coppery leaves that had outlasted winter. It was even darker here, the trees a wall around them, a dark roof above. They might have been in a church, for the silence and the dimness.

A man had been crucified on the wide beech bole.

Dark spikes of some black hardwood had been hammered through his wrists and ankles. His belly gaped, a gash with something dark as blackberries inside. He stank, but not so badly, for the weather had remained cool and he had, Michael estimated, been dead less than a week. His face was still human, though the crows had made off with his eyes. Slashes and burns at his elbows, knees and groin spoke of torture.

'They didn't eat this one,' Michael murmured.

The embers of a fire lay on the ground. They had worked on him a long time, judging by the depth of ash.

Blackthorn sprays had been twisted into a ring and pushed down on to his head until they tore the flesh.

Michael's spine prickled. He moved closer. What he had taken to be the tongue was in fact a piece of wood jutting from the mouth. He tugged gingerly at it. A cross.

'He was one of the Brothers,' Cat said tonelessly. 'That is why they did not feast on him. They were afraid, so they killed him the same way his god was killed, to destroy his magic.'

'Magic!' Michael snorted. A deep rage smouldered into life within him. 'Was this your bloody forest people? Mirkady and his like?'

She shook her head. 'This is not a good place, Michael. We should go. The tribe will need warning.'

'Warning of what?'

'*Grymyrch*. Goblins. They may be watching us now.'

He whipped the Ulfberht out of its scabbard, the iron a black bar in the dim light.

'Let them, the bastards.'

'Don't be stupid. If they wanted you they would take you in the night, or when you were alone. They are not strong in themselves, but are deadly in numbers. And they would swamp you. We must go.'

'Just a moment.'

He hauled out the spikes and let the corpse fall to the ground.

It was hard bending the arms down to its sides, and when he felt the skin slide under his hand he had to pause and reswallow burning bile. He covered the body with leaves and branches, then lashed up a cross of sorts with ivy and burnt sticks, jamming it into the ground. Strange how it outraged him that a priest should die this way, when he had thought little on seeing that other one die in the village with an arrow in his throat. Perhaps it was the isolation of it, the knowledge that he had almost certainly died alone—for the bones that carpeted the ground nearby were much older. Perhaps it was the barbaric nature of his death.

Still a farm boy, he thought with a bitter smile. Still capable of being shocked. The violence in the air was as palpable as the smell of putrefaction. It sickened him, and fed the anger. Who had the corpse been? A hermit seeking enlightenment, or a missionary out hunting souls?

They left the thicket and breathed in the clear, cold air of the valley with relief. The day was wearing round and they hurried on their way back down to the camp, Cat pausing once to listen, head cocked. But it was only a breeze wheezing through the trees. And the pattering on the leaves was not feet, only the first heavy drops of rain, the beginning of a shower that was to fall steadily until dark.

The rain gathered in puddles and streamed from the canopy overhead. The women set about erecting their hide shelters, suspending them from the nearby boughs and placidly tending the fires against their men's return. Those warriors who remained stood guard, leaning on their spears with the rain dripping from their noses and streaking their face paint. A child cried until it was given its mother's thin breast. Michael and Cat sat in silence before their fire while the world beyond became blue with evening and the heavy cloud gathered, lowering over the valley. They had told old Irae, who was in camp, that there might be *grymyrch* nearby and he was walking the rough perimeter, doing the rounds.

The wood was ominous this evening, the shadows full of malice. Michael felt that the tribe was stepping where no men were supposed to go. He hoped the hunters were safe.

Grymyrch. They were of the Wyrim, Cat told him, and yet were not. They belonged to some branch of the Forest-Folk who had long ago broken away from their cousins and followed a different path, a darker way. Mirkady's people were capable of savagery, but were just as ready to tolerate, even to welcome, an outsider, a human, depending on how he tickled their fancy or challenged their wits. They were a capricious, finicky people, as unpredictable as the weather; whereas the *grymyrch* were black and wholly evil, scarcely above animals. The Wyrim and the *grymyrch* had become enemies, and loathed each other, the hatred fuelled by what they recognized of themselves in the other race.

For the Fox-People goblins were a story, a legend to go with the store of other legends they held in their heads. The Forest-Folk they knew of; they were a part of the Wildwood that was familiar. But these new, unseen monsters which Michael had told them of and Cat had afterwards described had Irae looking grey and worried. On the whole, he told Michael, he preferred the dangers of the Knights to the perils of this new land, this unknown region of the wood. The tribes had not been this far south since the Great Journey, when they had trekked steadily, a great multitude of them, from the far mountains in the south, northwards to where the woods were friendlier. That was before the villagers split off to found their settlements, before the Knights or the Brothers, before the Four Roads had been laid down.

For a moment, as he spoke, he reminded Michael irresistibly of Mullan, and he might have been talking wistfully of the horses moving up to Ypres in 1915. The resemblance was striking, but it lasted only a second, and Irae was a grey-haired savage again, his skin stained with madder and his teeth rotten in a weather-lined face.

The hunters returned in the late part of the evening, grins breaking out across their faces as the women welcomed them, laughing at the burdens they bore on poles. Three does, thin but full-sized. The tribe would eat well for a few days.

Ringbone came over to where Cat and Michael hunkered near one of the rekindled fires. He was chewing on raw meat and the dark blood drooled down his chin. The fox man offered Michael a chunk and he took it politely, biting into the juicy flesh and feeling the blood slip down the back of his throat. At the other fires the people were butchering the deer. The animals had already been gralloched, the organs replaced in the chest cavity. Now they spilled out glistening in the light of the flames. Knives flashed wet as the women expertly skinned the beasts, cramming odd bits of meat into their mouths as they did so. By the fires the older children were readying what earthenware the tribe possessed while two of the men were stoking up the embers in the smoke tent. There was almost an air of festivity about the place, and Semuin was looking relieved. The hunting was his main concern and if it failed he would be held at least partially responsible.

Ringbone sat opposite Michael at the fire, taking off his headdress and scraping his short-haired pate. He caught a louse and threw it to pop in the flames. His face had grown serious. He wiped the blood from his chin and told Michael that he had been speaking to Irae. The old man was perturbed. This was not a good country they were in, he had said; it was too full of beasts and strange things. They should go back north and take their chances with the Knights. What had the *Utwychtan* and *Teowynn* to say to that?

Michael hesitated. It was true, he told Ringbone, that there were strange beasts and strange peoples in this part of the world, and the tribe had best be on its guard for there were *grymyrch* nearby in all likelihood. He told Ringbone what he and Cat had found at the lip of the valley.

The fox man's face went blank, as it always did when he was thinking something over. He asked Cat if she knew of these *grymyrch*. Were they dangerous to a band of warriors such as this? What were their customs, and how close did she think they were?

Cat answered perfunctorily. She did not know much more than she had told Michael or Irae. Ringbone's face grew blank again. He would have to think on this for a while, he said—until tomorrow at least.

Then Michael said in a rush that he was leaving the tribe, pushing on south alone with Cat. He was going into the Wolfweald. He could feel Cat's glare on his face as he said it.

The fire cracked and spat, branches slumping with a noise like rattled tinsel. It was a very quiet night now that the rain had stopped.

What the *Utwychtan* sought to do was his own affair. No man could tell another one where to go, Ringbone told them, but his eyes were as black as jet pebbles in his face, fixed on Michael's. For a second Michael thought his habitual reserve was going to break and a flood of questions spill out, but the fox man remained silent, only shaking his head a fraction and staring momentarily into the glowing logs. When he looked up again there was grief in his eyes. He thrust an arm out over the fire and Michael clasped it, the flames scorching hair from their skin.

Things would be readied to aid them on their way—food, clothing, shelter. And their horses would be rubbed down for them and given the last of the barley grain. Then Ringbone rose fluidly and padded off to the butchery and feasting at the other fires.

'So you will do this thing, no matter what I say?' Cat asked Michael in a low, stilted voice.

'I have to. I don't think I have any choice. It's what I came here for, I think.'

A memory of Rose with the lightning flickering in her eyes. *You'll look for me no matter what they tell you? Promise?* She was here all right. Somehow she had known what was going to happen to her.

'I'm sorry, Cat.'

'You'll be the death of me, Michael.'

'Don't say things like that.'

True night fell, the silent pitch of night in a windless forest.

Michael had come to love and fear it. There truly were bogey men in the world. They were not just a fairy tale, and they roamed the darkness at the edge of firelight. But there was a beauty in the trees and the snuff of woodsmoke that eddied about their trunks, a peace he had not known even in the placid Antrim countryside. He wondered sometimes if he would ever again be able to live content without it.

The camp was still, the fires burning down and most of the tribe asleep, their bellies full. Even the horses stood with their eyes closed, resting one hindquarter.

Michael had slipped into the light doze that had been his equivalent of sleep for the past months when Cat's gentle shake woke him. He was sitting up in a second and fumbling for his sword, blinking. About the camp silent figures moved out to the perimeter in the dying flush of the fires. The warriors.

'What is it?' he whispered to Cat. Then he realized.

Lights. Flickering blue witch lights in the trees. They guttered and leapt like candle flames but burned as blue as deep ice.

'Bale-fire,' Cat muttered. They had seen them before, of course, but never in such numbers. Michael's grandmother would have called them 'will-o'-the-wisp' and told him that they led travellers to their deaths. Here in the Wildwood they were the toys of the Forest-Folk, harmless if they were ignored. But there were hundreds of them out there and, standing up, Michael saw that they ringed the camp entirely, like the watchfires of a besieging army.

He sought out Ringbone whilst Cat settled her bow and quiver on her back, crushing dried kingcup on the flint arrowheads. It was not an especially potent herb, but the best they could do. The most effective weapon in the camp was Michael's iron sword.

Owls called in the trees, and once they heard the howl of a wolf a long way off; but otherwise there was no sound. The Fox-People built up their fires until the campsite was as bright as sunlit amber in the night. Women gathered their children in close whilst the men patrolled the perimeter.

An hour passed, and nothing happened. Michael staggered where he stood, eyelids fighting to drop. Cat was on the alert, however, and the fox men were leaning on their spears talking quietly or squatting with their backs to trees. The fires burned low for want of fuel, for Ringbone would let none leave the camp to gather more and the ground within was bare. A few women had put green boughs on a fire, only for it to smoulder and smoke uneasily. Most of the children were asleep, an amorphous huddle cloaked with hides and furs. The tension had left the air.

Someone screamed, a high yell of pain cut off in mid-flow. At once half a dozen warriors congregated on the area of the sound, flashing noiselessly over the ground and casting about for its source. They found a spear lying on the earth and a spatter of shining blood. Further away a trio of fingers lay pale as grubs amid the decaying leaves.

'Jesus,' Michael said.

The flickering bale-fires suddenly went out. In the moments it took for his eyes to adjust to the deeper darkness, Michael could feel the beating of his own heart, a fast pulse at his throat.

Then madness erupted.

A boiling tide of squat, dark shapes seemed to rise out of the very soil around the confines of the camp and swarmed forward. They were pitch-black, broad as tree trunks, and they loped along on tiny legs and overlong arms, agile as apes. They glinted with bone weapons and ornaments, and made no sound.

One warrior was caught by the bristling horde and immediately swamped. They engulfed him like a mass of black maggots; he went down with one arm still swinging his club. They came on into the dim fire glow at terrifying speed, and here Ringbone's people made their stand: whilst the women helped or carried children into the branches of the trees the men stood in an ever-shrinking circle and began to fight for their lives.

For Michael it was an unreal nightmare of half-guessed shapes and clawing limbs. The goblins thronged before him waist-high and so dark-skinned that even with the aid of the low fires he could make out little in the way of features. He felt the rake of claws, the agonizing bite of fangs, and he kicked back bodies that were compact and heavy, furred as finely as rabbits. He saw the shine of eyes that were without pupil and as blank as stones, and all the time he swung the heavy sword down again, again and again, hearing the crunch of bone, the pulp of broken flesh, and his breeches became soaked with blood. Only when they were hurt did they make any sound, a thin, high squealing like a hare caught in a trap, and after three had fallen before him in quick succession they started to avoid the deadly iron of his blade—one nick was poison to them—and concentrated their attacks elsewhere. His leaden arm came down and for an instant he chanced a look around whilst the fox men battled on at his shoulders.

They were being overrun. He saw Cat flailing about her with her stone knife, her hair a raven billow about her head. He watched, aghast with fear for her, as she slashed the throat of an adversary, booted another aside and stabbed a third through the heart, all the while avoiding the deadly flicker of the bone skewers the goblins bore.

Nearby Ringbone fought with a grim economy of effort, his face bitten with a frown of concentration. He had lost his headdress and blood slicked his torso. His or his enemies' Michael could not tell.

Semuin went down, tripped up and stabbed in the eye with a bone sliver. Michael leapt into his place and split a long-eared skull, smashed back a snarling face with the sword pommel, ground the point into the mouth of another. They drew back, snarling. Even their fangs were as black as ebony.

The circle was shrinking fast. At their backs were the trees at the centre of the campsite, their branches full of children and women, though some of the women had taken up weapons and were fighting alongside the men. Michael saw one woman dragged into the black throng of the enemy and then carried off screaming by a dozen of them. Her mate lurched after her, but his mad thrust only put him in the middle of his foes and they slashed at him until he collapsed.

We'll die here, Michael remembered thinking with perfect clarity. He was fighting at Cat's side now, and his body was looking after itself. He was filled with a sense of exaltation as he spun and swung and stabbed and kicked out. Perhaps it was the unreal, nightmarish quality of it, but he felt that were he to die here he would wake up in bed at home to an autumn morning.

Tired, though. He was tiring quickly, blocking more attacks than he launched, lunging less violently so the creatures before him were able to evade his thrusts. One set of claws fastened on his arm and tugged him forward to where the ravening maws waited. He stumbled, punched, cutting his knuckles on a set of teeth, and fell on his knees in the scrum, unable to swing the sword properly. A bone knife was pushed with incredible force into the top of his thigh and he shrieked with pain and anger, toppled helplessly and felt the black bodies close over him.

But then Cat and Ringbone were there battering the enemy aside, clearing a way to him. He was dragged backwards, one fist closed about the bone that protruded obscenely from his thigh, the other hanging grimly on to his sword hilt.

Clear. He screamed again as he yanked out the bone sliver and a jet of blood followed. For a moment he felt faint, and the night swam in his eyes. Ringbone and Cat had already returned to the fray.

Children were wailing above his head and looking up he saw that the goblins were in the lower branches of the trees. The circle had broken. The horses were neighing in terror and Fancy reared madly with a black form clinging to her neck. The defenders were no longer a line, but straggling knots of people surrounded by a swarming sea of bestial monsters. A child was thrown from its perch and swallowed up by the teeming crowd. A warrior beat at the jaws that had fastened about his wrist. A man dragged his unconscious friend away with a goblin clinging to his shoulders.

That's it, Michael thought. It's over.

A massive roar rose over the noise of battle above the screaming and the striving, and a hulking shape loomed to the rear of the goblins with two lights blazing in its head and two long arms sweeping terrible destruction on every side. It plucked two goblins from their feet and swung them like clubs, breaking the attacking mass to pieces and picking up two more when the first pair fell apart. The enemy recoiled in confusion, and Michael heard some of them cry out in fear.

Above, along the branches and trunks of the trees, a green light shimmered like arcane electricity, and the goblins that were grappling with the children there shrieked as they felt its touch. They smoked and burnt, fell to the ground in flames and bounded off trailing fire towards their fellows. When the flame, still burning and filling the air with the stench of charred flesh, hit the rest of the goblins it leapt from one to the other as though alive. The wood was lit up by the hellish light of the creatures cavorting and screeching in molten agony, though the fire did not seem to harm the trees.

The attack was melting away. Scores of the monsters were afire and many were streaming away like demented fireflies into the forest. The huge, hirsute shape that had wreaked such havoc upon them was clearly visible now. The face was brutal but merry, the eyes green glints under an overhanging crag of a brow and the lower jaw out-thrust to accommodate the laughing tusks.

'Dwarmo!' Cat shouted joyously. A twig smote Michael on the head and he looked up to find Mirkady peering down at him from the branches of the tree.

'Told you I'd keep an eye on you,' he cackled. The bark around him flickered harmlessly with green flames.

'Yeah, right,' Michael muttered. The world was a swimming dance in his eyes, shot through with the retreating light of the flaming goblins. Their screams were dwindling, fading into the forest. Dark shapes moved about, and he was conscious of Cat talking at a great rate, reassuring what was left of the warriors. '*Cymbr*,' she was repeating: 'Friend.' And Dwarmo was still grinning all over his great troll's face. But the women were weeping and the air stank of blood and burning. It swooped in on Michael like a cloud, and he sailed away into the core of its darkness.

FIFTEEN

HOT, CLOUDLESS, THE sky lowered smog-grey on the topmost floors of the highest buildings, buoyed up by the traffic roar and battened down by the crushing sunlight. He swallowed carbon with every breath, was bumped and jostled like a pinball in his progress up the street. Big steps, little steps, never one long, uninterrupted stride. Big steps, little steps, the pavement awash with litter and blaring reflected heat up into his face.

Time flies, he thought. No: it does not fly; it is flushed away and carries so much with it. Memories stay, though, even when they are unwanted. They are a stain no bleach will fade. An aftertaste.

He was slipping back and forth, his mind awash with images from the past. The beating sun was forgotten as he stood, one hand on the bottle within his pocket, and remained unyielding and unaware of the glares from obstructed passers-by. He was in the cool woods again, and their dark smells were choking his brain.

He looked behind him, at the crowd and scurry of the street with its towering two-deckers and beetling cars. Impossible to tell if it were following.

The Wildwood was here, in the city. Wolves in the alleyways. A fairy catching a train. He laughed harshly, and lurched into motion again.

She was waiting for him when he dragged himself to his door that night, there on the landing.

He caught his breath at the sight of the raven hair, the pale cheek semi-lit by the dim bulb overhead, and in that moment he sobered entirely, an entire evening's alcohol obliterated in an instant.

Then she turned, and the fearful wonder, the budding joy, twisted and burned to ash. It was that bloody girl again. Maybe she'd left her lipstick behind. The alcohol began to trickle back into place, fuzzing the edges of his mind.

'Mike! There you are.' The use of his Christian name was forced, an unfamiliar word in her mouth.

'Here I am.'

He reached the top of the stairs, breathing hard, and painted on a grin which might well have been a leer. His grinning muscles were not exactly overused these days.

'Good timing. I just got here. I was trying to remember if it was this floor.' She was diffident, nervous, and looked away from him as she spoke.

'It's late,' he said with gruff gentleness; a last-ditch effort to be decent.

'I know.' She gestured to the shut door. 'Can I come in?' He shrugged. So be it.

He winced at the mess inside, threw on a low light and kicked a cushion out of the way as he went to the window and opened it wide. For a second or two he stared down and out at the teeming city, the orange street lights and the eyes of cars. He wondered where the wolves were tonight, where that Wyran was, if it was here at all and his mind was not just playing games with itself.

A cough. He turned, smiling apologetically. 'Sorry, I was wool-gathering. Sit down. Have a drink.'

She sat on the edge of the big sofa. He meandered his way to where the bottles stood on the dresser, thought better of it, sighed and took a seat. Here we go, he thought.

Young. She looked painfully young sitting there in her city clothes, her shiny shoes and sheer tights, a smart jacket. And a briefcase, for

God's sake, resting on her thighs like a secret weapon. Had she been working to this time?

Black hair, thick, just touching her shoulders. Big eyes, dark, under brows that would be heavier if she didn't pluck them. A round face with a snub nose and well-painted lips. Not a businesswoman. More like a business child. He tried to remember what she had been like under the power dressing. He had a vague impression of white curves, softness. Breasts bordering on the large. He had laid his head between them, almost content for a while.

She was talking to him.

'...don't make a habit of that sort of thing, and then when you didn't call or anything, I thought that—'

'Why did you leave in the middle of the night?'

She hesitated. In the low light, he thought she flushed. 'You were drunk. You were talking nonsense, about trees and fairies and cats. And then you began talking gibberish, like a foreign language. I was scared. I thought maybe it was Gaelic or something. I thought I'd hopped into bed with some kind of lunatic.'

Unwillingly he smiled again, and this time she returned it. 'Did we actually...?'

'No. You were too drunk. It was sort of sweet. You apologized over and over.'

'I see.'

Silence, but for the city noises. He suddenly wanted this girl to stay with him, to see out the night. But there was another indignity.

'I've forgotten your name.'

The eyes flared briefly, a flash of temper. He expected her to get up and go, but instead she said quietly: 'Clare.'

He nodded.

'I wrote it down, and my number. I left it beside the bed.'

'Why did you come back?' he asked, too tired to beat around bushes.

'I don't know. To see if you really were a lunatic, I suppose.'

They looked at each other, strangers ashamed of past intimacy. And yet that, oddly enough, lent an air of companionship to the room.

'How about that drink?' Michael asked, as if he were requesting a truce. She shook her head. 'I'll have some coffee, though.' For the first time, the briefcase descended from her lap.

She was twenty years old. Her accent spoke of expensive schooling and her smell of expensive perfume. He let her talk, conscious of his own bedraggled appearance, hoping she would not notice the bulge of the empty bottle in his coat pocket or the bulge of the stomach over his belt. Vanity, he thought wryly, is an irrational thing.

It grew late, and the city began its brief sleep. The tiredness tugged at his eyelids and he realized that he had ceased to listen to what she was saying. He was aware only of that nicely cultured voice and the silence it held at bay. He was willing to sit and fight off sleep all night, just to have it continue. As long as she talked and sat there smelling elegantly the wood was kept out of the room, and his ghosts stayed in the memories where they belonged.

But she stopped talking at long last, and sat balancing her empty coffee cup on her knee as though she were in a monarch's drawing room. One hand slipped down to touch the briefcase as though it were a talisman.

'I have to work in the morning.'

'So do I.' There was a pause, long in mute communication.

'I have to get up early.'

'I've an alarm. Works most of the time.'

Another pause. Those dark eyes bored into him. He knew with a sudden flash of insight that in her way she was as frightened of the lonely night as he was. But he kept his face neutral, sure that he had overstepped the mark, transgressed some mutual contract of flippancy.

Finally she smiled; a wide, generous smile. 'Promise me you won't speak Gaelic in your sleep?'

'I promise.'

And this time he was not too drunk, or too tired. They made love carefully, courteously, anxious not to offend. The earth hardly shifted, but afterwards he laid his head between her breasts and gloried in the feel of her arms around him. No wilderness had worn her lean, no wounds had scarred her skin, and he nuzzled the ripe bloom of her body as though he could bury himself in it, whilst outside the dawn broke open the black sky and in shadowed corners of the streets below the woodland creatures kept their vigil.

A LONG WHILE, it seemed, he floated in some indeterminate place, a Never-Never Land that swirled with known and unknown faces. Cat was there, but she had changed somehow, had grown plump and wide-eyed. His grandfather was present, also—old Pat. And Rose was there. She was crying.

'*Come and get me, Michael. Take me home.*'

Home.

The Horseman rose up like a black wall, blotting her out. He was immense, black as a starless night. Up and up he towered, tall as a hill—and he became a castle, high-walled and ruinous upon a granite crag, so high that the clouds played about its battlements and grey moisture beaded it like sweat. Around its knees the trees rose, huge and old, tangled as wire, their roots grinding deep into the loam and rock of the earth. So thick was their canopy that it seemed like a textured carpet for giants to walk upon, and from its dim depths came the sound of wolves howling, as they bred and slaughtered in their thousands.

He opened his eyes with a cry and Cat shushed him, held him close.

'It's all right, my dear. You are all right.'

It was day. He could smell the acrid fire reek in the air, and there was a woman keening softly somewhere, people moving around, muttered talk.

'Mirkady,' he croaked from a dry throat.

'Here, my man.' And the diabolical face grinned a foot from his own.

Michael closed his eyes again and let himself be held by Cat's warmth. Ringbone's voice close by. There was a sound of bustle. He opened his eyes and looked into Cat's face.

'They're leaving, aren't they? Going back north.'

She nodded. Behind her a shape loomed, hulking and tusked.

'This part of the wood is no fit place for human man,' Dwarmo said. 'And their hurts are many.'

'They will be more numerous still ere they win their way back to the Forests of Men again.' Mirkady twinkled. Michael felt an urge to strike him. He sat up instead. The pain in his thigh was a hot red thing that impaled him to the ground, and allied to it were three or four other little agonies that gashed his limbs. The Ulfberht lay to one side.

Looking round he could see the funeral pyre ready to be fired, the other, blacker mound nearby that comprised the enemy dead. Hundreds, there must have been. The pitiful remnants of Ringbone's folk were packing up their meagre belongings, many women bleeding from grief cuts and red-eyed, the men like walking corpses, some with wounds oozing. No more than two score had survived. Michael could count less than a dozen men able to stand. In the midst of their camp were the two horses, gashes and bites marking their flanks. They had survived, at least.

Ringbone squatted before him. There were bark dressings about forearm and bicep. No one in camp seemed to have escaped hurt, Cat included.

'*Cadyei*?' the fox man asked him. He said he was well.

Ringbone bent his head to the ground for a moment, and then asked him if he and Cat still intended to go on south.

Michael glanced at her and she winked at him, though Mirkady's eyes had darkened. Ringbone ignored the two Wyrim as if they did not exist.

The people were going north, he said. They would not survive if they stayed here. He stopped and Michael saw an obvious struggle on the normally impassive face.

Let the *Utwychtan* and the *Teowynn* come back north with the people, he said as though the thought had just occurred to him.

Michael shook his head.

Ringbone nodded to himself, and broke into one of his unaccustomed smiles. If—when—they came north again, they would find the tribe four days' walk west from the burnt village. It had been decided that it was better to face the Knights than the Forest-Folk—and here his gaze did slide sideways for a second at the silent Mirkady.

'*Dhanweyr moih*,' he said finally. And Michael wished him good travelling in his turn. Then the fox man stood up in one swift movement and was gone, off to organize what was left of his people.

And so they melted away, not so much disappearing into the trees as dissolving. Forty souls in search of sanctuary. Michael got the feeling that he was watching an ancient ritual, oft repeated. It was as natural as the turning seasons that men should shift and move, seeking a better place. Even if it destroyed them.

It was quiet when the last of the Fox-People had gone. Michael, Cat, Mirkady and hulking Dwarmo moved up the slope of the valley, away from the stink of the dead and the smoke of the funeral pyre, and lit a fire of their own to boil water and tend their wounds.

Night swooped in on them. At the edge of the firelight Dwarmo stood tireless guard like some broad megalith whilst Mirkady sat listening to the wood noises, his long ears moving back and forth.

Michael and Cat drank infusions of wood poppy to deaden the pain and cleaned out each other's hurts with a heated knife. There would be scars, Michael knew as he treated the gashes on Cat's legs, and he mourned the marring of her perfection. She was as thin and hard as a greyhound and her breasts seemed meagre—dark nipple and very little else. He kissed her navel as she lay under the knife, and covered her over again.

'You need feeding, Cat.'

'What about you? With that beard you look like a half-starved prophet, though your shoulders are nearly as broad as Dwarmo's. Where did you get that size from?'

'It's in the bones.'

They ate reheated venison and forest onions along with some barley spirit that Ringbone had given Cat. Powerful stuff, it was precious to the tribe for it could only be obtained through trade with the villagers. It was clear, but smelled strongly of alcohol, like methylated spirits that had somehow been infused with a hint of corn and summer dust. They trickled some on their wounds, stiffening and grimacing at the pain, which made Mirkady chortle. He declined a drink, recalling for them the sweetness of the mead in his own Howe.

They fed the fire as the night deepened, heavy cloud being blown in from the west to hide the stars and promise rain before morning. The trees tossed and turned uneasily in the wind, their tops undulating and swaying like the waves on a vast, dark sea. Their campfire was a tiny jewel, a bright pinhead in the midst of the forest murk, for the pyre had burned to ash now, and Ringbone's dead were being scattered through the air like a cloud of dark moths winging towards some distant light.

'So it is south you are headed,' Mirkady said at last, the humour gone from his voice. Michael nodded. His arms were full of Cat and he was resting his chin on the crown of her head. Her cold fingers were clasped over his.

'You have an idea, maybe, of the country you will be entering,' the Wyran went on. 'It is not named the Wolfweald for nothing. And wolves are the least of the things you will encounter in there.'

'We know,' Michael said firmly. He thought Cat shuddered in his embrace, and hugged her tighter.

'Do you now...? Sister Catherine, you know. You have heard the stories. Can you not talk this man out of madness?'

Cat leaned forward from Michael's arms and poked at the fire with a stick.

'There is no talking to him. He has a quest in mind and means to follow it.' There was a sort of weary bitterness in her tone.

'The kinswoman taken by the Horseman. I see. So you hope to find her, *Utwychtan*.'

Michael did not speak.

'Let me tell you a story, Farsider, an old one your lady might not know. Like all the best tales it is a true one, and it may yet give you an idea of what you are clamouring to get into.

'Some years ago—nine times fifty or less, which is a raindrop in a storm to the Wildwood—the Brothers took it upon themselves to convert the men in the wood to their way of thinking, and they sent out missions to the outlying villages. The villagers were easy to win over, for the crosses and holy words of the Brothers kept the beasts at bay. And so the men who are now of the tribes, though they were called *Myrcans* in the beginning, these men who had been the guardians of the villagers were left purposeless. They were and are a proud people, and when they saw they were no longer wanted or needed, they drew apart from those who had once been their wards. The people began to mistrust them, for they were warriors without compare in those days, consummate soldiers whom even the Wyrim respected. They were ostracized, and degenerated into the wandering folk we know now.

'But that is getting away from the story. These Brothers sought to convert the whole world in their arrogance. Their numbers grew and grew, and men began to flock to their service. Soon it was that villages which hesitated to convert, or who desired to cling to their Myrcan warders, were overcome by force, and the soldiers of the Brothers of the Wood were named the Knights Militant.

'Even the Forest-Folk, who loathe and despise the Brothers for their holy poisoning of the wood, even we have known good men amongst them, men who preached harmony and who wished to live in peace with everyone, the Forest-Folk included. There were more of these in the beginning. But as time has gone on tolerance has declined on both sides. First it was the Wyrim who were decried from the pulpits, and now it is the tribes. There is a war of sorts in the Wildwood.

'Again, I draw away from my story. Forgive me. The Wyrim are ever a prolix folk when they get going. A tale to them is as good as drink, worthy of savouring. It is a thing to be embroidered and delved into. It is a thing to be mined and smelted and reforged with every telling.

'Well such, as I have said, was the arrogance of these Brothers and their armoured henchmen that they decided they would spread their good news to every glade in the forest, and this, they thought, should include the forbidden places to the south where the beasts roamed undisturbed. This part of the wood was less perilous in those days, and humans hunted and farmed within it in communities so small as to be hardly worth noticing. Some even ventured as far south as the Wolfweald itself—and never returned. It was not known what manner of place the wood was in those days. There were only the tales to go by, the myths of the Wyrim and the stories of those men who had become of the tribes. And yet the people preserved stories of their passage through it on their way north from the mountains. It was a terrible place, they said. No man survived there. Why, they could not say.

'The Brothers did not come across the mountains, Farsider. They came from your world, or one like it; they came from a door in the north and so never knew the terror and the hardship of the passage of the southern woods. Their crosses would keep any beast at bay, they said, and they would rid the villagers of this superstition of theirs concerning the Wolfweald. They would bring it under the wing of their church.

'And so an expedition was arranged and a Brother called *Bishop*, who was very high in their authority, led a company south into the forbidden forests there.

'Five and twenty Brothers went, and with them half a hundred of the Knights and more than twice as many followers. They had mules and horses to carry their baggage and they drove flocks of sheep and a herd of cattle with them, for they had a mind to build a holy settlement of sorts, part church, part fortress. It is rumoured they also carried with them a piece of their God's flesh as a talisman, but I doubt if even the Brothers could be so barbarous.

'So off they started one morning in the spring, singing as they went, and into the woods they disappeared, two hundred souls. They were never seen again.

'Over the years the rumours came to the people in the villages. They had built themselves a fortress and were beleaguered there. They had turned back to savagery the same as the tribes had. They had died at the hands of the Wyrim, or the goblins. The Brothers' magic had failed them in the deep woods. They had gone on south and had crossed the mountains to the land beyond. The Horseman had taken them to his castle.

'Another expedition was rigged out two years after the first. Only three Brothers went with it, three young men, one of whom had once been a Myrcan: Phelim, Finn and Dermott. Forty Knights accompanied the trio. The forest swallowed them also.'

The fire cracked and spat before them, a bright blaze against the encroaching dark. Dwarmo stood immobile, but his head was cocked as he, too, listened to Mirkady's tale.

'That was the end of the expeditions to the south. From then on it was a land for no man to venture into. Gradually men left the woods bordering on the Wolfweald—these woods around us. There were tales of black shapes in the trees, vampires that stole children and drained cattle of blood. Ghouls that preyed on human flesh.'

'Goblins,' Michael said.

'*Grymyrch*. Yes. They were more furtive in those days. They have grown in confidence since, and in numbers. It is the Horseman has seen to that. It is said that the ghosts of the lost expeditions still wander the trees, their souls kept in the Horseman's castle.'

'What happened to them?' Michel asked, sure that the Wyran knew.

Mirkady smiled unpleasantly. 'Why do you think I have that knowledge about me?'

'You people seem to know everything.'

'Oh, we do,' the other replied airily. 'It is just that we do not choose to disclose it to everyone.'

'What happened?' Michael repeated.

The little creature stared into the flames of the fire.

'Our people trailed them for a while, kept at a distance by the crosses and the masses and such. They came upon isolated farmsteads, hamlets, tiny villages whose folk were known to us and whom we had let be. Some of us had even got to know the people within them. They were hardy souls. They had to be, living in what was then the very eaves of the Wolfweald. They lived with the forest, not in spite of it, and there was a truce between them and the Wyrim. These people were converted to the Brothers' cause, either by persuasion or by force. In the larger settlements a Brother and a pair of Knights would stay behind to make sure this faith of theirs grafted, and the column rode on.

'By the time they were well into the Wolfwood itself they had left over a score of their number behind them. They erected wooden crosses on cairns at the close of every day's march, and their thinking was to build a road between them some day. These things they magicked with their incense smoke and their water and they may stand yet in places, for the Brothers used oak and built to last.

'They had few problems for the first days. They saw the balefires and ignored them, set up a fortified camp every night, which was no small labour in the thicknesses of that part of the forest. But things began to happen. The livestock became difficult to manage and some were lost. Men disappeared in the nights, having ventured beyond the camp's perimeter. A pair of Knights vanished when sent out to look for them.

'After that they were more careful. They had to slaughter their herd for food, for game was non-existent and they could not range out to hunt for it. The wolves followed them in great packs, and the brothers had to stand watch in the nights to ward them off. They began to tire, and the constant watchfulness took its toll of tempers and spirit.

'They were deep in the Wolfweald now, glimpsing strange animals they had never encountered before. The trolls shadowed them, and goblins peered from the branches of the trees. The camp followers began to murmur against the Brothers, saying they were on a fruitless errand, that there was nothing in the trees but death. Some were for turningg back, but Bishop and the head Knight quelled their opposition. In the night a large number did leave, having suborned a pair of Brothers and a few Knights. They forged into the trees intending to retrace their path and find the Woods of Men again. None returned.

'Weeks passed, and every day there were fewer at the morning mass. When scarcely a hundred were left Bishop decided that they had best turn back, and his decision was greeted with rejoicing. But that night a fog came down, thick as cream. Some men panicked and rushed into the trees. Some the Knights slew as they tried to loot the supplies. The Brothers themselves became mortally afraid, and with their fear their powers waned. Beasts penetrated the perimeter, and in the fogbound night men blundered around leaderless and were taken one by one. Only a few young Brothers kept their faith, and around them gathered the hardiest of the Knights and followers. By morning barely twenty of them were left alive and Bishop himself had been taken. The camp was a wasteland of gore and wrecked supplies and dead animals, but not a single man corpse was to be seen.

'It is not clear what happened after that. The faith of those that remained was strong, and they did not fight among themselves. The Wyrim left them to the *grymyrch*, but I have heard tales and rumours that this tiny band kept together and went on south, seeking an end to the trees, a glimpse of open sky again. Some among my own folk maintain that they got away, that the goblins lost them in the darker parts of the weald and that they found their way at last to the Mountains of the World's Rim. But that is mere conjecture. One thing is known: never a one ever came again to the Woods of Men. Likely enough they left their bones in some glade where even the goblins do not go, that or the Horseman took them. And this is what happened to the second expedition also, that led by the three Brothers. The Wolfweald swallowed them all.'

'You speak as though you had been there,' Michael said, staring at Mirkady closely.

The Wyran laughed: a brittle, dangerous laugh.

'Wyrim did help the goblins, the wolves, the manwolves. We are children of the same father, after all.'

There was a silence, during which Dwarmo came over to the fire and helped himself to the bulging wineskin Ringbone's people had left them, gulping deeply and smacking thick lips over his fangs. There was a look of bliss on his face.

'You know now what it is you are walking into, Farsider. What you are taking our sister into,' Mirkady said softly.

'They are watching us,' Dwarmo added. 'They fear the Wyr-flames, or they would have been upon us hours ago.'

Michael started up, gasping at the pain in his thigh. He drew his sword, but when he looked out from the fire all he could see was a screen of tangled trees, impenetrable as a wall. An owl hooted, and somewhere there was the harsh choke of a pheasant. He might have been in the wood back home, were it not for the height of the trees. They were massive here, towering giants with trunks wider than he was tall. He sheathed the sword and rubbed Fancy's nose absently. The horses were picketed well within the limits of the firelight and they seemed calm enough considering the madness of the night before.

'I'm still going, even if I have to go alone.'

'You will not go alone,' Cat said heavily, and she frowned out into the forest.

'So be it,' Mirkady said, and he spat into the fire.

There was a hiss out of proportion to his spittle, and the fire cracked sharply. Michael spun round.

'What are you doing?'

'Keeping both your skins whole for as long as I can. Wyr-fire, Michael Fay. I am granting you a boon.'

The fire rose higher, waist height, shoulder height, and then it was above Michael's head, a thin spiral of flame that was rapidly deepening in colour. It darkened to blue, then green, and their faces were suddenly bathed in a flickering, undersea light. It was the same hue as the flames which had consumed the goblins.

'Wyr-fire,' Mirkady said. 'A gift of the forest to the Wyrim. The sap of the earth refined in light.'

He leaned forward so that the very flames were caressing his wedge-shaped face, running up through the thatch of hair and licking at his eyes. Their emerald light was almost identical to the firelight. For a few seconds it looked as though the flames were pouring in and out of his eyes like twisting tears. Then Mirkady breathed in sharply, his bird-like chest expanding enormously, and the green flicker of the fire was sucked in through his open mouth, running down his throat like water. The yellow of ordinary firelight returned, but Mirkady was standing there swollen to bursting. He stepped over to Cat first, and abruptly placed his black, leathery lips against hers, making Michael start. Then he seemed to blow. Cat jerked away, but the little creature's fingers fastened on her shoulders and held her close. A huger, heavier hand on Michael's nape prevented him from getting up, and behind him Dwarmo rumbled: 'You have nothing to fear. It is a privilege Mirkady is according you, a boon indeed. Be still.'

Mirkady released Cat and she tumbled backwards with the whites of her eyes flickering under the lids. Michael jerked convulsively, but Dwarmo's massive strength held him.

Mirkady's lips were leaf-dry and light on his own. He felt as though a gale had somehow been funnelled into his mouth; a hot wind that raced down his throat and warmed his gullet like wine. It wheeled through every nerve and vein within him and he thought he might be becoming lit up and luminous, a neon decoration, a Christmas tree overhung with lights. It exploded in his brain and fireworked through every passageway, every neurone, every cell—and the wood was in the light, in his mind. He raced from hot darkness through rock and clay and sediment, strata clicking past madly, through the slow reach and tangle of root systems, up the trunks of trees, the seasons mere blurs to be felt like a quiver of wind through the thick bark. And then out to the whirling leaves, feeling the sun warm and stir him, the air move in his veins like blood. And he was cast loose, floating down, back to the soil and the clay and the deep gut rock again, to begin from another beginning.

And the firelight was warm and yellow on his face and the weight on his shoulder was Dwarmo's hand stopping him from falling. He glanced round, dazed, saw Mirkady reclined by the fire, smirking and serious at the same time. Cat looking as bemused as he felt, shaking her head as though a fly buzzed at it.

'What did you do?' he asked Mirkady, and staggered as Dwarmo's grip finally released him.

'I gave you a gift that the forest things will smell for miles around. Wyr-fire. You can call it up yourself now, you and Catherine—but once only between you. The wood creatures will think of you as Wyrim until you finally let slip the fire, should you do so. When it leaves you, you will both be human again, mere cattle in this part of the world. Remember that.'

'How do we release it?'

'You will know how, Farsider, when the necessity is great enough. But remember it can be used once only.'

Dwarmo spoke, a deep bass from the edge of the firelight.

'It is... an honour you are being done. It is not a thing given lightly by our people.'

'Why?' Michael asked Mirkady.

'Because I love your lady.' He and Cat stared at each other whilst Michael looked on, baffled.

'And because I think you are doing something important. Something that is meant to happen. I do not think it is mere whim that has brought you here; nor do I think that you yourself truly know the reason. There is more to it than that.'

The Wyr-fire was a distant singing in Michael's bones, a tingling.

'Do you know the way to the Horseman's castle?'

Mirkady nodded. 'We all do. And so does Cat. It is like a shadow at the edge of sight, always in the comer there.'

Michael looked at her. 'You know, then? You know it exists, that it is real?'

She said nothing. Her mouth was a tight, angry line.

'How far?' Michael asked Mirkady.

'A bad dream away. Distances are deceptive in this land, and straight lines are fatuous things. You will walk until you find it—and all who come here find it sooner or later, if the Horseman wants them to. It could be a league away, or ten thousand. You will find it when he wishes you to. When he deems you ready.'

'Ready for what?'

'Ready to give up your soul.'

MORNING CAME AND Mirkady and Dwarmo were gone, though a smiling face had been scratched into the earth by the fire. Michael listened for a while. The valley was full of thick mist that rolled like an ocean below him, the trees towering out of it, shaggy giants wading ashore. The wood was quiet and a pale sun was just flinging the first of its beams over the eastern horizon, cutting rainbows from the vapour in the air.

Cat lay on the other side of the dead fire, watching him. It had been cold without her warmth in his arms, but she had been distant since the Wyr-fire had been kissed into her. Was it Michael's imagination, or was there something different about her—something that had more to do with Mirkady's folk than with humanity? Could it be that her eyes were more narrow, her ears longer, more pointed?

But when she got up, throwing her furs aside, he castigated himself for being absurd. She was the same lithe, lovely girl he had always known, and he ached for her.

'Cat?'

'What?' she asked, not looking up from her packing.

He touched her arm and paused without meeting his eyes.

'No, Michael.'

'Why not? It's been an age.'

'I'll not love you while you're selling your soul for some other woman.'

She was crying, the tears coursing down one cheek, though her face was unmoved, set hard.

'She's kin to me. Damn it, Cat, I thought this had been settled. I thought you had stopped worrying about it. You're the one I love.'

'Then find me my soul, Michael.'

'What?'

'If I am a changeling, then my soul is also in the Horseman's castle. Would you go on a quest for it?'

He could not answer her. He felt winded, wholly at sea. She was as unpredictable as the rain. Damned if he knew what to say to placate her.

He turned away. 'I'll get breakfast,' he growled, bewildered with hurt. Nothing was as it appeared in this place. He began to wish he had taken up Ringbone's invitation and gone north.

If Ringbone was still alive. He and his people might well be a jumble of corpses by now.

Cat's hand was on his nape, and he turned at once to kiss her. They pressed into each other hungrily, and he made short work of tucking her tunic aside.

'I'm sorry,' he said as he slid inside of her, and she repeated it, so that they were apologizing to each other as they made sudden love, transforming it into a litany until it seemed they were sorry for all that was to come as well as all that had been. They were sorry that things were going to turn out the way they would.

SIXTEEN

It was a quiet night. He was at his station, pulling pints behind the bar; or he would be pulling them if anyone wanted one. The pub was almost deserted, a few die-hards staring into their glasses, a game of darts in the corner with old men taking their time to shuffle to and from the board.

Outside the long day was winding into a clear blue night, and the traffic had eased from the five-o'-clock mayhem that he hated. There was the roar of a red bus now and again, ploughing along the road outside.

He leant on the bar and lit a cigarette, though the landlady forbade it.

Clare. There was a thing.

Not a good idea to get involved with a girl ten years your junior, one who believed in true love and honour and suchlike.

Nice, though.

He liked her elegance, the city cut of her. There was not an ounce of hayseed in her make-up. The city was her everything.

A face appeared briefly at the window of the bar. It grinned hugely, the eyes becoming slits filled with green light, the ears pointed as leaves.

Mirkady?

He hobbled from behind the bar and crashed open the door, glaring out into the calm night, the lamplit street.

Nothing.

His heart was labouring, fighting to expand out of his chest. He pressed a fist to his breastbone, panting, whilst the world leapt and jumped in his sight, the street lights spangling into stars.

He staggered back to the bar. Stares followed him.

There was an iron band around his chest, tightening unbearably, squeezing shut his lungs. He lurched to the row of optics and clinked a glass below the brandy, clicked it up. Then the stuff was searing his throat and heating up his gullet.

A pair of customers at the bar were asking if he needed help. He waved them away. Christ, he thought, I'm getting old. I'm dying here.

Had it been Mirkady out there, in the street? He was no longer sure. After so much time one fiendish face looked very much like another. And his lips stretched in a ghastly, mirthless grin. His chest loosened, lungs opening. The world steadied again and he was able to laugh at the concern of the old blokes, make a joke of it. The rest of the brandy finished his recovery, and one of the pensioners bought him another. No mean gesture. He raised it in salute.

What was happening to him? He was seeing monsters in every shadow. There was something about the city after dark that reminded him of the Wildwood. That watchfulness. It was not his imagination. Walking with Clare around nightfall he had been sure they were being followed, soft feet padding the pavement behind them. Nothing to see, of course.

And there had been that one night he had woken to the sound of hoofbeats in the road below his flat. There had been no clash of iron. The hoofs had not been shod, as no horses were shod in the Other Place.

He cried off work early, his excuse of illness backed up by the customers in the bar. The landlady took one look at his face and let him go without comment, surprising him. It was only when he was on his way out that he noticed his reflection in the mirror behind the bar: a sight he hated, these days. His face was as lumpish and heavy as always, the fair hair sliding ever further up his scalp, but it was as white as snow, the eyes popping in their sockets. His mouth was twisted with self-disgust and fear as he stepped outside.

Into the lamp lit darkness, the traffic, the long streets dotted with people, some hurrying, some dawdling.

Too damn quiet, even if Mirkady were here somewhere, watching over him.

Would Mirkady watch over him, though? He and his kind had withdrawn, had abandoned Cat and himself after what had happened in the Wolfweald. Perhaps he was allied to the manwolves and the Horseman now. They were in it together.

A few years ago these thoughts would not have come to him. The memories had not been there then, at the top of the heap. They had been buried somewhere deep down, and the thought of fairies or goblins had been absurd. Not now. It was no mere fairy tale.

He eyed shadowed corners fearfully as he walked, but nothing disturbed him. It was only whilst negotiating a wholly deserted square that he thought he caught the flicker of a deeper darkness off to one side, and he halted, watching. But there was nothing there.

And Clare was at the door for him, and tugged him inside to the light and the cooking smells.

She was vegetarian, and as he sat down to his candlelit pasta he found himself smiling to think what Cat would have made of this—or himself, for that matter—once upon a time. Clare was talking about work, about bosses, about weather, for God's sake. Clearly his silence was making the meal heavy going for her. But he smiled, toasted her in red wine—finer, thinner stuff this, than the vintage he had drunk in the Wildwood—and it seemed to make her happy. Though she kept stealing worried glances at him when she thought he could not see.

Afterwards they lay on the sofa, the television flickering like a blue-flamed campfire in their eyes. She seemed oddly heavy lying on top of him, and he thought that her flesh was strangely soft, with no hard muscle underneath.

He blinked, and slid far down the road before sleep. His mind retrod old ground on the edge of dream and nightmare. He thought he was staring open-eyed across the room to a dark corner, and in that corner Cat sat watching him. He tried to get up, but Clare's weight pinned him to the sofa. She seemed to be asleep.

Cat's eyes gleamed green in the dimness and her ears lanced up through her hair, as long as a deer's.

He heaved Clare off him and she fell to the floor with a thump. He scrabbled over to the corner. Nothing. A dream. A memory from a long-ago time when he had consorted with wood spirits. Wood spirits! Christ, he was going mad, that was it. He was hallucinating, reliving some childhood fantasy.

'What the hell was that about?'

Clare. He turned. She was rubbing her hip and glaring at him in anger and puzzlement.

'Sorry. Had a—a bad dream. It shook me up a bit—'

'Another one?' Now she was concerned. Her hand stroked his face. 'I thought something was wrong as soon as you came in. You were so pale, Michael. You looked as though you'd seen a ghost.'

He almost laughed aloud at that, but settled for a smile and kissed her on the mouth. She pulled him closer, all big dark eyes and tumbled hair, skin smooth as china. Peaches and cream, he thought. English roses. He doubted if she'd spent a night outdoors in her entire life.

The television burbled along to itself as they shed their clothes and for a moment its light washed her skin in green so that it might have been the light of the Wyr-fire in the forest. But it lasted only a second. She was moving on him now, eyes shut and lower lip caught between her teeth as though she were caught up in mental arithmetic. Her breasts, dark-aureoled and full, swayed with her thrusts. He balanced his hands on her hips and closed his own eyes as the familiar sensations took hold. But as his body responded to hers, as they moved together to some desirable culmination, he was with one clear part of his mind seeing Cat's face in the firelight. He was watching sunshine in trees as tall as office buildings, feeling the cold breeze of spring on his face.

He could remember everything, as clear as day. Everything that had happened in the Wolfweald.

SOUTH THEY HAD gone, with the sun rising on their left every morning and the first light taking its time to filter down through the immense trees. It pushed through the branches overhead in great spars and shafts, splintering into spears and arrows as it struck the sprays and twigs, the budding leaves, and finally spangling into a swaying dapple that carpeted the forest floor.

The canopy grew thicker as they travelled, however, the branches entwining together ever more closely and the tops of the trees fighting for space and sun, and they began to move in what seemed like perpetual twilight. The horses' hooves made little sound on the soft humus of the ground, clumping steadily, and the nights were black as pitch, the stars invisible overhead, blocked out by the interwoven ceiling of the trees.

It was dank and chill in this underworld, as if the trees had sealed in the end of winter, the cold air and the dampness. Their lower branches were dead and rotten through want of light, and the dead wood itself was like wet paper, stinking. It became almost impossible to find dry wood for the fire and often Michael and Cat huddled together in the endless darkness of the nights with the horses crowded round them, unsettled and restless.

Navigation became a problem. Though Cat, if pressed, would indicate the rough direction they were to take, Michael felt it necessary to glean information from every glimpse of the sun or stars, for he had a fear they would otherwise go in circles till they left their bones in the leaf mold. He marked trees with the Ulfberht in a desperate attempt to keep them going in a straight line; but he had a feeling that it was unnecessary, that they were travelling a course which had been plotted for them a long time ago.

He climbed a tree once, to try and see the sun, and scaled a hundred feet of an old forest giant, his fingers digging into the rotten bark and the black, evil-smelling stuff grinding in under his nails. He caught a hint, a wisp of sunlight, and knew that up there somewhere the world rolled on. Dawn came every morning and the moon rose. But the highest branches were too flimsy to bear his weight and he had to descend, grubs and mites from the tree infesting his clothing and biting his scalp.

They had enough dried meat and forest roots in the saddlebags to keep them chewing for a few weeks, which was as well since the forest seemed empty of animal life. Not a bird sang in the gloomy mornings, and never a game trail did they find. It was as if the massive bulk of the trees sucked the vitality out of the land, leaving room for no other life. Michael voiced this thought to Cat as they sat shivering one evening with their pitiful campfire guttering at their toes. She nodded.

'Can't you feel it?'

'Feel what?'

'The power here. It is in the very air. The trees are part of it, and thrive with it, but nothing else can unless it is a beast of the Horseman. This place is rotten with magic, Michael. It is sick with it, like a stagnant pond.'

Water became a worry. There were streams in the forest, narrow and choked with roots and mud, and the water in them was dark as porter. They drank nonetheless, but after two weeks of it Michael fell sick. He remembered little but the ground swooping up to meet him as he slid off Fancy's back, and Cat's face bent over him for what seemed an interminable time of vomiting and sweating. Then things became blank, and his mind lost all links with his body. He had convulsed, Cat told him later, which was why there was a chunk bitten out of his tongue, and the healing wound in his thigh had sprung open again like the rind of a rotten fruit.

Two days he was like this, waking on the night of the second to the smell of his own stink and the taste of blood and vomit in his mouth, Cat a red-eyed manikin beside him. Around them the trees loomed as huge and silent as ever, and the reek of the forest seemed somehow worse than that of his own wastes.

They boiled their water after that, though Cat had seemed unaffected by the stuff, and drank it in sparing sips. Michael's bowels remained loose, the constant riding an agony to his reopened thigh and chafing buttocks. He ate some of the horses' barley, which helped, but the horses themselves were growing gaunt through lack of food. The undergrowth, sparse as it was, did not tempt them, and they gnawed at sapling bark and fleeting clumps of wiry heather that clawed for life in the murk of the forest floor. Great ticks fastened on them, white and heavy-jawed. If left to feed they would become as big as Michael's little finger, bloated on blood, before dropping off.

Cat caught frogs in some of the unwholesome streams, and they skinned and ate them warily. Though they tasted to Michael like rotten pork they were not poisonous, and soon they halted to try their luck every time they heard the trickle of water, eking out the smoked venison they had left.

One day, however, they heard the clear tinkle and bubble of free-flowing water, quite unlike the slow seep of the streams they had so far encountered, and steering towards it they came upon a brook running crystal clear between banks of green grass and overhanging briars. They halted, amazed, and drank their fill of the delicious, clean water, better than wine after the filth they had been imbibing. And, even more astonishing, there was a hole in the impenetrable canopy overhead so that for a few minutes a ray of sunlight actually lanced down to set the water alight and gleam off the polished stones in the stream bed. Michael laughed aloud, but Cat was silent and presently she threw up, her whole body arching in agony.

'What is it? What's wrong?' He felt fine himself, as though the clean water had flushed the forest muck out of his belly.

'The water,' she croaked. 'It's burning. It burns me. Oh, Michael—it's *holy water*.' She collapsed into convulsive retching again.

Mystified and alarmed, he examined the stream, sniffed at it and saw the cross in the water arranged out of black stones.

'The Brothers did this. They put it here when they came this way. They poisoned the water,' Cat gasped. Saliva trailed in a bright bead from her chin.

'Don't be stupid, Cat. It's good water, the best we've tasted in this God-forsaken place.'

'Your god forsook it, not mine.' And she collapsed again.

He stood confounded and almost angry, glaring at nothing. The horses were greedily cropping grass. There was nothing wrong with them. He set a hand on Cat's shoulder but she shook it off, lost in her own suffering. Michael cursed and spun away.

A shape in the trees. Someone standing there in the shadow.

'Cat!' He drew his iron sword.

Not a man, or even man-like. It was tall and thin, as black as tar. Cat was deaf to him.

'Damn you, Cat.'

A post, taller than he was, standing like a thin megalith ten yards from the stream.

A cross, it had been. Dead briar was wound round it, and honeysuckle. At its base the arms lay, rotted free of the central post and decomposing with the stubborn slowness of oak. He felt a rush of... relief? Some skeletal piety, perhaps, a remnant of the church-going child he had once been. He touched the old wood with something like a caress. So the Brothers and the Knights had come this way, untold centuries ago. They had drunk from the stream and left their markers behind.

'It's all right, Cat. We're all right here.'

'You are. This place—' She broke off, heaving. He was torn between concern and irritation.

Michael's respite was short-lived. The next day they left the stream and its marker behind and the twilit dankness of the forest took hold of them again. Cat was pale and silent, still racked with occasional shudders, though Michael had filled his skin with the delicious water.

So she truly was different. For so long he had refused to think of her as anything but an ordinary girl; a wild, fiery one, maybe, but a girl just the same. He could no longer convince himself that it was true.

The trees unfolded endlessly, and the silence rang in their ears until it became a noise in itself, never-ceasing. Michael longed for song, laughter, anything which did not belong to the towering trees and festering mold. Anything to break the spell of the stillness. But there was nothing. Though this place was named the Wolfweald, they had not seen or heard a single wolf in weeks, which was unusual even in the inhabited parts of the Wildwood. He began to wonder how many of the tales and legends of this place were founded on ignorance and imagination. This dead emptiness, filled only with the huge presence of the trees, was somehow harder to bear than all the wolves and goblins in existence.

Cat's bout of sickness passed quickly, but Michael's lingered on and on, despite the good water in his skin. Weight fell off him pound by pound and he felt weak and lethargic, needing Cat's help to rub down and unsaddle the horses in the evenings. It was as if the forest were invading his flesh, wearing him down.

Cat seized his face in her hands one morning as he lay in the furs, scanning it with grief and worry written over her own. 'What is it?'

'Your hair. The beard. They're going grey, Michael.'

He paused, her cold fingers hovering over his cheekbones. 'I'm getting old, Cat. I'm getting old quickly in this place. I should be scarcely fifteen and I feel like an old man. It's the forest. It's this damn wood.'

'No,' she said. 'It is the Horseman. He rules here, and he knows we are coming.' She stared at him intently, and he knew what she was asking.

'I'm not turning back. Not now. I'm not sure it's possible anyway.'

She left him, throwing aside the furs and letting the cold air bite. 'It's on your own head then, Michael. Yours alone. I am just a follower.'

They continued, Michael leading, Cat following; and there was little talk between them.

They came upon two more of the cross markers left by the Brothers' expedition, and once there was another of the clear running streams for Michael to drink from, but for the most part the wood was monotonous and dim with great trees hanging with moss and ivy, fungi riding up the trunks like steps or sprouting in profusion between the roots; and in the nights the only light was that of rotting, phosphorescent wood.

It was at the beginning of one such night that Michael was kissing Cat and their bodies were entwined like holly and ivy. Then her hair fell back, and in the light of the little fire he saw that her ears were pointed and long, fine dark hairs fringing them. And with the fire behind her there was a light leaping out of her eyes, green as the heart of a sunlit emerald.

Mirkady had been wrong, he thought. He had said that Michael's love would make Cat into a human, a mortal like himself, but here in the Wolfweald she was reverting to the other half of her nature. She was starting to leave her humanity behind.

They began to notice signs of life in the trees. Michael found the tracks of what seemed to be large deer in the dirt of the forest floor and Cat kept her bow to hand in case they should chance across any. Sometimes there were scufflings and scrabblings beyond the firelight at night, and once the wink of glowing eyes.

They were riding along silently the morning after seeing the eyes when Michael became aware of something up ahead: movement among the trees, distant cries, the first sounds they had heard from voices other than their own in weeks. He and Cat halted at once, dismounting cautiously.

'*Grymyrch*,' Cat hissed.

'Are you sure?' Michael could make out nothing.

'I smell them.'

They crept forward. A dark knot of the creatures was struggling and snarling over something. There were four, perhaps five of them. Michael drew his sword and out of the corner of his eye saw Cat's arm drawing back her bowstring.

A sound of air being sliced, and one of the goblins squawked and tumbled away with an arrow through the back of its neck. The others straightened, and Michael lunged forward with the Ulfberht. He stabbed one fanged, midnight face that already had blood plastering it and it disintegrated. Another he slashed down the spine as it turned to run, and a third he kicked aside as it leapt for his throat, impaling it as it struggled back to its feet. Another arrow took the last one in the eye. Cat swept the surrounding trees with her gaze, another arrow notched and ready, but the wood was silent again. Michael bent and examined what the goblins had been fighting over.

A goat, or what was left of one. The goblins had just about torn it limb from limb. A glint of metal caught Michael's eyes, and he reached into the hairy, sticky mess to pull away a metallic object that rang and clinked in his hand.

A bronze bell, and what remained of a rawhide collar. The goat had been wearing it.

Someone keeping goats in the Wolfweald? He shook his head.

'There are tracks here,' Cat said, staring at the ground around the goblins' bodies. 'They lead off to the west. That is where these came from.' She looked at Michael questioningly, and he nodded.

An hour's careful travelling brought them into an area of woodland they had almost forgotten could exist. The trees were farther apart, and in between them the ground was covered with ferns and briars, yarrow and kingcup, the haze of bluebells close to the ground, primroses in bloom—reminding them that it was spring—and the purple of wood anemones. But most of all there was the light. The canopy overhead had thinned, and the blessed sun poured down on them in a thick stream so that Michael laughed aloud and raised his face to the sky as though drinking it in. Sunshine after these weeks of gloom. It was like a draught of wine.

Cat noticed it first. A faint hint in the air.

'Woodsmoke.'

'Where?'

'Up ahead.'

They dismounted, tethered the horses, who were cropping the good grass greedily, and made their way forward with weapons drawn.

A rude fence, the smell of goats. The trees opened farther. A neat stack of firewood and a bronze-bladed axe. There were small structures dotted about a tiny clearing, some tacked on to the trunks of the immense trees and with bark and turf roofs, like those of the villages farther north, and thick tree limbs for supports. No walls. They were little more than lean-tos, open to the air. One of them could only be a forge, with a squared boulder for an anvil and leather bellows propped beside a stone-built hearth.

They startled a strutting chicken and it clucked crossly at them.

Michael and Cat stared at it hungrily for a second. 'Michael?'

'What?'

'I smell the Brothers' work in this place. It is one of their sanctuaries.'

He raised his eyebrows at her. This deep in the Wolfweald? They halted as one. From the trunk of one of the trees a deep hollow had been carved, and in the hollow was a wooden cross, the bark still clinging to it. Before the tree a man in a woollen robe stood, his back to them and his arms uplifted to the air. Cat raised her bow but lowered it, frowning, at Michael's glare.

They waited, and after what seemed an age the man blessed himself and turned round.

'*Pax vobiscum.*'

They stood, staring. A wild sight, Michael knew they must be, weeks of hard travel and fighting written over them, their clothes thick with mud and in tatters, their hair filthy, the smell of horse and sweat as thick as mist about them—and the sword drawn, the bow strung. He was obscurely embarrassed, as if his grandmother had caught him with a dirty face on a Sunday morning.

The man smiled. He had a round face, as full and rosy as an apple, and his shoulders under the rough habit were as broad as a labourer's. He was short, stocky, and his hands were thick-fingered. He would have looked at home in Antrim digging peat with a flat cap on his head, were it not for the lively intelligence in the eyes, the shrewd lines at their corners. He spread his arms wide.

'Welcome, travellers. You have no need of your weapons here.'

It was as if a great load had slipped from Michael's back. He sheathed the Ulfberht. Cat hesitated, then replaced her arrow in its quiver, though her face remained tight with suspicion.

'I am Brother Nennian,' the man said. 'I have little enough here to offer you, but what I have is yours.'

Water sprang into Michael's mouth at the thought of the goats and the chickens. He felt like a rude savage, a barbarian at the dinner table.

'Thank you,' he said with what gruff grace he could muster. 'We've come a long way.'

[illegible] a great deal had [illegible] which [illegible]
[illegible]
[illegible] were [illegible]

[illegible]

[illegible]

[illegible]

SEVENTEEN

BROTHER NENNIAN HAD a more substantial building farther back in the trees, a long low hut which Michael would have to stoop to enter. A fine rain had begun, misting up the wood and starting a distant thunder as it hit the trees. They saw to the horses first, unsaddling and rubbing them down whilst the Brother silently ladled out what seemed to be a good half-peck of barley grain for them.

Brother Nennian's living hut was not much different to many Michael had seen the tribes construct, but it was cleaner and airier, due partly to the innovation of windows cut in the turf and mud of the walls and glazed with animal stomachs stretched thin. Firewood occupied one corner, a pile of goatskins another and a well-built wooden table a third, with the inevitable cross standing there. In the middle of the place was a sunken hearth in which coals gleamed red, and around it were various utensils, including a surprising number made of bronze, Michael noted, and earthenware vessels of one sort or another. It was dark, stuffy, smoky, smelling of old food and old fires, but the hard earth floor had been swept bare except for the ubiquitous tree roots poking up through it, and none of the vermin usual among the tribe's huts seemed to be in evidence. Michael hoped that he and Cat had not brought too many of their own with them. The warmth was making them more active already.

Cat sat with that green glow in her eyes, her quiver on her back and her face as still as stone. She kept her gaze averted from the cross on the low table, and eyed the clay pots around the fire with a mixture of longing and apprehension.

The Brother deftly resurrected the fire and set a heavy bronze pot on to warm, stirring the contents. The flames lit his face from below, making it at once cherubic and daemonic. Michael could hear the sound of rain on the roof, heavy now, pattering against the cloudy windows.

'Goat stew,' Brother Nennian said suddenly. 'You arrive at a good time. Usually it is porridge, or cheese and bannock, but one of my charges died yesterday and thus she makes her contribution.'

'Was it goblins?' Michael reached into a pocket and brought out the bell, black with dried blood.

Brother Nennian paused. 'That would have been Meif. She was always a one for straying. Yes, the *grymyrch* like to prowl the borders of the sanctuary in the hope of a stray. They have been busy these past few weeks. Something in the wood has agitated them. But do not be afraid. We are safe here.'

'We were not afraid,' Cat said coolly.

Brother Nennian smiled. 'I believe you, child. Anyone who has come as far as you must needs have rope in place of nerves.'

'Anyone who lives alone in the depths of the Wolfweald is not short on them either,' Michael said, making it into a question of sorts.

The Brother inclined his head slightly and stirred the steaming pot. 'We each have our own way of getting by. Me, I have my faith. You, I think,' he said, speaking to Cat, 'have something else. Another blood in your veins, perhaps. It does not make us so very different, believe me.'

'It makes us enemies,' Cat said. Her ears poked through the black hair and her eyes were feline-bright. She looked hardly human. With a sense of shock, Michael realized that he had become accustomed to her appearance. Only now, seeing the quiet, ordinary-looking man stirring his stew, did he grasp how truly strange she appeared.

'I have made you welcome in my home, though I could smell the Wyrim blood in you. Do I not rate some trust in return?' Nennian asked.

'Folk such as you have been persecuting the tribes and the Wyrim for centuries. You think we can easily throw that aside?'

'Cat—' Michael began, but she ignored him.

'We are the Folk of the Forest. What does that make us in your eyes? Even the water of the forest you taint. I can smell what you call the holiness of this place, the thing that keeps the beasts at bay. It does not keep me at bay, holy man, for I am half human, a changeling, and my soul is already forfeit.'

Brother Nennian stared at Cat out of his round face, the humour gone; in its place was something like sadness.

'Child, we three are a mere spark in the darkness of this wood. It would crush us if it could. I see something in you both that should not be there. Maybe it has preserved you thus far, but be careful that in the end it does not destroy you.'

His steady stare fell on Michael, who was sitting mute but tense, prepared to intercept any spring of Cat's. She was crouched like a cornered leopardess, her fingers gouging the dirt floor. Outside the rain had risen to an endless rush and roar. It was beating on the roof like a live thing, a minion of the forest striving to batter its way inside.

'You,' the Brother said to Michael. 'You are not of this world, though something of it is in you. I sense an old piety in you, my friend. Can you not tell your lady that I mean her no harm?'

'It's true, Cat. He's telling the truth, I'm sure of it.'

Cat glared at him, her pupils black vertical bars in the green blaze of her eyes.

'Please, lass.' He took the savage face in his hands, searching for the girl he loved. She struggled and one hand fastened on his wrist, trying to pull him away. Once she would have succeeded, but despite his recent weakness the forest had bred strength into him and she could not. He kissed her, pulled her head down on to his shoulder and felt her shudder.

'It's all right,' he murmured. 'We're all right here.'

He heard the rain slacken outside, and knew that somehow the moment had passed. Mirkady's gift was double-edged, he thought.

'Don't let him do anything to the food,' Cat muttered. 'I'm hungry.'

'Plain fare it is then, unblessed and untouched,' Brother Nennian said. 'Eat with me, and be welcome no matter who or what you are. There are not so many travellers in this part of the world that I can be choosy as to the company I keep.' His smile was back again, and the appetizing smell of the steaming food was wafting through the length of the hut.

THERE WERE TURNIPS and cabbage in the stew, bannock and buttermilk to follow, and they ate in silence whilst the sound of the rain dwindled. The afternoon was waning, the light that came in at the windows fading into blue. They heard a wolf howl off in the wood, the first since leaving the Fox-People, and Michael started, fearing for the horses, but Brother Nennian shook his head.

'Nothing will enter the sanctuary that I do not wish to. Your animals, and mine, are protected.'

'How do you come to be here, alone so deep in the wood? This wood, especially.'

Brother Nennian chewed on a bannock. 'I came here a long time ago, and I was not alone. I had a young novice with me, but he has left. If he is alive, he should be in the Woods of Men again by now.'

Michael remembered the tortured corpse he and Cat had found by the Fox-People's camp, but said nothing. He could feel the brother's stare on him, though.

'Why the Wolfweald?'

'I am alone here, and I love the great trees: it is a good place to stay and think. Also, I have long wanted to find out the fate of an expedition sent here many years ago. I roam the woods looking for traces of it sometimes. And sometimes I have found old bones that have never been buried, but lie half sunk in the leaf mulch.'

Brother Nennian did not seem disposed to explain farther, but Michael was sure he had not told them everything. There was something else, something more which had led or driven the man here.

'You too are a long way into the Wolfweald,' the Brother said. 'A long way from home as well, if I do not miss my guess.' His eyes flicked to Michael's sword.

'Maybe.'

'Two things keep a man alive in this place. Faith, or the forest magic. I wonder often if the two do not blur together. Our Lord was hung on a tree, after all. And two things bring a man here. Either he is fleeing something, or pursuing it. Those two also have a way of blurring together in the Wolfweald; the hunter becoming the hunted. It is a strange place. The roots of these trees are deep. They go to the centre of the world. There is wisdom here, for those who are hardy enough to look for it, or lucky enough to find it. And power. There is so much power that most of the beasts cannot endure it.'

'Some endure it,' Cat said unexpectedly. 'Some are born out of it.'

'Indeed?'

'The Wyrim say that the forest is the Horseman's bride, and they are children of both him and the trees, part of the land itself.'

'And you, my child, what do you believe you are?' the Brother asked with great gentleness.

Cat glared hotly back at him. 'I told you, I am nothing. I am what the Wyrim call a halfling and the villagers call a changeling.'

'It cannot be easy, being caught between two worlds.'

Cat did not reply. She ducked her head toward her bowl of buttermilk with surprising docility. The Brother regarded Michael again, and again took in the long length of the Ulfberht.

'A soldier by the looks of you, and yet something about you tells me you are not. The tribes still have something of the soldier in them: a pride, a hardiness not seen even among the Knights of the Church... You have encountered them, our Knights Militant?'

'I know of them,' Michael said curtly. He was beginning to distrust this holy man. 'Are our answers the payment for your hospitality?'

Brother Nennian seemed genuinely pained. 'Forgive me. I find I am prying. It is a hazard I run when I meet so few folk in this part of the world. I glean what I can from them, to digest when I am alone again.'

They finished their meal in silence, the blue evening deepening outside and the air loud with the sound of water pittering down from the treetops. The fire lit up their faces, becoming brighter as the light fled. Again Michael heard a wolf call in the gathering dusk. It sounded desolate. A lonely soul, lost in the deep woods.

Cat helped the Brother to wash up with an odd defiance, as if she dared him to contradict her. She brushed away the trickle of wet that was starting to crawl in the doorway and replaced the wooden sill. Outside, the beaten dirt of the clearing was awash with rainwater, puddles shining in the firelight that spilled from the windows. Wind stirred the water into restless rings. Michael saw the two horses standing resting under a lean-to, a line of movement off in the twilight where the goats shifted in their pen and the flutter of the chickens nesting under the eaves of another hut. The coming night seemed peaceful. He might have been in any part of the Wildwood—except for the immenseness of the trees.

How could a man live here, year after year, with nothing but the seasons and the changing weather to mark the time? He had thought once that this journey would be an idyll of sorts, with castles and knights, fairies and goblins. It had not quite turned out that way.

He remembered home, the farm. It seemed so long ago.

Another world.

For two pins, he thought with sudden vehemence, I'd go back now. Leave the whole thing behind and go home, forget about fairies.

And Cat? And Rose?

Things were not as neat and tidy as that. This place lapped over into the world he called his own. That was why he was here, in the end. He was not merely a tourist.

To his surprise, when he turned back to the interior of the hut, he found Brother Nennian smoking a long clay pipe, much chipped and blackened. The holy man grinned, showing square teeth with black gaps between them.

'A weakness of mine, the weed. I grow it, though a small, withered offering it is.'

Michael remembered Mullan's beautiful Peterson, red as fresh blood. The Brother's smoke was surprisingly fragrant. He mixed herbs with it, he told them, and soaked the whole in honey to flavour it. He had skeps of his own farther along the clearing. Bees were one thing the Forest-Folk always respected. Except for the bears, and they were rare here. A troll had sat at the edge of the hallowed ground the whole of one morning and had told him a tale in return for a comb of honey. And the beeswax made the best candles in the world. (Here he gestured to the slim palenesses on a shelf near the low ceiling.) But for some talk, the firelight was best.

'Sitting here alone of an evening, with only the fire and the trees for company,' he mused, 'I know that I am not a good priest. It comes to me. My faith is strong enough to keep the beast at bay, if it is faith indeed. But I wonder sometimes if it is not also a love of the wood, for all its horrors. To live here with no man to speak to, in this deep, black forest, this for me is peace... Maybe it is even prayer.' He looked keenly at Cat. 'You speak the truth about the place, you and your people. The wood is alive, especially here in the Weald. It remembers things.'

A picture of Rose asprawl in the leaves, a man atop her.

Michael lowered his head. The Brother continued:

'I have seen the end of the Brothers' first expedition here, on gloomy days. I have watched their last stand about the cross as the goblins slew them. I have seen the unholy feast that followed. And I have seen the Horseman watching over it.'

The Brother's face had darkened. Despite the round goodwill of his features, he seemed grim, forbidding, the firelight carving his visage into canyons of brightness and shadow.

'He comes here now and again, sits on his horse at the edge of the clearing and watches me at my work. No prayer or cross of mine will shift him. I have seen him in the dead of night when the moon is up, and there are werewolves fawning around his steed, goblins black and silent at his back. He sits watching. But then I think of the wood's memories that I have seen: my own people butchered like cattle, corpses by the score defiled and mutilated, and it steels me. I can stand there with that faceless stare on me, kneel scant yards from him and pray... My pipe is out.'

He bent to relight the long pipe with a twig from the fire, and in the stillness they cocked their heads to listen. Something on the wind, far away. Nennian puffed smoke placidly but his eyes were chiselled glints under his brow.

'Him,' he said, so low it was almost a whisper.

Hoofbeats, far away but getting closer. A horse galloping. 'Speak of the Devil and he will surely appear,' Michael murmured, an old saw his grandfather had used.

Nearer now, and they looked up towards the roof as they realized that the hoofs were beating on the empty air above their heads, on a level with the canopy of the trees. For a moment it seemed as though they were directly overhead, a soft thunder, and Michael thought the roof trembled. Then they were receding again, dying into the wood.

Nennian chuckled. 'Most nights he passes by, on the way to his castle. I am a thorn in his flesh, I believe. An itch he cannot yet scratch.'

'His castle?' Michael repeated. He could feel Cat's stare on him, the green eyes luminous and inhuman.

'Yes. It is not so very far from here. I saw it, once, through the mists that enshroud it. A black place, high as a small mountain, with the trees thick and tangled round its foot. I tried to approach it, but grew afraid and my faith faltered. I had to retreat. There is a dread sorrow in that place, and power. It is as though the earth were split open there, and all the blackest of its magic were oozing slowly out—and the castle the scab on the wound. And yet... and yet—'

He stopped.

'That is where you go, is it not? To the Castle of the Horseman?'

Cat laid a hand on Michael's arm as if to silence him, but he spoke up.

'Yes. That is where we go. We have an errand there.'

'An errand.' The humour came back into the Brother's eyes. 'A very high one I'm thinking, to bring you this far to the edge of life.'

'Indeed.'

The fire cracked and spat, faggots falling into its molten heart.

Brother Nennian opened his mouth around his pipe.

'You are welcome to be my guests for as long as you please, to build up your strength for what lies ahead.' But he kept his gaze in the fire, and Michael had the impression that for a moment he had been about to say something else.

Morning arrived grey and dripping, the clearing a bare patch of mud with only the print of Brother Nennian's sandals marking it. Michael felt fuzzy-headed and dull, the results of sleeping under a roof for the first time in weeks. Through the window he could see Nennian feeding his animals, a skin bag slung round his shoulders and a cloud of chickens following him hopefully, the cock crowing the morning in again and again. The horses were nosing at a log trough with gusto, their breath a plume of steam in the cold air. Winter was in full retreat, but here it seemed to be leaving a rearguard behind, fighting for every day.

Cat nuzzled the back of Michael's neck, tiptoeing to reach.

Her hand, warm from the furs, slipped down the front of his breeches to cup him there. He swelled at the touch of her fingers, but pulled away.

'Don't, Cat. Not here.'

'What's wrong? Is this place too holy for you?'

'It's not right, with him here. This is his home, and he's a priest.'

She laughed without humour, patted his bulging crotch and went to pack their things.

'Are we leaving today?' she asked.

He stared out at the clearing. A mist hung in the tops of the trees, drifting in swathes as thick as muslin. He could smell more rain in the air, and his body ached with sickness and wounds. He felt old, indecently old, worn as a cast-off shoe. He wanted to slip back into the furs and sleep the grey morning away.

'No. We'll stay for today. The horses could do with the rest.'

'The horses,' she repeated sardonically. 'Of course.'

'Oh, shut up,' he whispered wearily.

They had honey on their bannock for breakfast, a treat which even Cat savoured. Nennian turned aside for a moment to say grace over his own food whilst Cat wolfed down hers. Michael tried to eat his in a more leisurely fashion, but even so he was long finished when the Brother was still munching. Nennian doled them out fresh bannock without a word, refilling their mugs with foaming buttermilk. The taste brought memories of crowded breakfasts by the warm range in Antrim, the farm hands clumping in and out. But they were distant, like pictures seen through a grimy window.

'I took the liberty of examining your sword while you slept,' Nennian said through mouthfuls of bannock.

'What for?'

'The edges are blue and discoloured. That is because it needs quenching. The iron in it is going soft.'

'So?'

'So I will quench it for you. I have a forge here of sorts, and I can get a good flame going.'

Michael examined the Ulfberht. The lovely lithe lines of the pattern welding were like a swirl of water on its surface. He had read of it a long time ago. Bars of iron were twisted together and heated repeatedly to drive as much carbon as possible out of the metal and to make it similar to steel. But the metal needed occasional 'quenchings' to keep its hardness.

'All right,' he said.

Cat would have nothing to do with the forge, and instead wandered about the clearing talking to the animals whilst Michael helped the holy man stoke up a fire out of charcoal. Then Nennian spent half an hour piling up a mound of wet clay—there was plenty after the night's rain—and measuring it against the sword blade.

'A notch here I could hammer out, and the blade is a little out of true. It has seen hard service, this weapon.' He ran a finger down the edge appreciatively, for a moment wholly a craftsman, the other part of him hidden. His habit was covered by a leather apron and his face was aglow with exertion in the cold, as red-cheeked as Santa Claus.

'It was a Knight's weapon. I killed him,' Michael said, tired of the game.

'I know.'

Nennian set the blade in the charcoals and Michael began pumping the crude leather bellows. The stone hearth became a little sun of white and red heat in the mist of the cold morning and soon Michael was sweating, his forehead hot and the heat soaking through his jerkin. Cat was singing somewhere across the clearing. The coals flared and blazed.

'Enough.'

Nennian hooked the blade out of the fire and slapped it down on his stone anvil. He took a surprisingly small bronze hammer and began tapping gently, his face close to the white-hot edges of the blade. Sparks jumped, but he ignored them. He squinted and examined, his face shining with sweat, then replaced the blade in the coals and wiped his temples. Michael began plying the bellows again.

'How do you know?'

The Brother smiled: his natural expression, Michael was coming to think. 'No one save the Knights and a few nobles has a weapon as fine as this. Ulfberht died a generation ago. These things become heirlooms, the sword passing from father to son. I could name you perhaps three families with a sword such as this.'

'You don't seem bothered that I killed a Knight of your church.'

'I am always bothered by bloodshed, but you do not strike me as the murdering type. Our Knights can be overzealous at times. You and your lady have the look of people who have lived among the tribes. My guess is that you maybe became embroiled in a tangle that was not your own.'

'Maybe we did,' Michael admitted.

Once again the sword was hooked out of the fire, and this time Brother Nennian plunged it into the mound of clay he had built up. There was a hiss and bubble and a small spume of steam rose up. The Brother regarded it with satisfaction.

'Water forms a barrier of steam too easily, and the metal does not cool down rapidly enough. Clay is better, and urine, also. And some say the best quencher of all is blood.'

Michael wiped the sweat from his eyes. The forge fire was a blare of heat, shimmering the air.

'Why did you really come to the Wolfweald?'

'I might ask you the same question. I might also ask you where you came *from*.'

'As far as I can guess'—and this time it was Michael who smiled—'I come from the same place that you Brothers first came from. A place called Ireland.'

It had taken a while for him to realize, but he was convinced now that it was true. These monks or priests were from his own world, all right, and his own country, too. The angular tonsure, more complete than that of British monks of the period, proved it. A long-past century had bred them—perhaps that of the Viking raids—but they had slipped through a door as easily as he had, a community of them fleeing the Norsemen, perhaps. The stories he had heard thus far in the Wildwood said that they had been fleeing something or someone.

Brother Nennian digested this in silence for a long while, retrieving the sword from the day and replacing it in the fire. He tapped his hammer on the stone anvil, his round face closed.

'What do you hope to do at his castle?'

'I'm looking for someone from my own world. He took her there, I'm sure. He has her soul.'

The Brother's eyes quickened at that, but he retrieved the blade without a word and plunged it into the clay again. Cat was still singing, walking with a crowd of chickens at her feet and feeding them with barley grain.

'So you bear this Horseman no love? You or your lady?'

Michael was puzzled. 'Of course not. Who does?'

Nennian stared across at the slim, dark girl singing near the trees. She had stripped off much of her heavy clothing and her arms were bare. She looked like some long-limbed animal, a beautiful gazelle. Her hair had swung to cover the pointed tips of her ears and in the daylight the fire of her eyes was less pronounced.

'She comes of two worlds, your lady, and the deeper she travels into this wood the more she will be drawn to the world of the trees and the Horseman. I have seen things in the wood's memories. The Wyrim and the *grymyrch* fighting side by side, wolves and Tree-Folk at each other's shoulders, to expel what was the first expedition. This near to the centre of things the differences fall away. It is as she said: they are children of the same father. It is what has preserved you both, I think.'

'I am not one of them. I can't even drink the water in this wood.'

Nennian smiled his customary smile, warm but faintly condescending. 'Yet the blood of the Wyrim flows in you also. It has not yet taken root, but it is there.'

Wyr-fire. Michael shook his head helplessly. 'What are you saying? That when we reach the castle we'll be mere minions of the Horseman, glorified goblins?'

'No. Not you. You have, as I said, an old piety in you that goes deep. But the lady there...'

Michael grabbed him by his apron and shook him, but the holy man did not blink. 'What do you want, *Brother*?'

'To come with you.'

Michael released him, not wholly surprised. 'Why?'

'We can help each other, you and I. Your lady's Wyrim blood will get us to the castle and my faith may help preserve the human side of her when we reach it. We can confront the Devil in his lair.'

'That's it. That's why you came to the Wolfweald. To confront the Horseman.'

'Yes. But I am not strong enough on my own, and my novice was a young fool, a coward of little faith.'

'He's dead.'

'I don't doubt it.'

'For a priest, you don't strike me as being too holy.'

'I am *holy* enough to have survived in this wood. And I know the way to the castle. I can guide you there. Without me you might wander the wood till you die of old age, or until the Horseman is ready to receive you. He controls the paths of all who walk here, unless they have the faith.'

'*Faith!*'

'Yes. Faith. It has kept me alive here for twelve years, a broken, limping thing at times, but still potent. *Let me come with you.* It can do no harm, and may do great good.'

'You would set yourself against him, would you? Now there's hubris... Cat would never let you come.'

'Tell her I am to be your guide, no more.'

Michael hesitated. He thought of the changes in Cat, the way she seemed to be metamorphosing into something else. He wanted it to stop. He did not want her against him if he ever made it to the damned castle in the end. The thought was more than he could bear.

And yet he was sure he did not trust Brother Nennian. He had not come this far to be a mere means to someone else's end.

'I'll see what Cat thinks,' he said at last.

Brother Nennian bowed slightly, then with one swift movement drew the Ulfberht out of its bed of clay. He thumbed the edge.

'It would draw blood from the wind now. A weapon fit for a Crusader.'

MICHAEL FOUND CAT with the horses. The brief rest was already filling them out, though Fancy had a tendency to gorge herself. Nennian's hay had been dampened by the winter's rain and had little goodness in it. Cat doled out the Brother's barley grain as though it were water, and Michael had to restrain her; too much of the stuff would give their mounts colic. It was rich after the short commons of the previous weeks.

They stood leaning on a rail very like a hitching post before the horses' lean-to whilst the mist vapour thickened and beaded Cat's hair with grey drops. It made spiders' webs into tangible, jewel-like things and hid the tops of the tallest trees so that they might have been beans talks racing up through cloud to some giant's castle above.

Cat was goosepimpled, and Michael embraced her from behind, burying his nose in her hair.

'So you are not so shy now in this holy place? Has the priest given his permission, then?' But she relaxed in his arms, tilting her head back so he was able to kiss the side of her neck.

'We'll leave soon,' he said, his voice muffled by her flesh.

'Mmm.'

'Brother Nennian is coming with us.'

'*What?*' She pulled out of his arms and faced him. 'What did you say?'

Tiredly, he told her that the Brother knew the way. He would be their guide, no more. Otherwise they would be wandering until the Horseman was ready to receive them.

'Why is he so charitable to us, knowing what I am? He wants something, Michael. It is in his eyes. He is not offering to do this for nothing.'

'Maybe. But we need him, Cat. We can use his help.' Seeing this did not convince her, he said: 'We'll leave him behind once we sight the castle. We'll lose him in the forest. He won't come the whole way.'

She seemed slightly mollified.

'What's happening to you, Cat?'

'What do you mean?'

'Nothing, nothing.' Again that weariness, the sense of years piled on his shoulders before they had any right to be there.

Cat touched his beard gently. Her eyes had softened. 'You're grey, my lovely boy, all grey and grown. The wood has made you into a man, a warrior. You belong to it now, Michael.'

It's killing me, he snarled silently, but he bent his head to receive her kiss and she pressed her body against him. Hard and soft, bone and breast. He wanted to bury himself inside her and forget about castles and quests, horsemen and goblins.

And the wood. He wanted to forget about that most of all, and scrape the gathering moss from his memory.

EIGHTEEN

ANOTHER NIGHT IN the smoky hut, a meal composed of the last of the goat stew. Michael woke the next morning with the bright rectangle of the window a lambent blur in his sleep-gummed eyes. Cat was in his arms, their bodies a tangle of limbs and raven hair. He blew dust from her eyelashes gently, saw it dance and glow in the sunshine that poured through the door, and smiled with simple, momentary happiness.

It was cold, sharp and frosty. He got up and looked outside, stretching. The mud of the clearing had frozen hard, the puddles iced over, though where the sun hit them there was only a shimmer of ice thin enough to be broken by a spider's foot. Mist again, but it was a hazy, gossamer thing this morning lit by the sun. It hung in a broad band halfway up the trees and their tops were crystal clear against the pale blue sky, their trunks the washed-out colour of a pastel painting. As he watched he saw a heron take flight from the stream at the far end of the glade, the great wings wide. Brother Nennian was talking to his goats in a low voice, the sound carrying like a bell in the stillness. After a while he came trudging back to the living hut leading what looked like a large donkey and carrying a rough basket.

'Eggs for breakfast,' he said, grinning.

They started off in the middle of the morning, the food warm in their bellies, and set the sun in their left eye. Within an hour the character of the forest had changed again, and the sun was cut off. Michael's heart sank as the early light was lost, hidden by the encroaching treetops, and the forest floor became bare and dark once more. He felt he was riding into some endless cavern that went deeper and deeper into the heart of the world, a tunnel without end.

Their saddles were piled and hung with supplies. Bannock, honey, cheese, smoked meat and dried vegetables as well as skins of the blessed water which Cat could not drink and a pouch of the Brother's fragrant tobacco. Nennian's donkey, a patient, flea-bitten creature, clanged and clanged as they ambled along, irritating Michael. There was a copper pot and various bronze implements hanging from its pommel. Brother Nennian looked like a tinker on his travels.

'What about the animals?' Cat had asked him coldly as they left the sunlight of the hollow behind. Nennian had opened the goat pen before they left.

'They will wander, but there is good grass in the dell and most of them know well enough not to stray into the deep part of the forest. The billy will keep them together, and I have left caches of barley grain here and there. The chickens are good at fending for themselves.'

'You'll have a lean time of it for a while when you return,' she told him.

'Everyone must make sacrifices.'

TRAVELLING AGAIN. THE rhythm of movement claimed them once more as though they had never paused in Nennian's sanctuary. They had strayed off the direct route south to find his clearing, and now the rotund Brother led the way, taking them back on the southward path, but as far as Michael could make out veering off it after a while to the south-east. Within a day Michael's navigation was based on glimpses of the stars and surmise, though the priest led them clanking onwards without faltering, as though the lair of the Horseman were a beacon standing high and bright in the distance.

Little things irked Michael. He was constrained with Cat in Nennian's presence, and to her frustration could not make love to her in the nights beside the fire. In the mornings they were delayed by the Brother as he said mass for himself off to one side, and Michael felt oddly distanced from the ceremony, as though it were a fossil he had left buried behind him. He had enough belated piety in him to quiet Cat's protests and let the priest pray undisturbed, though it cost them travelling time.

He and Nennian ate well, though for some reason—bloody-mindedness, perhaps—Cat insisted on foraging for food, and they looked somewhat askance at her forest roots and skinned frogs. Only the honey could tempt her, and she would wolf down a sticky bannock with relish, refusing everything else and drinking the forest water without fear. It was as if the trees had claimed her once more, and she was slipping into the ways of the wood now that the transient civilization of the sanctuary had been left behind. It worried Michael. When be lay beside her in the nights he could almost believe she was changing in her sleep, shifting in his very arms. She would twitch and shake, and sometimes he thought he heard her snarl.

Mirkady's gift, he thought. It had not been as generous as it seemed. Occasionally he thought he could feel it working in his own flesh, making him loathe the stocky priest on his donkey and causing the clean water to bubble in his throat.

The signs of life they had noticed on approaching Nennian's glade disappeared, and the forest became an empty, stark place, a hall with a thick-raftered roof upheld by the pillars of the trees. Spring was beaten back here, and they travelled in a never changing dark of winter, the cold air moving in trapped eddies and currents under the canopy, the leaf mold on the ground, millennia of autumns, degenerating into thick mud that sucked at the horses' hoofs and exhausted them so the travellers had to dismount and pull the weary beasts along by their bridles ankle deep, calf deep, sometimes knee deep in black glutinous ooze. It did not take very many days for the neat and plump Brother Nennian to begin to take on what Michael had come to think of as the wanderer look. His cheeks seemed to fall in on themselves and the mud-thick habit became looser around the stomach. He stuffed his sandals with rags against the cold and his eyes seemed to sink in his head. Cat took a grim satisfaction out of this transformation, as if it were evidence that the holy man's magic was not proof against the power of the forest.

Their camps at night became at once hugely desirable and achingly uncomfortable. They were tired enough to sleep where they fell at the end of the short daylight, but had the horses to see to, a fire to coax out of sodden wood, the worst of the sludge to sluice off. The trunks of the trees ran with moisture, bringing out the mites that infested the bark—blind, white, burrowing things with painful bites. The travellers lay with the wet soaking through the furs—furs which were themselves hard with caked dirt and reeking of mould—and focused their eyes on their guttering campfire before dropping off. Watches were kept, each of them waking and watching for several hours every night. Michael had a suspicion that Nennian slept through most of his, though he was so in need of sleep himself that he was never able to remain awake and test the theory.

They spoke little, eating their food silently in the evenings, Cat dining on toadstools which clustered at the foot of the trees in scarlet profusion. They looked deadly, but she consumed them with something near relish and drank the reeking water of the stagnant ponds without coming to any harm. It was as if she were made to exist in such a place, or it was made for her.

'Damned if I know why they call it the Wolfweald,' Michael said. 'The place has fewer wolves, fewer of anything, than anywhere else I've ever been in this place. There's nothing here. Nothing.'

'There are the trees,' Cat told him, her eyes ashine in the gloom.

They were sitting in the dark, the tinder having defeated their attempts at lighting it. The horses were shifting and blowing through their noses a few yards away and further still they could hear Brother Nennian murmuring his devotions. There was a faint rush and hiss of wind in the treetops, but no other sound in the forest.

Michael wondered if the first expedition had come so far. He doubted it. There was hardly any forage for horses here, let alone cattle. There was nothing a sane man could do in such a place, except cut down the trees to let some light in. Michael was beginning to hate the trees, but he kept that to himself because he could see the awe and reverence with which Cat regarded them.

The Wyr-fire was there, inside them both. Michael had a feeling he could live on toadstools and stagnant water as easily as Cat, if he only surrendered to the wood; but he preferred to eke out the last of Nennian's supplies and keep his mind his own.

The priest finished his prayers and rejoined them. He was shivering as he sat, though his face was impassive, calm. Not once had he seemed at a loss for the right path in their travelling, even in the thickest of the swamp or the blackest part of the wood. It was as if he had some kind of internal compass, its needle pointing infallibly at their goal. Michael was getting to the point where he did not care whether they reached it or not, as long as they returned to clean beds and decent food again.

'How much farther?' he asked Nennian, as he had been asking often these past few days. The sanctuary was almost two weeks behind them and there was no sign of the wood changing.

The Brother's expression was hard to read in the dim light, but Michael could hear the uncertainty in his voice.

'Farther than I had thought. It took me a week of travelling to come within sight of it the last time I tried. We are on the right path. I cannot be mistaken about that. I can feel the power of the place like some black sun beating on my face. But it seems to be retreating, or the forest is growing larger even as we traverse it... I don't know.'

He sounded weary and baffled, his ready smile in ashes. Cat snorted in disgust.

'Is this some will-o'-the-wisp in a brown habit we are following, or is he just leading us on a grand tour of the Wolfweald?'

'Cat,' Michael said warningly, but he was too cast down by Nennian's uncertainty to argue. All this time he had been telling himself that it was not far, that they were nearly there. Now they could be a thousand miles away. He could have howled with frustration and despair.

'We were better on our own. We made better time, and the forest hardly minded us. Now that he is here it is watching us, our every step. Can you not feel it?'

Michael thought he could. It was a silent regard, an eyeless stare that made him hunch his shoulder blades as though expecting a blow between them. There was something in the air of the Wolfweald that made it heavy to draw into the lungs, like the opposite of high altitudes. Thick air, leaden with dislike, dripping with power.

'I feel nothing,' Nennian said. 'I have lived in this place for a dozen years and I have never felt such a thing. The Wolfweald knows me, and I know it.'

'You are a fool,' Cat said contemptuously, and Michael thought he saw the priest's face tighten with anger.

'Stop it,' he said, angry himself at their bickering. 'How much longer will your supplies last?' This to Nennian, who was a tense crouched shape, the habit making him look like a moss-covered boulder.

'Water for two, maybe three days. Food for another four.'

'Toadstools and pondwater.' Cat laughed. 'You'll be sinking them soon, unless you'd like to try chewing your sandals!'

'Shut up,' Michael hissed, and surprised them with the venom in his voice. 'No more arguing. We boil the forest water as soon as we can get a fire lit, and we eat anything we can find. Beetles if need be. But we keep going, even if it means riding south to those high mountains that are supposed to be on the other end of this damned place. All forests finish, and we'll get to where we're going even if we end up eating the horses and walking our feet down to the bones.'

His outburst seemed to subdue his companions and Cat's back was turned resolutely towards him that night, but he did not care.

He could sense the tendrils and shoots of the wood worming their way into him, infiltrating his will, and the effort of shutting them out was exhausting him as much as the endless travelling. The wood was telling him to abandon the Brother, to leave him here where the trees could take him. It urged him to wander without a path, to let the weald resculpt him in a more fitting form for the meeting that was coming. Sometimes he thought its voice was an actual sound, an audible whisper that carried above the creak of tree trunks. He had to abandon himself to the Other Place and forget all that he had learned in his former life. He must forget about Ireland, about home, about mass on Sunday and the bustle of a surrounding family. He was merely an orphan in between parents, and he needed the wood in his veins to be accepted within it. *Give up; give in*, it said. Drowning is easier if you do not struggle. You will find your goal the quicker, and be a happy man at journey's end. The message was as persistent and annoying as tinnitus.

The ground under the trees rose and fell as they continued, becoming a range of wooded hills and giving them drier campsites. Here and there patches of moss-covered stone thrust out of the humus and dead leaves like the bones of the land pushing through decaying skin. Nennian was convinced that these heights were the foothills of the terrible southern mountains, and that they were near to the edge of the forest. It could not be far, he told them, with something of the old confidence back in his voice. Cat ignored him, and even Michael paid him little heed.

The trees grew strange. They diminished in height, though their roof was as thick as ever. They looked as though they had contracted some leprous disease. Instead of soaring straight up they twisted and curved like arthritic fingers, and the bark had dropped off them in places, scab-like, revealing black wood underneath. Their roots crept and crawled over the thinning earth, coiling around stones. They had become contorted, tortured things clawing for life, and Michael's imagination conjured the misshapen trunks into mottled faces and bodies, distorted limbs.

'Can you feel it?' Cat asked in a whisper. Her face was full of awe.

'Feel what?' Nennian demanded irritably.

'The power here, thrumming in the air. Even the trees cannot stand it. It's like a hot air. Michael, can you feel it?'

He could. It was like the light tapping of a drum in his temples, a far whisper. The wood was alive and watching them. He felt that they had wandered into the maw of some gargantuan beast, a whole land become sentient and cunning. And hostile. It leached the strength from his limbs and sucked out what courage he possessed, so that he might have been seven again, seeing the dark shapes crossing the river at twilight, the fear rising to block his throat.

'Mother of God,' he murmured. Brother Nennian was reciting Latin in a low voice.

Their camp was at the base of a rocky bluff, the fire reflecting off wet stone and lighting up a tiny semicircle of the world. Around them was the darkness, the wood, and in the night they could feel the presence of the trees as though they were a vast silent crowd of onlookers, baleful and disapproving. They were *alive*. Michael could think of no other word to explain it.

'We are close, here. Very close,' Nennian said, staring at his unlit pipe. Cat was calming their mounts at the edge of light, whispering in their ears and wiping the rank terror sweat from their flanks.

'Did you not pass through this region when you approached the castle?' Michael asked him.

'No. It is... it is new to me, this place, but I have followed the path I took then, I swear. It is as if the forest could move and shift, the land itself change.'

'He doesn't want us to find him,' Michael said. 'He's delaying us, letting the trees work for him. Do you think your people got this far?'

Nennian shifted his eyes to the encroaching darkness, as thick as felt. 'I do not see how they could. I think we have passed the site of their last battle. It must be well to the north of us. I think no man has ever come this far. It is an unholy place.'

There was silence for a while, and Cat rejoined them. Though the atmosphere had dampened her spirits slightly, she seemed far less apprehensive than either Michael or Brother Nennian. She chewed on a toadstool impassively, and for a moment Michael hated her for not sharing their dread.

The night passed with little sleep, no real rest despite the fact that the woods were as still as an old grave. Their travelling continued uninterrupted, the supplies dwindling. When the water gave out they began boiling the noisome trickle of the forest streams, and when the food ended Cat caught them small creatures to eat. Nennian refused them at first, and even Michael's hardened stomach balked at the tiny carcasses of mice and newts, the glistening hide of the great snails that slimed along the damp stones, but soon they began to look more appetizing and the goat stew, the buttermilk and honey of Nennian's sanctuary became a dream, a brightness at the back of Michael's mind. His belly contracted and he could almost feel the slow but inevitable shrinkage of the muscles that padded his frame, whilst Nennian's face began to take on the aspect of a skull. Only Cat continued to thrive, though her body became more spare, the bones at the back of her hands more prominent.

The horses had trouble bearing the weight of their riders, and so they walked in file leading them. Only Nennian's donkey was still in fair condition, for it could stomach tree bark more readily than Fancy or the grey. It and Nennian took the lead every day, picking their way up steep, rocky slopes that were nonetheless choked with the stunted trees, or wading through the black sludge that accumulated in the hollows between the high places.

Twenty-six days out of Nennian's sanctuary the rain started again, pouring from the overhead branches and reducing the ground to something like soup. They staggered through it with their eyes fixed on the tail of the steed to the front, sometimes grasping its tail to help them through the thickening mud. Often they had to congregate around one of the two horses to lever and shove it out of the mire, pulling free the embedded hoofs and beating the poor beast onwards. They slipped and slid, falling often and covering themselves with black, tar-like sludge, while the rain continued to pour down without stint. For Michael it assumed the aspect of a nightmare, something that could not possibly be real. He was so tired that even the discomforts he was suffering were far away, back behind the looming need for rest, real sleep, a chance to close his eyes. The tiredness became a physical pain, and he had to fight to keep himself from sobbing aloud as he tottered onwards.

The rain filled the forest with noise, a rushing roar of water hitting the canopy and streaming down from the trees. It ran down his face unheeded, dripping from his nose and filling his eyes. He tried opening his mouth and drinking it in, but it proved to be as filthy as the forest water, bringing with it the taste of the leaves it fell upon. He spat it out, grimacing.

Nennian had halted before what seemed to be an impenetrable thicket of trees and saplings. The priest was bent over clutching his knees, his chest heaving. Michael staggered to his side as Cat came up, dragging the grey after her. Black hair was plastered over her face, giving her a wild look.

'We can't go on,' the Brother was gasping, the roar of the rain almost drowning out his words. 'We must stop, rest.'

'There's nowhere to rest. The ground is too wet. We can't. We have to get to higher ground,' Michael found himself saying, though he too craved a halt, a pause in their agonizing progress.

'I can't... can't do it. Sweet Jesus...'

Even as they spoke the waters that puddled the surface of the mud were joining up, becoming a lake. The ground seemed to be liquefying under their feet, sucking at their legs. Michael had never seen such rain. It was like a barrage. It stunned the senses. Already the trees were losing limbs. Twigs were floating thick in the widening pools and in the midst of the water's roar they could hear the rend and shriek of breaking branches, weak limbs being battered away. Flooding would come next as the rain poured down off the hills that surrounded them.

'Michael!' It was Cat, tugging at his arm. 'The trees! Look at the trees!'

'What is it?' He squinted past the rain in his eyes, knuckled it away impatiently. What was she wanting now?

Faces. Faces in the bark.

'Holy God!' He squelched forward with her and left Nennian bent towards the mud. The tree trunks were knobbed and gnarled, shining with wet, but their rough ridges and contours were recognizable as features, faces set in expressions of terror and agony. If he looked closer he could see the vague outlines of hands, arms, legs, an impression of clothing—but the faces were the most clear. Mouths gaped and screamed, the rainwater overflowing from them, and the eyes wept as drops filled their hollows. It was as if men had been engulfed by the wood, fossilized like dinosaurs in rock strata.

The topmost branches began to sway and reach in a gathering wind and drops were flung so hard through the air that they stung Michael's cheeks. He found it hard to see and the air he breathed seemed devoid of oxygen.

'This is what became of the last of Nennian's kind,' Cat was shouting, and there was a strange kind of exultation in her voice.

The wind strengthened. The forest bent and roared, the trees swaying like reeds under the growing gale. Michael felt stupefied. The wind was level with his eyes, sweeping under the treetops and lashing spray from the deepening lake that was the forest floor. He had the impression that the birthing storm was contained within the wood itself, that it was the trees which were whipping up the current. It was waxing by the moment, becoming a shriek of mad, blasting air. Twigs smote him in the face and he shielded his eyes, knocked back a step. His hand lighted upon one of the wooden faces as he swayed and he snatched it away again in revulsion. Then he was *pushed* by the wind, shoved backwards. He sprawled into the water and the muck as it detonated in wind-driven packets all about him.

'Cat! Help me!'

He wallowed in the mud and felt Cat's strong grip on his arm. A bough from a nearby tree splashed into the water and blinded him.

'He's coming, Cat. It is him doing this!'

It was their storm, raised for them alone. As Nennian had once said, things in the Wolfweald had a way of turning around. They were no longer hunters, if they had ever been.

Cat was staring into his face from six inches, trying to make out his words. But her eyes had changed. They had narrowed to thin slits and angled up towards her hairline at their corners. A green fire spilled out of them. Her ears had become as long as horns. She was grinning, and her teeth seemed to stretch across her entire face. Michael yelled and shoved her away so that she fell into the water.

'What is it?' she shouted at him.

Could she not feel it working in herself anymore? Was she now so possessed by the forest that she was blinded by it?

'Nennian!' Michael screamed, but the wild wind snatched the words out of his mouth.

Here, now. The Horseman was here. He had come for them.

A thumping that might have been a thick branch striking a tree bole, except it was regular and unceasing. Like a heartbeat.

It was a heartbeat. It was the sound of the living forest, and it was getting louder.

Nennian was fighting to keep their mounts under control.

The animals were whinnying in terror and rearing up before him. Michael splashed over too late. The chestnut bowled the priest out of the way and the three of them galloped off through the trees. Cat started after them, but got bogged down after ten yards, thigh deep in mud and water with her hair lashing about her face. She struggled there.

'Michael! Help me!'

Brother Nennian was moving feebly, dragging his limbs out of the ooze. His face was as black as coal, the eyes wild white circles in the midst of it.

'Michael!' Cat screamed.

He was frozen, rooted to the spot as firmly as one of the forest trees. The heartbeat of the wood was a massive thumping rhythm in his head. Around him the trees groaned and bent under the preternatural hurricane. The air was full of water and flying branches, scraps of bark, dead leaves, and the light was dimming moment by moment. Soon they would be floundering in near darkness whilst the water rose to engulf them and the mud sucked at their bones.

You cannot fight. You cannot win. Join with the wood.

Nennian was struggling to pull Cat free of the mud. The pair were shouting words Michael could not hear. Still he stood motionless. The water was kissing his knees now, was pouring down the inside of his clothes. He was saturated. The rain did not slacken, but battered him with unbelievable force, hitting the surface of the water and rebounding into the air.

Cat was free of the mud. She and Nennian lurched towards him, almost unrecognizable, their faces encrusted masks of filth.

And Michael knew. In the instant before it happened his frozen limbs freed themselves from immobility and he managed to bawl a warning.

'Look out! He's *here!*'

There was an explosion of silt and water that fanned the air like a geyser and was shredded immediately by the wind. Michael caught a glimpse of an angular black shape, all ravening muzzle, before it dived towards Cat and Nennian.

His sword was in his hand and he was wading through the dark water, but there was another detonation of spray almost at his feet and he was knocked down by the impact of something as hard as stone that crashed into his chest. For a second the water closed over his head and there was an immense weight on his torso, but he rolled out from under it and, still blind with muddy water, swung the blade and heard it connect with a sharp crack, like an axe clicking off wood.

Wood.

He wiped the water from his eyes and saw Cat jabbing with her stone knife and Nennian half-sunk in mud with a black beast worrying at him. His face was distorted by stark terror.

Other fountains of water and mud detonated around them, and other four-footed black shapes appeared, hard to make out in the murk and the spinning spray. He thought they were dog-like. Or wolf-like.

They were everywhere.

He thrust forward with the sword, trying to get to his companions, but the brutes dodged his blade, snapping at him with a sound like breaking timber. Cursing, he took a wild swing at the nearest and hit it on the side. He saw with strange clarity the chips and splinters of black wood that flew from the blow, and the animal buckled as the iron blade bit. It toppled to the surface of the churning water and sank out of sight with unreal swiftness.

One of its comrades sprang forward to snatch at Michael's arm, but it caught only the furs he was wearing and tore them from his forearm, unbalancing him. He yelped as another bit into his foot, and kicked out frantically as the teeth drew blood until it let go. He regained his balance and stabbed at another, but missed. There was a torrent of snarling and snapping, hollow sounding but carrying above the howl of the wind. Another creature leapt for his throat, but he threw up his free arm and smashed it back with a strength he never knew he had. The others rushed in. He swung the sword desperately but they came in quick, lunging and leaving gashes in his flesh from which the blood flowed freely, staining the water.

He caught a glimpse of Cat fighting, a raven-haired fury laying about her. Nennian was swinging a broken branch, thigh-deep in filthy water, his habit ripped from one shoulder and the blood pulsing from his neck. Then a great weight smashed into Michael from behind and toppled him forward. He went under, feeling the teeth rake the back of his neck, and in the ooze he lost his grip on the Ulfberht. It slipped from his fingers. His mouth filled with water and he fought to his feet, elbowing one of the beasts from his back. Another fastened on to his thigh where the old wound had been and that leg buckled, throwing him under again. His breath bubbled out of his nose and mouth and his face was pressed into the muck that underlay the churning water. He floundered to the surface, buffeted by hard bodies. A set of jaws closed round his wrist and he ripped it free, the teeth raking his flesh from the bone. He saw Cat fall, her stone knife splintered into shards, and the wolves crowded in on her. Nennian screamed and went down with half a dozen of the beasts tearing at him. Michael was knocked to his knees again, a wolf lunging for his face. Incredibly, his fingers came upon the hard blade of his sword under the water. He gripped it and stabbed his attacker in the throat, then swept it through a hundred and eighty degrees with a wordless bellow, decapitating another, slicing the foreleg from a third. They drew back.

'Cat!'

He floundered forward like a maniac, cutting and thrusting, and beat off the pack that was attacking her. She was barely conscious, her face covered in blood. He grabbed her hair and pulled her head above the water, but he was tired and the shock of his wounds was setting in, weakening his limbs. Where Brother Nennian had been there was a crowd of the beasts tearing at something which was now submerged. Scraps of the brown habit were flung about, chunks of something unrecognizable, and the water was black with gore.

'Cat! The Wyr-fire!'

In his extremity he could feel it, simmering at the forefront of his mind. But it was trapped there. It was as though it was bulging behind the bone of his skull.

They closed in on him again. He was sobbing as he fought, Cat a dead weight dragging at his wounded arm, the sword becoming heavier and clumsier in the other. The wolves were implacable, fearless, and behind his immediate attackers he could see more explosions, more columns of spray and muck, as fresh foes rose out of the very earth to join them.

So this was how the tale would finish.

This land does not go out of its way to provide happy endings.

Indeed. But he would fight it to the end. He would die with his soul his own.

Cat was stirring, trying to sit up. He was too busy fighting off their enemies to spare her a glance but he felt her hand gripping his knee. She was trying to pull herself to her feet. Her fingers slipped into the open wound on his thigh and he screamed in agony but did not cease his efforts for a second. He spun round and the world began to flicker darkly in his sight. The wolves were black snarling shapes that crowded his vision and the wind beat unceasingly at his head, his eyes squinting against spray. He felt his life was trickling out of him, leaking away into the muddy water and being soaked up by the forest.

I'm dying, he thought.

Then Cat was standing at his shoulder, supporting him. The green fire was flaring out of her eyes, a flood of emerald.

'Wyr-fire, Michael. Use it.' And, unbelievably, she was smiling at him through her mask of blood and mud.

And it was *there*, ready and waiting for him. The world was a verdant brightness. The fire was glaring from his own eyes now, spilling out of his wounds like phosphorescent gore. The Wyr-fire was singing in his veins, steadying him. It formed a halo, a globe about the pair of them, and within it the wind dropped, the ceaseless roar diminished. Those wolves which were caught by it flared like struck matches, and the smell of burning scorched the air. They howled in pain and collapsed sizzling into the water. But the green fire continued to burn so that the lake round Michael's feet was a chiaroscuro of viridian, full of green flares. The rest of the beasts backed away, but the flames raced across the water as though it were inflammable and caught them also. It licked round their flanks and poured out of their maws and eyes, gutting them. They sank out of sight, shrieking.

The Wyr-fire flowed about the trunks of the trees and became a whirling immensity of light, whipping up the water further. Cat and Michael were the eye of the hurricane. They watched as the trees bent and broke under its onslaught, saw the remnants of Brother Nennian's body flung through the air like a tattered sack and felt the water retreat, sucked away. It became a wall around them, spinning and light-filled, white horses breaking off to dash against the trunks of the trees, spray filling the tortured air. Then there was a massive paroxysm of energy that staggered them and made the wood shudder. The water erupted outwards, toppling nearby trees and wrenching their roots out of the ground, sending heavy trunks hurtling and crashing in the-air. Michael and Cat were blasted off their feet and lay with their heads pressed close to the ooze, clinging to each other. A high wind hammered them, smeared them along the ground for ten feet before Michael stabbed his sword into the earth and halted them. They clung to it, this iron spike in the world's heart, and thought they heard the forest groan. A spinning branch struck Michael on the elbow and one numbed arm slipped free of the hilt, but Cat scissored his waist with her thighs and gripped the blade until the edge sliced her fingers to the very bone and her blood was blowing in drops across Michael's face. Even in that moment he was able to realize that she was proof against iron. The Wyr-fire had left her and she belonged to him again.

Then the wind eased, descending from its scream note by note. The trees stopped thrashing like demented things and began to sway more naturally. The Wyr-fire had spent itself. Michael raised his face from the dirt to see a scene of devastation and wreckage. Dead leaves and shattered twigs were scudding through the air but the gale had broken. He could breathe again.

Cat moaned softly and he turned her in his arms to see the seeping tear in her scalp, the cut fingers, the ripped flesh that left her collarbone all but bare. But her eyes were open, and they were human, warm and green, full of tears.

'We're alive,' he said softly. 'We survived.' And she smiled up at him.

The wind fell further. In moments it was a mild breeze that tugged gently at their hair, and there was a warmth in it they had not known in weeks. The last sounds of tearing wood and crashing trees ceased.

He was bleeding, and his left hand was a useless lump of meat at the end of his forearm, but he was almost unaware of it. He thought he could still hear the forest keening to itself. A clearing had been blasted in its canopy, the trees fallen like skittles with their roots black tentacles clawing at the air. But the sky above was blue and empty, and the sunlight was pouring down on them, beginning to raise steam from the bare mud. A day in spring, sunset long hours away. He cradled Cat in his arms, half lifting her from the cold earth.

'Come on. We're getting out of this place.'

NINETEEN

THE MUD HAD stiffened on them, making Cat's hair into a helmet of spikes and clogging the raw, ragged edges of their wounds. They sat beside a high fire that it had taken the better part of two hours to light and carefully cauterized every break in each other's flesh with the pink glow of the Ulfberht's point. Even that brief flaring agony brought no more than a moan from them. Pain had become an everyday thing, as unremarkable as the need for sleep.

They had no food, nothing to drink. The pot they had boiled their water in was lashed to the back of the grey gelding, lost in the forest. The fact barely registered. There was only this present, the night that darkened around, them, the trees leaning close.

It had gone. The brooding presence that had been dogging them for days had disappeared with the unleashing of the Wyr-fire, and now there was no longer any sense of being watched. It was as if the consciousness of the forest had retreated. To lick its wounds, perhaps—or to consider a new mode of attack. They could not say which.

Why did they call it the Wolfweald when it had no wolves? Those things were the beasts the forest had been named for; the beasts that had sprung out of the ground. Wooden wolves. They were the guardians of the Wolfweald, extensions of the trees' enmity.

The scene of the fight was a scant hundred yards away—all the distance they could stumble in their beaten state. Here the ground was less sodden, for the waters had retreated. They lay on a thin layer of twigs and moss and around them the faces of lost souls strained out of the tree trunks, mouths open in silent screams. Nennian was there. A loud crack in the gathering dusk, and a layer of bark had fallen off a nearby bole to reveal his broad features caught in the wood, cords standing out on his neck as though he were striving to free himself from the clutch of the tree. Cat had screamed on seeing his face, but now they ignored it. The sturdy priest had shared the fate of his brothers. Perhaps he was exchanging stories with them in some tree-bound hell.

Tiredness bound down their limbs like some mind-thickening drug, and yet they could not sleep. There was no going on, Michael knew. He had had enough. They had not the strength to continue. He was not sure if they had the strength to go back, either.

He would leave Rose here; abandon her. He could do nothing else. That knowledge was a bitter taste in his mouth, the tang of failure. Cat knew it also, but he did not think she knew that he was going home. Somehow he was going home, and if he had to leave her behind then so be it. At present all he wanted was to be a boy again, unscarred and unafraid of the dark. He wondered if it were possible.

Cat shifted painfully beside him and even in the uncertain light and the shadow of the fire he saw the dressing at her collarbone darken further as the blood seeped through it. He could have wept to see her like this, bone thin and ravaged with hurt, but all that came was a hot stinging in his eyes. He would betray them both, leave her and Rose behind. His quest had failed utterly.

IN THE MORNING they lurched upright like stiff marionettes, unspeaking. There was light in the forest. Somehow the canopy seemed to have thinned and the weak sun was filtering through overhead. Cat broke Michael a rude crutch from one of the trees and they set off northwards at a snail's pace, leaving Nennian's face howling in the tree behind them.

Luck of some sort was with them, though. They found a trampled trail in the leaf litter that only the horses could have made, and pieces of equipment and scraps of harness were scattered here and there. And in the afternoon they came upon their three recalcitrant mounts standing trembling with their saddles askew and their manes matted with mud and twigs. They rode them for part of every day after that, striving to husband both the animals' strength and their own, and made better time. After a week the more shallow of their wounds were healing well and they were becoming healthy enough to sicken of the forest spawn they consumed to keep the life in them alive.

Ten days from the site of the battle they came to a decision and butchered the priest's donkey, ladening down the two other animals with its bleeding flesh and eating their fill of the stringy meat in the evening. Fancy and the grey were too exhausted to balk at the stench of blood and from then on they picked their way through the wood with the dismembered limbs of their comrade swaying from their flanks.

The meat put new strength into Michael and Cat. Tough though it was, it represented the most filling meal they had eaten since the days of Nennian's goat stew and honey. They stuffed themselves morning and evening and soon Cat was able to walk at the side of the grey all day, though Michael's mangled thigh kept him on a horse's back for most of their travelling.

Time passed. The forest left them alone, and the huge trees of the Wolfweald paraded endlessly by. Two weeks from the scene of Nennian's death they came upon his clearing in the trees, cutting almost in half their outbound journey—as though the wood were eager to be quit of them.

It was a chill afternoon when they stumbled across it, the light growing steadily stronger as the trees thinned until they startled a goat grazing at the edge of the glade and made out the humped shapes of the priest's outbuildings. Chickens pecked the ground contentedly there, but the forest had made inroads in the Brother's absence.

The bare central yard around which the buildings clustered was already thick with grass and green briar. Tufts of vegetation were sprouting over the sleeping hut, and young ferns were springing in the very doorway. The rough enclosure that had held the goats was fallen and overgrown, and saplings of hazel and lime, birch and beech, had broken out of the ground with amazing speed. They were almost waist high, trembling in a slight breeze. There was a thick, growing smell in the air, like freshly turned loam. The place looked as though it had been deserted for a year.

They unsaddled the horses, fed them from Nennian's store and let them loose in what was left of his goat enclosure. Then they both drank their fill of the clear water that still ran in his stream. It was delicious, paining their teeth with its coldness. Michael met Cat's eyes across the stream and knew she was human now, or as human as she could ever be. He wondered if there was a chance for the pair of them, a place for them both in his own world. He felt as guilty as a murderer with his secret resolution to go home. Could he make her come with him?

They ransacked the place for what food remained: smoked meat, mainly; the vegetables in the garden that the weeds had not yet buried, and a pot of honey. It was not enough for Cat's sweet tooth, and she attacked the bee skep determinedly, scooping out handfuls of honey and wax with the outraged and cold-sleepy bees blackening the air about her head. When she and Michael settled down for the night her hair was matted with honey and her face had swollen with stings. But her sticky face grinned at him across the fire. He felt a kind of disgust.

In the night something walked in the trees surrounding the glade, and the horses were restless. Michael hobbled from the fire with drawn sword, listening to the bending vegetation, the muffled footfalls. Something big circled the outermost reaches of the firelight; he could sense the breathing, the wary eyes, and a hint of the rank smell. But perhaps there was some of Nennian's faith clinging about the sanctuary, for the thing left them in the early hours, and swished off into the forest.

'What is it?' he had asked Cat.

'Troll, maybe. Who knows? There are reputed to be beasts in the Wolfweald no one has ever seen. Like the tree wolves we encountered. I think our time of being ignored is over, Michael. It starts again now.'

They left Nennian's home with regret, their saddles weighed down with all the supplies they could claw together. Braces of chickens were dangling trussed and indignant from their saddles, and a pair of freshly slaughtered goats.

As they departed from the glade Michael looked back once and saw that Nennian's cross had sprouted green shoots which blurred its outline. It had become a tree, alive and growing.

THE JOURNEY CONTINUED without ceasing, like a forty-year stint in the wilderness with no Canaan at its end. Michael's thigh wound slowly healed, and he cast aside his crutch. The horses gathered strength from Nennian's barley grain and began to fill out. They made better time, which was just as well for there were shapes in the trees at the corner of sight, darker shadows lurking in the dim light of the wood. They took to keeping watches in the blackest hours of the night, and all the time were aware of the movement at the limit of firelight, the odd noises. But the Weald was being left behind steadily.

Twice they were attacked by goblins, the squat shapes boiling out of the night to be met with Michael's blade and Cat's arrows. Both times they threw back their attackers with grim slaughter, piling their corpses around their campsite. The assaults were disorganized, febrile, the *grymyrch* launching themselves in knots rather than in waves. Michael and Cat received hardly a scratch in return.

At last the wood opened out and the land dipped. The trees grew smaller and there was light enough for undergrowth between them. There were birds and game and clean water. Cat laughed aloud, throwing back her black mane of hair. It was like a paradise after the gloomy fastness of the Wolfweald. They felt as though they had been freed from prison and given a glimpse of the real, brilliant, vibrant world once more.

They dawdled, taking time to hunt and gorging themselves on fresh meat. The horses cropped good grass and drank from the streams. When they were unsaddled in the evenings they rolled in the wetness of the grass, rubbing the fresh scent into their coats and wiping off the mud and mold of the weald.

They, all of them, almost died.

A wolf pack came upon them unawares as they were warming meat at a morning fire: eight rangy beasts with eyes as yellow as pus and black muzzles. Whilst Michael struggled with the horses Cat shot two down with the last of her arrows and disembowelled a third using a knife they had salvaged from Nennian's hut. Another fastened itself on the grey gelding's near hind leg but was kicked away. Michael gutted one that tried to attack Fancy, but as it collapsed it took the Ulfberht with it, ripping the hilt from his fingers. Another sprang at him, but Cat pounced on it in mid-air and bore it to the ground. They rolled, snarling in unison, and when the thrashing tumble had stopped she got to her feet with one arm blood to the elbow. The rest of the pack fled.

They were more wary after that, remembering belatedly that the Wildwood proper had its share of horrors too. But they were hungry for the sight of human faces, the sound of voices other than their own.

They had not long to wait. Three days after returning to what Michael thought of as the normal wood, they came upon a wide track going south to north. Following it (a relief to ride without ducking under branches and leaping fallen trees), they saw lopped stumps in the wood, abandoned brush huts, and finally they came across a village set back from the road in a tiny clearing. They snuffed woodsmoke and heard children squealing.

'Civilization,' Cat said.

The children burst into view from the trees—a trio of tiny ragamuffins. They stopped as one and stood stock-still on seeing the pair of mounted strangers, then they gave a collective wail and ran off, crying out in the forest language, '*Fiesyran, fiesyran*!'

The word could mean either strangers or enemies. In the Wildwood the two were seen as virtually interchangeable.

'Do we seem so fearsome?'

'Have you seen your face lately, love? You look like a grey-bearded killer.'

He thought Cat was making fun, but her own face when he looked at it was sober. Grey, he thought. I'm a grey man now.

He supposed they did look fearsome—mounted, for one thing. Few but the Knights went mounted in the wood. And armed as well. And they were scarred, their eyes wild, their faces filthy. Their clothes were bloodstained and ragged, black with mud, resewn a hundred times. They had taken to wearing short capes of deerhide with the hair turned outwards to ward off the rain, and dangling from their pommels were lumps of smoked venison, inadequately wrapped in one of Nennian's spare habits. Cat's beauty was hidden behind a mask of dirt and a tangle of matted hair. It was hard to tell if she were a woman at all, for she was as slim as a tall boy and the long blade of Nennian's bronze knife hung wicked and glinting from her waist.

Men came hurrying out of the trees with their tools grasped in their fists. Half a dozen, then ten, then fifteen—they gathered in a silent crowd with the children and a few women behind them. Michael felt very weary.

'*Pax vobiscum*,' he said.

They started at that, muttering amongst themselves. The Ulfberht drew many stares. Finally one man stepped forward. He was as barbarous looking as the rest, clad in deerskins and rough wool, but his head was shaven.

'*Et cum spirito tuo*.'

The Brother's name was Dyrnius, and he made them welcome despite the reservations of the other villagers. They stayed for three days, resting the horses and themselves. Cat caused a minor sensation when she cleaned herself up and the men saw her face properly. She was as lovely as ever, but it was a fine-edged loveliness now, as sharp as frost. She was as slender as a sapling, her eyes huge in her pinched face. Purple-pink lesions, healed and half-healed, old and new, striped her body, and in the nights Michael kissed each one, mourning. He made love to her as though he were afraid his weight would snap her in two.

The village was the last settlement of men before the Wolfweald, a forgotten place that Brother Nennian had come to twelve summers before and that the Knights rarely visited. The people were hungry for news once they had overcome their initial fear, and they were consumed with curiosity about the fact that the two travellers had come from the south, from the terrible depths of the weald. Michael and Cat had little to say to them.

On the third night, lying entwined in the hut that had been set aside for them, they heard hoofbeats off in the wood, galloping faint and far away, and the wolves baying at the new moon. They knew they were still pursued, and left on the fourth morning with the priest's blessing upon them.

Endless days, ceaseless travelling. They would stop for a while, and then move on as the beasts got close. The settlements grew in size and frequency; they passed other roads in the wood, saw the spikes of churches through the trees and bypassed troops of Knights who patrolled the forest tracks. They made slow time, always headed north, sometimes running across the signs of the tribes in the woods, glimpsing figures in the trees that were as wary as animals. Three times they came upon the remains of men burnt at stakes, and once they found an entire encampment destroyed, stinking with the unburied dead, alive with gore crows and foxes. The Knights were exacting revenge for the attack of the Fox-People. It seemed like years ago.

'Where are we going?' Cat had asked him, and he had answered: 'To find Ringbone's people.' But that was only a half-truth. As spring edged into summer and they discarded the heaviest of their furs he told her at last that he wanted to go home. He wanted to return to the morning he had left and be given his boyhood back again. They were heading for the cave mouth they had entered this place from, the one unchanging door that would lead him out at the bridge in his own world. And he asked her to come through it with him.

He thought for a moment that she would fly at him. Her eyes blazed. But it was her sudden tears catching fire from the sunlight. She said nothing and they travelled the next two days in a stiff silence, nor could he draw her on the subject. It became absurdly, maddeningly taboo.

They became aware of being watched again, but it was not the wood this time. There was hooted laughter in the trees that degenerated into snarling, and they thought they saw faces in the branches looking down on them as they rode. Little things began to go wrong. The biggest waterskin somehow developed a leak. The horses went intermittently lame. Michael's saddle girth split in two and he discovered that teeth had gnawed it thin. Cat shouted Mirkady's name into the trees, sure that the Wyrim were behind it, but there was no reply.

'They've left me,' she whispered. 'I'm not one of them any more.' Nothing Michael could say would cheer her. The guilt of it twisted like a cold blade in his stomach. Whatever life she had led here before his coming, he had destroyed it—and now he planned to desert her. She must come with him. She had to. There was nothing here for her.

Midsummer came and went. Michael's hair turned almost white, though his beard was salt and pepper, grizzled as an old sea dog's. Cat looked like his daughter... no, his granddaughter. They travelled north like a pair of exiles seeking rest, and all the while the pursuit never left them. It was a distant noise in the night, a rank beast smell in the dark hour before dawn. Though they had recovered from the worst ravages of the weald, they grew worn and irritable with the constant watching. The day they finally chanced upon one of the fox men out on a solitary hunt, Michael almost killed him, riding him down in a mindless reflex. It was only when the bruised tribesman shouted '*Utwychtan*!' desperately that he lowered his sword, the red haze leaving his eyes. Recognition took him, and he heard his own joyful, relieved laughter creaking out of his mouth.

Celebrations. Feasting. A glad day that seemed free of shadow. Ringbone greeted them both with a grin splitting his usual reserve, and he and Michael embraced like brothers. Cat and Michael were feted as heroes, and Michael felt that this, at least, was a homecoming of sorts, a return to familiar things.

They were greater in number, the Fox-People. They had taken in refugees from the Bear-People whose camp the Knights had gutted. There were almost four score of them, a healthy number, and a far change from the defeated, fearful people that Michael had last seen on the borders of the Wolfweald. They had fought their way back north, losing people in ones and twos all the way, but now they were in their traditional hunting grounds again and neither the beasts nor the Knights with their iron swords would shift them.

The battle at the village had been made into a song, a savage plainchant, and Michael realized that he and Cat had been elevated into something of a legend with these people. They were greeted with awe by the newer members of the tribe. *Utwychtan,* the man who slew Knights with fire and thunder and who dared the Wolfweald. *Teowynn*, the Tree-maiden who knew the forest better than any of the hunters. They had become the beginning of a myth.

But they had to move on. The beasts were closing, and Michael did not want to bring the Horseman down on these people's heads.

Ringbone and some of his men escorted them through the wood—an aboriginal honour guard—and as the summer wound down into autumn they found themselves far to the north, the cold weather creeping up on them again and the nights becoming longer. But they became separated as the pursuit quickened and drew close. Wolves attacked Cat and Michael, taking the grey gelding that had carried Cat so far. They finally met up with Ringbone's folk once more with Michael feverish and wounded yet again.

And something else had happened. Little by little the forest language that had leaked into Michael's head and made a place for itself there was disappearing. Words at first, then the construction of sentences. It was easier to understand it spoken than to speak it, but as the autumn drew on into an early winter he had to use Cat as an interpreter between himself and the fox men. As though this land were washing its hands of him, shutting him out now that he had decided to leave it. The thought made him bitter and sad.

They had to seek sanctuary in a Brothers' retreat, which the fox men refused to enter. Strangely enough, Michael could understand the Brothers' speech as he always had. It was something to do, perhaps, with their shared Christianity.

There most of the tribesmen left, only Ringbone staying with them to the end, to the Utwyda. It was cold by then, and the woods had seen the first snows. With the fox man at their side, Cat mounted on a borrowed mule, they had stared out at the land beyond the forest, weirdly open and empty after the months and years spent under trees. And there they had said goodbye to the savage who had started off as a child's nightmare and who had become a friend, one of the precious few Michael had known. Ringbone seemed not to recognize the finality of this parting. He had never thought to see them again after they had disappeared into the southern woods, but they had survived and no doubt they would one day come back from this new journey.

'*Ai neweht yewenian*,' he said, and that much Michael understood. Until the time you return.

And then Ringbone melted away into the thick dimness of the trees, the wood that was his world. Cat refused to watch him go, and her face was white and closed, admitting nothing. The pair struck out across the bare hills for the last stage, to where a river issued from a cave mouth and formed Michael's road home.

Looking back once, they saw the Horseman seated silently, watching them from the shadowy eaves of the Wildwood as the dawn broke open the sky above his head.

* * *

THEY MADE GOOD time, for Cat's mule was a willing brute. By the evening of that day they were up in the hills, and the sylvan world they had sojourned in for so long was a vast dark carpet on the land below, its higher contours dusted with snow. It was eerie and exhilarating to be able to see in all directions, to have no dark hollows or overhanging branches to worry about. If the wolves continued their pursuit they would be obvious for miles away. Of the Horseman they could no longer see any sign.

The cave and its river had not changed. For some reason Michael had expected it to be different, perhaps because the boy who had come through it that morning was gone. Now there was only a hulking, grey-bearded man with scarred limbs and the eyes of a killer.

They made camp, lighting their fire by the riverbank and heating the meat of a two-day-old kill. Then they drank barley spirit that Ringbone had given them on parting, toasting him and his people.

Still Cat said no word about Michael's impending departure. They sat on opposite sides of the firelight, leaning on their saddles whilst Fancy and the mule grazed peaceably nearby and the night swooped in overhead in a spatter of glinting stars. It was cold these nights. This far up in the hills there were banks of snow everywhere in the lee of stones and knolls, and the welkin was clear and sharp with oncoming frost. If it snowed again it would become warmer.

These things he told Cat in a desultory fashion, knowing that if it snowed he would not be here to set his footprints in it. It was his last night in this world. In the moments before dawn he would take Fancy and swim up the chill river into the cave mouth, and he would never come back. Cat must know that, but she refused to speak and the twisting grief and guilt within him began to glow into anger against her stubbornness.

'I'm going home in the morning, Cat,' he stated bluntly at last. She poked at the fire with a stick. The yellow light threw into relief the hollows under her cheekbones, the seamed scar at her neck where a wooden wolf had almost ended her life.

'Will you come with me?'

'No.' She looked up, and her pale face was shut against him. She seemed middle-aged, gaunt, like a saturnine spinster.

'Why not?'

'It's not my world there. I don't belong. You will be returning as a child, a boy, and I will remain the same. My place—my home—is here. Once I thought yours was also.'

'I never said that.'

A dry smile bent her mouth.

'I told you before: I didn't think it would be like this. I didn't know what it would do to me. Christ, Cat, I thought it would be some sort of fairy tale complete with knights and castles.'

'But it is.'

'Not the way I imagined them. How could I stay here? You saw the Horseman at the edge of the wood. He'll never leave me alone and you neither, maybe.'

'I'll take my chances.'

'There are no Wyrim to look after you, Cat. Mirkady and his folk were on the Horseman's side all along. That's why they gave us the Wyr-fire. So it would transform us into something like them—something the Horseman could control.'

'It saved our lives,' she said, her face becoming animated.

'It wasn't meant to. We turned the wood's power against itself.'

'Michael'—and her voice was full of scorn—'you don't know a thing about what you're speaking.'

'Don't I? I've had a long time to think it out. You nearly became one of the Forest-Folk yourself, and even I felt the change that was possible. If it hadn't been for Brother Nennian—'

'The priest who was going to confront the Horseman in his castle, the one who would have challenged the whole Wildwood if he could.' She was contemptuous.

'Yes. That was what he wanted, and he saw us as a means to his end. But he kept me sane, Cat, or I would have been drinking that black water and having green fire fill my eyes just like you. *I felt it too.*'

'But truth and justice and the God you follow won out?'

The hostility in her voice shook him, but he ploughed on regardless.

'If you like. Those wooden wolves attacked us because we were almost at the castle, and I was not going to change. The Horseman had failed, so he was going to destroy us. He didn't think the Wyrfire was a two-edged sword.'

She was silent, her face a mask of baffled anger and grief.

'We can't stay here anymore, Cat,' he said softly, willing the words across the fire as though they were missiles. 'I love you, lass. Please come back with me.'

There was a brightness in her eyes, as though the firelight had caught there and writhed behind their windows.

'We've come a long road together, you and I,' she said. 'And yet we're back where we began. As though we came no distance at all. Like a dream.'

Perhaps it was like a dream, he thought. A dream of trees and dark beasts, of other wonders. He could not speak. It was as though the width of the flames were a yawning gulf, Cat an unbridgeable distance away, lost for ever.

'Oh, Michael—' she said, and her voice broke.

They both moved in the same moment, crossing the distance, and were in each other's arms. He could feel her bones under his hands, the lean warmth of her, and he kissed the satin skin below her ear.

'I can't,' she whispered. 'I don't belong. This place is where my bones must lie.'

You will be the death of me, she had once said. The phrase came back to him and he felt as helpless as the boy he had so recently been. There was to be no happy ending, for either of them. This world did not work that way.

They made love for the last time at the side of the fire, whilst around them the cold wind picked up and moaned round the treeless hills. When they slept at last the sky was crowded with dark cloud, the stars invisible, and in the darkness the snow began to fall, kissing their upturned faces and shrouding the hard earth.

* * *

In the last dark moments before the dawn he left, the water iced around the banks of the river. Its chill grip made him cry out, and he clung to Fancy's mane as the mare struggled through the slow-moving current towards the dark cave mouth and the world that waited on the other side. He was going back to his home, his boyhood, the land he had been born into, but half of him was still with the dark girl who watched from the snowy bank behind him. He felt bruised and bleeding, torn in two, and as the black entrance closed over his head he was weeping like a child into the icy river.

Cat remained standing and watching long after he had gone, the cold spreading numbness into her limbs. When at last she turned back to the dead ashes of the fire she saw without surprise that the Horseman was there behind her, his steed breathing quiet clouds of breath into the frigid air. He reached out a hand towards her, and she had no longer the will to flee.

The Horseman

PART THREE

TWENTY

MICHAEL CAME THROUGH on the other side with a high wind tearing at his hair and the black branches of the overhanging trees roaring. Fancy powered through the freezing water and scrabbled to the bank, shaking herself. Michael hauled himself slowly in her wake. His clothes were hanging on him, hampering his limbs. He was weak and chilled. He lay on the bank in a grey pool of river water with his feet clutched by the swift current. His tears were a rawness in his throat. She had not come with him. He had lost her.

Dawn was coming. Though the river hollow was full of the noise of the rushing water the sky was vast and empty beyond the trees, light glowing in the east and making its sure way upwards. He struggled to think, to remember how things had been when he had left all that time ago, but his mind was as numb as his soaked body. He threw off his stinking furs—much too big for him—and found the sword scabbard empty. The Ulfberht had been lost in the river. Remembering his family history, he knew it would not stay lost for long.

His shudders of cold and the sobs that racked him merged into one and for a moment he stayed kneeling on the sodden riverbank, his face buried in his hands. He could feel the lithe freshness of his body, the lessening of his muscles' bulk. He was a stripling again, a thirteen-year-old with middle-aged eyes. His chin felt weirdly smooth as his palms touched it—as smooth as Cat's had been. And he had no scars.

I'm a blank slate, he thought.

No, not quite. He had those memories. He knew he would never lose them, even if he wanted to.

Those first days in the Other Place, riding across a vast empty landscape with the air as clear as spring water.

Firelight in a whispering wood, Cat's face an inch from his own, her body pressing against him.

Hunting in the Wildwood with Ringbone, watching the mist rise through the trees and the antlers of a stock-still stag become black branches against it.

And the other side, the dark side.

The eyes of the werewolf burning into him like malevolent coals.

The Horseman waiting in the dark trees while gore crows flapped around his head.

Brother Nennian's face before he died.

Dream or nightmare, he would never forget. It was burnt into his brain.

'Cat,' he whispered. And the cold had him shuddering again.

Fancy nuzzled him, and he lurched to his feet. Things to do.

He led her out of the hollow, and the rush of the water faded. There was dew-wet grass under his naked toes. He stopped to stare at the quiet meadows, the dark woods. Cattle moved in the field, staring at him and chewing cud. The birds were in the middle of their dawn chorus.

The wind had a tang to it, a faint aftertaste of smoke and metal. He had forgotten how different it was here.

He clinked open the gate and led the docile mare into the yard, unsaddling her once he had reached the straw-deep stables. She seemed none the worse for wear, as well-fed and sleekly groomed as the morning he had galloped off in Cat's wake. But her saddle was scraped and scored, hung with rawhide bags that gave off a sour, wet stink. The shotgun was still there also, rust along the barrel. He cleaned the tack as best he could, dumped the saddlebags behind sacks of grain in the tack room and patted Felix's huge flank as the heavy horse sniffed at him. Then he padded out across the yard, the wind cold on his skin. But the gale was dying. It would be a fine day once the sun cleared the eastern hills.

He eased into the house, clicking the latch of the back door. The kitchen was silent, the range glowing red and a clock ticking endlessly to itself. The house seemed tiny, enclosing, and for a second claustrophobia rose like a cloud in Michael's throat. There was movement upstairs. His family, waking.

He made not a sound as he ascended the stairs, wary as an animal. He closed the door of his room behind him, hearing the clump of feet on the landing. His grandparents, his Uncle Sean, his Aunt Rachel. All here.

How long had he been away? One, two years? Or the fragment of a morning?

He crept into his bed and found Cat's smell there on the sheets. He buried his face in them and wept bitterly.

'MICHAEL, MICHAEL, TIME to get up! You'll be late for school.'

And faintly, from down in the kitchen:

'Where are my clothes? Who's taken my trousers?' Uncle Sean, discovering Cat's long-ago theft.

'Someone's been in the larder. Mother of God, we've been burgled!'

Who's been eating my porridge? he thought, and smiled faintly. Cat would have laughed.

They forgot him, in the hubbub. When he came downstairs there was an early sun flooding the kitchen and the entire family, Mullan included, were toing and froing as more missing articles were noticed.

'My best pan.'

'That apple pie I'd just made.'

'We never heard a thing.'

'Must have been a tramp or something. All he took were food and clothes.'

'And my best pan!'

'No one heard anything. You're sure?' One by one they shook their heads.

'The dogs didn't even bark,' Pat added uncomfortably.

'I thought I heard the horses moving about, but it might have been the wind unsettling them,' said Sean, his dark widow's peak of hair tumbled down over his forehead.

'The horses!' Pat and Mullan cried at the same moment, and they both shot out of the back door.

Michael's grandmother shook her head. 'Never seen the like of it,' she said, and she sank into a chair.

None of them was different, Michael realized, none of them had changed. It was not a shock to see them again. He had a feeling that in a few days his memories would be like so many dreams.

His grandmother put on a huge pot of tea to brew and Sean went out to start work, muttering that the cows would not milk themselves. Michael was lost in thought, and when Aunt Rachel asked him sharply if he had washed his face this morning he barely heard her. She shook his shoulder, and he raised his eyes to stare at her.

'*What?*'

She backed away, pale as paper. 'Nothing, nothing.'

'Almost time for you to be off, Michael,' his grandmother said over her shoulder. She was frying bacon and eggs and the exquisite smell was drifting about the room, bringing the water into Michael's mouth. Presently she set a steaming plate on the table for him and smiled. Her smile drained away.

'Are you all right, Michael?'

Irritably he told her he was, and began wolfing down the food. In the heavy silence that followed he looked up to see Rachel and his grandmother staring at him, and realized he had been stuffing the greasy food into his mouth with his fingers. He wiped his hands on his shirt, a shamefaced grin on his face.

'Better be off,' he mumbled.

'Don't forget your bag,' his grandmother said faintly.

He grabbed it and ran, feeling the cool outdoor air on his face with relief. He had been sweating in the kitchen, and the walls had seemed too close, the ceiling too near his head. It was like being buried alive. This was better, though there was still that tang in the air that made him screw up his nose. He could smell the horses in their stables, the fragrance of Mullan's pipe, cow dung from the pastures and a hint of fox from the back field where most of the chickens had their nests.

That diesel smell—the tractor. And he spat to get it out of his mouth.

Mullan came out of the stables leading a pennant of smoke and striking sparks off the cobbles with his boots. 'Mike!' he called.

'What?' Michael was uneasy.

'Have you been mucking around with the tack? It's all ahoo in there, and there's a saddle looks like the light riding one but is scratched to shit. And then these—' He produced a rawhide bag shiny with grease and usage that Michael knew contained the remnants of a winter hare, caught in another world. The miasma of just-rotting meat wafted from it.

'Maybe the tramp that was in the house left it there,' Michael conjectured.

'A tramp or a bloody cave man.' But Mullan stopped and took the fragrant Peterson from his mouth. 'Christ Almighty, Mike. What happened to you?'

'What's wrong with me?'

'Your eyes. They gave me the shivers for a minute there. Have you not been sleeping?'

'I'm fine.' And an edge crept into his voice.

Mullan looked away hurriedly. 'There's something funny about this... You weren't out and about in the night, were you? You didn't see anything?' And now his old eyes were fixed on Michael's, though he seemed uncomfortable with that contact. 'Are you sure you're all right?'

The invitation to speak was there, and for an instant it was crowding on the tip of Michael's tongue—the horrors and the wonders he had been a part of. But if he spoke of them then his chance to live normally in this world would be gone. Nothing had happened to him. He had seen nothing. He was only a boy.

'I have to be going to school.' And he turned away and set his face to the road and the morning walk. Soon he would be in a musty classroom, staring at books, listening to the other children snigger, feeling the teacher watching him.

As Mullan was watching him now. He could feel the old man's quizzical gaze on his back as he strode out of the yard on to the road.

A passing car made him leap into the air with fright, and his hand went to a sword hilt that was no longer there.

Home sweet home, he told himself, and there was a deep and abiding pain at the thought. He shut down the workings of his mind, the vision of the unending days ahead in this place, living this way. And he trudged off to school like a man ascending the scaffold.

He laboured through the passing days like a sleepwalker.

But he missed Cat. He missed her face, her quicksilver grin, her barbed comments. He missed her body next to his in the nights, the joy of joining himself to her. He lay awake through the nights, unable to sleep in the too-soft, too-warm bed. He waited for her to come tapping at his window and went down to the river hollow at least once a day, hoping to see her lithe form splashing there or hear her singing off in the trees. But the place was dead, empty. All that was over. There was only this present reality, the world he had been born into with its maddening rituals.

School was a numbing ordeal to be endured. His teacher, Miss Glover, took him to task for not paying attention, but when he looked at her, the words dried up. He was left alone, the other children avoiding him out of some youthful sixth sense that told them he was less than ever one of them. He grew to be a silent, awkward figure, at ease only in the outdoors and in his own company.

* * *

BY HIS FOURTEENTH birthday he had taken to missing school to work for some of the outlying farms. His precocious strength and morose demeanour served him well. He looked older than his years, and his eyes were those of a pitiless savage. He hoarded his wages, for there was nothing he wanted to buy, but some far voice in him said that he had to get away. He was too near to the Other Place here, too close to the old bridge that was the way across. He considered returning sometimes, and sat for hours by the river, torn and agonized. He hated what his life had become, and yet the fear was deep in him, holding him back. He had to get away from the temptation.

Before he was fifteen he ran away, sleeping in the fields at night, doing casual work, but all the time wandering eastwards. In the dark nights he had nightmares full of wolves and monsters, Cat's screaming face, the grasping branches of trees. He kept moving. There was no remorse in him, no nostalgia for the life and the family he had left behind. The choking horror of his memories left no room for it.

He made it to Belfast, and wandered the streets like a bewildered primitive. Once two men came at him from a darkened alleyway and a knife had glinted in one of their hands. He had left them lying unconscious and bleeding, his body moving into the attack without rational thought. The money on their bodies had bought him a ticket on a ship, and he had sailed the following morning, seeing the sea for the second time in his life.

YEARS PASSED.

He worked his way slowly south through England, taking jobs here and there, staying a while and moving on. Always there was that knowledge that he must keep moving. At times, near dark, he would believe himself watched, and if he was in the countryside he would see—or thought he did—shapes moving in the night. He finally conceived a hatred for trees and woods, for empty places, and began to haunt cities more and more. The pickings were better there, anyway.

There were women. Here and there he would see a face and would be drawn like a moth to a candle. But in the morning the face was never what he had wanted it to be, and he would slip away, leaving it sleeping. Whether it lasted for a night or a month of nights, the result was always the same and left him feeling desperate and lost. That was when a drink would calm him and let him see clearly again.

But gradually it took more and more drinks to get him to sleep at night. He frequented public houses, becoming a regular in half a dozen towns—the big, silent man at the end of the bar. This was before he turned twenty. His powerful frame began to pad out and sag and his stamina seeped away, though his arms remained enormously strong. He became a strong-arm man, a bouncer, a security guard; a professional thug. Often the look in his eyes was enough to stop a fight, but twice he was sacked for using excessive violence, once landing in court and missing a jail sentence by luck and technicalities. He realized dimly that his values were wrong for this world, that his sense of right and wrong was not that of the other people within it. But the bottle made it a lot simpler.

As far as he could, he kept in touch with his home country. There was trouble there, a civil rights movement struggling to survive. Tinder waiting to catch fire.

ON THE FARM the family gathered for three funerals, and the cars and horse traps extended almost a mile for every one. Old Pat Fay, found lying dead in the buttercups of the lower meadow one morning with the horses nosing at his body and a smile on his face. And not long after Agnes Fay, her heart giving its last beat as she pumped water from the well into her bucket—a job Michael had once been entrusted with.

And Old Mullan. Two communities came together for his final journey at a time when they were pulling ever farther apart. Old men whose chests were bright with medals standing beside old men who had once been in arms against their like. It no longer mattered.

They had found Mullan's body down in the river hollow, his pipe lying cold at his side. Sean had discovered the corpse, and afterwards had needed half a bottle of whiskey to stop the trembling of his fingers. Mullan's face had been stretched in terror, his eyes bulging and the lips drawn back into his gums. He looked as though he had been scared to death, said Sean.

And one of the first things Sean was to do on inheriting the farm was to fell the trees in the hollow. He had never liked the place anyway. He dug drains leading down towards the river, cut and burned the thick undergrowth and felled the oaks and alder that clustered along the stream. Soon sheep were grazing there, cropping good grass right up to the water's edge.

The horses were sold, and even Rachel wept the day Felix and Pluto were taken away.

Sean did not keep the sheep in the hollow for long. A pack of feral dogs haunted it, he decided, after losing three animals in quick succession. And he sat out himself, shotgun across his lap, for more than one night watching them. Sometimes he thought he heard things, or saw shapes moving in the corners of his eyes. Once something big and dark splashed its way across the width of the river and he had been too paralysed to even raise his weapon. The hollow remained empty after that, the green things beginning the slow, inexorable process of regeneration.

MICHAEL HEARD OF the funerals one after the other, and though they pained him, his real grief, oddly enough, was reserved for what they represented: the end of a way of life. An older way, a way closer to the land and the growing things, was ended, and the country was about to be raped by a new method of farming and an unending guerrilla war. The home he had known would very soon cease to exist.

* * *

FOURTEEN YEARS. FOURTEEN years after the mornings he and the chestnut mare had struggled out of the womb of the freezing river he was here, in London. He was a prematurely aged man, a barman-cum-doorman with a smoker's cough and thirty pounds of flesh he did not need. He had sunken killer's eyes and a fighter's nose, blue veins knotting his thick forearms and the red lines of a heavy drinker breaking across his face. The boy he had been, even the woodsman who had hunted with Cat at his side, were a century and a world away; and neither they nor the monsters and marvels that had existed alongside them would ever return.

Or so he had thought.

TWENTY-ONE

CLARE WAS ASLEEP, and the city slumbered with her. It was hot in the room, a summer night hanging heavily in the air with the orange glow of the street lamps.

Michael padded to the window as he did so often in the nights, and pulled the blind aside to look out into the street.

Nothing.

He could feel them though, watching. Sometimes he thought that his senses were quickening again, that the old awareness was coming back and lending him another set of eyes. He sensed unseen things. At night outside his front door he would smell sometimes the reek of mould, the sweet stink of decay, and he would know they had been there.

Traffic, far off. The street was lit with the sickly orange hue of the street lights, but there were shadows everywhere.

He knew too much about that Other World. Maybe that was why they had come for him. Or perhaps it was revenge, a lust for the blood of someone who had wounded their beloved forest.

It still seemed like a dream at times, though. Brightly lit pictures spilling into his mind from another life, when he had been someone else in an impossible place. He had left Cat behind in it. Maybe Rose, too. That pain was real enough.

Impossible to separate them in his mind. They had blurred together with the passage of the years, becoming a single, hauntingly lovely face. Maybe they had always been the same. Perhaps the 'quest' he had taken upon himself had always been absurd.

Perhaps.

Michael lit a cigarette, turning to watch the sleeping girl in the bed. The sheet had fallen from her shoulder and he could see the jewel of sweat in the hollow of her throat. He had kept the windows closed, despite her puzzled protests.

Not fair to involve this girl, this lady of the city, in what he felt was coming. Hardly right. But he felt it might be too late for that. His smell was about her. He had marked her.

Clare turned over in the narrow bed, uncomfortable in her sleep. The sheet slid from her so he was able to see the curve of her hip, white and full, shadowed darkness cupped within it. Her body was soft and generous, so unlike Cat's. No scars there, no hardness on her feet, no nails broken or dirt-crammed.

And yet when he remembered Cat's flashing grin, the sheer life in her gaze, something in his chest seemed to stretch and ache, and he had to shut his burning eyes.

Still there, even now.

He wondered how the time had passed for her back in the Other Place, how quick or slow had been the passage of the years.

He had *seen* her, here in this room...

Or had that been his mind chasing its tail?

Mad, he thought. I'm going mad. It was a dream, and now I'm falling asleep again, reliving it with a change of backdrop.

A trio of young, merry men meandered down the street outside singing softly. He watched them avoid a shadowed corner without thinking, and knew that the darkness there was not empty. He smiled grimly, reached for another cigarette, and then thought better of it.

So they had finally caught up with him. He wondered what it was they wanted. Were they going to drag him screaming back into the wood like some latter day Faust?

The Wildwood. It had had its beauty, its bright moments. He remembered quiet campfires, Cat in his arms. He remembered glorious dawns, the nip of cold and the exhilaration of hunting in the first snows. Ringbone's face over firelight, the easy companionship of the Fox-People.

No. It had been a savage place. He was well out of it.

He returned to Clare in the bed. She was hot, moist with sweat. He threw back the sheet and she nuzzled against him. A buxom lass, comfortable to lie with, touchingly trusting. He was content with her, now he was no Adonis himself. She would never have to catch breakfast on the hoof, fight off goblins or clean wounds.

He smiled into the dark, thinking back. Piglet on a spit. Or that first day...

Call me Cat.

That's a stupid name.

You're a stupid boy.

He had missed that challenge, the sharpness. Perhaps he was too old to enjoy it nowadays.

Too old? He was not yet thirty.

An old sound out in the street, a sound he had never thought to hear again. The howl of a wolf.

'Jesus!' he said softly.

He disengaged himself from Clare's soft clutch and peered out of the window. Somehow it was darker than it had been.

The street lamps were dead.

He saw a flickering of shadows along the side of the street.

Far off there was the faint hum of nocturnal traffic, but the surrounding streets seemed as silent as the moon.

'Shit...' He backed away from the window, then turned and shook the sleeping girl on the bed.

'Clare, wake up! Wake up, Clare!'

She slept on, oblivious. He grabbed her shoulders, his fingers bruising her flesh, and half lifted her from the mattress. Her head lolled bonelessly to one side.

'*Clare!*'

He dropped her. No good. No good.

The time had finally crept round on him. He knew it was going to finish here tonight. All those loose ends were going to be tied up.

How? With his death?

They were coming for him, this very minute. It was not Clare's battle, so they had put her out of the picture.

Or so he hoped.

He was shaking. Where was that old stubbornness, that dogged courage? What would Ringbone think of him? Or Cat, for that matter?

They were coming for him. The big bad wolf. The bogey man. They were real. He had seen the stories walking woods at night.

God help me.

He pulled on his clothes with furious haste while his mind ran through the contents of the flat. Weapons. He needed something to fight with. Perspiration popped out over him as his clothes soaked up the heat in the room. He fiddled with the clinking keys in his pocket.

The kitchen. He pulled out the drawers, his eyes constantly darting to the windows. Christ! The door. Had he locked the door? He must have! He sprinted to it, skidding as he halted and banging it with his shoulder. The chain was on. Good.

Even as he stood there checking it, the hair rose on the back of his neck. In the little gap below the door the light from the landing had suddenly flicked out.

They were in the building.

He tried the switches in the flat. Nothing. So he would be fighting in darkness.

His mind had bifurcated. One part of him was calmly searching for weapons, gauging their strategy, sizing up the defensibility of the flat. The other was quietly but insistently denying that any of this was happening. Wolves do not prowl city streets. The Devil does not ride a horse.

The phone. He would phone the police, get people around him.

Dead, of course. The wood part of him had known it would be. There would be no help for him from the outside. It was his fight alone. The reason they had bewitched Clare.

Momentarily he wished Cat were here at his shoulder, to fight with him. She would have put some heart into him.

In the quiet he could clearly hear the thump and swish of his own heart. His hands were trembling around the grip of the big kitchen knife.

I've grown timid, he thought. I've been too far from the edge of things for so long.

In the wood he had lived with fear every moment until it had ceased to be fear and had been merely another bodily function. Fear had been an asset, then. It had concentrated the mind wonderfully.

Now his mind was clouded by it. It blurred his thinking. He wrenched a broomstick free of its head and began tying another of the kitchen knives to it with the tail end of a washing line. No crosses or holy water here. Nothing to keep out the beasts. It took faith to bar the door to them, and his home in Ireland had been strong with untold generations of it. But here there was no history, no strength of character. This building and the rest in the street were concrete shells, hardly touched by the lives within them. The things from the wood would need no invitation to cross this threshold.

Something scratched at the door, like a dog seeking entry, except that the scratching was at head height. There was a low growl on the other side, deep enough to hum through Michael's skull, and something began sniffing at the lock.

Other feet were padding on the landing, and he could hear the tick and scrape of the claws.

A heavy blow banged on the door. The floorboards creaked. There were scrapes and thumps. He thought he could hear breathing, coming in pants. And then the smell sifted into the flat, a rank, rotting smell of old meat, uncured hides, the stink of leaf mold and marsh.

A wind blew through the hallway heavy with the smell, and he almost gagged at its potency. It was as though the flat around him were mere illusion and what he really stood in was a damp wood, that charnel house stench hanging in the trees.

He closed his eyes. It was clearer. A looming tangle of mighty trees around him, dead leaves squelching under his feet. All quiet in the twilight, dusk deepening and shadows moving in the depths of the wood. The breeze stirred his hair.

No. He was here in the city, and the tiles of the kitchen were cool under his bare feet, though the broomstick was slick with moisture in his palms.

Here, in his own world. With teeming millions. Scores of people slept within earshot of him. And he knew they would never hear a thing.

There was no sound, but he could feel the heavy presence beyond the door. He left the kitchen and padded at a crouch over to the window, peering through the blinds.

—The momentary flash of a diabolic face, laughing at him. He recoiled, then cautiously looked out again.

On to an endless canopy of trees, bare with winter, the stars glittering bright and cold in the sky above.

He retreated from the window. Tricks. They were playing tricks on him.

A smothered giggle, like the laughter of a child, from the bedroom.

He ran in with the spear thrust in front of him, saw the disordered shape of Clare's nude form—and a black, spider-thin creature chuckling over it.

He shouted with outrage and stabbed at the thing, but it leapt away and scurried across the room, still chortling. In one claw-like hand was a black ribbon of hair.

It was hard to see. He prodded the corners, the loose clothes on the floor. The voice laughed again. Its owner invisible. Michael was shaking with rage and fear. He bent over Clare and saw that some of her dark locks had been cropped. Acorns nested on her eyes and a scarlet cluster of rowan berries had been placed in the dark pelt of her crotch. The bed was covered in shards of rotting leaves and broken twigs, the hard spheres of unripe winter berries. He brushed them away and shook her again, but she continued to breathe in even sleep.

Another smashing blow to the front door. There was a long, eager howl just outside, the sound of animals snapping and yelping. They were waiting for something, growing impatient.

The bedroom seemed empty, the creature that had been there gone. He kissed Clare with an odd feeling of fraud, and shuffled out of the hall.

There were leaves on the floor, pieces of twigs that jabbed his bare soles. Mushrooms and toadstools had begun to sprout in corners. The flat smelled dank, and the temperature had dropped until Michael was beginning to see the plume of his warm breath misting the mephitic air. There was that unwholesome breeze coming out of nowhere, carrying along with the smell of decay a hint of snow, the breath of the dark season. He might have been in the deep woods on a winter night.

Shivering, he went back to the window.

The forest was still there with a mist rising in it and the moon climbing over the tops of the tallest trees. There was a frost starting to sparkle on the bare branches, and the thin mist was set alight by the moon.

Michael sank to his knees in the gathering muck that was the floor of the flat. The Other Place had reclaimed him. He groaned, and thought he could hear answering laughter, silvery as bells, outside. But he would not look.

Why? Why had they come back for him? Had he done them and their forest so much harm that they must needs hunt him like this, following him over the years and the long miles, the separating sea? Why?

There was a rending crash, a splintering and tearing of wood, and then a dull boom as the front door was punched off its hinges and fell to the floor. A cacophony of howling and screeching broke out in the hall, and Michael leapt up.

In the living room doorway was a long-eared shape with shining teeth and glowing eyes. He stabbed the spear into it with all his strength and felt the knife slide sideways from the wooden shaft. But the iron in the blade did its work, and the beast tumbled sprawling to the floor.

More shapes behind it, the rank smell choking his throat. He drew the other knife from his belt and it flashed in the moonlight that splintered in wands and bars through the window blind.

Another great head thrust over the corpse of the first wolf and warm slobber spattered his chest. He stabbed again, but this time went wide as the animal swung to one side. Something hit him with tremendous force, flinging him across the room. The knife spun from his fingers. Bright lights stabbed into his head and the breath was crushed out of his lungs. Something raked his upper arm, tearing his sleeve to shreds and ripping long tears in his flesh. There was harsh fur against his face, pricking his cheek. A tremendous animal heat, hot breath, was clouding about him. The twigs that littered the floor pierced the muscles of his back.

And the eyes were a foot from his face. Vast, amber circles, they were slitted with pupils black as jet, red lines veining the yellow cornea. They blinked once, slowly, and Michael could see the massive muzzle; striped by moonlight, the faint shine of the teeth that lined it.

Terror galvanized him. He screamed aloud as his entire body convulsed with effort, the cords in his thick neck riding out of the flesh and near to snapping. His arms pushed up with enormous force, a strength dredged from the bowels of his fear, and the heels of his hands impacted with the wolf's throat. He felt something give way in there, a wet snap, and then the heavy beast was punched into the air. Air flooded his lungs, and he flowed to his feet with something of the old hunter's grace.

The others were lunging for him.

Without thought, he launched himself towards the window, adrenaline powering the neglected muscles of his legs. He hit the Venetian blind and felt the sharp edges slice at his arms and shoulders, and then the glass doing the same, but with a bright flare of pain, deep and cold. He was weightless, his stomach turning and his ears full of the demented howls of his attackers, anger in them, disappointment—and fear?

And so it ends, he thought, and he was smiling as he fell, a moment of free fall crammed with reflection. He wondered what the shattering impact of the concrete pavement would be like.

Branches whipped at his face, along his torso, cutting and whipping his flesh.

The wood. Still there.

He hit something hard and unyielding, a thicker branch. It crushed the breath out of him, popping his ribs like sticks, and then he was careering past it.

Again. This time a spray of twigs and lesser branches that lashed his face. And now he was being buffeted from branch to branch in a kind of arboreal pinball, yelling with the pain of his broken ribs.

And a final, enormous impact that left him lying on his back with his lungs flat and airless: the surrounding trees a wheeling kaleidoscope of shadow and moonlight.

He struggled, and finally sucked in a huge draught of air that fuelled his scream of agony. Then he was breathing quickly, carefully, his ribs an orchestra of white-hot daggers jabbing his sides.

But I'm alive.

He hauled himself to his feet, grimacing. Around him the trees reared up, a diffuse silvery radiance that was the moonlight illuminating the topmost branches high above. Down here he was enveloped in Stygian gloom. The ground gave moistly under his feet, mud and moss, the mulch of millennia's leaves. The tree trunks glowed faintly, phosphorescent mould plastering the bark. There was a reek of dampness, of rot and decay. It stirred memories. He squeezed his eyes shut until the darkness had seeped into them and he was no longer totally blind.

He was in the Wolfweald.

Something stirred in the wet earth at his feet. He jumped backwards, the lurch sending the jagged needles of his broken bones grating.

The leaves shifted there, mud rose up. He blinked furiously, trying to make it out. His injured arm dripped blood upon the earth but he hardly noticed.

Something coming out of the ground.

He remembered, and white terror flooded his brain. He saw Nennian's face as they tore him to pieces.

Two black horns or ears surmounting a broad skull. A long muzzle thrusting its way free of the ground. Powerful shoulders below the heavy head, all utterly black, mud-covered, stinking of decayed leaves and deep clay.

He ran.

He had time to think: This is the end. It finishes here. I am the last loose end. And then he heard the awful howl of the beast behind him and the patter of its feet on the dead leaves.

He blundered along like a drunk, careering into trees, tripping over roots and having his forehead slashed by low branches. His lungs worked and wheezed like a leaking set of bellows, and the pain of his injuries mingled with the chill race of his adrenaline to make a cocktail of energy, high-octane panic. He sounded like a mad ghost, all laboured breathing and the jingle of the keys in his pocket.

It was not enough. He was losing blood steadily and his air supply was constricted by the racked agony of his broken rib cage. And he was not fit. He was an overweight man who smoked and drank too much, who spent his days on one side of a bar or the other. The city living was heavy in his limbs, a millstone settling with fatal weight across his chest.

I'm going to die here, he thought. The fairy tale finishes.

Michael! This way!

What? A voice? Had he heard it or imagined it?

Michael!

There she was. Cat, plain as day, beckoning urgently to him. Just as she had once many years before in the wood beside his home. A laugh got past the strangled constriction of his throat. She was going to save him again. It would be all right.

Something struck him from behind and knocked him on to his face. His mouth was full of the stinking leaf litter and there was a dry snarling, like the rip of a chainsaw, in his very ear. He rolled in the filth of the forest floor. The beast was on top of him and there was a green light spilling out of its eyes. The black maw descended and he reached up to fend it off. It was like grappling with slimy mahogany, solid wood that nonetheless bulged with muscle. His fingers slid along its smooth throat. Stone-hard paws scrabbled at his chest, ripping his clothes away, popping buttons, tearing into his flesh. He shrieked with pain and fury. The teeth lunged for his face and he punched the wolf's head aside, skinning knuckles. The jaws fastened on his forearm and it was as though a razor-edged vice was crushing the bones. There was a metallic rattle as his keys slipped from his pocket.

His keys.

His free hand scrabbled for them, digging through the wet dirt and rotten twigs. Then they were, hard and cold in his palm. With absurd familiarity, the key to his front door was in his fingers. An old key, for an ageing Victorian red-brick. The locks had never been changed.

An iron key.

He stabbed it into one of the green-glowing eyes and saw the light sputter out.

The grip on his arm slackened, the teeth pulling free from his flesh. The wolf fell to one side with a sound like the splintering of sap-heavy wood. The weight was off his chest and he was breathing more easily.

When he looked again there was no trace of the beast, but only a framework, hard to see in the near-dark, like a skeleton of twigs, the flesh mere shards of rotting bark and something like dark fungus within the woody rib cage. Then it sank into the forest soil and was gone.

He lay back. His body was a massive labouring wound, and the blood was pulsing out of him to clot in ropy strings on the leaves. There was no feeling in the arm the wolf had bitten. Peering fearfully at it, he saw his flesh hanging in streamers and tendrils from the bare bone. His hand flopped like a dead spider at the end of his wrist. No movement. The bone was not bitten through, but the sinews and nerves had gone. He recorded the fact with an odd detachment. It did not matter. He was going to die here—that much was plain.

But there was something else to do first. He had seen Cat. (Or had it been Rose?) That was a reason to get up, to knot together the remains of his shirt and tuck his mangled arm within them.

It was hard even to stagger. Moonlight ahead, a brighter shade beyond the trees.

And behind him the howls of other beasts. A pack of them now, on his trail.

If only he had the Ulfberht. And the strength to wield it, he added to himself.

Sense and consciousness were coming and going like a blossoming red balloon in his mind. He was wandering, the pain tearing his mind free of panic and fear.

I'm dying.

But that did not matter either. If nothing else, he wanted to sate his curiosity before the end. And to see Cat again. Maybe he would have a fairy-tale ending after all and die in her arms.

He fell, cursing feebly, and then he was on his feet again. Had someone helped him? Was there an arm supporting him?

Never mind. It was easier to walk now. He came through the trees and then there was a brightness, a flood of silver light. The wood ended as though it were a carpet with clear-cut edges. And there was open country before him, rising into hills. Looming directly to his front, one hill reared up above its brothers and became a steep-sided crag, the rock faces on it black in the moonlight. There was a building at its summit, built so cleverly that it was impossible to say where rock ended and man-made wall began. A castle.

He smiled. Of course. It all fits.

He stepped out of the wood, leaving it behind just as the murderous shadows lunged at his back. They stopped at the eaves of the trees, snapping and snarling their frustration, but came no further. Michael grinned at them.

Fuck you.

Then he began stumbling and staggering south across the moon-bright hills, towards the Castle of the Horseman.

TWENTY-TWO

IT WAS COLD up in the hills. The moon sparkled off frost-coated grass that thickened as he limped onwards until it had become a covering of brittle snow. Soon the powdery stuff was above his ankles, soaking and numbing his feet. He stuffed handfuls of it into his mouth, trying to assuage a raging thirst. Its chill made his teeth ache and his head throb. His eyes were like hot globes of glass set in a freezing skull, but he felt little pain from his injuries. Dimly he thought he might be in shock.

He accepted without question the burning need in him to approach the castle ahead, and battled uphill grimly, slipping and sliding on the snowy ground—and once falling on his face with an impact that tore a shriek out of him. Back in the wood the wolves were still howling as though mocking his pain.

But I beat them, he thought. I got past them, somehow. Made it so far.

His breath plumed; a moonlit feather. As the rises became ever steeper he began scrabbling upwards on hand and knees. His passage left the snow scuffed and torn, speckled with blood. He was carving a brutal path southwards through the white, pristine covering, leaving a trail that would be visible for miles. The woodsman part of him was bothered by that, but the rest knew it did not matter. He had survived the Wolfweald, had seen the end of it after so many years. There would be no more pursuit.

The castle loomed slowly closer, bulking as black as pitch against a star-filled sky. There were no lights within, no sign of life. It might have been a ruin set at the edge of the world, a grim monument.

He worked his way higher. The hills began to level off after a while. He was walking across their crests now, with the occasional loss of altitude as they dipped. He was higher up than he had ever been in this world before, and looking round he could see the whole vast panorama of the earth filling every horizon. To the north the forest rolled for league after uncounted league under the moon, the treetops glistening with frost. To east and west there were the hills he was stumbling across. They were higher around him, and he realized that he was walking up a drumlin-filled valley with the real, stony heights of the others extending in higher tors and ridges to west and east. It seemed to be a pass extending through them, and dominating it all was the castle.

To the south, beyond the black crag the Horseman's Castle occupied, there was a white country of wind-scoured buttes and escarpments rising ever higher until at the end of sight the moon set alight the far shapes of mountains, snow-covered, sharp as horns. Even at this distance he could feel their height and coldness. Thousands of feet of barren, ice-bitten stone extending like some savage barrier along the south of the world. He knew now why some of the forest people believed them to be the rim of the earth with nothing but a star-filled gulf beyond them.

The castle overtopped him, towering and dark. He was nearly there, and his strength was almost finished. Pausing, he saw that there was a rime-white road leading around the circumference of the crag, winding like a helter-skelter until it disappeared far above.

He groaned. His injured arm had lost all feeling up to the biceps, but his broken ribs were protesting incessantly and the raking clawmarks of the wolf were oozing blood. Blood that was crystallizing even as he stood. The cold had deepened. It was a raw, numbing thing that ate towards his marrow. He could no longer feel his feet and he could sense tiny ice particles crackling in his nose.

'Jesus,' he stuttered, shuddering. He had not expected this.

Had he really seen Cat in the wood or had it been his own fancy? He looked up at the winding road ahead.

Can't—can't do it.

He was shoved forward roughly—he distinctly felt a pair of hands in the small of his back—but when he spun round there was nothing there. He cursed rabidly.

'All right! If that's what you want then I'll do it!'

And he started stumbling forward up the last, spiralling road.

He was swearing and mumbling as he went, trying to talk himself up it. But the steep incline and the bitter cold stole the breath from his lungs after a while so that he was wheezing and panting for breath, and he was clenched into silence. Stopping once to spit out the phlegm that was crowding the back of his throat, he saw it land dark and clotted on the snow and knew that his wayward ribs had punctured a lung. But still he battled upwards. There was nowhere else to go.

He slipped on slick stone and fell, his head cracking on the ground. The darkness whirled in on him and for a while he had the strangest sensation: that he was warm and beside the kitchen range at home. The heat was glowing over him and warming his toes. His shudderings eased. But the woodsman part of him would not let him rest. Hypothermia, it said. Get up. But it was not his own voice telling him that.

He opened his frost-whitened eyelashes to see Cat leaning over him. She was dressed only in the white shift he had first seen her in, but she did not seem to feel the cold.

He smiled. That white shift. She had worn it for so long. It looked like a hospital shift, the type they gave out to expectant mothers. He wondered why he had never noticed that before.

She was looking at him mutely and he sighed.

'All right.'

He wriggled to his hand and knees, then to his feet. There were white blotches on his fingers and the back of his free hand. God, he was tired.

'Damn you, Cat.' But he lurched onwards nonetheless.

It seemed as though he had been travelling for many hours, but there was no lightening of the sky to the east, no sign of the dawn, and as far as he could see the moon had scarcely moved. There was no Great Bear in this sky to tell the time by. He wondered if the Horseman was keeping the land in shadow to impede his climb. Or maybe his sense of time was awry. Everything else was.

And he was there.

Just like that. He wheezed a chuckle that turned into a bloody, agonized cough.

The castle walls reared up black and shining before him—fifty, seventy feet maybe, with not a joint or crack or squeeze of mortar to be seen. There were cobbles underfoot—the snow was a white skim here, no more—and a cold wind winnowed the crag around him. He was too far gone even to shiver.

A gateway yawned, black and high.

There was a dry moat, cut like a dark chasm in the very rock of the hill. Spanning it was a crumbling stone bridge that led to the gaping portal. Like the bridge at home, he thought. A doorway. He knew he must go through it, and knew also that he had to be swift, for life and consciousness were ebbing away. His body was hardy and stubborn yet, despite the years of abuse; but he was human, after all. Mortal.

He staggered through the gateway.

'Cat! Are you here?'

Vast buildings reared up around a huge courtyard. There was a barbican behind him with pointed towers, then a broad walk into the square. A well was in the middle, broken in on itself.

The buildings were in ruins, walls fallen in, roofs gaping, slates and rubble littering the cobbles along with the rotted ends of once-mighty oak beams. Michael scuffled through the detritus of centuries as he walked. Broken swords, fragments of chain mail, bones and skulls. Earthenware and copper pots, glinting trinkets that caught the moonlight and sparkled icily. All strewn across the cobbles like rice after a wedding. Derelict. The place was empty.

He groaned. 'Oh, Christ!'

And then, from somewhere close by, music. A tabor beating, someone accompanying on a mandolin, and the golden notes of a harp. Beautiful, tugging music that wrenched at his heart, and then faded away like an echo of silver bells, at once merry and elegiac. He had heard it before somewhere.

Walls rearing up in sunshine, white as chalk. There were battlements and flapping flags, and men in bright armour mounted on huge horses. There was a bridge spanning a glittering river with girls splashing and diving, sleek as salmon.

A picture barely viewed before it was gone. Why did he feel he had been here before?

His voice fell into a trough of silence when he called Cat's name again, the echo soaked up by the surrounding stone. Why had he expected to meet her here anyway?

Because he had sensed her. She had accompanied him all the way from the trees.

She was *here.*

His sight flickered. He was at the end of his strength. He sank to his knees on the hard ground.

The Horseman rode out of the shadows, his steed's hoofs clumping softly on cobbles. He seemed huge beyond belief, towering up amongst the stars with the moon haloing his head and his hood full of impenetrable shadow.

Michael's heart lurched sickly for a moment. He had been mistaken. Cat had not called him here. It had been some trick of the Horseman's. And now his soul was forfeit.

But he felt no fear. In the extremity of his pain and exhaustion there was a certain clearness, an icy logic to his brain. The worst had already been done to him. He no longer cared.

Grimacing with pain, he hauled himself to his feet.

'What the hell are you?' he muttered.

As if in answer the Horseman reached up and threw back his hood. Michael gaped.

There was nothing human there. The head looked like an overgrown stump of dark wood wound around with shoots of honeysuckle as though they were a necklace. Gleaming holly clung like hair mixed with mistletoe and dog rose. What might have been eyes were formed by red rowan berries, and a circlet of blackthorn coiled above them like a crown.

'I am the Wildwood,' the Horseman said softly, and his voice was like the rush of the great trees in a breeze. It had no depth, as though his chest were not airtight, but was some wide, leafy space.

'Cat,' Michael whispered. 'Where is she?'

Here, Michael. The words flitted past him like a wind-driven leaf.

We're all here, Michael.

He realized that the voice was coming from the Horseman. 'What have you done with her—with Rose? What the hell do you want?'

'You.'

Michael backed away, trembling. 'No.'

Without any sense of transition, it was Cat who was seated on the horse before him. Her scars were gone and her hair was shining in the flood of moonlight.

'It's me, Michael. I'm part of the wood, as I always was. I'm not any different—but I'm not afraid any more.'

'He got you, Cat. He got you at last. It was my fault. I'm sorry.' She seemed irritated.

'You don't understand, do you?' But her face faded away, and he was looking at the mossy features of the Horseman again. The Green Knight.

'I am the Wildwood,' the figure said again. 'And I am anything you want me to be. What you see is what you wish to see. Root and branch, my sap is the same as that of every tree nourished by this earth.'

And then it was Nennian who was astride the motionless horse, his broad face smiling slightly.

'You have changed, Woodsman. The world you live in now is not fit for you. You belong to the wood even as I do.'

'He took your soul,' Michael croaked.

The priest continued to smile, shaking his head gently. 'Still you understand nothing.' And he was gone.

'What about Rose? What happened to her? Is she here too?'

'She died in your world, but yes, she is here. She had a daughter who belonged to the wood.'

Cat. Michael had guessed as much over the years. She was his cousin.

'Let me see Rose.'

'She is dead.'

'So was Nennian.'

'The priest was a part of the wood, part of this world. He will never truly die.'

'So the quest was futile from the start. There was no way I could free Rose.' He was bitter, bitter and humiliated. All that suffering had been for nothing. He had thrown away his time in this world, maybe Cat's too.

The Horseman did not answer.

The cold was eating into Michael like a canker and the blood in his wounds had frozen into crystals, black as coal in the moonlight. He did not think he had much time left.

'Why am I here? You brought me, didn't you?'

The leafy head inclined slightly. His horse nosed at the white ground. Rime was forming around its muzzle but it seemed oblivious to the cold. Michael's face was becoming a mask of ice where his breath condensed around his mouth and nose. It cracked every time he spoke. He was very tired.

'When you die here, you will be mine,' the depthless voice said. 'You will belong wholly to the wood.'

It was the Wildwood speaking to him, Michael realized. The castle was a mere ruin, a peg to hang a legend upon. And the

Horseman was merely a cipher. The *wood* was the key, the centre of everything, the heart of this world. Its god. Poor Nennian had wanted to confront the Horseman, not realizing that he was only the embodiment of the wood's will. He did not steal souls—they were lost to the Wildwood. Nennian's had been lost also.

I love the great trees.

The Horseman was the wood.

I am anything you want me to be.

Rose had wanted a mysterious romance. Michael wanted Cat. Or Rose. It did not matter. He had wanted that dark girl, and the wood had given her to him.

But now it wanted something in return.

'You're not getting me,' he said steadily. The cold had tightened the muscles of his jaw and his words were bitten out of the frigid air. 'I won't become part of you unless you let Rose go.'

'She is dead.'

'You have her essence here. Her... soul. And you have my life. Give my life to her and let her go back. Let her go free and I'll be part of your wood. I'll do whatever you want.'

'Are you so strong you will bargain with me?' The words were a soft, threatening zephyr.

'I'm not Nennian. You can't blind me. My life for hers.'

The face stared at him. It seemed to be weighing things, considering. In that moment Michael knew that it was not evil, no more than the spring gale or winter blizzard were evil. It was as elemental as the sun.

'She will return to the moment she left, to a stillborn daughter and a life of disgrace.'

'But life, nonetheless.'

'When she returns you will be there also, a boy. The man you grew into will never exist. There will be another Michael Fay in your world. That land's history will have changed.'

Michael smiled. So his other self would have another chance, a life not ruined by his time in the Other Place. And Rose would be there with him. Who knows? he thought. Maybe he will even go to

England one day and meet a well-spoken girl who dreams of a man speaking Gaelic in his sleep.

'That's the bargain.'

The leafy growth around the face rustled with what Michael thought was silent laughter.

A happy ending for a fairy tale.

And Michael knew that he had won. His quest was fulfilled at long last.

Cat was there, and Nennian, his face open and grinning. And Michael was no longer cold.

I'll do whatever you want.

He left aside the battered remnant of what he had been, found Cat lithe and alive in his arms. The pair of them were standing in sunlight looking out over the vastness of the Wildwood that was the breath and life and heart of this wide world. And it was summer.

My life for hers.

EPILOGUE

THE SUMMER EVENING was finally darkening. She placed the last plate by the sink and listened to the birds at their evensong. Outside the air was becoming blue with dusk and the sun had long sunk behind the mountains to the west. Only a red glow, like the coals of some old fire, burned at the brim of the world's horizon.

The house was quiet. Most of the family were in bed, and old Demon was twitching and snuffling in his sleep under the kitchen table. A piece of harness lay gleaming with soap across one chair where Mullan had left it, and the clock ticked quietly in the empty stillness.

She padded upstairs, avoiding the steps that creaked through long practice, and paused on the landing. Slow breathing; more clocks ticking endlessly to themselves. She entered the smallest room and stood there for a moment gazing down on the head that occupied the pillow there. His mouth was open in sleep, one hand trailing on the floor. She replaced it under the blanket and kissed the boy's forehead, easing away his frown. Then she tiptoed back downstairs and let herself out into the yard soundlessly.

The sky was huge and cloudless. It had been a hot day, and the evening star was rising into a flawless vault above the trees. She could hear the river in its hollow, an early owl. Her bare feet made no noise in the grass.

The river was louder here, on the brink of the hollow, and night came more quickly in the shadow of the trees. She put her back to one and wrapped her bare arms about her knees, waiting as she had waited so often at dusk and dawn, not even sure what she was waiting for. All these years.

She thought sometimes she was watched, as she crouched there, by small shapes in the shadows; and once she was sure she had heard the soft thud of a horse's hoof. But the wood had been empty, the river coursing along within its banks to pour into the darkness below the bridge at the other end of the trees.

Nothing, yet again. Stiff with tiredness, she stood and began to walk back across the fields to where the kitchen light glimmered in the dark. She paused at the gate, looking back—and it was then she saw the movement and thought she heard her name called softly in the warm air.

She ran back, sure now, her heart bursting with inexplicable gladness and the joy hiccuping a laugh out of her as she went. Two shapes, standing in the eaves of the trees, the wood strangely thick about them, as though it were a copse transplanted from some other, older forest.

And she stopped. The man was tall, broad-shouldered and bearded. He was dressed in leather and cured skins and he leaned on a spear. The woman beside him was slender and dark. She carried a bow, and a full quiver hung at her back. They stood so still that they might have been part of the trees, their faces slightly lighter ovals in the gloom.

Then the man raised a hand, pale in the dim light, and said something in a language she did not understand. But it was a happy thing, the words an alien music that were as deep and as old as the hills. And the woman laughed, her voice a silver bell in the growing night. Rose's eyes filled with tears and the world became a blur. When it cleared again they were gone, and the wood was empty. But she ran back through the quiet fields to her home with the wild flowers skimming her knees and the earth clinging to her feet. The stars were filling the night sky with brilliance, and she was singing.

ABOUT THE AUTHOR

Paul Kearney was born in Northern Ireland. He studied Old Norse, Middle English and Anglo Saxon at Oxford University, and subsequently lived for several years in both Denmark and the United States. He lives in County Down, in a croft with a boat by the door.

PAUL KEARNEY'S
THE MONARCHIES OF GOD

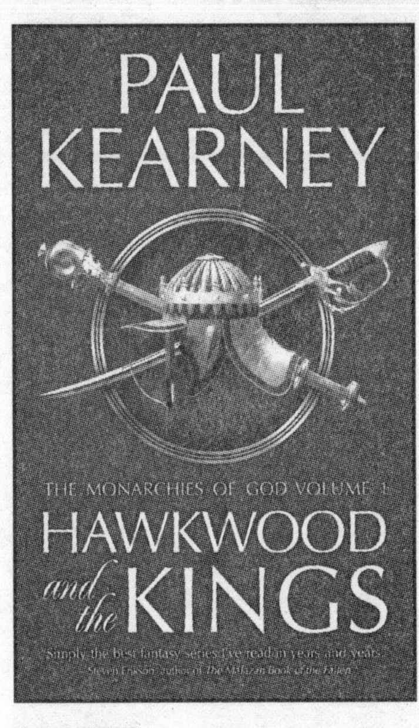

VOLUME ONE

HAWKWOOD AND THE KINGS

ISBN: (UK) 978 1 906735 70 8 • £8.99
ISBN: (US) 978 1 906735 71 5 • $9.99

For Richard Hawkwood and his crew, a desperate venture to carry refugees to the uncharted land across the Great Western Ocean offers the only chance of escape from the Inceptines' pyres.

In the East, Lofantyr, Abeleyn and Mark – three of the five Ramusian Kings – have defied the cruel pontiff's purge and must fight to hold their thrones through excommunication, intrigue and civil war.

In the quiet monastery city of Charibon, two humble monks make a discovery that will change the whole world...

"One of the best fantasy works in ages."

– SFX

VOLUME TWO

CENTURY OF THE SOLDIER

ISBN: (UK) 978 1 907519 08 6 • £8.99
ISBN: (US) 978 1 907519 09 3 • $9.99

Hebrion's young King Abeleyn lies in a coma, his capital in ruins and his former lover conniving for the throne. Corfe Cear-Inaf is given a ragtag command of savages and sent on a mission he cannot hope to succeed. Richard Hawkwood finally returns to the Monarchies of God, bearing news of a wild new continent.

In the West the Himerian Church is extending its reach, while in the East the fortress of Ormann Dyke stands ready to fall to the Merduk horde. These are terrible times, and call for extraordinary people...

"Simply the best fantasy series I've read in years and years."

– Steven Erikson, author of the *Malazan Book of the Fallen*

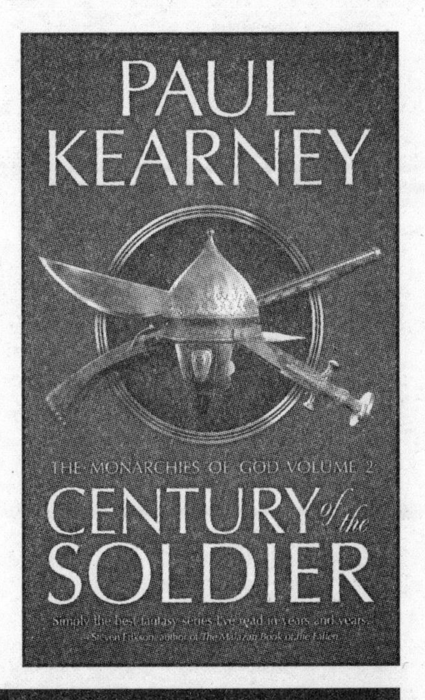

WWW.SOLARISBOOKS.COM

Follow us on Twitter! www.twitter.com/solarisbooks

PAUL KEARNEY'S
THE MACHT

BOOK ONE

THE TEN THOUSAND

ISBN: (UK) 978 1 84416 647 3 • £7.99
ISBN: (US) 978 1 84416 573 5 • $7.99

The Macht are a mystery, a people of extraordinary ferocity and discipline whose prowess on the battlefield is the stuff of legend. For centuries they have remained within the remote fastnesses of the Harukush Mountains. Beyond lie the teeming races and peoples of the Asurian Empire, which rules the known world, and is invincible. The Great King of Asuria can call up whole nations to the battlefield. His word is law. But now the Great King's brother means to take the throne by force, and has called on the legend, marching ten thousand warriors of the Macht into the heart of the Empire.

"A bold, strong new voice in fantasy."
– Robert Silverberg

BOOK TWO

CORVUS

ISBN: (UK) 978 1 906735 76 0 • £7.99
ISBN: (US) 978 1 906735 77 7 • $7.99

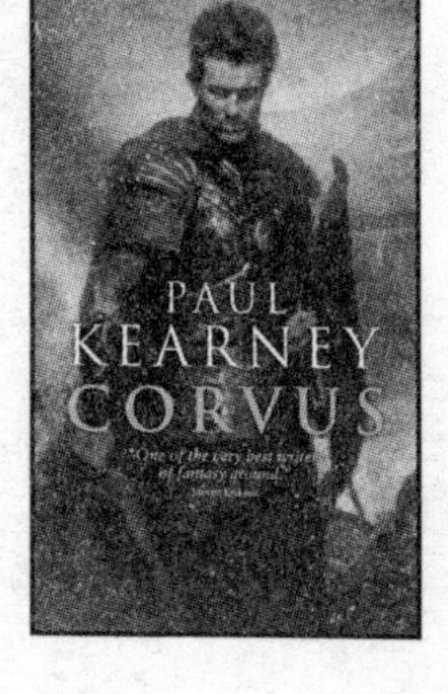

Twenty-three years after leading a Macht army home from the heart of the Asurian Empire, Rictus is now a hard-bitten mercenary captain, middle-aged and tired. He wants nothing more than to lay down his spear and become the farmer that his father was. But fate has different ideas. A young war-leader has risen to challenge the order of things in the very heartlands of the Macht, taking city after city and reigning over them as king. His name is Corvus, and they say that he is not even fully human. He means to make himself ruler of all the Macht, and he wants Rictus to help him.

"One of the best writers working in fantasy."
– SciFi.com

BOOK THREE

KINGS OF MORNING

ISBN: (UK) 978 1 907519 38 3 • £7.99
ISBN: (US) 978 1 907519 39 0 • $7.99

For the first time in recorded history, the ferocious city-states of the Macht now acknowledge a single man as their overlord. Corvus, the strange, brilliant boy-general, is now High King, having united his people in a fearsome, bloody campaign. He is not yet thirty years old. A generation ago, ten thousand of the Macht marched into the heart of the ancient Asurian Empire, and fought their way back out again, passing into legend. Corvus intends to do more. Under him, the Macht will undertake nothing less than the overthrow of the Asurian Empire.

"All the best parts of fantasy, with grit and realism and enough blood to drown a horse."
***– Fantasy Book Review's* Book the Month**

WWW.SOLARISBOOKS.COM

Follow us on Twitter! www.twitter.com/solarisbooks